Kiss of the Wolf

Kiss of the Wolf

MORGAN HAWKE

APHRODISIA

KENSINGTON PUBLISHING CORP.
http://www.kensingtonbooks.com

APHRODISIA BOOKS are published by

Kensington Publishing Corp.
850 Third Avenue
New York, NY 10022

All Kensington Titles, Imprints, and Distributed Lines are available at special quantity discounts for bulk purchases for sales promotions, premiums, fund-raising, and educational or institutional use.

Special book excerpts or customized printings can also be created to fit specific needs. For details, write or phone the office of the Kensington special sales manager: Kensington Publishing Corp., 850 Third Avenue, New York, NY 10022, attn: Special Sales Department, Phone: 1-800-221-2647.

Aphrodisia and the A logo Reg. U.S. Pat & TM Off.

ISBN-13: 978-0-7582-1546-8
ISBN-10: 0-7582-1546-0

First Trade Paperback Printing: February 2007

10 9 8 7 6 5 4 3 2 1

Printed in the United States of America

For my Angel of Inspiration
Angela Knight
—See what you made me do?

And a very special thank you to
Brent, Erin, Jet, and Maura.
—I could *not* have done this without all of you!

Prologue

It was so cold. . . .

Her breath steamed from her lips. Naked and shivering, she rose from her crouch. Her long pale brown hair that fell over her bare shoulders, and the tall white dog pressed against her side, were her only sources of warmth.

The windowless basement of the abandoned textile factory was thick with shadows. She couldn't see the walls or ceiling at all. The only light came from the circular design inscribed on the worn plank floor, blazing an eerie blue all the way around them.

She needed to get out of there.

Just beyond the edge of the glowing circle, her patched corduroys, sweater, boots, and squashed cap lay in a crumpled heap on top of her canvas shoulder bag still full of undelivered newspapers. Arms across her bare breasts, she padded across the icy planked floor toward the edge of the design, heading for her clothes.

Her dog, Whitethorn, followed her toward the circle's edge, her black claws clicking on the wood floor. The dog's head stayed low, though her tall pointed ears swiveled back and forth, her silver fur glowing like the moon in the odd light.

Two rings from the edge, she rammed face-first into—nothing. She stepped back and held out her palms. An invisible wall shivered and clung to her skin like spider webbing. She pressed against the shivery nothing. Current vibrated in her bones. She pressed harder against it. The buzzing current increased, vibrating up her arms, down her spine, and in her teeth. Her hair lifted from her back. Pain sparked sharply across her palms. "Ow!" She jerked back and rubbed her hands together. *Damnit!*

There had to be a way out of this.

Hands outstretched, she wandered the entire glowing inner circle, Whitethorn's claws clicking at her side. There was no opening in the nothingness, no way out, no escape.

Whitethorn shoved her head under her hand and rubbed, begging for a pet.

She knelt and swept her hand across the thick, silky ruff around Whitethorn's neck. Her silvery white fur was sleek, warm against her bare skin.

Whitethorn's yellow eyes looked into hers, and a long pink tongue swept out to lap along her jaw.

She smiled and kissed the dog's cheek. She didn't care that the men who had kidnapped them insisted that Whitethorn was their escaped wolf. She had found her. Wolf or not, Whitethorn was the sweetest, gentlest, and smartest animal she had ever known. *Finders, keepers . . .*

Whitethorn looked off to the side, laid her ears back, and growled. Her black lips curled back, revealing long curved fangs.

Together they hurried to the design's center. No one had touched them, other then to take Whitethorn's collar and her clothes, but that could change. She'd heard horror stories about what men did to naked girls.

A tall man stepped out of the darkness in a long black over-coat. Under the curving brim of his bowler hat, the circle's blue light reflected on his dark spectacles. His orange beard and handlebar mustache seemed to glow. "My apologies for keep-ing you waiting." He pulled his gloved hands from his pockets.

She hunched down and clutched her dog around the neck, pressing against Whitethorn's soft, furry side. She glared at their kidnapper, the man who had put them in this cage of light. "Are you going to let us go now?"

"Let you go? But I only just acquired you." He walked around the glowing circle's edge.

She turned her head to follow him and shouted. "Who are you people, and what do you want with us? I'm just a paper-boy, and she's just a dog!"

He stopped, and his red brows rose. "How many times do I have to tell you, young lady? That is not a dog." He peeled off his black leather gloves. "That is an arctic wolf, *canus lupus arctos,* from the Alaskan tundra."

Her fingers tightened in Whitethorn's fur. "Fine, whatever you say. What has that got to do with us?"

"I am the Doctor." He shoved his gloves into his coat pocket, and his smile turned cruel. "And you are my test sub-jects."

A chill shivered down her spine. "You're a scientist?"

"After a fashion. Allow me to show you." He lifted his hands and recited a string of words in a language she didn't know.

The design started to shift and move, rotating in counter cir-cles. The light brightened from blue to white.

Every hair on her body stood up.

Whitethorn's fur ruffed out, and she snarled.

The light on the floor blazed to blinding brightness.

Pain exploded in her heart and ripped through her. She fell, screaming.

Whitethorn collapsed on top of her, yelping in obvious pain.

Consumed by fire, their terrified voices joined—and ended in a single long agonizing howl.

1

November 1876

The Fairwind, *American Line steamship*
En route to Constantza, Romania

Thorn gasped and jerked upright, knocking the pillows off the small brass bed and onto the floor. Her entire body shook. She pressed one palm over her slamming heart. "A dream . . . just a dream." She shoved the long pale brown strands of hair from her damp cheeks. It was long since over and done.

She jerked the white cotton sheets from her naked, sweat-soaked body and slid from the cot to stand. The waxed hardwood deck of the steamship's tiny iron-walled cabin was cool and rocked gently under her feet. She turned to stare out the cabin's porthole. The moon floated among rags of cloud, and the sound of the sea rushed in her ears.

Once upon a time, she had been Kerry Fiddler, an ordinary girl, with an ordinary paper route, who had found an extraordinary white dog. And then the Doctor had found them.

But that was years ago.

She couldn't stop shaking. She moved to the corner and the small washstand. "It's over and done, over and done, damnit!" She had long since become used to being someone else, some-*thing* else, something wilder, something fiercer, something feral. She splashed water on her face.

The moon's light silvered the mirror's glass. Beneath her dark slashing brows, her dark gold eyes caught the light, and the hearts caught fire, glowing like two green-gold coins—wolf eyes.

The night shadows within the ship's small cabin seemed to close in on her. Her sweat-slicked skin chilled in the cool air of the cabin. She shivered and gasped for breath. She couldn't get enough air. She shook her head and forced herself to take deep, slow breaths. It was over, it was done, and she had escaped. It was nothing but a memory.

Thorn turned to look back at the moon floating outside her small window. The damned nightmare came whenever she spent too much time in too small a space. She needed to get out of this tiny iron box. She needed to run.

She took three long steps to the cabin door and jerked it open. The wind from the ocean caressed her naked skin and swept through her waist-length hair. Moonlight tinted the fine straight strands with silver. She lifted her face to the moon and let her wolf rise from her soul in a tide of fur and joy. She dropped to four paws and shook her silvery fur into place. Ears forward and long tail lifted, she trotted down the deck, her black claws clicking on the slick wooden surface.

"A large white dog was seen running loose on the ship last night." Seated behind his elegant golden oak desk, carried on-board for his express use, Agent Hackett, fine, upstanding representative of the United States Secret Service, wrote with a hasty hand. His Parker fountain pen scratched busily across the very fine parchment. "What do you have to say for yourself?" He did not look up.

Thorn Ferrell's hand tightened on the brim of her charcoal-gray leather hat. "I needed some air."

Agent Hackett scowled at his writing while working the top back onto his fountain pen. "So you ran around the deck on four legs? You couldn't do it on two like a normal human?"

Thorn didn't bother to answer him. He wouldn't have liked the reply. Why should she act like something she wasn't?

In complete contrast to her farmboy appearance, he was fashionably dressed in the attire of most governmental associates. His restrained frock coat of midnight green was buttoned over a severely understated waistcoat of black damask, and a floridly knotted cravat of black silk was tied around the high collar of his white shirt. With his blond hair combed back into a ruthless wave, and neat mustache, he was considered handsome by many.

Thorn considered him a self-righteous prig.

Agent Hackett tucked the fountain pen inside his jacket's breast pocket. "This makes four times you've exposed yourself." He gently blew across the damp ink.

Thorn rolled her eyes. "They saw only a dog. . . ."

"That is not the point." Agent Hackett ruthlessly folded the paper and reached for his stick of sealing wax. "If you cannot be trusted to control your baser urges and at least act like a human, I do not see why you should be treated as one." He struck a lucifer match against the side of his desk.

The stench of sulfur burned in her nose. She winced back. The bastard knew damned well she hated the smell of those things.

A smile twitched at the corner of his mouth. "Perhaps your return trip should be done at the end of a leash." Melted wax dripped onto the folded paper. "Or better yet, in a cage."

A leash? A *cage*? Thorn's temper flared white-hot. Did he

honestly think she would allow either to happen? She swallowed to hold back the growl that wanted to boil up from her chest. His attitude clearly begged for a reminder of whom, and what, he was dealing with, but a show of temper would only work against her. She needed something far more subtle.

She dropped her white canvas pack and dark gray, black fleeced, sheepskin coat on the expensive carpet. Casually she stepped slightly to one side, choosing a spot by the corner of his desk very carefully. She adjusted her position to allow the light from the small oil lamp to shine directly into her highly reflective and inhuman eyes. It had taken ages to figure out the exact angle, but the results were always worth the effort. Pleased, she jammed her thumbs into the pockets of her faded dungarees, relaxing into her pose.

"Now then, Courier Ferrell . . ." Agent Hackett looked up from his desk and froze, staring into her gaze. The pupils of his eyes widened, and the acrid scent of his sweat perfumed the air, betraying his instinctive alarm.

Perfect. Thorn smiled. Yes, my dear Agent Hackett, your brain may be dense, but your body knows very well that it's in a small room with a dangerous predator.

Agent Hackett tore his gaze from her eyes and lunged to his feet. Scowling, he yanked open a desk drawer and pulled out a small brown-paper-wrapped parcel with a white card. He came around the desk to tower head and shoulders over her and offered it to them. "This is the package. You already know the route. The card has the address you are to deliver it to. It is vital that you arrive as swiftly as possible."

Thorn took the package and card from his hands and then knelt to tuck them into her small canvas pack. She knew the "preferred" route, all right. It hadn't taken much to memorize the map they had provided and to deduce that she would cover the territory a hell of a lot faster if she didn't bother with roads. But Agent Hackett didn't need to know that.

He held out a second card. "When you return to Constantza, I will be at this address." His blue eyes narrowed, and his painstakingly neat mustache twitched. "No delays on the return trip, either, you wanton little beast. I don't want to remain in this godforsaken country any longer than necessary."

Still kneeling, she looked up at him. He was standing so close her lips were but a kiss away from his crotch. Well aware of her suggestive position, she smiled. "Do I really look like a wanton to you?"

Agent Hackett's eyes widened, and the perfume of lust rolled off him. She could smell the evidence of an erection growing under his knee-length midnight-green coat. He jammed the card into her hand and jerked back a step. "You look like a street urchin." His voice dropped to a growl. "However, your reputation for shameless exploits precedes you."

"Dungarees are better suited than skirts for what I do, Agent Hackett." She rose to her feet and dragged on her fleeced coat. "And I'm not ashamed of my exploits." She shouldered her pack and smiled. "I like sex."

He jerked his chin up, refusing to look at her. "Why in God's name did they saddle me with you?"

Thorn snorted. "My guess is you pissed off somebody upstairs."

His cheeks flushed, and his jaw clenched. He pointed at the stateroom door. "Get out of my sight!"

Thorn headed for the door and jammed her hat on her head, chuckling softly. Agent Hackett simply could not accept his physical attraction to her. His morals wouldn't let him. Too bad. He obviously was in dire need of a good fuck.

She stepped out onto the steamship's crowded deck and blinked against the late-afternoon winter brightness. The icy wind from the dark Romanian port city smelled bitterly of coal smoke. The Black Sea, behind her, smelled just as strong, but far cleaner. Damp chill crept down past the collar of her sheepskin coat and up the legs of her faded dungarees. She'd thought to bring her good boots and flannel shirts, but she should have brought a heavy sweater, too.

Among good-natured farewell shouts and horrific blasts from the steamship's horns, she eased in among the ship's debarking third-class passengers and marched toward the narrow roped walkway leading down from the steamship to the dock. Setting her hand on top of her battered hat to keep the wind from blowing it away, she tromped down the gangplank into a maelstrom of humanity.

Keeping her head down, she jogged across the busy docks, dodging drays hauling freight and coaches with passengers. The occasional steam carriage chugged by, disturbing the horses with their whistling pops and loud, grumbling hisses. The train at the far end loosed a long, high whistle that raised the hair on her neck.

She entered the city proper and jogged swiftly through the wasteland of crumbling buildings, garbage heaps, and casual violence. She dodged gazes as she hurried by, just another kid in a battered sheepskin coat and faded dungarees. She snorted. The illusion would have been a lot more effective if she'd been a little more flat-chested and narrow-hipped.

Thorn reached the city's limit just at nightfall. Farmland stretched before her, and, beyond that, clean forest. Strands of her hair escaped her braid and flitted around her cheeks. Snow scented the wind.

The next leg of her journey was the easy part. Run. A lot.

The snowstorm finally ended, and moonlight bathed the snow-covered mountains and forest, creating near-daylight brilliance.

The she-wolf ghosted out from under the snow-heavy, ground-sweeping conifer, her silvery winter coat blending perfectly with the fresh snow. The chill hadn't been a problem, not with her thick arctic coat, and the long nap under the draping tree had given her a much-needed rest. She gave herself a firm shake to settle the white pack strapped to her long slender back and then launched into a gliding lope.

Her long strides and wide paws carried her atop the snow and through the moon-bright forest with blinding haste. Her sensitive nose caught occasional traces of the far smaller, and darker, red-coated European wolves that lived in the small mountain range she was passing through. They weren't too difficult to avoid. They stank from eating human garbage. She smelled them long before they could scent her.

A trace scent of human drifted on the breeze.

She stilled and lifted her nose to sift the wind. What the hell was a human doing all the way out here? Along with wool and sweat, there was something odd about the scent, something subtly wrong. . . . Her tail switched in annoyance. She figured out where the scent was coming from and moved away, deeper into the trees. She preferred avoiding humans as much as possible. She had no interest in their noisy, cramped spaces, their stinking food, and their lies about what they wanted and didn't want.

Her loping pace ate distance, and the moon drifted across the sky, marking the passage of hours. Her long strides carried her out of the forest and higher, into the mountains. The pass she was headed for was impassable for humans in winter but not for a wolf.

She moved swiftly upward over rock and snow. Her muscles burned with the effort. Her time on the ship had held far too much inactivity. She was going to need to rest again. Dawn was only a few hours away, so finding a safe place to sleep through the day was probably a good idea. She could start out again at sunset.

Halfway up the mountain, among the cliff heights, she found a small opening in the rocks. The opening proved to be the mouth of a small tunnel. She squeezed into it and wove her way into the back, where she found a rather roomy cave. There wasn't one speck of light, but her nose told her that a tiny runnel of water slid down one wall and a crack offered a draft for a small fire.

Perfect.

She shivered into her human form. Her breath steamed out and chill bumps washed across her naked skin. It was way too cold to play human, even with a fire. She hastily dragged her pack off her back and pulled out her sheepskin coat. Throwing it on the rocky floor, she slid back into her wolf form. Warm and comfy in her thick fur, she curled up, nose to tail, on the black fleece lining of the gray coat and promptly drifted into sleep.

Scrabbling among the rocks at the mouth of the cave's tunnel jolted her out of a sound sleep and onto her paws. The fur along her back rose, and she snarled loudly. Whatever was trying to enter needed to get the hell back out or she would kill it and eat it.

Shifting stones betrayed that whatever had entered was moving deeper into the tunnel.

Her tall ears flicked forward, and her tail switched in annoyance. Just how stupid was this creature? Other than a bear, she was the biggest predator on the mountain. Her snarl should have given that away. She snarled again and gave it some serious volume.

It progressed closer.

She jolted, dancing back on her paws, thoroughly alarmed. Whatever it was, it wasn't heeding her warnings. That meant it thought it could take her in a fight. What the hell thought it could take out a wolf? It couldn't be a bear; a bear was too big to fit in the cave. It had to be her size or smaller. Was it insane?

Scent drifted into her section of the cave: wool, leather, dust, earth, old blood, and cold human.

A human? She sifted through the more subtle scents. The human was male, with silk, oil, steel, and gunpowder. A gun. She snarled in pure reaction. A stinking hunter? This high in the mountains in winter? The scent of oiled steel smelled small, like a pistol. What kind of idiot went into a wolf's cave carrying only a pistol?

She crouched, her muscles bunching tight, in preparation for a lunge. If he wanted to kill her, he was in for a nasty shock. It took a hell of a lot more than a mere pistol shot to kill her. Her voice dropped to a deep, rumbling growl. *Last chance to escape death, moron.*

Light flared in the inky blackness of the cave.

She blinked and flinched back, but her growl remained.

A man with long straight silver-white hair, swathed in a bulky black wool coat, knelt at the tunnel's exit with one gloved hand held palm up. A tiny ball of light floated above his hand—a ball of light that did not smell like fire.

Her ears flicked forward briefly. Light without heat?

He spoke in a language she didn't know, but there was no mistaking his meaning. "Wolf."

She curled back her lips and flattened her ears to her skull. Stupid human. What else did he think was growling, a bunny rabbit?

His eyes opened wide and reflected the light above his hand with an emerald-green shimmer.

Every hair on her body rose. This might look human, but it wasn't human. Human eyes reflected red, like a rat's, and they did not reflect easily.

The light rose from his palm, floating toward the cave's low ceiling.

Her gaze followed the curious floating light.

The man smiled, showing long upper incisors and shorter lower ones, the teeth of a hunting predator.

Her gaze locked on the creature's bared fangs. A deliberate

challenge? Snarling in anger, she dropped to a crouch. *Fine, die.* She lunged, teeth bared to rip out his throat.

He caught her by the fur of her throat and was bowled over backward by the momentum of her charge. He snarled, baring his long teeth in her face.

She snarled right back, writhing in his grasp, snapping for his arms, his face, his throat, anything she could reach.

Twisting with incredible dexterity, he kept her fangs from his skin while holding her with ferocious strength.

She writhed and stretched her neck. Twisting suddenly, she sank long teeth into his forearm, tearing through the wool of his coat to reach flesh and blood. *Got you!*

He threw back his head and shouted in pain.

His blood filled her mouth, thick and hot—and nasty. It burned in her throat like whiskey. She pulled her fangs free but couldn't escape the taste.

His black eyes wide, he stared straight into her eyes and shouted.

A black spike slammed into her mind and sizzled down her spine. She yelped in surprise and pulled back.

His fingers closed tight in her neck fur, holding her gaze locked to his. He spoke. She didn't know his language, but the meaning was crystal clear. "Be still."

Black pressure smothered her anger. Her growls stilled in her throat, and she froze, trembling.

He spoke again, his words an indistinguishable waterfall of liquid syllables, and yet she knew their meaning. "Your bite is deep, but my blood is strong, yes?" He sat up slowly, easing her back and off him while holding eye contact. Gripping her neck fur with one gloved hand, he stroked his other gloved hand down the silver fur of her shoulder. His voice dropped to a low croon. "Yes, wolf, be stilled. Be at ease."

Languid ease infiltrated her mind and spread, making it hard to think, making it hard to stand upright. Off balance, she rocked on her paws.

"Yes, very good, you are a brave wolf." He stroked her neck and shoulders with both hands. "Rest. Lie down, and sleep."

Pressure increased on her mind. She wanted to rest. She wanted to lie down and sleep, just like he said. She stilled. Like he'd *said?* It was him; he was in her head! She jerked back.

"Wolf?" He caught her by the neck fur. "What disturbs you?" His narrowed gaze pierced into her mind, probing her thoughts with smoky black fingers.

She twisted sharply, fighting to break away, and a frightened whine escaped her throat. *Get out! Get out of my head!*

"What?" His silver brows rose and then dropped. "A wolf should not have such thoughts."

She froze. He could hear her? He was listening to her thoughts?

His gaze focused. "Human intelligence? How is this?" His curiosity drove fingers of darkness deeper into her mind, questions looking for answers.

Panicked, she twisted her head to break eye contact. *No, no, no! My secret!*

"A secret!" He gripped her neck fur and fought to keep eye contact. "Tell me your secret!"

No! She reared up and back, dragging him with her.

"Yes!" He wrestled her to the cave floor and pinned her on her side, holding her down with his greater weight. He caught her long muzzle and forced her gaze to his. "Tell me now!"

A steel spike of power slammed through the center of her skull. She howled in agony—and changed.

Thorn snapped aware, naked and curled up on the icy stone floor. She shivered and opened her eyes.

The silver-haired man poised above her on his palms, framing her naked body with his. His expression was one of complete astonishment. His eyes narrowed, and his long teeth appeared. "Who has done this sorcery?"

She wrapped her arms about herself and trembled with cold and fear. He had forced her to change into her human form. Would he kill her now?

2

She shivered in the bitter cold and couldn't stop her teeth from chattering.

"Glory to the night, you will freeze!" He jerked open his coat. Catching her shoulders, he pulled her up and into his lap, wrapping his coat closed around them both.

Thorn froze in surprise. What was this? He wasn't going to kill her?

His arms closed around her. "Be still."

Thorn could feel the pressure of his mind on hers and didn't bother to fight it. He wasn't going to kill her, and that was all that mattered. She curled into his embrace, wrapping her arms around him. His body was not particularly warm against hers, but it was better than nothing. He smelled of wool and man and shadows. The shirt under her cheek went to his knees and was made of heavy silk. She could smell a small amount of dried blood on it. Her body heat filled his coat, and her shivering eased.

"You are warming, good." Holding her close, he looked around. "Ah, a coat and a pack; yours, I assume?"

Thorn nodded.

"Good." He inched forward, cradling her in his arms, and eased down. "The fleece will hold warmth."

The softness of her sheepskin coat pressed against her back. His body draped atop hers, a heavy and solid blanket of flesh and muscle. His coat covered her past her feet. He was far broader and much taller.

He lifted onto his forearms and gazed down at her. "Where has your fear gone?"

Thorn stared up at him. Stupid question. If he was going to kill her, he wouldn't have wrapped her in his coat to warm her.

"Very practical." He smiled, carefully hiding his teeth. "And quite lovely."

So was he. With wolf's eyes she had not noticed that his mature face was one of carved beauty. She lifted her hand and pressed it to his cheek to explore the exquisite line of his jaw and throat. His skin was soft under her fingers.

He started and then smiled. "Ah, a sensualist." He rubbed his cheek against her palm. "When I followed you, I did not know you would prove such a treasure."

He'd followed her? Thorn frowned up at him. Was he out of his mind? What was he thinking, going into a cave with a wolf?

He smiled. "I was thinking to feed upon wolf, but I find myself hungering for wolf maiden."

She frowned. He was still following her thoughts?

He brushed a stray hair from her brow. "Yes. You have tasted my blood. Your mind is open to mine."

She froze. Wait a minute . . . did he say *feed*?

"Oh, yes." He groaned and shifted his hips against hers. The length of his swelling erection pressed against her belly. "You shall satisfy my appetites most pleasantly."

The heat of awakening lust coiled in her belly even as alarm washed through her. She did not want to get eaten! She twisted under him. If she could break loose, she could escape back into wolf fur.

"What is this?" He caught and pinned her hands above her head. "Now you are afraid?"

She snarled and bucked hard under him.

His legs closed tight around her, holding her firmly beneath him with an ease that was simply not possible for a normal man. "More wolf than maiden."

She bared her teeth and snapped. If he did not let her go, she would take his throat!

He pulled his head back and scowled. "Be at ease, I do not intend your death. Have I not proved this already?"

She stilled. He had a point. She looked up at him in suspicion.

"Good." He nodded, releasing her hands, and then shifted his hips, settling himself between her thighs. The rigid heat of his fabric-trapped shaft pressed against her bare and moist flesh.

Delight sparked from the friction of his trousers against her. She sucked in a breath.

He smiled and very deliberately rubbed against the softness of her core. "Ah, yes, very much a sensualist."

She bit her lip against the heat throbbing in her flesh. She didn't trust him. She didn't know what he was or what he meant by "hungers" and "feeding."

"My hunger?" He smiled. "Allow me . . ." He dropped his head, and his mouth opened on her bare breast. His lips claimed a nipple, and his tongue flicked the captured tip.

Heat speared straight down and clenched deliciously in her belly. She arched up toward his mouth, her lips opening on a moan. Oh, he meant *lust*, hungers of the flesh. This she understood.

He groaned and sucked hard on her breast. *Yes, I hunger for your lust.*

She blinked. Was that his thought? She could hear his thoughts?

As I hear yours. His hand slid between their bodies, and his fingers closed on her thigh. *Open.* He caught her nipple in his front teeth and tugged.

Fire burned from her nipple straight down to throb in her clit. She gasped and parted her thighs. She couldn't help herself.

Yes. . . . He leaned back onto his side and pulled her with him, tugging her thigh over his hip. He raised his knee, spreading her and holding her open. He reached down to cup her feminine heat and then slid one finger along her moist folds.

She clutched at his shoulders and shifted against his fingers, rubbing her moistening flesh against his palm.

"Yes, yes . . . that is what I want." His fingers played among her intimate folds, lightly stroking the tiny sensitive nub, encouraging her body into bucking response until her cream slicked his fingers. He flashed a smile. "Excellent." He insinuated a finger deep into her, found something deep within, and flicked.

She jolted under his touch and writhed in delight. It had been too long since she had played with a skilled lover. She dug under his shirt to sweep her hands across his muscular chest. She found his hard nipples and rubbed her palms against them.

He groaned. "Now I am being seduced!"

She smiled. Did he think he was the only one with skills?

"Ah, a challenge." He flashed a brief smile and lowered his head to scrape his sharp, overlong teeth along her breast, his tongue following the path of his teeth.

She moaned. The light sharp pricks of his fangs and the delicious wet velvet of his tongue added to the delight of his fingers, coiling into a lascivious trembling pleasure just shy of ecstasy. She bucked against his hand and released a soft cry, begging for the release that was so close.

He lifted his head from her breast to catch her gaze. He pressed her onto her back, his hips cradled between her spread thighs. Staring straight into her eyes, he lowered his head.

She raised her chin, offering her lips.

His mouth took hers, his tongue surging in to take possession. Propped up on one forearm, he slid his other hand down her waist and over her hips in a long caress.

She sucked and nipped on his tongue. He tasted of fresh water, strongly aroused male, and, oddly, of blood. There was another more subtle flavor beneath it, something dark and dangerous. She found it painfully exciting. Her tongue found a long fang, and she explored carefully.

He groaned, and his hand moved between them. He jerked at himself and grunted. The hot length of his extremely rigid cock pressed against her soft belly. He lifted his mouth from hers and centered his cock at the moist entrance to her body. Heat and intent narrowed his gaze. "I am going to take you."

She nearly grinned. "If you don't, I'm going to take you instead!"

He blinked, startled. "Oh, you are American, yes?" He spoke in heavily accented but perfectly understandable English.

Her mouth opened in surprise. "Yes."

"You are very far from your home." He nodded, clearly pleased. "Very good."

Her brows shot up. "Very good?"

Coiling one arm under hers, he grasped her shoulder from underneath, rose over her, and smiled. "Yes, very good for me." He thrust, with power.

His cock speared into her with a strength she hadn't encountered before, striking something deep within. Pleasure slammed her with a hammer's blow. She arched and gasped. "God!" She clutched him under his shirt and dug her fingers into his bare back. "More!"

He flashed a broad smile and slid his hand under her to cup her ass. "Very good." He thrust again.

She cried out and bucked under him in response without bothering to hold back.

He gasped, and his fingers tightened on her shoulder. "Night! You have strength!" His other hand closed on her ass, his fingers digging in. "Very good, very much a pleasure for me." He ground his rigid cock into her.

She grinned and rolled up under him. "A pleasure for me, too. Finally a man I can't break."

He licked his lips, and his eyes narrowed. "Oh, I will not . . . break." He tightened his grip on her ass and slammed into her with a thoroughly male grunt, then again, and again. . . .

She wrapped her legs around his hips, bucking violently under him, matching him stroke for stroke, and moaning in greedy delight.

His face a tight mask of concentration and hunger, he groaned and thrust, fucking her brutally and without reservation.

She replied with ferocious counterthrusts. Sliding her hand down and into his loosened pants, she felt the muscles of his ass flexing under her palm and dug in her fingers to encourage him.

He responded with swifter thrusts and soft groans.

The sounds of damp flesh striking damp flesh filled the cave, underscored by masculine grunts and soft feminine cries. The raw scent of sweat and lust thickened the air.

She writhed under him, his hard thrusts delivering lightning flashes of pleasure. Erotic tension coiled tight in her belly. She was going to come, and come hard.

His mouth dropped to her throat, and his tongue made exciting wet swirls against her pulse. His hand slid down from under her shoulder and came around to close on her breast. He trapped her nipple between thumb and forefinger and squeezed with ruthless strength.

The bright stab of delight from her nipple jolted her clit hard. Her breath stopped, and she trembled uncontrollably, balancing on the edge of the abyss.

He reached under to cup her ass with both hands. "Come for me!" He slammed into her. "Now!" He thrust again.

Release struck, burning up her spine to explode in the back of her skull. Drowning under a molten wave of carnal euphoria, she threw back her head and howled, bucking wildly.

Holding her tight and riding her frantic body, he sank his teeth into the side of her throat.

The bright hot pain of his bite slammed her back up and over into a second violent climax. She clawed at his back and shrieked.

He sucked on her throat, and a deep groan escaped. He thrust powerfully and then thrust again and trembled violently.

She felt his cock releasing within her and writhed under him, shuddering with tremors.

He pulled his mouth away from her throat with a gasp. "Night!"

They collapsed together, trembling with the ebb of passion.

"Forgive me, I am undone." He pressed a kiss to her shoulder. "Your taste is intoxicating."

She panted with his heavy weight in her arms. "Thank you. You're pretty impressive yourself." She raised a hand to her stinging neck.

He reached out and caught her wrist. "Do not. The wound is still fresh." He slid to her left side and pushed her hip. "Up. Up on your side."

She rolled onto her side and pillowed her head on her arm. Languorous repletion washed through her. "God, I haven't let go like that in . . ." She frowned. "In ever."

"I, too, have long been . . . cautious, in my affairs." He tucked his long coat over them both. Wrapping an arm around her, he leaned up behind her. "It was a very great pleasure."

She snuggled back against him. "It was incredible."

He leaned down to stroke the wounds on her throat with his tongue.

She pushed her hair out of the way and lifted her chin to give him better access.

He started. "You do not mind?"

She snorted. "I am a wolf. I lick all my wounds."

"Ah, yes, of course." His head dropped, and his tongue swept across the wounds on her neck. He stopped. "You are healing very quickly."

"I do that." She sighed and closed her eyes. "You could have told me you wanted a taste of blood."

He leaned up on one elbow to look down on her. "If I had told you such, would you have let me?"

She turned and looked up at him. "I am a wolf. I understand the occasional need to taste blood during sex."

His brows shot up. "You need to taste blood?"

She smiled. "Occasionally."

He brushed a finger across her cheek and chuckled. "Oh, yes, you are perfect for my needs."

"What?" A chill slithered down her spine. That better not be what it sounded like.

He raised a brow and smiled. "Fear not, I will take very good care of you."

She caught his arm and dug her fingers in. "I can't stay with you."

He frowned. "And why is that?"

She avoided his gaze. "I have responsibilities. . . ."

He caught her chin and made her look at him. His silver brows lowered, and his eyes narrowed. "To whom?"

To her government; she had a package to deliver. She scowled and jerked her chin from his hand. "That is none of your business."

He perched his chin on his hand and pursed his lips. "Ah, you are a messenger, a courier for your government." He shrugged. "I care not."

She twisted out of his arms and sat up. She'd forgotten that he could pluck the thoughts from her head.

He smiled. "I will show my kindness. You may deliver your package; then you will return to me."

"What?" She curled her lip at him. "I am not a dog to come to your heel. I am a wolf! I wear no one's collar."

He smiled and caressed her thigh. "And your United States does not have a collar on you?"

She stilled. They did but not for much longer. She glared at him. "That was a low blow. My contract ends after this delivery."

"Excellent." He smiled, showing a hint of his long teeth. "You will be very good for me."

"You're assuming that I'll come back after my delivery." She closed her arms about her breasts. It was chilly in the cave, and only the bottom half of her was covered by his coat. "What if I don't?"

"You will return." He grinned and tugged her down into his arms. "Or I will find you."

It was too cold to fight, so she didn't bother. She snuggled into his embrace. "Fair warning: I am not so easily tracked."

"Ah, but I am not so easily lost." He tucked his coat around them both and curled against her back. His hand slid up to cup her breast. "Do you have a name?"

She started. She didn't know his name either. "I'm Thorn, Thorn Ferrell."

He chuckled softly. "A good name. You may call me Yaroslav."

She turned to look at him. "No last name?"

He smiled. "I have many, and all difficult for your American tongue. Better to use Yaroslav." He pressed her down and held her close. "Sleep."

She yawned, and a question tugged at her. "What are you?"

He chuckled against her throat. "You could not tell?"

"You're not human. . . ."

"No. I am *upir*, vampire."

A vampire? Not likely. She snorted. "You're nothing like a vampire. Well, other than drinking my blood."

"I assure you, I am *upir*. And you are werewolf, yes?"

She frowned. "Yes."

"Much that is told of your kind is incorrect, yes?"

She nibbled on her bottom lip. "Yes." The big one being that she didn't need to eat people.

"Same is with *upir*. A very great much that is told of my kind is incorrect."

"I see." She frowned. If this man was a vampire, then somebody definitely had their definitions wrong. Just for starters, Yaroslav was very much alive.

"Thorn?" His voice was soft against her neck. "I would be very much interested in who has made you such."

Thorn stared into the shadows. "So would I, Yaroslav." Her jaw tightened. "So would I."

"You do not know?"

"I know what he looks like, but I never got his name. He called himself the Doctor."

"Ah . . ." His lips pressed against her shoulder, and his arms tightened around her. "Sleep, sweet Thorn."

She dreamed . . . *of fire.*

A city was burning in the night. Smoke and red-tinted shadows leaped, towering over acres and acres of wood and stone buildings. A roaring red wind full of ash tore the city apart, nearly obscuring the sound of screams. . . .

Thorn jerked awake, shivering. She took deep breaths and forced her slamming heart to calm. *A dream, it was just a dream.*

Yaroslav moaned softly at her back. His hands tightened around her.

Thorn looked over her shoulder. Yaroslav was asleep and apparently having a bad dream, too. She turned in his arms and slid her arms around him. She pressed her lips to his brow.

He pressed closer, rubbing his cheek against hers, sighing softly. He shivered, hard.

She winced in sheer sympathy. It must be a really bad dream. She frowned. He had said that her mind was open to his and his was just as open to hers. Could she have seen *his* dream? Her brows lifted. Could she deliver a better dream?

What could it hurt to try?

She closed her eyes and pressed her brow to his. Concentrating, she pictured mountains, her mountains, the snow-peaked Adirondacks under a midnight summer sky full of stars bright enough to touch. Forests of tall, straight trees marching up steep mountainsides filled with white-tailed deer. Sparkling waterfalls falling into pools of mist and meadows of wild-flowers . . .

Yaroslav drew in a breath. "Is this your America?"

She smiled. He could see it. "Yes, these are my mountains." She concentrated harder, focusing on the cliff heights and the storms that filled the valleys. . . .

"They seem . . . big."

She chuckled. "It takes months to walk from one end of the Adirondacks to the other. The Rockies, at the other end of the country, are much bigger and take over a month just to cross."

His lips brushed her ear, and he sighed deeply. "You give me good dreams."

She leaned back to press her cheek against his. "That was the idea."

His breathing deepened, and his body relaxed.

She smiled. He'd fallen asleep. *Good.* She snuggled into his embrace and her memories of home.

3

Thorn's eyes snapped open. She was curled up tight in a cave under a warm and heavy weight. She turned her head. A man was sleeping practically on top of her. Oh, yes, Yaroslav—the vampire. She looked up. His tiny, glowing, heatless light still floated above them.

Light trickled down the cave's tunnel. Her wolf instincts suggested that sunset was not far away. It was time to go.

Thorn wriggled out from under Yaroslav. Her breath steamed out, and chills raced across her skin. It was seriously cold. She grabbed her pack and then turned to stare at the black and gray sheep-fleeced coat Yaroslav was sleeping on top of. She couldn't leave without that coat.

The pressure in her bladder forced her into her wolf shape and outside. The late afternoon sun was bright and the sky a clear, hard blue, but she could smell a coming snow on the wind. A quick sniff and a hasty dig turned up a hibernating rabbit for a breakfast snack. However, at the speed she was traveling, she was going to need to eat something larger than a rabbit before the day ended.

She dove back into the cave. She needed to go.

Yaroslav was sprawled belly down across her entire coat.

Thorn laid back her tall ears. She needed that coat as a human. Braving the chill, she assumed her human form and gripped the edge of her coat.

Yaroslav opened his eyes halfway and yawned. "Ah, a naked woman; how pleasing."

Thorn shivered. "I need my coat. I have to go."

"I see." He winced, rolled over onto his back, and sprawled in a full-body stretch. He smiled and held out one hand. "You may leave after I have a kiss."

Pushy bastard. Thorn rolled her eyes. "Oh, all right." She crawled over to grasp his hand.

He tugged hard.

She fell, sprawling, on top of him.

He grinned and rolled her under him.

Thorn grabbed his shoulders. "Hey!"

He pouted ferociously. "What? I am merely trying to keep you warm."

Thorn lifted her brow. He was a hard, substantial weight atop her, and heavily aroused. "Oh, is that all?"

"But of course." He lowered his head. "I will have my kiss now, if you please."

She wrapped her arms around his neck, leaned up, and met his lips and then his warm, velvety tongue. Her eyes drifted closed, and she explored the softness of his lips and tongue.

He groaned in appreciation and fit his mouth to hers, his tongue stroking hers as though he could not get his fill.

Heat flashed and coiled tight with merciless greed. She moaned. Her thighs parted, and her knees lifted to let him rest between them.

His hips shifted, and his hand slipped between them. He grunted and the heated weight of his unrestrained shaft pressed against her moistening flesh.

She pulled from his lips. "I thought all you wanted was a kiss?"

He smiled. "I am not such a fool as to turn down a woman who clearly wishes more than a kiss."

Her mouth opened. "Who, me?"

"Was I mistaken?" His fingers explored her sensitive folds and ripe clit.

Her body jolted under the sparks of delight that danced through her. She gasped, pushing up against his fingers.

He smiled. "Shall I stop?"

She groaned. "You do, and you die."

His brows lifted. "Ah, now you are demanding?" His fingers gently rolled her swollen clit. "This sweet fruit I look forward to tasting when there is a bed and a fire."

She choked and bucked hard. His brutally tender caress was so pleasurable it was closer to pain.

His finger entered her and flicked within.

She shuddered with violent urgency and writhed against his deliciously stroking fingers. "All right, you win." She lifted her legs, hooking her heels around his waist. "You can have more than a kiss."

His fingers stroked deep into her. "Are you quite sure?" His thumb swept across her swollen clit.

She jolted right to the edge of ecstasy. With a gasp, she threw back her head and arched up hard. "God, yes! Please, damn you, fuck me already!"

He grinned. "Such a sweet invitation. . . ." He shifted and set the broad head of his cock to her slick entrance. "How can one resist?" He thrust.

She met his stroke with an upward push, and he sheathed himself deep within her.

They both groaned in satisfaction.

His mouth took her breast, and his teeth worried at her swollen nipple.

The exquisite torment of his tender bite speared into her belly. She tightened her legs around him and burrowed under his shirt to pull him tighter to her.

Stroke and counterstroke were agonizingly slow, yet deep, punctuated by heartfelt sighs and greedy moans.

Climax rose and held on the trembling edge. She set her heels into the floor and pushed to encourage him to a quicker pace. She was right there. . . .

"Not so quickly." He groaned and slid down his hands to cup her ass. "Control your greed."

"Please!" She writhed, fighting his hold. "I'm right there!"

"In time." He dug his fingers into her cheeks, holding her rhythm to his brutally slower pace. "I wish to savor."

"Damn you . . ." She fought to get closer, but he held her back with his slow yet powerful strokes. Frustration made her shudder beneath him.

He opened the collar of his shirt and then tugged both the shirt and his coat down, baring his right shoulder. He cupped the back of her head and pressed her mouth to the hard muscle of his shoulder. "Bite, and taste my blood." He thrust and groaned. "As I tasted yours."

So close to the edge of bliss, and held back from reaching it, she seriously wanted to bite him. She opened her mouth and bit down, hard.

"Yes. . . ." He gasped. "Yes . . . yes. . . ."

His skin parted under her teeth, and his blood, thick and sweet, slid over her tongue. It barely tasted like blood at all, and it burned, like potent whiskey. She jerked back.

"No." His hand cupped the back of her head, keeping her mouth against his shoulder. "Drink."

She didn't want to; he didn't taste right. She pushed against him.

His fingers locked in her hair. "Drink."

Her mouth filled; she had to swallow or choke.

"Drink!"

A spike of darkness shoved at her mind. She whimpered in alarm and swallowed. The thick liquid burned all the way to her stomach. She groaned.

"Ah . . . yes, very good." He shuddered, and his thrusts increased in power. "Again."

Her mouth was already filling with his burningly potent blood. She swallowed, and languorous heat spilled down her throat and spread from her belly. Her thoughts drifted apart.

He stilled, hard and deep within her, holding her fiercely tight. "Now, come!"

Climax rose and clenched violently within her, stopping her breath.

His mouth closed on her throat, and his teeth sank viciously deep. He thrust, slamming into her without mercy.

The sharp bite pushed her over the edge, and her release exploded in a horrific torrent of fire that burned up her spine, spilling over her in a wave of unexpectedly ferocious, carnal euphoria. She hammered up to meet his violent thrusts and screamed her delight.

Moaning, he thrust deep and held, his cock trembling within her. He swallowed, drinking the blood pumping from her throat.

Clinging tightly to his shoulders, she moaned through the aftermath of her ferocious pleasure and the aching sting of his feeding.

He pulled his teeth from her throat and shuddered. "Night and blood. . ." His tongue swept across her wounds.

She sprawled under him, struggling to think through the fog in her mind. An odd heat coursed through her.

He leaned back and smiled down at her. "Yes, very good." He licked his lips and then nodded. "In fact, most excellent."

She stared up at her bite on his neck. His wound had already stopped bleeding. Apparently he healed as fast as she did. She frowned, reached up, and slid her hands through his hair. His hair was no longer pure silver but streaked in black, and his face had smoothed. She pressed her palm to his cheek. "Are you getting . . . younger?"

His brows swept up, and then he shrugged, his gaze drifting from hers. "I am a vampire, and your blood is . . . potent."

She frowned. "Is that a yes or a no?"

He dropped his head and smiled. "That is a yes. The magic in your blood feeds mine."

Thorn licked her lips and tasted the sweet potency of his blood. "Magic?"

He snorted. "But of course. That is how one makes one such as you. That is what allows you to move between bodies. How else would two souls and two bodies be joined?"

She looked away, remembering the glowing ring. "But the Doctor said he was a scientist." She looked up at him. "I thought what he did was science?"

"Your Doctor . . ." he curled his lip, "is magi, a user of magic."

She frowned. "Are you sure?"

He smiled sourly. "I am without a doubt." He lowered his head and softly brushed his lips against hers. "We will speak on this at another time." He took her lips, pressing her mouth open under his. He explored her mouth and lapped at the traces of his blood on her tongue. He pulled back, dropped a quick kiss on her brow, then lifted up on his palms. "Now you may go."

She scowled. "Oh, gee, thanks."

He tilted his head, and his gaze brightened. "You do not wish to go?"

Of course she did. She opened her mouth to say so and felt reluctance. She frowned. She *didn't* want to go. She didn't want to leave him. But she had to deliver her package. She leaned up on her elbows. "I have to go."

A smile lifted the corners of his mouth. "I am in anticipation of the delights of your return."

She smiled. "So sure I'll come back?"

Yaroslav sat up and then leaned back on his heels to straighten his clothes. "I am."

"Is that so?" Thorn lifted her coat from the floor and shook it. She winced against the thrown sand. "I may not."

"You will." Yaroslav lifted his chin to button his dark silk shirt. "There is much you do not understand about what you are and what I am to you."

Thorn rolled her coat into a bundle and grabbed her pack. "And you know all the answers?" She shoved her coat into her pack.

Yaroslav winced. "Not all the answers, no." He focused on her. "However, I have no doubt that you will return to me."

She rolled her eyes and slid her arms into the straps of her pack. "You're awfully sure of yourself."

"You will come . . ." he leaned forward on his knees and caught her face, "because you cannot resist me." He smiled from only a kiss away.

She lifted her brow and bit back a smile of her own. "Really?"

He leaned close and brushed his lips against hers.

She answered his caress without thinking. Their mouths joined in a sweet, hot kiss. Warmth coiled around her heart. She jerked back, startled. What the hell was that?

"There, you see?" He released her and smiled tiredly. "You already have love for me."

She froze. *Love?* Her mouth curved up into a cynical smile. "I'll admit to lust, but I am not in love with you."

"Of course you are." He nodded and tugged at his coat. "I am of great age. I know love when I feel it." He waved a hand toward the cave entrance. "You must go." His smile broadened. "I will follow with the night."

She sat back on her heels. "You're going to follow me?"

He groaned and sprawled out on his back. "Later, when full night has come. Now I will sleep." He folded his arms behind his head.

She scowled and shivered, but she couldn't tell if she trembled from the cold or from the idea of him following her, of her seeing him again. She shook her head in confusion. Later; she would worry about it later. Her wolf rose from within in a wash of joy, heat, and power.

Standing firmly on four paws, she leaned back to stretch her long forelegs and then leaned forward to stretch her back legs. Oh, yes, the rest, and the bed sport, had done her a world of good. She shook hard to settle her fur and her pack.

Yaroslav looked over at her. "You have great beauty as a woman and as a wolf." He held out his hand. "Come, I would touch your glorious coat."

She padded over to him, though not sure why. As a wolf, she normally did not want to be touched.

His fingers slid through her fur in a long caress. "You are silver, like the moon, and so large."

Pleasure stirred along her spine. His touch felt good. Too good. She had to resist the urge to rub against him for more. She moved away.

He waved his hand. "Yes, yes, you must go."

She turned to the cave mouth and scrabbled her way out and into the setting sun. The chill wind ruffled her fur. She turned her nose toward the pass and hesitated. Her tail switched. She didn't want to leave him alone and undefended.

She shook herself hard. He had defended himself just fine against her fangs. He could handle anything else. She stepped away, and each long step became easier to take. She bounded up onto the snowy ledges, and the joy of running in fur took her.

The sun fell completely, and the stars filled the blue velvet of the night sky.

She reached the pass at the mountain's peak just as the moon rose. Standing atop snow that would not hold a man's weight, she looked back. The cave was very far away and well down the mountainside. She lifted her nose to the waning moon and sang. Her voice sailed into the sky, deep and strong, and then high, like the whistle of a hawk, echoing across the mountains. *I am here. . . .*

Laughter echoed in the back of her thoughts. *Why, so you are.*

The journey down the mountainside was swift and full of bounding, joyful leaps from cliff edge to cliff edge. Visibility was excellent. The moon on the snow made the night very nearly as bright as day. The cliff heights became rolling, heavily forested foothills, and the snow thinned underfoot.

A small deer started before her, and she gave chase. She needed to eat. She had changed too many times in too short a period. The deer fell under her fangs, and she feasted on sweet, hot meat.

The scent of wolves drifted on the breeze.

She lifted her head and detected movement in the deep shadows under the trees. She licked her lips, cleaning her teeth. She turned and left her kill for them to feast on. She couldn't eat the whole deer anyway, not on a run. It was better this way; no waste.

She entered the farmland valleys. Ears forward and tail straight out, she bounded across snow-covered fallow fields. Dogs barked in the night. Small villages dotted the valleys, but she continued by. She was looking for something much larger, a town with a railway station.

The night passed, and dawn colored the thick, dark clouds in bruising shades. There was snow on the wind.

The bitter scent of coal fires and the distinctive scent of train steam warned her that she was coming to the town she was looking for. On a small rise she stopped to look. Her wolf eyes were not particularly keen on details, but there was no mistaking that she was looking at a good-sized town, nestled deep in a valley, surrounded by the mountains she had just crossed. However, the sour scent of burning scrap-wood overwhelmed the sharp scent of burning coal. More people were using cheap wood rather than coal to heat their homes.

Or, houses were burning.

She didn't see any leaping flames and only traces of black smoke. Puzzled but determined, she trotted toward the town.

Head low, she followed the muddy road into town but stayed among the hedges to avoid being seen by the early morning farm traffic. Wolves tended to draw bullets. Luckily her coat blended in with the winter terrain.

A row of massive factories squatted right on the town's edge. Steam whistles announced the stoking of the factory boilers and the change in shift. People bundled in heavy coats, caps, and mufflers slowly made their way in and out of the multistoried brick monstrosities.

Slipping out from the brush, she bounded over railroad tracks and skirted the walls of the factories, avoiding the pools of light cast from the tall paned windows. She spotted a gate into the town proper, but people and wagons moved in and out of it. A momentary lull in traffic came. She bolted across the icy cobbled yard and into the town.

Shouts followed her down the street.

She ducked into an alley, her claws clicking on the cobbles. She lifted her head, searching the backs of the cheek-to-jowl buildings for an abandoned stable. It was time to assume her human form.

Slender red-coated wolf dogs drifted slyly from the backs of the scattered houses. They were half her size and weight and stank of the human garbage they ate.

She lowered her head but kept her ears up and her tail lifted in deliberate warning that she would kill any that came too close.

They eyed her and kept their distance.

Behind a crumbling, fire-scorched house, she found a stable in relatively good condition. She ducked inside and changed. Shivering in bare human skin, she padded into a stall and tugged off her pack. Dressing with haste, she pulled on her warmest socks and her thickest creamy flannel shirt before stepping into her dungarees.

One of the odd advantages of moving between shapes was that it kept her clean. Dirt, and fleas, left with the shift between bodies. There was no trace of the blood, and other things, from her lovemaking with Yaroslav. She smiled. Trying to find clean and unfrozen water to wash in before dressing would have been a nightmare.

She pulled back her pale brown hair and secured her braid with a thong and then tugged on her gray sheepskin coat. She stopped and sniffed. The black fleece lining smelled of Yaroslav. She smiled, and her belly warmed with memory. She doubted she would see him again, but what they had shared had been well worth the delay.

She shrugged her pack onto her back and stepped out of the stable into gray morning daylight. Jamming her hat on her head, she pulled the card from her coat pocket. It was time to find her delivery address. She strode out to the main road.

There were Russian soldiers everywhere.

From the mouth of the alley, Thorn watched line after line of them march by without stopping. The local townsfolk stared at them in confusion. Apparently no one had any idea what the Russian army was doing there, but they didn't seem to be bothering anyone, and they all appeared to be heading for the main gate out of town.

Thorn shrugged—the Russian army was not her problem—and started searching.

4

She reached the busy steel and glass train station at the very end of town just as the tall cast-iron gas lamps were being lit. The face of the train station's clock tower was bloodstained with sunset.

Exhausted, she sat down on the steps of the ticket office and cursed, using every foul word she could think of. She had wasted the entire day searching for an address on a street that didn't seem to exist. The town was a freaking rat's warren of unnamed streets, and she didn't speak the local language. Worse still, the address was written in English, so the locals couldn't read it. She stomped the cobbled walk with her booted foot and cursed some more.

A double line of Russian soldiers marched out of the train station and kept going.

Thorn blinked. Oh, so that's where they were all coming from. . . .

"Is something the matter, young sir?" The accent was British, and the voice was right behind her.

She jolted and whipped around.

The man at the top of the stairs was head and shoulders taller than she and dressed in a heavy caped coat that was buttoned all the way up and draped to his heels. A bowler hat was perched on his head, and dark round spectacles covered his eyes.

The hair lifted at the back of her neck, and she jumped to her feet; then she looked again. His clean-shaven face was long and narrow, not square and florid, and a neat braid of dark brown hair fell over his shoulder. No trace of bright orange. She released her breath. "Sorry, you surprised me."

"Oh, an American?" He smiled and came down the steps. "And my apologies to you, young *lady*." He walked over to the curb and then turned back to eye her clothes. "It's the trousers, you see. . . ."

Thorn smiled. "Dressing like a boy is safer when you're . . . traveling."

"Ah, yes, how clever. . . ." He lifted his chin, looking past her at the passing Russian soldiers. His gaze chilled. "Considering that there are a lot of, shall we say, less than civilized soldiers marching about." He sighed and shook his head. "The Turks and the Russians are at it again." He waved his hand in clear dismissal. "Well, never mind that. . . ." He touched his hat and smiled. "I'm Max, by the way, Max Rykov, a linguist with the British attaché."

She nodded politely "I'm Thorn Ferrell, and I'm . . ." She winced. She was not going to say lost. "I'm looking for a specific address, but I can't find it."

Max arched his brow. "Perhaps because a great many of the streets are not marked?"

She snorted. "That could have a lot to do with it."

Max clicked his heels smartly together. "Maybe I can be of assistance? Where did you wish to go, Miss Ferrell?"

Thorn held out her card. "I'm trying to find this. . . ."

Max took it and frowned. "Oh, this is . . ." He lifted the card to his nose and stilled. He reexamined the card and then looked at her and smiled. "You are a quite a ways from this address."

Thorn scowled. "Oh, wonderful." She nibbled on her bottom lip. Why had he sniffed the card? It only smelled of paper . . . and her. Suspicion niggled, but she squashed it. A human did not have her sense of smell. All he would be able to detect is the scent of the paper.

Max looked up past her shoulder. "Since I just happen to be on my way to visit Colonel Ives, why don't you come with me?"

"Come with you to see . . . Colonel *Ives*?" She stilled utterly. He couldn't mean *her* Colonel Ives, the cavalry officer that had found her living feral in the mountains so many years ago? It had to be a different Colonel Ives. It couldn't possibly be the same man she'd called father until he'd betrayed her to the U.S. Army.

"Certainly." Max lifted his arm and waved his hand, signaling to someone behind her. "Why walk when you can ride?"

The hissing chug of an approaching vehicle came from behind her. She darted back against the wall. A bright yellow and ornate, horseless vehicle on tall rubber-tire carriage wheels came bumping up the cobbled road billowing gouts of steam. Brass headlamps speared the mist rising from the road. A driver in a heavy overcoat, wearing a squashed cap, sat up high in the front holding the long, curved steering pole.

Thorn eyed the oncoming vehicle. It was a steam carriage. She'd seen Mr. Dudgeon's steam wagon rattling along the roads back in Long Island City, but this one was a far finer vehicle, and it didn't make half the noise. The tall wheels were not huge wooden disks, like those on Mr. Dudgeon's steam wagon, and the passenger compartment was a proper carriage. "Wow. . . ."

Remaining exactly where he was in the road, Max looked over at her at her and smiled. "Steam cars, Miss Ferrell. Wave of the future, don't you know."

The vehicle came to a hissing stop right in front of Max, and two loud bangs echoed from the rear of the vehicle. The driver tipped his hat. "She's all warmed up and ready to roll." His accent was thickly Eastern European, but it was clear he had learned his English from a Brit. "Where to, Master Rykov?"

Max rattled off the address Thorn had spent the day hunting.

"Ah . . ." The driver nodded. "That's by the new brass factory."

Thorn frowned. Good god, did he mean one of the factories all the way back over on the other side, where she'd come into town in the first place? She groaned.

Max stepped to the side of the carriage and tugged open the door. He looked over at Thorn. "Coming, Miss Ferrell?"

Thorn's mouth fell open. "In your steam car?" She hesitated. Everyone knew you didn't go anywhere with strangers. She balled her hands at her side. She was a werewolf. If he caused a problem, she'd rip him to rags. "I'd love a ride." She strode to the open door. "I have had enough running around today."

Max held out his hand to help her up the steps. "Well, we certainly can't have you running around anymore, can we?" He smiled.

Thorn glanced up at Max, but his dark spectacles made it impossible to see his eyes, and the cologne made it hard to read his scent. She shook her head and climbed up. She had more important things to worry about than him. She was going to see a Colonel Ives, possibly the last man she'd ever wanted to see again.

Thorn ducked into the small door. The carriage's interior was done entirely in brass-tacked leather with leather-curtained windows. Two leather-upholstered, cushioned benches with curving brass armrests faced each other. She went to the far side of the carriage and sat in the front-facing bench by the curtained window. Everything reeked of saddle soap, brass polish, and money.

Max climbed in and sat on the bench beside her. He reached up and tugged a cord strung along the roof's edge. A bell sounded outside the window.

A piercing steam whistle answered.

"Here we go!" Max grinned and grabbed the strap by the window on his side of the car. "You'd best hang on. The carriage moves rather jauntily."

The car lurched under them, throwing Thorn back against the seat cushions. She grabbed onto the leather loop by her window with both hands.

The steam car chugged forward, rocking side to side as it bumped along the cobbled road.

Thorn shoved her head out the window to see. The car's lurching and rocking increased with their speed until the chilly breeze against her cheeks became a strong, icy wind. The car chugged along insanely fast, practically flying past streets and buildings. Moving horse carts appeared to be at a standstill. It was frightening and thrilling. "Holy smoke!"

"I love modern science!" Max laughed. "Do try not to lose your head on a lamppost. Some of these streets are very narrow, and my driver tends to make sharp turns."

The steam car chugged to an intersection and slowed just a little to go around a corner. The entire carriage rocked to the side, practically lifting off its wheels.

"Whoa!" Thorn jerked her head back in. "I see what you mean!" She settled back to watch from her seat. Streets passed, shops passed, and as they went, people pointed, horses spooked, and shadows lengthened.

They bumped off the cobbled way and jounced along the packed dirt of the town's main road. The street got darker, narrower, and misty. The gaslights of the factories appeared at the far end of the road.

Thorn turned to look at Max. "I see it!" She was forced to

shout over the noise of the steam engine. "I can see the factory lights ahead!"

Max nodded and smiled. "Almost there!"

Thorn grinned. "It took me all day to cross town, and here we are in less than an hour."

The car bumped back onto a cobbled road and then lurched and chugged past a busy factory, and then another, and then another. . . . Workers in heavy coats and mufflers were everywhere. People stopped and stared. Some pointed, and others waved.

Abruptly the car turned onto a narrow gaslit street lined with two-story brick houses. The car's steam whistle sounded and then whistled again.

Max tapped Thorn's knee. "Brace yourself. We're getting ready to stop."

The car gave a hard shudder and released a squeal. The bumping, chugging, and rocking eased to a trembling putter and then a hard stop.

Max smiled. "We're there."

Thorn followed Max out of the carriage on wobbly knees.

The driver leaned over the side of the car. "Eh! Enjoy your ride?"

Thorn turned to wave at the driver. "Yes, thank you!"

Max looked up at the driver. "You know where to go?"

The driver nodded. "I will make very sure the car is secured for travel." He frowned. "Are you sure you won't need me to come for you?"

Max shook his head. "I will be taking a different route back to the lab."

The driver stiffened, and his eyes went wide. "Oh, of course."

Max waved his hand. "Carry on!"

The driver nodded and tipped his squashed hat. "Yes, sir, farewell, sir!"

Max strode past Thorn. "This way, Miss Ferrell!"

"Coming!" Her white canvas pack over her shoulder, Thorn trotted after Max, following him into a tiny front garden and then up two steps to the front door of one of the brick houses.

Max lifted the brass knocker and pounded twice.

The door opened, releasing light, warmth, and the stench of cigars. The man answering the door wore a brown wool dinner jacket with a carelessly knotted tie around his collar, but his iron-straight stance and watchful gaze were pure military. He stank of cheap soap and expensive gun oil. "Good evening, may I help you?" He spoke English with a strong Yankee accent.

Thorn frowned. Definitely American military, but normally they wore their uniforms even in foreign countries. Apparently Colonel Ives didn't want to announce his presence in town.

Max smiled and did not offer his hand. "I'm Max Rykov, and this is Miss Ferrell. I believe we're expected."

Thorn eased past Max to face the man at the door. It was code-phrase time. She pasted on her best "I'm just a kid" smile. "The snow is pretty deep in the Adirondacks right now."

The man blinked; then his jaw tightened, and he nodded. He stepped to one side to let them pass him.

Thorn followed Max into a plain but spotlessly scrubbed foyer. Before them, a narrow, dark, paneled hall led past a steep staircase on the left side and continued to the back of the house.

The man closed the door behind them. He turned to Max. "This way, sir." He strode into the narrow hall.

Thorn set her hands in her pockets to wait right where she was.

Max stopped. "Coming, Miss Ferrell?"

Thorn smiled. Not if she could help it. "In a minute."

Max frowned but followed the man down the hallway and to the left. A door clicked open and then closed.

The man returned and nodded at Thorn. "This way, courier."

Shit. . . . She'd hoped he would simply ask for the package so she could leave without seeing anybody. Thorn sighed and followed the man down the hall to a door on the right.

The door opened on a small room lined with empty bookshelves. In the center of the room was a massive desk set with two oil lamps and completely covered in sheets of cheap writing paper. The floor all around the desk was littered with strewn newspapers. Behind the desk, seated in a large leather armchair, was a dapper older man in a wine-red, quilted smoking jacket. He had shoulder-sweeping golden curls and a painstakingly trimmed goatee. A lit cigar burned in a broad glass ashtray close to his right hand. "Thank you, Brentwood, you may leave."

The hair on the back of Thorn's neck lifted. It was him, Colonel Ives, the man she'd once called "father"—her betrayer.

The man, Brentwood, nodded once and then turned smartly on his heel and left, closing the door behind him.

Colonel Ives lifted his head and smiled. His midwinter-ice-blue eyes crinkled in the corners. "Hello, Kerry, it's been quite a while, hasn't it?"

"My name is Thorn Ferrell." Thorn crossed her arms. "Colonel Ives."

The colonel lifted his cigar and winced. "You're still mad at me."

A growl rumbled in Thorn's chest, but the sound was far too low for a human to hear. "Because of you, I'm a slave to the army, old man." She should never have trusted him with her secrets.

Colonel Ives's gaze narrowed. "When I found you, you were little more than a wild animal." He shook his head and shoved aside papers. "I did what I thought was best for you."

Thorn stepped up to the desk and set her palms on it. "You did what was best for your career. You gave the army something they could use, and use me they did." Her lengthening nails dug into the desk. "I haven't stopped running errands for the Secret Service since the day you left me in that office with that . . . agent."

His gaze narrowed. "You have a roof over your head, clothes on your back, and you're paid a decent wage. . . ."

Thorn slammed her fist on his desk. The desk gave a hollow bang and a crunch. She pulled her fist from the splintered dent she'd made in the wood. "I live in a room with bars on the windows and a bedroll on the floor. The only time I'm let out is when the military needs something carried across terrain no one else can cross. As for pay, whatever agent is acting as my handler gets it, not me."

The colonel raised his icy gaze to hers. "If you hadn't kept trying to run away, bars and handlers wouldn't be needed."

Thorn clenched her jaw. She could feel the teeth lengthening in her mouth. Her humanity was slipping with her temper, baring the beast that shared her soul. "You're a total bastard, you know that?"

Colonel Ives snorted. "I'm a colonel; it comes with the job." He sighed and then looked down at his desk and shuffled some papers. "You'll be free to go wherever you like when your term is done."

Thorn pulled her pack from her shoulder and dug out the brown-paper-wrapped box. She set the package on his desk. "There, my term is done. You're the last delivery." She turned on her heel and headed for the door. She had to get out of there before her temper got the better of her and she ripped him apart. "Good-bye, and good riddance."

"Halt!"

Thorn froze out of sheer force of habit. *Stupid military reflexes. . . .* "What now?"

"I have a return delivery."

She turned slowly to face him and knew damned well her smile was full of long teeth. "I guess you're just going to have to use a normal courier."

Colonel Ives rose from behind his desk. "Until you have been officially served your walking papers, you are a U.S. courier and subject to my orders. Is that clear, soldier?"

Thorn let her wolf rise under her skin, let the crackle of energy dance along her bones, exposing the predator within her. "You want to try to make me follow those orders, colonel?"

Colonel Ives bared his flat and yellowed human teeth. "Not a whole lot of people know it yet, but there's a particularly nasty plague going around out here, and I don't want that happening in America. You're the only one that can get what little I have on this European plague back over those mountains."

Thorn scowled. "Oh, gee, what a surprise, another life-or-death mission." She folded her arms over her chest. "Don't you think I've saved enough lives for you?"

"Don't you have any human compassion?" His jaw tightened. "Or does the beast do all your thinking for you?"

"I did have human compassion once." Thorn lifted her chin, knowing damned well that the light from the small oil lamp on his desk made her eyes reflect and glow like green-gold coins. "I saved an old man lost on a mountaintop in winter. It got me a job at the end of a military leash."

Colonel Ives dropped into his chair and wiped a hand down his face. "I was trying to provide for your future."

Thorn turned her back on him and faced the door. "I'll carry your package, old man, but after that, I'm done with you. I don't ever want to see your face again." She grabbed the brass door handle. "Or anyone else's."

"Where are you planning to go?" His voice was soft.

Thorn sighed. "To the kitchen. I just had a hard three-day run. I'm hungry."

"No, after you quit the military. Where will you go after that? You can't go back to your family in New York; they kicked you out when they found out what you were."

Thorn kept her back to him. "And whose fault was that?"

"If you hadn't lost your temper when I came to get you, they wouldn't have seen you that way."

Why is it always my fault? Thorn's hands fisted on the door-knob, denting the soft brass. "Where will I go, now that I can never go home? Someplace you can't find me, Colonel. Someplace where no one will ever find me again." She pushed the door open, stepped through, and closed it quietly behind her.

5
———————

The kitchen at the back of the house was warm, brightly lit with gas lamps, and scrupulously clean. The massive cast-iron Franklin stove that took up the entire far left wall was manned by the huge gruff cook, Tom. He and his two assistants, Dick and Harry, in white aprons over their dark corduroys with their white shirtsleeves rolled up over their elbows, were well into preparing dinner for the rest of the house's staff.

Perched on a flour barrel at the end of the rough-sawn plank table, Thorn was given a huge bowl of beef stew and a small loaf of warmed bread. She picked up her spoon and eyed the three men. "Tom, Dick, and Harry. You're kidding, right?"

Dick over at the sink under the row of shuttered windows grinned and waved a soapy hand. "It was an accident, I swear!"

"Speak for yourself!" Tom laughed and set a mug of milk frothy with cream before her. "So, you're a courier? My wife carried letters on occasion during the War Between the States." He smiled with obvious pride.

Thorn nodded. Wives and daughters had often done courier

duty when no one else was available. Sometimes family were the only people you could trust with something sensitive.

Scrubbing away at silverware, Dick turned to smile briefly. "You must be good if they're sending you on overseas missions."

Tom banged open the oven and poked at the roast within. "She made it here through the mountains in winter. I'd say that's pretty damned good."

Thorn shrugged. "I get the job done." She lifted her spoon. "Any idea why the Russian army is here?"

The men exchanged glances.

Tom turned his back to her. "They're probably on their way out to burn more towns."

Thorn froze, her spoon halfway to her mouth. "What?"

Tom shrugged. "There's a plague. That's how they're dealing with it."

Thorn frowned. "The colonel mentioned the plague, but burning towns?"

Tom slammed something on the stove. "It's their country. Not a whole lot anybody can do about it."

Thorn stared at her soup. "Well, yeah I suppose. . . ."

Harry abruptly sat down at the table to mash a pot of buttered potatoes. He nodded at her uneaten loaf. "Something wrong with the bread?"

Thorn wiped her mouth on a cloth napkin. She knew a deliberate change in subject when she heard one. "Not at all. Bread is just one of those things that doesn't agree with me."

Tom pulled the pan with the roast from the oven and set it on the sideboard by the sink. "How can bread not agree with you?" With a pair of carving knives, he lifted the meat from the pan onto a wooden cutting board. "Everybody eats bread!" He shot a scowl at her.

Thorn rolled her eyes. Cooks prided themselves on their

bread. "Anything with grain in it, corn, wheat, rice . . . it all puts me in the outhouse in a matter of minutes and keeps me there."

"What?" Dick grabbed the roasting pan for scrubbing. "How can you live without bread?"

Thorn shrugged. "I can't drink any kind of beer for the same reason."

"No beer?" The cook shook his head sadly and sliced. "Now there goes all the joy in life."

Thorn smiled. "No one seems to mind drinking my supper portion for me."

Dick stopped in the middle of washing the roasting pan and inched one of the window shutters open. "Whoa, looks like we have a fair blizzard going on out there!"

Tom whirled, carving knives raised. "Get your nose back in, and close that! It's after dark, you idiot!"

Dick slammed the shutter closed and put down the wrist-thick bar. "Oh, yes, of course, sir."

Thorn frowned at the row of windows along the back wall over the sink. The entire row was shuttered from the inside. Shutters were perfectly understandable—on the outside of a building, they protected the window glass—but these were closed on the inside and heavily barred. She looked over at the red-cheeked cook. "Are we expecting some kind of an attack?"

Tom frowned. "You mean you don't know?"

The small hairs rose on the back of her neck. "Know what?"

The cook and his two assistance exchanged looks, and their cheeks paled. The acrid scent of cold sweat suddenly filled the kitchen.

Alarm surged through Thorn. They were hardened war veterans, and they were afraid, all of them. "Guys, what's going on?"

Tom sighed and set his hand on his hip. "The dead have been walking at night and eating anyone they find."

"What?" That had to be some kind of a joke. Thorn's hand tightened on her spoon, bending it just a little. "That's insane! The dead can't walk."

"It's true." Harry slammed his masher into his potatoes violently. "We have the house shuttered upstairs and down because the damned things are attracted to light."

Tom shook his head. "They broke into a bunch of houses and killed everyone in them before anyone knew they were even there."

Thorn set down her spoon. She wasn't hungry anymore. "Why doesn't someone hunt them down?"

"They have been, but it doesn't seem to do any good." Dick scowled and applied his scrubber to the roasting pan. "They're real good at hiding during the day, and at night they're practically unstoppable."

Harry bared his teeth at his potatoes. "You can chop them to bits, and all the bits keep moving."

Tom turned to look at Thorn. "And if they bite you, you're dead in a day and a walking corpse the following night."

Harry shook his head. "Nobody can get them all because when people get bit, they hide. They don't want to get shot by their neighbors."

Dick sprinkled soap on the roasting pan. "And then they die anyway and end up eating their neighbors."

Tom stacked slices of roast onto a plate. "The only thing that destroys them is fire. That's why the Russians are burning towns."

Thorn couldn't believe what she was hearing. *This* was the plague the colonel was talking about, a plague of walking dead? She shook her head. "If this is really happening, why don't they clear all the people out of this town?"

"Evacuate the whole town?" Tom waved his carving knife. "And send them where?" He pointed his knife at the barred windows. "In case you haven't noticed, it's winter; there's no place for them to go. Staying home and locking the door is safer than going out in the open and freezing to death or getting eaten."

"Don't you worry." Dick nodded toward Thorn. "Come spring when the passes open, this town will empty out real fast."

Harry stood up with his pot of potatoes and walked around the table. "In the meantime, everyone barricades themselves in their houses at night, and in the morning they go out and burn the houses that couldn't keep them out." He set the pot on the sideboard by Tom's carving board.

Thorn blinked. "They're burning houses? You're lucky this whole town hasn't gone up in flames."

"They've been real careful about only burning the houses that get broken into." Tom left the sliced roast on the sideboard to check on the two pots simmering on the huge Franklin stove.

Thorn shoved her bowl back. "What about tenements—you know, where piles of families all live in one building?"

Dick turned to grab her bowl from the table. "Oh, those all got burned with the first snow last month. Most of the factory workers, and their families, are living in the attics of the factories."

Thorn shook her head. "So everybody just goes on like normal during the day and hopes they don't get eaten at night? That's crazy! How can you live this way?"

Dick waved his soapy washcloth. "Oh, don't worry, this house is brick. Unless someone lets them in, they won't get in here."

"And we'll be leaving real soon." Harry's jaw tightened. "Snow or no snow."

Tom moved the two pots off the stove. "All right, ladies, let's get supper upstairs in the dining room!" In a clatter of china and silverware, the food was set on trays, hefted on shoulders, and carried out of the kitchen.

Alone in the warm kitchen, Thorn listened to the winter storm rattling the window glass. The dead were walking? It had to be a hoax, a joke, a scary tale you told the gullible. But the stink of their fear was real enough. Something was definitely going on in this town at night.

Footsteps sounded on the stairs into the kitchen.

Thorn snapped sharply awake from her nap. Curled up under her gray fleece coat in the corner between the firewood and the pantry shelves, she held perfectly still and ready to leap, just in case.

Brentwood stepped into the kitchen and frowned. "Courier?"

Thorn released her breath and eased to her feet in silence. "Yes?"

Brentwood's right hand dove inside his jacket, and his head whipped around to stare at her, clearly startled. He took a breath to compose his expression and eased his hand out from under his jacket. He cleared his throat and held out a small brown-paper-wrapped parcel with a letter tucked under the string. "This is your return package. You're to deliver it to your superior officer without opening either the package or the letter."

Thorn took the parcel and snorted. "I know better than to open anything I deliver." She smiled tightly. "Being tortured for information is not my idea of fun."

"You'll leave at first light." Brentwood stepped back and held out his hand toward the stairs. "A room has been prepared for you. This way, please."

Thorn knelt to shove the parcel in her canvas pack. "I'd rather leave now." She had no interest in remaining under the same roof as Colonel Ives any longer than absolutely necessary.

"Now?" Brentwood's eyes widened, and he stiffened. "But you can't go out now!" The scent of cold sweat drifted off him.

Thorn looked up at him and frowned. He was afraid. "Why not?" Was the cooks' story true, or was it something else?

"Why not?" Brentwood glanced at the barricaded windows and then frowned at her. "You must have seen them, or at least heard about them, on your way here?"

"Them?" Thorn picked up her hat and folded her fleeced coat over her arm. "I didn't see anything on my way here but trees, snow, and the occasional wild animal." And a solitary vampire, though she supposed he could be considered a wild animal, too. She very nearly smiled. "I went cross-country."

His frown deepened. "Cross-country . . . ? Then you didn't pass through any of the towns?"

Thorn rolled her eyes. "Are you saying that the story of the dead walking at night is true?"

Brentwood looked her dead in the eye, and his mouth tightened. "There have been reports of attacks in just about every town in this region."

Thorn's brows lifted. True or not, hard-nosed and trigger-happy Brentwood believed in the walking dead. "All right, I'll leave in the morning."

Brentwood dropped his shoulders and released a breath and then turned to face the stairs. "This way, please."

Thorn followed Brentwood up the kitchen stairs and then into another, narrower stairwell straight up to a cramped and shadowed hallway at the very top of the house, right under the eves. A miniature oil lamp on a small battered table at the far left was the only source of light in the hall. He pointed to a narrow blue door at the far right end of the hall. "Water closet."

Thorn blinked. Did this mean they actually had indoor flushing toilets or just an indoor bathtub?

Brentwood led her to the other end of the tiny hall. He stopped at the table and pointed her up an even smaller stair, not much more than a ladder. At the top was a very small door. "Your room." He handed her the tiny oil lamp from the table.

"Thanks." Thorn climbed the narrow stair and opened the door into a room barely large enough for the carpet and the straw-filled mattress resting on top of it. A tiny circular window, shuttered of course, occupied the far wall, and the chimney spanned the right wall, so the room was actually warm. However, the ceiling was very low, and the slope from the chimney down to the left was very steep.

Thorn smiled sourly. A grown man would not have been able to stand upright comfortably, but it was perfect for someone as small as her and probably the only absolute privacy available in the whole house.

At the bottom of the stairs, Brentwood coughed softly.

Thorn turned around and smiled. "It's perfect, thank you."

Brentwood nodded. "Sleep well." He walked away, headed for the staircase.

Thorn stepped into the room, closed the door, and investigated the feather pillow and the battered gray wool army blankets that had been tossed on the mattress. After last's night's cave floor, the straw mattress was going to feel like heaven. She shucked out of her clothes, tossing them at the end of the bed, blew out the tiny oil lamp, and burrowed naked between the blankets. She sighed.

Something moved under her blankets carrying the scent of wool, man, and midnight.

Thorn's eyes snapped open. *What the hell . . . ?* She twisted sharply in her blankets.

Powerful arms closed around her waist, trapping her. Warm skin pressed against her bare back, under the blankets. Breath brushed against her ear. "Ah, how pleasant."

She froze. She knew that voice. She knew that scent. "Yaroslav?" She turned to look over her shoulder.

The vampire smiled less than a kiss away, the tips of his

long teeth neatly hidden behind his full, pale lips. "Thorn." In the deep shadows, his long hair was a curtain of black silk with two streaks of silver at the temples, framing a youthful and achingly beautiful face. He focused on her lips and leaned close.

"Whoa, hey!" She turned away, avoiding his kiss, and glanced about. The shadowed ceiling was sharply pitched and heavily thatched over bare beams. The moon was bright through a square and open window. She was not in her garret room but under some other roof. Hay crunched under the blanket spread beneath them. "What am I doing here?"

His lips landed on her throat, and his tongue swirled, raising shivers. "You have come to visit me in a dream." Under the wool blanket, his long hard leg slid over hers, and the hot hard length of his erection pressed against her spine. Apparently he was naked. His teeth grazed her pulse.

She gasped and shifted in his arms. "This is a dream?" It had to be; it couldn't be anything else, but it was so real. Heat pooled low in her belly and clenched with rising interest. He felt good, too good. It was fast getting difficult to think past the carnal hunger tightening within her.

Yaroslav sighed against her throat. "Is a good dream, no?" One hand slid up to cup the fullness of her breast and squeezed. His other hand swept down over the gentle curve of her belly, and delved between her thighs, encouraging her legs to part for his knee.

The hair rose on her body, and her nipple tightened deliciously under his palm. A moan slipped out of her mouth. "What are you doing?"

"I should think it was obvious." He chuckled, and his fingers captured her swiftly hardening nipple. "Giving my love to you." He pinched.

Fired sparked in her nipple and echoed down in her clit, startling a soft cry from her lips. Moisture slicked her thighs.

She had to take an entire breath to recover her thoughts. "But I don't recognize any of this." She'd never seen this attic before.

His lips brushed against her ear. "Because this is my place of rest. You have come into *my* dream." He cupped her hip to pull her snug against his erection and then palmed her feminine curls. A long finger investigated the tender folds to her body's entrance. "Mmmm . . . you are becoming very wet, my sweet." With the pad of his finger, he rubbed against the tiny nub of sensitive flesh.

Hot bolts of pleasure jolted her. Her back arched, and her soft cries filled the small attic. If he kept this up, she was going to come. . . . She grabbed for his wrist and some small part of her sanity. "Are we in a hurry?"

He chuckled and eased his wrist from her grasp. "Dreams have a habit of being short-lived." His fingers once again began their demonic dance on her damp flesh.

She moaned. "Is that a yes?"

His tongue stroked against her throat. "It is a yes."

She writhed under his hand. "Oh, I see. . . ." A hole in the thatched ceiling overhead caught her attention. His "place of rest" appeared to be an abandoned house in a village some- where.

There have been reports of attacks in just about every town in this region.

Alarm spilled ice water down her spine. She grabbed his wrist to stop his inciting fingers. "Yaroslav, wait!"

He gently twisted his wrist free of her hand and wrapped his arm around her. "No waiting." He cupped her butt cheek in his other palm. "Sleep is fleeting, and I would have you before I wake." He shifted against her back, his rigid cock sliding down along the seam of her butt to ease between her thighs. The broad, hot tip nudged at her moist entrance.

"Please!" She twisted sharply onto her back and grabbed his shoulder. "Just for a minute!"

"A minute is too long." He rolled on top of her, resting on his forearms, and his head dropped with the clear intent to kiss her.

She pressed her hand over his descending mouth. "I have a question, damnit!"

He smiled, and his wet tongue swept across her palm.

It tickled. She yanked her hand back. "It's important!"

He sighed and rolled his eyes. "Very well, one question." His gaze narrowed. "Then no more of this waiting."

She looked up at him. "Are the dead really walking?"

He froze above her, every muscle in his body stiffening. "Yes." His brows dropped low, and his mouth tightened to a thin line. "It is a plague with no cure but fire."

Thorn felt a chill sweep along her body. "You're saying it's true, that the dead are walking around eating people?"

"I am." His lips curled back from his long teeth, and a growl rumbled in his chest. "This evil came to my mountain and destroyed my people. I was forced to burn my villages, my forests, and my house to the ground. There is nothing left on my mountain but ash."

She stared, horrified. A forest fire had happened in a valley at the far edge of her mountains at high summer, years ago. The monstrous flames had lit the night sky for miles. The blackened and shattered ruins left behind had been the most horrible thing she'd ever seen. And he'd set an entire mountain on fire? Could this have been what she had seen in his dream? "My god . . ."

The hearts of the vampire's eyes seemed to leap with flames. "This evil forced me to destroy everything I once called mine." His sharp nails dug into her shoulders. "Now you know why I am here. I hunt the heretic sorcerer who cast this plague of evil, to destroy him!"

Thorn shivered hard. She knew hatred when she saw it. She frowned. "Wait a minute, a *sorcerer?*"

"Enough of minutes! Enough of questions!" His mouth came down on her parted lips. His tongue filled her mouth, seeking hers, kissing her with ruthless skill as though starved. He pressed the entire hard length of his body against hers, his cock urgently rigid against her belly.

Thorn moaned under the onslaught. Erotic hunger roared forth. Her nipples rose to hot, tight points, and her belly clenched with sudden ravenous appetite, forcing a gasp from her throat. She grabbed his forearms, digging in with her long nails.

He pulled his mouth from hers, and his eyes blazed with heat. "I wish to think of nothing but the sweetness of your flesh." He reached down to catch her thighs and pushed them up over his hips, spreading her. "I wish to hear nothing but the sounds of your pleasure."

Startled, she grabbed onto his shoulders, her fingers tangling in the silk of his hair. "Yaroslav?"

"No more waiting!" He reached down to set his cock against the slick entrance to her body. "Now." He grunted and thrust.

She arched under him, opening her body, welcoming the relentless push of his broad shaft.

He grunted and thrust deep, the hard length of his cock stretching her tender flesh. "Yes. . . ."

She bucked hard, sheathing him all the way to the root, and gasped.

His hands closed tight on her thighs. He arched, withdrawing, and then thrust, and thrust . . .

She locked her legs around his hips and writhed against him, feeling his rigid cock moving powerfully in her depths. She moaned with the agonizing delight of having him within her.

He sighed against her right ear. "Yes, that is what I wish to hear." His hands slid down her thighs to cup her butt, his nails digging in. He pulled, his cock sliding outward, and thrust back in brutally hard, then again, and again . . .

She bucked in his arms, straining to meet his pounding rhythm. She could feel every muscle in his back, ass, and thighs flexing as he took her with desperate violence. It was the most erotic thing she'd ever felt. A man upon whom she could unleash the full strength of her passions. A man she would not break.

Pleasure sparked with incredible speed and coiled tight with boiling fury in her core. She dug her nails into his back, and the scream built in her throat. She could see the blood running down his back from her nails. The sight inflamed her. Her gasps became cries as pressure and need rose to the explosion point.

His grunts became gasps. "Yes, Mother Night . . . yes!"

She writhed as her body came to the razor's edge—and refused to fall. *Damnit!* She wrapped her legs around him and clawed his back with her nails in violent urgency. "Please . . . !"

He groaned but the amusement was clear in the sound. "Please, what?"

"Please!" She shouted and bucked hard. "I need it!"

He ground into her. "What do you need, love?"

She shuddered, tormented by the pleasure she couldn't reach. "Bite me!"

His head lifted, and his bared teeth gleamed white. His head fell lightning fast. His teeth sank into her, and he slammed his cock into her with merciless strokes.

Fire exploded in her shoulder. She screamed with the bright hot pain of his bite even as her body flared with an overwhelming wave of clenching carnal heat that threatened to eat her alive. Lightning rushed up her spine and exploded at the back of her skull. Her body shattered from the inside in a release so profound it felt as though her heart had burst. She howled, shaking and clawing at the man holding her in his pitiless grasp.

He sucked on the wounds on her shoulder, growling, and

then released her, licking his lips. "Mine." He thrust into her, grunted, thrust again, and then held. He gasped, shuddering, his cock pulsing in her body. His eyes closed briefly, and then he threw back his head and screamed with a voice that was not even remotely human.

6

Thorn gasped, and her eyes snapped open with the echoes of Yaroslav's feral scream in her ears. Panting for breath and soaked with sweat, she clutched the blankets, shaking. Her heart slammed in her chest.

Her gaze locked on the sharply pitched ceiling and then the brick chimney rising along the wall next to her. The vague sound of barking dogs echoed in the night beyond the shutters. She was back in the garret. It *had* been a dream. She smiled and shook her head. That had been one intense dream, and he hadn't been kidding about being in a hurry either. She'd never in her life met a man that could get her that excited that fast.

She sat up on the straw mattress and groaned. Her entire body ached and trembled. She dragged a hand through her wet hair and sighed. She was sticky with sweat and stank of sex. She thought about changing to get herself clean, but she really didn't want the appetite that came with it. Out in the wild it was fairly easy to grab a rabbit or two, but among humans it meant going down to the kitchen and rummaging for food.

Her brow lifted. There was a water closet at the end of the

hall. She doubted that the boiler was lit, so the water would probably be ice cold, but it was better than nothing, and there might be a flush toilet available.

She rose from the bed and wrapped the blanket around her. Nudity didn't bother her one bit, but she knew for a fact Colonel Ives would have a stroke if she were seen by his men. For an entire breath she seriously considered doing it just to piss him off. She sighed and walked to her door. It wasn't worth all the yelling and screaming. Not to mention that the colonel had a nasty habit of using a cane for discipline.

She opened her door and peered down the shadowed hall with eyes perfectly suited to see in full darkness. Nothing moved. The only sound was the wind rattling the window glass beyond the shutters.

Clutching her blanket, she padded down the hall along the wall. Floors tended to squeak when you walked down the middle. The door to the water closet opened into a good-sized room with a black-and-white-tiled floor and a claw-foot bathtub against the left wall. The right wall held a tiny two-spigot sink and beyond it, miracle of miracles, was a pull-chain flush toilet.

Thorn walked over to peer into the china toilet bowl. There was actually water in there. She marveled for a whole three breaths and then turned and eyed the tub with a pang of regret. She doubted there was enough hot water left in the basement boiler to use it.

She padded to the sink and twisted the spigot on the sink marked H. Warm water came splashing out with an incredible amount of noise. Someone must have used the hot water not too long ago if the water in the pipes was still warm. Not that she was about to complain. She shoved the cork into the drain to hold the water.

She grabbed the cloth hanging from the sink and the soap

and scrubbed her entire body. The flower scent of the soap was a bit strong but not unbearable.

She used the toilet, just because she could, and pulled the chain. The toilet made horrific sucking noises, even louder than the sink, but as far as she was concerned, indoor plumbing was well worth the racket it made.

After wrapping the blanket back around her, Thorn stepped back out of the water closet. Outside beyond the shuttered windows, the neighborhood dogs were barking up a storm. There was fear and anger in their voices. She frowned. They were sounding an alarm. She concentrated on listening closely and realized she could also hear someone breathing on the stairs that led to the lower floor.

She froze and then took a deep, silent breath to sift through the aromas. She smelled masculine feet, body-warmed wool, some silk, sweat, and traces of expensive cologne, but the strongest scent was gun oil. If she'd been in wolf form, she would have detected a hell of a lot more, but this was good enough to let her know that Max was standing barefoot on the stairs with a gun. She was pretty sure he was the only one in the house wearing that particular cologne.

What should she do? A normal human probably wouldn't have noticed him. She sighed softly and tucked her blanket around her securely. Dealing with human limitations was such a pain in the ass. She stepped forward and moved past the staircase without looking.

Weight shifted, making the stair squeak loud enough for a battalion to notice.

Thorn looked toward the stairs. Yep, Max was there, all right, three steps down, in his shirtsleeves and wool trousers with the leather suspenders flopping at his hips, and he was barefoot. She didn't see the gun, but his britches seemed to be sagging in the backside. That was probably where the gun was, tucked in his waistband at the small of his back. She smiled. "Oh, Mr. Rykov, did I disturb you?"

"Miss Ferrell . . ." He kept his gaze low and smiled, keeping his hands behind him. "My apologies. I was just coming up to use the water closet."

Thorn blinked. With a gun?

Outside, the sound of the dogs got louder and more frightened. They sounded like they were barking right under the house. She frowned and turned toward the shuttered window.

"Something wrong, Miss Ferrell?"

Thorn shook her head absently. "The dogs . . ."

Max chuckled. "Oh, they're barking because of the dead."

Thorn turned back to look at him. "The dead?" Did he mean the walking corpses everyone had been talking about?

"Yes, Miss Ferrell." Max looked to the side and smiled. "The dead are walking."

Thorn scrambled for something, anything to say. "And people leave their dogs out with those . . . things?" She winced. That was not the brightest of comments.

Max snorted. "The dead seem to have no interest in eating dogs. Humans, on the other hand, they find quite irresistible." He lifted his chin and closed his eyes. "The barking is right below us." He smiled broadly with crooked teeth. "The dead will be banging on the windows very soon." There was a strange scent mixed with copper rolling off Max.

The wolf sharing Thorn's soul snarled in alarm, and the hair rose on her body. Something was not right with Max.

Max eased up onto the next step. "They're drawn to light and the smell of blood, you know."

She backed away toward her door. "Mr. Rykov?"

He scratched the back of his head and gazed at her sideways. "You do have the package, right?"

Thorn frowned. Should he know that?

"No need for alarm." Max came up the next step and waved

a hand. The scent of copper drifted from him. "I was the one who brought it to the good American colonel, and he assured me that he had the best courier in the world right here in the house. Someone who could cross mountains in winter." He lifted his chin and stared straight at her. "That could only be you."

Thorn froze. Something was wrong with Max, all right. His left eye was a mild ordinary brown, but his right was bright copper, shiny as a new penny, and completely inhuman in shape with an upward slant. It was the eye of a predatory animal.

Max raised his left hand, and the scent of copper became overpowering. There were curved claws on his fingertips, and blood was smeared from his palm all down his forearm. He licked the side of his thumb absently. "Don't you think it's time you got dressed and started running for your life?"

Thorn knew better than to turn her back on a predator. "Am I supposed to escape, Mr. Rykov?"

Max stopped licking and sighed. "Actually, yes. That package really needs to get into American hands." He waved his other hand down the hall. "Go get dressed. Oh, and I suggest climbing out the window and traversing the roof, seeing as I left the front door wide open."

Thorn stared at him. "You left the front door open? But those . . . things will get inside and kill everybody!"

Max smiled, and this time his mouth was full of jagged teeth. "Oh, don't worry about them." His voice dropped to a low and inhuman rumble. "They're already dead."

Icy sweat erupted all down her back. "They're . . . dead?" Tom, Dick, Harry, Brentwood . . . Colonel Ives? "All of them?"

Max nodded sadly. "Died in their sleep, every last one of them." He rolled his eyes and waved a bloodstained hand. "Well, so to speak." He frowned. "Brentwood and Ives gave me a bit of trouble. . . ." He licked his stained palm.

Anger burned away her fear. *Murderer. . . .* But she was not so easily killed. Thorn let the wolf rise under skin in a hot rush of power, stopping at the very brink of transformation. She fisted her hands to hide her lengthening nails. "If I may ask, Mr. Rykov . . ." She spoke carefully to hide the fangs in her mouth. "What are you?"

He chuckled. "Why, my dear Miss Ferrell, I'm a wolf in human clothing." He tapped his chin with a clawed finger. "I think they call us werewolves." He smiled with a mouthful of jagged teeth. "Yes, I believe that was it; I'm a werewolf—just like you."

Thorn froze in complete shock. He knew *she* was a werewolf?

His brows lifted. "My goodness, you look positively shocked."

Something smashed downstairs.

Max turned and peered down the stairs. "Oh, dear, it seems we're out of time." He turned to her. "You better go make your escape while they're busy eating." He held up his hands. Both were stained with blood to the elbows. "And if you'll excuse me, I really do need to use the water closet." He stepped up the last stair and into the hallway.

Thorn backed away from him.

Max turned toward the water closet and kept walking. He entered and closed the door behind him.

She bolted into her room, threw on her cream flannel shirt, and dragged on her other dungarees, shoving her boots and socks into her pack. She would need to use her clawed feet as well as her hands to go traveling across rooftops.

Max was a werewolf. There were others, werewolves . . . like her.

The wolf in her soul snarled in anger. *Not like me. Not like me at all.* There was nothing right or sane about something that killed and ate its own kind.

Thorn stopped in the middle of shoving her arms into her coat sleeves. Max was eating . . . people?

The wolf had lived in the remote wilderness for most of her life. She knew the stench of humans that ate humans when she smelled it.

Thorn felt her gorge rise. *Cannibalism.* . . . She shoved it down and buttoned her coat. Never mind the dead things that might be down two fights of stairs, Max was just at the end of the hall. She shoved her hat on her head and tied the string under her chin. She didn't bother braiding her hair; there wasn't time. She had to get out of there before Max decided to eat her. Yes, she was a werewolf, but he was the same, only nearly twice her size. There was no way she could take him in a fight.

Not the same. The wolf within sneered in derision. *Disconnected. Out of balance.*

Thorn agreed. Max was definitely not balanced. Only the insane ate people. She jammed her arms into the straps of her pack. Why would anyone *want* to eat one anyway? People tasted nasty. She'd bitten enough of them to know.

She went to the window and pushed up the bar to open the shutters. The window was a simple framed piece of glass with a hinge on one side and a latch on the other. It was fairly small, too, but she could go through it. However, the snowstorm still raged just beyond the glass.

She winced. *Great.* She unlocked the window latch and pulled open the small circular window. Snow blew in, driven by the wind.

She looked down. People shambled along the narrow street. Snow stuck to their faces, their bare feet, and their bare arms. The snow should have melted on contact with their skin. They couldn't be living; they had to be the dead. Her heart stuttered in her chest. The dead . . . *walking.*

Thorn closed her eyes and took a deep breath, sifting the wind for a scent. She couldn't smell anything beyond the cold.

She shoved farther out the window, gripping the snow-encrusted sill. Never mind them! There was a huge werewolf that ate people at the end of the hall. She needed to find a way to get her ass up on that roof. She twisted around to look up. The roof's edge was right there, within easy reach, but the roof's pitch was incredibly steep—and covered in snow. She would definitely need claws and strength to get up there, never mind walk across it.

She closed her eyes and let the wolf rise, but slowly. She needed the wolf's strength but didn't want to lose the human shape that would allow her to climb. Muscle bunched and expanded. Her shirt tightened in the arms and shoulders. The pale thin hair all over her body lengthened and became more like fur. Her hands and feet changed in shape and grew hard pads. Her nails extended and hardened into true claws.

She opened her eyes and took a deep breath. She could see as if it were full daylight. She wrinkled her nose. The scented soap she'd used earlier smelled a hell of a lot stronger and somewhat nasty. She could actually smell the fat and the lye used to make it.

Her waist-length hair, blowing in the breeze through the window, had gone from pale brown to silvery white. She readjusted her hat to suit her taller pointed ears and then scrubbed the roughened heel of her hand over the slight ruff along the edge of her jaw. There were three buttons on the seat of this set of overalls. She opened them and eased out her tail and then shook hard to settle the light fur that had grown all over her body. In this form, her fur wasn't near thick enough to run around naked, but it would make nice insulating layer under her clothes.

The commode flushed down the hall. She was out of time.

Thorn shoved her head out the window and twisted around to grab the eaves above her. Her claws sank in, and the wood shingles crunched. She pushed with her feet braced on the windowsill and pulled with her claws, dragging herself up onto the snowy roof.

She clawed her way to the peak on the roof to look. She couldn't see much; her wolf eyesight was somewhat near-sighted, and the blowing snow wasn't helping. What she could see was the next roof over.

The wolf within assured her that the jump to the next build-ing would not be difficult.

Thorn bolted down the opposite slope and leaped, her body stretching out to cover the distance. She hit the side of the next roof, her toe and finger claws digging into the snow-covered shingles to keep her from sliding. She climbed to that roof peak and ran down the side to launch herself at the next roof, and the next . . .

Her other half had been right. The jumps were almost ridi-culously easy. She wasn't worried about getting lost—her wolf soul knew exactly which way she needed to go—the question was, were there enough roofs to get her there?

She had lost count of her jumps when she finally hit a snag. The next roof was on the other side of a fairly wide street. It was too far to jump. Worse still, even if she made it across to the house, the damned thing was made of brick, making it a real bitch to climb.

She hunched down and stared through the falling snow at the ragged people shambling along the street below her. They were definitely dead. She shivered hard.

If she couldn't get up on the next house, she'd have to run for it. Her fastest speed was on four legs, but four legs did not work properly in human clothing. If she took off her clothes and later reassumed her two-legged form, she'd have to take the time to get dressed again. In full wolf form she wouldn't even feel the cold, but the fur on her half-human body was not near thick enough to keep her from freezing.

Her tail switched back and forth in annoyance. Damnit, what should she do? Either she had to take off her clothes and hope she could stay out of their reach all the way to the far end of town or find a quick way onto the next roof. Maybe she could outrun them on two legs until she could get back onto a roof?

Behind her, an eerie howl echoed in the night. The fur all up her spine and across her shoulders rose. That sound was not from any dog, and it certainly wasn't a wolf. It had to be Max. She looked back. Her scent trail across the snowy roofs was probably as obvious to him as red paint on a white dress. There was no doubt in her mind that he would follow it.

Shit! She slammed her fist onto the roof by her foot. The shingles crunched. This whole assignment had been one circus-freak act after another! She looked down at the road and then up at the house directly across from her. She had to do something. She could not stay where she was.

The eerie howl echoed again from a lot closer.

Max was definitely on her trail. She was out of time. Thorn looked down at the street. There was only one shambling figure, and it was in bad condition, partially blackened, as though some of it had burned. She looked left and right. She didn't see any others beyond this one.

Thorn hunkered down for a long jump. She really, really did not want to go down there, but she didn't have a choice. To get to the other roof, she still had to go down first. She launched off the roof and landed smack-dab in the middle of the road, rolling in the snow. She lunged back onto her feet and pelted for the house on the other side.

A weird howling moan sounded behind her.

Thorn did not want to know what it was. She hopped over the low stone wall into the garden and made for the house's windows. If she could get ahold of the windowsills, she could climb. . . .

A loud report blasted from the house. She jumped to the side and looked up. A window shutter was open, and someone had a gun pointed at her.

She rolled away from the gun's sight and pressed her back against the garden wall. *Shit! Now what?*

That weird moan sounded again.

A gun blast hammered in her ears, and something wet exploded far too close.

Thorn didn't bother to look. She bolted around the house to the back and headed for the wall and the next house. From what she could see, it was clapboard. She could claw her way up, as long as the wood wasn't too rotted. She hopped up on the low wall and faced three dead things only an arm's length away.

Their mouths opened, their arms lifted . . .

Thorn yelped in complete fright and jumped off the wall, launching right over their heads. She landed against the side of the house, claws first, and dug in. Her heart beating in her throat, she scrabbled her way up the side, scoring the hell out of the house's wooden siding.

She made it up onto the snowy roof and rolled onto her back, panting for breath. *God in heaven, that was way too close.*

Groaning, she rolled onto her hands and clawed her way up the snow-covered shingles onto the roof's shallow peak. Her eyes opened wide. She'd somehow found her way onto a long line of two-story row houses. No jumping, at least for a while. She frowned. There seemed to be dark spots on some of the roofs in the distance, but her wolf eyes couldn't quite make out what it was.

She sighed. No matter, it was running time. She got up onto her feet and started down the line of roofs.

7

In the blowing snow under churning clouds, Thorn lifted her head and looked out from under the brim of her hat down the line of roofs. The icy wind slashed against her cheeks. The wolf sharing her soul was insisting that they were drifting off course. By following the curving line of row houses, they were slowly but surely heading away from where she had originally entered the town. Sometime soon she'd have to leave this set of row houses to get back on track.

She rose to her feet and looked behind her. Sporadic and hysterical barking echoed in the night, but she hadn't heard Max's eerie howl in quite a while. Not that she was complaining. It would have been nice to think she'd lost him, but she couldn't see how. Her barefoot trail in the snow should have been easy to follow, if only by scent. It was more likely he'd found something more interesting to chase. Hopefully it wasn't human. She trotted down the line of roofs.

Hours passed—she had no idea how many. It got colder, and the snow showed no sign of letting up. Dangerously unstable roofs with burn holes became more frequent, and progress down the line of row houses slowed to little more than a fast walk. Thorn's bare hands had started to tingle, even with the extra protection of the coarse pads, and her feet were definitely getting numb. She shoved her chilled hands in her pockets, but there wasn't a damned thing she could do about her bare feet. And she was getting hungry.

A long, loud steam whistle sounded.

Thorn skidded to a halt and suddenly realized she was only one house from the end of the row. She had run out of roofs.

And she was way off course.

She scowled. She'd meant to get off this row of houses before she'd gotten this far. *Damnit. . . .*

She walked across the last roof and crouched on the edge. A broad cobbled thoroughfare wide enough for six vehicles stretched before her, bordered by a monstrous brick wall. Beyond the wall, left and right, as far as her eyes could see, were acres and acres of monstrous brick, steel, and glass factories soaring four to twelve stories high with a forest of tall smoking chimneys.

The open countryside was just beyond. She needed to find a way past the wall and through those factories.

She looked down the side of the building she stood on and spotted a windowsill below her and another below that. Getting down wouldn't be difficult, but it would be a solid four-foot run from then on. There was no way in hell she'd be able to climb up on top of those factories.

Thorn looked up the broad snow-covered road. She squinted, trying to see through the swirling snow. Nothing moved, living or dead. The only sound was the hushed whisper of wind-driven snow. She nodded. All right, time to find a place to change out of her clothes.

Thorn trotted back along the roofs and started looking for a burned house with some of the second floor still intact.

Four houses back, Thorn crept close to the edge of a blackened hole in a roof to peer within. The wood under her feet trembled and squealed alarmingly. Right up against the brick wall, one whole room on the second floor was still there. She eased back, away from the hole. She couldn't jump down from there. Attempting to go through the crumbling hole could collapse the whole roof. She went to the side of the building and looked over the edge for the room's window. Luckily the glass was already smashed out of it.

Her claws crunching deep into the roof shingles, she eased backward down onto the windowsill and then into the small room. The floor was gray with ash, but it felt pretty stable, compared to the roof, anyway. The room's door stood wide open onto a half of a blackened hallway with only the top of a staircase intact. She smiled grimly. Unless those dead things could jump straight up almost an entire story, she was pretty safe to change.

Thorn peeled out of her clothes, rolled them up tight, and tucked them into her pack as fast as she could. It was seriously cold. Shivering hard, she shoved her arms back into the pack's straps and then crouched down. She closed her eyes and opened her soul to her wolf side. The delicious warm rush of shifting muscle and thickening fur arched her spine, drawing a deep groan from her chest. The heavy winter coat was a very welcome addition. Already halfway there, it took only two breaths to complete her change into the long, elegant silver wolf.

Twisting sharply, Thorn shook her body from nose to tail, stretching her muscles and settling her fur under the pack. Her stomach clenched and rumbled. She really needed to eat. If she was lucky, someone might have left a goat or a calf in a shed somewhere.

Her nails clicking on the bare boards, she trotted over to the window and set her forepaws on the windowsill. She stuck out her head and looked but didn't see any movement. The factory machines and the rushing wind were the only sounds she could hear. The only thing she could smell was the charred wood of the building she was in.

She took a breath and then launched through the window, landing smoothly on the snow-covered street.

Movement exploded all along the edges of the street. Tangled humps covered with snow rose relatively upright and lurched toward her on twisted and rag-covered limbs.

Thorn froze, and the fur all down her spine lifted.

Dozens of dogs, short-coated, floppy-eared mutts and lean, red-furred wolf breeds, lunged out from under the buildings. Barking insanely, they rushed at the moving dead things.

Thorn had no interest in getting caught between the dogs and the dead. She wheeled and bolted down the street in a flat-out run, snow flying from her paws. She took a sharp turn into a long narrow lane between crumbling row houses that stank of charred wood and then took another turn into an even narrower street, little more than an alley. The sound of her panting breaths and her paws scuffing snow echoed between the buildings. Beyond that was only sporadic gusts of wind.

Huh? She stopped and turned to look back up the street. Nothing moved behind her. Neither the dogs nor the dead had followed her. Her ears lifted, and her head tilted in confusion. What had happened to them? She took two steps back toward the main road and stopped. Did she really want to see what had happened between the dogs and the dead? She turned away and trotted up the narrow road between the row houses through the falling snow. No, no, she didn't.

Two streets later, Thorn realized she was even farther off course than before. She turned her nose firmly in the right direction and trotted into an alley going the right way.

She crossed a couple of empty gardens, a few barren yards piled with old refuse, and came face-to-face with a tall stone wall with a spiked ironwork grille at the top. Factory sounds drifted from the other side.

She stood up on her hind paws, leaning on her front paws for balance. The wall was nearly three times her length. It was far too high for her to jump, and the brick was almost glass smooth. Hands, even with claws, would be of no use to climb it. She needed to find a way over it or a door through it.

She sighed and dropped back onto her feet and trotted alongside the wall. She passed the backs of four clapboard houses before she realized she was going the wrong way again. A low growl escaped. What was wrong with her? She turned around and loped back the way she'd come.

The wall ended at a cross street. She looked left and then right. Nothing moved but the snow on the wind.

She took a step and stopped in confusion. Her inner directional sense urged her to go right along the wall toward the eastern edge of town and the distant mountains, but something else was urging her to take the narrow alley directly in front of her toward the north.

She took a step to the right and halted. She didn't want to go that way.

What? She shook her head, flapping her tall ears. Yes, she did! She took a determined step toward the east and the mountains. And stopped cold. To her absolute horror, she eased back a step and turned to look to the alley leading north, the way she shouldn't go.

No, damnit! She laid her ears back flat and turned her nose in the correct direction. *Home is this way!* But she couldn't make herself take another step. A troubled whine escaped her throat. A howl of frustration very nearly followed. She clamped her jaw closed. The last thing she needed was a loud, clear announcement to the world in general as to where she was. God only knew what would try to find her, the other werewolf, the shambling dead, something worse . . . ?

Unable to go in the right direction but not wanting to go in the wrong one, Thorn walked in a circle in the middle of the snow-covered lane. This need to go in the wrong direction didn't make sense. The urge wasn't something she was hearing or something she could smell. It was more like a pressure around her heart, something pulling her body. She'd never felt anything like this before, as a human or as a wolf.

Clearly she was being driven insane by this town. The walking dead, the deranged werewolf, people eating people . . . All of it was crazy! She needed to get back to the forest and sanity.

But something else wanted her to go to the north, and it wasn't taking no for an answer.

She turned to face the north alley and snarled, baring her long teeth. Fine, then she'd go north. She trotted down the narrow lane, her ears flat back, anger making her shoulder fur stand stiffly. But whatever was pulling her north was going to be very sorry when she got there. She stretched out into a ground-eating lope.

The alley opened onto a wide thoroughfare that had once been a wealthy neighborhood. It had been completely decimated. The mansions on both sides of the street were blackened piles of rubble behind shattered walls. Even the trees on the once-stately lawns had been burned to char. It looked like a war zone without the battle wreckage.

The only building still standing was at the far end of the broad street—a massive and ornate gothic church several stories tall. The soaring sides were supported by the arched ribs of decorative flying buttresses. The medieval circular stained-glass window, centered between the two rising spires, appeared to be intact.

Whatever had forced her all the way to the north end of town was there.

She loped right down the middle of the street, getting angrier with each long stride. Damnit, she was *hungry!* She'd caught the scent of more than one penned-in goat, but this tether was pulling her too strongly for her to step aside long enough to raid a backyard chicken coop or rabbit hutch.

An eerie high-pitched, baying howl shattered the silence.

Thorn skidded to a stop and turned to look.

Behind her, a hideous manlike creature in a long black coat was bounding up the street in an ungainly lope. Tall, pointed ears parted ragged red-brown hair framing a repulsive face bearing a short doglike muzzle with far too many teeth and not enough fur. Oversize clawed hands extended past the coat's sleeves, and the trousers were ragged past the knees, showing misshapen clawed feet. She couldn't smell anything from it; the wind was going the wrong way—but it was coming straight for her.

Thorn turned and bolted.

"Wait! Wait!" The bellowing voice was oddly pitched and the words barely recognizable. "Please!"

Please? Thorn very nearly tripped. She skidded to a stop and turned to look back at the man thing. It wasn't growling, and its ears were up; it didn't seem to be trying to attack her, but it was so very wrong looking.

Four lengths away, the creature shambled from an uneasy trot to a walk, sniffing. "Smell right. . . ." It stopped a body length away, and its bestial yellow eyes widened. "Oh, pretty. . . ."

Thorn skittered away from it. *It must be nearsighted.* The clumsy thing wasn't acting aggressively, but she had no intention of letting it get close enough to grab her.

The thing stumbled after her. "Wait! I . . . I'm . . ." It pressed a clawed hand over its eyes. "Think . . ." It dropped its hand and took a deep breath. "Yes." It opened its yellow eyes. "Go!" It lurched toward her, waving his clawed hand. "That way!"

She danced away, circling around it. What the hell was this thing trying to do?

"No, no, no!" The creature twisted around to follow her on its misshapen feet and very nearly fell. "That way!"

The wind shifted, and she finally caught its scent. It smelled of dog, old blood, and something else, some*one* else, someone familiar. The hair rose all over her body. It smelled like . . . Max.

What? This hideous man creature couldn't be Max. She dodged around the creature to catch a better scent and immediately wished she hadn't bothered. It was hard to detect under the stench of dog, old blood, and gun oil, but it was Max all right. What the hell was wrong with him? He shouldn't look this . . . deformed. He didn't even have a tail for proper balance.

The wolf that shared her soul snarled in disgust. *Disconnected, warped, divided, imbalanced . . . insane.*

Thorn snorted and circled out of grabbing range. There was no arguing with any of that. Max was definitely not well-connected in the head. She was just glad he wasn't trying to eat her. So what *did* he want?

Max stopped and lowered his head, panting from his deformed muzzle, and wavering on his clawed feet. He took a breath and spoke slowly and with effort. "You are going the wrong way."

Oh! Thorn stopped circling. Was that all? She moved in front of Max and lifted her head. Ears up in a happy, non-aggressive manner, she gave him her best tongue-lolling grin. Very carefully she nodded her entire head in the human manner.

Max straightened, and his head tilted to the side. "You know?"

Thorn nodded again.

Max's ears flattened back. "Why?"

Thorn rolled her eyes. She had no earthly idea why she was out here. She turned to face the church. All the answers were there. She turned and trotted away from the ungainly wolf man.

"Hey!" The word was more bark than speech.

She stopped and looked over her shoulder at Max. *What now?*

His ears lifted. "Follow . . . you?"

She gave him a broad, friendly, panting grin. *Sure, why not?* Whatever had brought her out here could say hello to Max, too.

8

_____

Alert for unusual movement, Thorn padded down the street across the top of the fallen snow, heading straight for the big church at the very end.

Behind her, Max grunted with every step. The snow was up to his calves, and he was foundering in it pretty badly.

Thorn snorted. _Idiot._ If Max had simply assumed a wolf form, he wouldn't be having nearly this much of a problem with the snow. She stretched out into a lope. If he couldn't keep up with her, that wasn't her problem.

Thorn stopped at the ironwork gate to the church's walled enclosure and stared.

It wasn't a church. It was an honest-to-God gothic cathedral. The iron-studded double doors at the top of the steps were a full story high and banded with iron. The huge circular stained-glass window between the tall bell towers had to be at least three of her body length wide. Gargoyle drain spouts stared down from under the eves. Intricate vines and decorative coils framed every arched window. What she could see of the churchyard appeared to be crammed with overgrown bushes and statuary.

It was actually rather pretty in a creepy sort of way.

Whatever was pulling her didn't feel like it was coming from inside the church, so it was somewhere on the grounds.

The wrought-iron gate was chained and locked, but the surrounding stone wall was fairly low. She set her front paws on top and took a quick look. She didn't see any upright glass shards cemented into the broad flat top, and there weren't any iron spikes. A small jump took her on top of the wall. Her wolf's body was long but very narrow. She had no problems balancing.

The churchyard was one huge graveyard crammed tight with headstones. Funerary statues and a few oak trees rose above clumps of winter-bare bushes and the occasional thorned holly. Massive oaks bordered the far edge. Whatever was calling her was just beyond that line of trees.

Panting for breath, Max blundered up to the gate and stopped cold in his tracks, staring at the church. He shuddered, cringed a little, and stepped back.

Huh? Thorn's ears lifted. What was wrong with him now?

Max covered his muzzle with a paw and stumbled farther back. "Bad . . . smell bad."

Thorn sniffed. The smell of church incense was pretty strong, but it didn't smell *bad*.

The wolf in her soul radiated smugness. *Unnatural, unwelcome.*

Unnatural? Thorn snorted and tipped an ear back. *Hello, kettle, this is pot; we're both covered in soot!* She was just as unnatural as Max. And what did she mean by unwelcome?

Different. The wolf within firmly disagreed. *One body, one heart, accepted.*

If you say so. . . . Thorn had no idea how any of that could possibly make a difference, but Max clearly did not like the church. She turned and jumped down from the wall to the top of a broad, snow-covered stone sarcophagus. Either he followed her into the graveyard, or he didn't. She had other things to worry about.

If she didn't eat something really soon, she was going to have a real problem staying in wolf form. Those bowls of stew hadn't been near enough to keep her fed. Hopefully she'd find a rabbit or something hibernating under the roots of one of the bushes.

Out on the street, Max made a sound that sounded suspiciously like a frustrated whine.

Thorn eased through overgrown snow-dusted bushes between the headstones. She ended up fairly close to the cathedral's mortared stone wall and followed it back and back and farther back. . . . The building was a lot longer than it was wide.

Whispers of pipe-organ music drifted from the windows she passed. She turned an ear toward it. Someone was up late. Dawn was still a number of hours away.

Thorn reached the tree line and found a downward staircase that curved to the right. The stairs were broad and shallow. She went down them carefully, barely making a footprint in the snow. Pale gray, moss-stained, marble walls rose to either side, decorated with carvings of flowers and vines.

Thorn stopped only a few steps from the bottom. Before her was what looked like a deep round amphitheater bordered by walls of smooth marble. Sunk into the wall were more than half a dozen grave vaults with grilled cast-iron doors framed and decorated with Roman-style pillars and carvings. Trees and bushes bordered the upper edge of the wall, nearly a full story above, blocking the wind and quite a bit of the blowing snow. The stairs appeared to be the only way in or out.

She couldn't smell anything—the wind was going the wrong way—and she didn't see any movement, but the hair lifted along her spine. She knew a trap when she saw one. She turned to leave.

"At last." The voice was deep, masculine, and accented with an Eastern European lilt.

She froze. She knew that voice. She turned back to look.

The door to the farthest vault on the right swung open. A shadow parted from the darkness within to become a tall dark-haired man in a fur-lined, hooded, ground-sweeping black coat. A sword was belted at his hip, and a pistol was tucked into his black sash. The long black hair, spilling from under his hood, lifted in the wind. He smiled. "Thorn."

Yaroslav? Thorn's ears lifted. All the silver had gone from his midnight hair, and his proudly masculine face had smoothed to the beauty of a fallen angel. He looked . . . young. She shook her head. Never mind that, what was he doing *here?*

"This ground is blessed. The unclean dead cannot abide here." Yaroslav held out his hand. "Come. We have little time."

The pull in Thorn's chest was coming from him. He was the one that had forced her to this place. She braced her feet, dropped her head with her ears laid flat back, and growled. She was not taking one more step.

Yaroslav dropped his hand and sighed. "You are angry."

Thorn curled her lip, baring her teeth, and growled louder. Damned right, she was angry! She was not some dog to answer his call. She had a job to do, damnit, and he was getting in her way.

"What is this . . . job?" He frowned. "I believed that you were done with your U.S. Secret Service?"

Huh? Thorns ears lifted. *How the hell did he . . . ?* Was he listening to her thoughts again?

Yaroslav waved his hand and scowled. "Yes, yes, of course I hear you. You carry my blood." He lifted his chin. "Come, we have much to accomplish before they arrive."

Thorn dropped her ears and snarled. *I can't stay. I have a delivery to make!* She suddenly realized what else he'd said. *They? They—who?*

Yaroslav lifted his chin. "*They*—of the high prince's court."
His jaw tightened. "You cannot leave; they will kill you."

Prince? What prince? Thorn rolled her eyes. *Never mind. . . .*
She snorted. *I'm just a wolf; nobody will notice me.* Not to
mention that she was more than a little experienced in bypass-
ing troops on the field.

"They will indeed notice you." Yaroslav snorted and folded
his arms. "They are watching for that which is out of the ordinary, and this land does not have such large white wolves." He
lifted a black brow. "And certainly none bearing a backpack."

Thorn curled her lip. *Then I'll wear a human form long
enough to get past them.*

The vampire shook his head. "They have come to burn the
unclean dead. They will kill any wandering human they find."

What? The fur along her spine lifted. *Burn the dead?*

Yaroslav looked down and scowled. "Fire is the only way."

Fire? Thorn shivered. He couldn't possibly mean they were
burning *this* town; a lot of people lived here.

Yaroslav met her gaze. "Most of the living population has already been fouled. Death, for them, is only a matter of time."

They can't burn the whole town! Thorn lowered her head
and flattened her ears. *How would you know how many people
are . . . fouled . . . anyway? You haven't been here!*

He shook his head. "To those who can see, it is . . . unmistakable." He closed his eyes briefly. "The poisoned living must
be destroyed, along with the unclean dead, or they will conta-
minate every town within reach of the railway." He sighed
heavily. "If they have not already done so."

Brentwood's words came back to haunt her. *"There have
been reports of attacks in just about every town in this region."*

Yaroslav lifted his hand. "Come, I wish to examine your aspect before the prince's men arrive."

Thorn stiffened against the pull. *Examine my . . . what?* De-
spite her resolve, she stepped down to the bottom of the stairs.

"Your existence proves that there is a heretic sorcerer doing forbidden magic. The heretic's sigil, their signature, will be incorporated into your aspect."

She froze, her muscles shivering with tension. She did not want whatever made her a werewolf taken apart.

Yaroslav frowned. "Thorn, please, stop this resistance. I have no intention of harming you. I merely wish to see who has done this to you."

She snarled at him. *Why?*

He took a deep breath and released it. "It appears that my prince has somehow come to the conclusion that I am the creator of the walking dead."

You? She tilted her head. She couldn't see how. Come to think of it, she couldn't see how anyone could make the dead walk in the first place. She'd read in one of the papers that electricity could make dead frogs twitch, but make a whole town of corpses move? She tilted her head the other way. *Why do they think you did it?*

Yaroslav looked away and shrugged. "I do possess the knowledge to design an infectious spell to do such."

A *spell? Wait a minute, you're saying this is all—magic?* Thorn's ears lifted, and her mouth opened with a wolf's grin. *Magic made the dead walk? You can't be serious? That's fairy tales and make-believe!*

Yaroslav tilted his head and lifted his brow. "Werewolves and vampires are also fairy tales and make-believe, no?"

Thorn closed her mouth, and her ears folded back. He had a point.

Yaroslav waved a hand. "So, as I am one of the very few with such knowledge, it is only natural that I am, of course, under profound suspicion."

The anger bled out of Thorn in a cold rush. *But that's stupid. You wouldn't do something like that.*

Yaroslav smiled sadly. "I am so glad someone believes so."

He folded his hands behind him and looked up from under his hood. "Now, will you allow me to examine your making?"

Fine, all right. Thorn dropped her head and leveled a glare at him. *But you have to let me go first.*

Yaroslav frowned. "Let you . . . go?"

Thorn trembled with hunger. *I need to eat. I need to hunt.* And she needed to do it fast, or she was going to lose her wolf shape. For some reason, hunger drove her into her half-and-half form rather than her human body.

Yaroslav's brows lifted. "Ah, this I can provide. Come." He turned and strode for the farthest vault.

Thorn's ears lifted, and she trotted after him. *You have food?*

Yaroslav glanced over his shoulder and smiled. "I have that which will assuage your hunger." He opened the ironwork gate leading into the vault.

Thorn stepped passed him, and her claws clicked on the stone floor with a slight hollow echo. Her eyes took only moments to adjust to the darkness. The interior of the grave vault was raw-hewn stone, with a curved ceiling, and not very large. It was little more than a middle-sized room. The back wall held nothing but bronze plaques covering the interred, some marked with writing, some not. The side walls each featured a long bench carved directly from the stone wall. A good-sized carpet bag flopped across an arm of the bench on the right wall near the very back. Other than that, the shadow-filled stone room was empty.

Yaroslav followed her in and strode past her to the bench against the right wall. He pulled his gun from his sash and set it on the bench.

Thorn looked back at Yaroslav with curiosity. Why were they in here?

"Here is better than out in the snow." He unbuckled and removed his sword belt, setting it by the pistol. "The cold is not good for your human body."

Huh? My human body? Thorn strode toward him, one ear forward, one ear tilted back. What was he planning?

"I am planning to feed your hunger." Yaroslav unbuttoned his heavy fur-lined, hooded coat and shrugged out of it, revealing a deep blue, high-collared tunic that draped very nearly to the floor. The tunic was buttoned from his heavily embroidered collar down to his broad black sash and then parted, showing his plain black trousers and knee-high, pitch-black, pointed-toe boots. "However, to drink my blood you will need a human mouth."

Thorn stopped cold. She didn't want to drink any more of his blood. It tasted . . . wrong. *I can feed myself.* If he'd just let her go, she could raid a shed.

Yaroslav draped the coat over the bench and sat down. "Thorn, there is no time for the raiding of sheds." He shoved the tunic's full sleeve up past his elbow, baring his left arm. "My blood will give you what your body needs." He held out his hand. "Come."

Thorn braced her feet. *No, thanks.*

His brows lowered, and his mouth tightened. "This stubbornness . . ." Staring hard at her, he raised his wrist to his mouth and bit down. He turned his arm over and held it down, exposing two somewhat ragged tears and two small holes, marks from his upper and lower fangs. Scarlet slid down his arm. The warm scent of blood perfumed the air.

Thorn's nose twitched. His blood smelled savory, rich, and delicious. Hunger burned in her belly, and her mouth watered. A whimper slid from her throat. Thorn knew damned well that his blood would taste nasty, but it smelled so good, and she was so very hungry.

Head low, she went to him. Before she could even think about hesitating, her long tongue was out, and the flavor of his blood burned on her tongue, as potent and heady as whiskey. It was not a pleasant taste, but it wasn't as bad as she remembered.

She lapped the blood running down his arm. Warm spilled into her belly and spread.

"Good." His hand settled on her head and swept down the thick fur of her neck. "Such a stubborn heart."

Her eyes drifted closed, and a shiver moved down her spine. Without thought, she eased into her half-human muscular, furred, and fanged form. She normally didn't like people to see this shape, but at that moment with the warmth curling through her, it didn't matter quite so much. Crouched at the vampire's feet, she grasped his arm with both clawed hands and sucked. Her thoughts drifted very far away.

Yaroslav used his free hand to push the straps to her backpack down her arms. "This is an annoyance. . . ."

Distracted by the drugging warmth spreading through her, she let her pack fall to the floor.

"Very much better." He leaned over her to wrap his arm around her and lifted her onto his lap, settling her against his chest like a child. He eased slightly to the side and dragged his coat over them both. He pressed a kiss to her brow.

Thorn barely noticed.

9

Held in the vampire's embrace, wrapped in his fur coat with her tail tucked up against her thigh, Thorn opened her eyes to look up into his face. The burning need in her belly had eased into the oddest feeling of warm satisfaction. She licked her lips. Though it had only been a small amount of blood, she actually felt full and strangely content, almost sleepy.

He smiled, carefully hiding his long teeth, and pressed his hand to her cheek. "We are feeling better, yes?"

She blinked at him and then nodded. She couldn't quite get up the energy actually to speak.

"Very good." He nodded and slid his fingers into her long silvery hair and let it spill past his knees to the floor. "Now, to look upon your aspect." He gently eased her onto her back across his lap and parted the coat draped around her. He spoke a single incomprehensible word and touched her brow.

A strong shudder took her.

He smiled. "Be at ease." His fingers trailed down her throat. A trail of warm tingling followed, tightening her nipples. He pressed his palm over her heart briefly, and then his hand glided lower to settle on her belly. Misty pale gold light seethed under his palm.

What the hell . . . ? Her eyes widened, and she grabbed on to his arm.

He frowned and tightened his arm under her. "Calm, be calm. I will not hurt you."

Warmth curled within her belly. It didn't hurt at all. It actually felt kind of good and a little . . . exciting. She arched under his palm and groaned.

He smiled. "Such a welcoming response. . . ."

Warmth bloomed in Thorn's cheeks. She bit down on her lip and looked away. Jagged stripes of blue were glowing on her arms. She raised her arm and rubbed her rough-padded palm against the stripes. She couldn't feel anything but her fur. The blue glow was coming from under her skin. "What is this?"

Yaroslav trailed his fingers along the marks blooming on her arm. "This is that which binds you into a creature of two natures."

Thorn turned her arms over and then noticed the blue stripes surfacing across her belly and spilling upward to frame her breasts. "This is . . . magic?"

Yaroslav frowned. "Indeed."

She watched them trail downward, appearing on her hips and then down her legs, too. "I've never seen anything like this."

The vampire's frown deepened, and his fingers traced an intricate snarl of lines forming on her belly. "If you would stand for me?"

"Yeah, sure. . . ." She pushed to sit up and then turned to slip off his lap. She wavered on unsteady feet and shivered slightly. It was cold in just her light fur. However, the chill cleared some of the fog from her thoughts. "Maybe I better put on my clothes?"

"In a moment." He leaned forward and urged her to turn

her back to him and then brushed her hair away from her back, pushing it over her shoulder. He tsked. "This making could not have been . . . pleasant."

Thorn clenched her jaw. "It wasn't." She looked over her shoulder at him. "Did you find what you were looking for?"

"Oh, yes." He sat back on the stone bench and rubbed his jaw. "What I am trying to discover is why it is functioning." He threw out his hand, his frown deepening. "This pattern is incorrect."

Thorn turned around to look at him. "Huh?"

He crossed his arms. "According to what is written here, you possess two distinct and fully aware souls."

"Well, yeah." Thorn crossed her arms against the chill and gave him a tight smile. "I do."

The vampire shook his head. "This is not as it should be. You should have but one soul comprised of two elements. You were improperly made." He looked up at her. "You should be . . . embattled within." He tapped his heart with a long, elegant finger. "But you do not appear so." He lifted his long fur coat and stood to drape it over her shoulders.

"Embattled?" Thorn gripped the edges of the warm coat. "The wolf and I get along just fine."

Yaroslav's brows rose. "Get along . . . ?"

"We're friends; we like each other." Thorn shrugged. "We argue on occasion, but usually over the human stuff. A lot of it doesn't make sense to her." Thorn smiled. "If it doesn't make sense, she doesn't see why she should bother with it."

"I . . . see." A slight smile tilted the corner of his mouth. "This . . . friendship is good." He stepped past her to pace, rubbing his brow with his hand.

Thorn frowned, her hands tightening on his coat. "Having two souls is bad?"

Yaroslav folded his hands behind him and frowned at the floor. "Those with such a division tend to be malformed, flawed in body and heart." He peered at her from under a fall of black hair. "You are not so."

"Oh. . . ." Thorn frowned. Flawed in body and heart . . . ? That sounded familiar. It sounded like Max.

He lifted his head to stare hard at her, his entire body stiff. "Who is this . . . Max?"

Thorn flinched but only a hair. He was still paying attention to her thoughts. She lifted one shoulder in a half shrug and glanced away. "He's another werewolf."

Yaroslav stilled. "There is another?"

"Yeah, but . . ." she shook her head, "he's all wrong. He looks wrong, and he does . . ." She looked at the floor. "He does bad things."

Yaroslav moved to stand before her. "Bad . . . things?"

She looked up from under the fall of her silver hair and swallowed. "He eats people."

Yaroslav's brows lifted. "And you do not?"

Thorn's mouth fell open in shock; then white-hot rage seared up her spine, straight from her wolf's soul. "Fuck, no, I don't eat people!" She curled her lips back from her teeth. "That's . . . disgusting!"

Yaroslav blinked. "Not at all?"

"Hell, no!" Thorn stomped her foot. "Wolves don't eat people any more than they eat other wolves!"

Yaroslav tilted his head to one side and folded his arms before him. "In this country, wolves do indeed eat people, especially in winter."

"Then your wolves are more dog than wolf." Thorn sneered. "Dogs are scavengers; they'll eat anything, including people." She lifted her chin. "True wolves are hunters; they won't eat garbage unless they're forced to."

Yaroslav snorted, a smile tilting the corner of his mouth. "Humans are garbage?"

Thorn curled her lip. "Animals and people taste like what

they eat, and people eat mostly garbage." She made a sour face. "I hate biting people because the taste makes me gag."

"Ah. . . ." Yaroslav raised a hand over his mouth, his brows lifting. "So this is why you do not like to drink my blood?"

"Well, yeah." Thorn raised a brow at him. "And it tastes strange, stranger than normal people blood." She looked away. "It does things to my head, too."

Yaroslav snorted and then rubbed his jaw. "I should like to see this other werewolf."

Thorn shook her head. "Oh, no, you wouldn't."

Yaroslav's brows rose. "No?"

"He looks . . . bad. He's all twisted and blown out of proportion." She curled her lip. "He doesn't even have a tail." She lifted her chin. "And he eats people, remember? He might try to eat you."

Yaroslav's mouth tilted up into a half smile. "But not you?"

"Oh, I'm sure he would, if he could catch me." Thorn rolled her eyes. "He doesn't have a whole lot of control over that big body of his."

Yaroslav frowned. "Clearly a malformed soul. Perhaps made by the one who made you?"

"God, I hope not." She shuddered. "The Doctor was a nasty, nasty man."

"Ah, but most important . . ." Yaroslav strode to her and set his hands on her shoulders, "this Doctor is a heretic sorcerer." He smiled in vicious triumph.

"Count Feodor Yaroslav Iziaslavich. . . ." The voice that came from the door of the small vault was soft with a Mediterranean lilt. A shadow wearing hooded dark robes eased into the stone room. "So, this is where you've been hiding."

Yaroslav stiffened, his fingers digging into Thorn's shoulders. "I have been waiting for you, Antonius." Yaroslav glanced to the side but did not turn. "I have something here you might find interesting." The vampire smiled down at Thorn. "I know my prince will."

The shadow became a smallish man, with impossibly broad shoulders, holding the naked blade of a short sword. "Is that so?"

Thorn leaned to the side to look past the vampire. Her fur lifted down her spine. She didn't want to be seen between forms. She grabbed for her soul and sought to bury her wolf under her skin.

It wouldn't go.

What the hell . . . ? She closed her eyes and pushed the other way to bury her human nature.

Nothing.

She opened her eyes to stare at her clawed hands. *Damnit!* She couldn't make herself change either way. She bared her long teeth and whispered, "Vampire, what did you do to me?"

Yaroslav lifted his chin a hair. "Remain calm; it is not permanent."

The shadow-draped man, Antonius, silently eased closer. He was a full head shorter than Yaroslav but still taller than she and far broader in the shoulders. "You're looking positively youthful, count." From under his hood, a sky-blue gaze focused on Thorn. "You must be keeping excellent company."

Thorn met his gaze levelly, but her palms were slick with sweat. She did not like people seeing her this way. They had a nasty habit of screaming and then shooting.

The man shoved the hood back from his head, revealing coal-black curls tumbling across the pale brow of a youthful angel. His lips parted, showing overlong incisors. "Yellow eyes. . . ." His straight black brows lifted. "Good god, is this a . . . werewolf?"

Thorn's fur lifted down her spine. He had fangs. Was he another vampire?

Yaroslav swept his hands down to her arms. "Thorn, this is

Master Antonius Aralias, a *Tribuni Angusticlavii*, and, yes, he is *upir.*"

Antonius rolled his eyes. "Nobody uses that title anymore." He winked at Thorn. "It's an old-fashioned name for a knight. These days, I'm just a cavalry officer."

Yaroslav nodded toward her. "Master Antonius, may I present Miss Thorn Ferrell, an American."

Antonius sheathed his short sword and grinned, showing his fangs. "Ah, so that is why we're using English." He nodded. "Good evening, Miss Ferrell. I spent quite some time in your America; beautiful country, big mountains."

Thorn focused on his long teeth, her hand fisting at her sides, but she nodded and smiled without showing her fangs. "Master Antonius."

Antonius tilted his head to the side and gazed up at Yaroslav. "She is a very finely made ... companion." He frowned, and his voice softened to barely a whisper. "But shouldn't she be ... bigger?"

Bigger? Thorn frowned. Just what was Antonius trying to say?

Yaroslav smiled briefly. "Thorn has indeed become my companion." Yaroslav turned to look at the smaller man but kept his hands on her shoulders. "But she is not of my making."

Become his companion? Thorn's frown deepened. Since when?

Antonius crossed his arms. "Not ... yours?"

Yaroslav's smile chilled. "Alas, Thorn proves that I am not the only sorcerer capable of committing criminal acts."

"Criminal acts ... ?" Antonius curled his lip. "No one thinks you are a criminal, Count Yaroslav. We are not here to arrest you. The prince merely wants to talk to you."

Yaroslav turned to scowl at the smaller man. "Would not a letter have sufficed for such an invitation, rather than the fully armed battalion that came to my mountain?"

Antonius groaned and rolled his eyes a little dramatically. "We were told you were under attack, and we were sent as support." He set his hands on his hips. "Imagine my surprise when we found your entire mountain smoking ash and you nowhere to be found."

Yaroslav's brows dropped low, and his jaw tightened. "I am unaccustomed to uninvited . . . support."

Antonius snorted. "Apparently so."

Yaroslav looked away. "I left to discover the source of this . . . plague."

"I thought that might be why we couldn't find you." Antonius looked down. "I'm sorry for your personal losses. I do know how you feel."

"Of course." Yaroslav looked away. "I thank you."

Antonius sighed. "I would just let you go on about your business, but Prince Rafael wants to see you." He folded his hands behind him. "In fact, he insists."

Yaroslav took a deep breath and closed his eyes briefly. "I am ready."

"Good." Antonius nodded. "We don't have a lot of time. The Russians were a little more enthusiastic here than usual."

Thorn looked up at Yaroslav. "Does this mean I can get dressed now?"

Antonius tilted his head and delivered a cupid's-bow smile that exposed a dimple in his cheek. "No need to dress on my account."

Yaroslav shot a glare at Antonius and pushed Thorn back a step, away from the other man. "You may dress." He released her and turned to face Antonius with his arms crossed. "And you may leave while she does so."

Antonius snorted. "Aren't we being a little . . . overprotective?"

"Where you are concerned?" Yaroslav pointed at the door. "No."

Thorn blinked. Was that actually jealousy?

Yaroslav shot her a glare.

Thorn bit back a smile.

Yaroslav sighed and looked away. "Do you have a fear of great heights?"

"Heights?" Thorn snorted. "I lived on a mountaintop. That's about as high as you can get."

"Not quite." He smiled tightly and then walked over to the bench to collect his pistol and sword. Then he lifted the carpet-bag.

Thorn followed him and picked up her fallen backpack.

Yaroslav turned to drop a kiss on her brow. "I will wait for you outside." He strode for the door and then walked out.

At the very back corner of the vault, Thorn knelt and dug into her pack for her other dungarees.

A small paper-wrapped package tumbled out onto the floor. *Shit. . . .* She'd forgotten her damned delivery. She shoved the package back into her pack and then looked over at the door. She needed to get past Yaroslav and Antonius and then leave the town at top speed. She definitely needed to change but not into clothes.

Scowling, she dropped the oversize fur robe to the floor. Her body was still lined in blue light. Whatever was making those blue stripes appear on her skin was probably what was keeping her from changing shape. Crouching down, she closed her eyes and looked inward.

The wolf within her awakened and shifted soul against soul, but far too closely. They were merged too tightly for one to ascend the other. Bound together, caged in one form—trapped. . . .

No! White-hot rage seared up her spine and flooded outward, fighting the prison that bound them into one body. She would *not* be trapped. The cage stretched, and the lines seared her skin. She fell to her clawed hands and snarled in defiance. This pain was nothing compared to their first awakening.

Lightning crackled around them, leaving the dry burned stench of ozone.

Thorn collapsed on the icy floor. Panting, she stared at her extended arm. She was human once again, and the stripes were gone. She was free. She shoved up onto her shaking knees and scrambled to get on her pack. Her human body could not bear this cold for more than a few minutes. Crouching up on her bare feet, she called on the wolf.

She came in a rushing flood of fur and joy, the change from naked human to silver-furred wolf swift and comforting.

Thorn stretched her long limbs and shook out her fur.

The door slammed open, and the vampire filled the doorway. "Thorn!"

She lunged forward, sleek, swift, and determined.

Yaroslav grabbed for her.

She ducked under his hands and slipped out the door into the falling snow.

10

Thorn burst through the doorway into the open amphitheater of mausoleum vaults. Snow blinded her eyes, and the sour scent of burning wood filled her nose, but there was no missing the more than a dozen black-robed men standing in groups. Where had they all come from?

"What the hell is that? A dog?"

"Whoa, it's huge!"

"That's no dog; it's a wolf!"

Thorn darted past them, startled.

"Don't hurt her!" The voice was Yaroslav's. "It is Thorn!"

"What?" Antonius appeared right before her. He gasped. "Mother Night, she *is* white!" He twisted to grab for her and missed. "Catch that animal!"

She dodged dark-clad bodies and grasping hands, her paws finding purchase atop the snow where their booted feet sank more than ankle deep. She had no time for any of them; she had a duty to fulfill.

"The damned thing's white! I can barely see it!"

Antonius turned to glare at Yaroslav. "Damnit, Count, you didn't tell me she could do this!"

Yaroslav grinned under his hood. "She *is* a werewolf!"

Antonius stopped to wave a hand. "I know, but you didn't say she could become a real wolf!"

"That's the werewolf?"

"Shouldn't it be bigger?"

Bigger? Thorn growled out of sheer reflex. She'd never met a wolf larger than she was; just how big was she supposed to be? She rushed for the stairs, the only exit out of the pit of mausoleums.

"Don't let her escape!"

"She won't get far!"

Thorn lunged up the steps, and the falling snow darkened and dampened, sticking to her fur. Heat washed against her muzzle. At the top of the stairs, it was as bright as sunset and far too warm. All around, the fallen snow had melted into filthy puddles, and black, wet ash fell from the orange-stained sky in place of snow. A roaring filled her ears. The stench of burning wood was overpowering.

Thorn rushed past the enormous church. The massive stone walls and every headstone in the graveyard were awash in angry orange light. She leaped atop the wall enclosing the churchyard.

On every side, just beyond the ruined buildings, flames leaped higher than buildings, painting the sky with blood and ash. The world was on fire.

She froze, horrified.

"Thorn!"

She jolted and turned to look back.

Yaroslav shoved past gravestones, his long coat flapping open, the furred hem catching on the overgrown weeds and bushes. "You cannot leave that way. The town is ablaze!"

Thorn laid her ears flat. She wasn't about to let him trap her a second time. She turned away and leaped down, landing on the other side of the wall. Mud and half-melted dirty snow spattered up from her paws. She loped up the wet cobblestone street just a bit. There had to be a way through this. She couldn't be that far from the town's edge. She lifted her nose, but all she could smell was burning wood and heated brick.

An unearthly, inhuman scream erupted.

Thorn turned.

From behind a pile of broken timbers, Max, deformed and filthy with mud, came rampaging for her, his claws out and his crooked teeth bared. "Stupid bitch!"

She dodged, easing past him without even trying.

He twisted to grab for her and skidded on the slick cobbles. "Give it back!"

Her head lifted. *Give what back?*

Yaroslav vaulted over the churchyard wall, landing in the mud. "Thorn!"

Max whirled and spotted the vampire. He snarled in fury.

Yaroslav stiffened and then bared his teeth and shouted out an incomprehensible stream of words.

Max ran toward the vampire, his mouth wide with long teeth, and his fingers armed with claws as long as knives.

Thorn's heart stuttered in her chest. Max would kill him— and eat him. *No!* Red rage slammed into her heart and pounded in her skull. *No!* She rushed after the werewolf. Coming up behind him, she sank her teeth into his calf. The foul taste of his skin and blood filled her mouth. She bit down anyway, dug her paws into the slick muddy road, and pulled, yanking his leg out from under him.

Max fell forward and slammed face-first onto the muddy stone street.

Thorn jerked back with a sharp twist of her head, ripping her fangs free, tearing muscle and sinew in her wake.

Max wailed and rolled onto his back, his hand claws raking for her head. "Kill you!"

Thorn twisted up on her hind legs and grabbed his wrist with her teeth. She stared into his one human eye for a split second and then crunched down, shattering the bones in his wrist.

Max howled and fell back, kicking out with his uninjured and clawed foot.

Thorn leaped clear and circled. She didn't want to risk his fangs in a grab for his throat. If she could get him on his stomach, she could get his neck from behind. She shook her muzzle, trying to clear his foul blood from her mouth.

The sour-armpit stink of human fear boiled up from the fallen werewolf. "Need it . . . back!" He reached over to his side with his uninjured hand and scrabbled at the waist of what was left of his breeches. His hand emerged with a heavy revolver.

A gun? She snarled. She'd known he'd had one—there was no mistaking its reek—but using a gun was a human method. He was supposed to be a wolf; he should fight like one!

"Thorn, get out of my way!"

She lifted her head to look for Yaroslav. He strode from the churchyard wall with a pistol in his hand, pointed past her at Max.

Behind her, the sound of a gunshot hammered in her ears.

Something burned viciously across the top of her left shoulder. *What . . . ?* She leaped away from the burn, but her left front leg wouldn't move right. She overbalanced and nearly fell. Ferocious, biting pain erupted in her shoulder. The scent of burned fur and fresh blood washed over her. She snarled and looked over at Max. He'd shot her. *You bastard!*

Max's revolver smoked, and he was already sighting for a second shot. "Silver bitch!" He gasped for breath. "Silver bullets! Kill you! *Take* it back!"

A second shot echoed in the fiery night.

Max's gun fell from his bloodied hand. He shrieked.

"I, too, have silver!" Yaroslav stalked toward him, his fangs bared, his gun aimed at Max. "And I do not miss!"

Antonius appeared at the churchyard wall with several men

108 / *Morgan Hawke*

behind him. His mouth dropped open. "Two? There are two of them?"

Muddied and bleeding, Max rolled onto his belly. He snarled, spitting foam, and reached for his gun lying on the wet cobble-stones.

The vampire's gun barked loudly.

The gun jumped away from the werewolf's hand, landing in the mud.

Max pushed upright and backed away. "Kill you! Eat you!"

Yaroslav grinned, showing his teeth. "You think so?" Step-ping closer, he aimed his gun carefully for Max's head. "I think not!"

"Count, don't kill it!" Antonius vaulted over the wall. "We need it alive!" Four robed shadows came after him, carrying heavy chains.

Yaroslav pulled back the hammer of his pistol and kept com-ing. "You may need this thing alive; I do not!"

Thorn bolted to intercept Yaroslav. She couldn't let Yaroslav get too close. Hamstrung or not, if Max was anything at all like her, he would recover from her bites very fast. Pain ate at her with every stride, and a rushing filled her ears. Her sight dimmed to a narrow tunnel until she couldn't see. She slammed into Yaroslav's body and yelped in surprise.

Yaroslav caught her in his arms. "Thorn!"

Exhaustion hammered at her, and her wolf sank back within, leaving a bleeding human body behind. She grabbed Yaroslav's coat with both hands. "Keep away . . . from Max."

Yaroslav scooped her up into his arms. "Foolish child! Max is not my concern!" He rose to his feet and backed away from the downed werewolf.

Antonius and his men rushed past Yaroslav and Thorn to surround Max.

Limping badly, Max staggered back from the men. "I smell your stink!" His gaze darted around. "Vampires!"

Sword out, Antonius stalked toward the werewolf and sneered. "We smell your stink, too, plague beast!"

"Plague . . . beast?" Max kept moving back from them and laughed, an ugly sound. "Not today!" He turned and fled for the nearest burning alley.

Antonius and his men chased after him.

Yaroslav knelt in the street and shoved her hair out of the way to look at the wound on her shoulder. "Merely a graze; the bullet struck your pack. This is very good." Holding Thorn against him with one arm, he struggled out of his coat and flung it around her shoulders over her pack. "For I plan to beat you for your foolishness!"

Thorn's mouth fell open. "Beat me?"

The vampire buttoned his coat closed around her. "You could have died from the werewolf, a bullet, or the fire—take your pick!"

Thorn grabbed for the vampire's wrists. "You wouldn't . . . !"

He seized her by the arms and bared his teeth at her. "You will not sit for a week. This I so swear!" His fingers tightened on her arms, and he pulled her up onto her feet. "You will never put yourself in such danger again, do you hear me?"

Thorn blinked up at him. "I hear you! I hear you!"

"Good!" Yaroslav grabbed her and pulled her into a hug. "I only just found you; I have no wish to lose you so soon."

Wrapped in Yaroslav's coat and enclosed in his arms, Thorn didn't know if she should laugh or cry. He cared, he honestly cared for her. It was sweet and scary at the same time. Thorn shivered from something other than cold.

Antonius came back with his men, empty-handed and snarling out a list of invectives in several languages. He stalked stiffly toward Yaroslav and Thorn, his face a mask of anger. "Fuck! That beast is the plague carrier."

Yaroslav tightened his arm around Thorn. "You are sure?"

Antonius scowled. "That thing has been seen in every town

with a major outbreak." He turned and raised his arm, shouting to his men. "To the church; Master Kober will be here any time now!"

Yaroslav leaned down and again scooped Thorn up into his arms.

Surprised, Thorn threw her arms around his neck. "Hey!"

Yaroslav glared at her and growled, showing his fangs. "For once, you will be silent and obedient. Is that understood?"

Obedient? Thorn scowled and looked away. *My ass!* What the hell was he so pissed off about?

Antonius led the way back toward the church at a flat-out run. He and his men vaulted over the low wall and then headed through the overgrown graveyard.

Following close on Antonius's heels, Yaroslav eased Thorn over the wall, setting her on the other side among the weeds.

Thorn pushed through the snow-melt-soaked weeds on bare feet.

The vampire jumped over the wall and scooped her back up into his arms.

"Hey!" Thorn pushed at his shoulder. "I can walk, you know!"

Yaroslav bared his teeth. "If I could trust you, perhaps I would let you do so."

Thorn's mouth fell open. "Trust me . . . ?" What the hell was that supposed to mean?

The vampire strode between the gravestones carrying Thorn. "Did you or did you not run away?"

Thorn growled, her fingers clenching in the silk of his blue shirt. "I told you I had to go!"

Yaroslav scowled. "And I told you you could not!"

"Hey!" Antonius turned and glared at the vampire and Thorn. "Quit fighting, you two, and get over here!"

Yaroslav rolled his eyes and angled toward a small wooden

door in the side of the church, held open by one of Antonius's black-robed men.

Arriving at the door, Antonius turned to look at Yaroslav. "Master Kober has arrived." He glanced at Thorn and smiled tightly. "I hope she's good with heights." He didn't wait for an answer but turned and headed into the narrow, incense-scented hallway.

Arrived? Thorn frowned. How could anyone have arrived through that fire?

Yaroslav carried Thorn into the oak-paneled hallway, following Antonius at a fast walk, passing several closed doors guarded by more of Antonius's robed men. An open door at the end of the hallway led to a tightly spiraled upward stairwell with steps worn down with age and planked over for ease of climbing.

Yaroslav marched up the staircase after Antonius, the rest of the men falling in behind. They reached a door and stepped out under the blood-tinted sky at the top of one of the square bell towers forming the corners of the church.

Thorn frowned at the burning town all the way around them. A massive wall of flames consumed every building in view. The refuse littering the broad street had begun to burn, set alight by blowing embers. Only the churchyard remained unscathed, though it was clearly only a matter of time before the fire reached there, too.

Where were they supposed to go from here?

Yaroslav let Thorn slide down from his arms to stand on the damp rooftop in the circle of his embrace. "Be good." He looked up.

Be good . . . ? Thorn scowled. *Right.* Pressure began to deafen her, as if she were up in a higher elevation. She swallowed, and with a slight pop, a loud humming vibration filled her ears. *What in hell . . . ?* She glanced around. All of them, Antonius and all his men, were looking straight up. She followed their gaze. Directly above them the sky seemed to shimmer and dance, as if she were seeing it through a sheet of rippling water. She clutched at Yaroslav's sleeve. She'd never seen anything like it.

Yaroslav leaned close to her ear and spoke loudly. "Are you well enough to climb?"

"Climb?" Thorn turned to look at him. "To where?"

Yaroslav pointed upward.

Thorn looked up in time to see a rope and post ladder unrolling downward from the wavering sky. Two of Antonius's men grabbed the ladder and braced it between them.

Thorn blinked. "Where did that come from?"

Antonius turned to face Yaroslav and Thorn, grinning. "Ready to go for a ride?" He waved them toward the ladder.

"A ride?" Thorn stiffened. "In what?"

"A dirigible balloon airship." Antonius looked up. "Designed by Master Kober exclusively for the High Prince of the Penumbral Realm."

Thorn frowned. "Who's that?"

"Go." Yaroslav urged her forward, past Antonius. "Someone you will meet very soon."

Thorn walked forward and looked up again. A *balloon?* She'd seen them before, during festivals and fairs. Humongous floating balls of air wrapped in bright silk with tiny boat-shaped baskets, or gondolas. However, other than the weirdly shifting heat waves, she saw only flame-tinted clouds and rising sparks. "There's a balloon up there? Are you sure?"

"It is there." Yaroslav urged up the ladder. "Climb; I will follow you."

Thorn set her hands on the smooth wooden pegs of the ladder and then looked over her shoulder at the vampire. "Wait a minute; aren't balloons supposed to be made of air and cloth? Won't it catch on fire?"

"The craft is under a protection enchantment. That is why you cannot see it, but you can feel it. Here." Yaroslav tapped his temple and pushed her upward.

"I see." So it was the spell on the ship that was causing the weird altitude pressure in her ears. She rolled her eyes. "Whatever you say. . . ." *More make-believe and fairy tales.* Unfortunately she didn't have much of a choice. To stay was to die. Thorn tugged the edges of Yaroslav's overlong furred robe to the side to step up onto the ladder, and climbed.

11

Thorn climbed the rope ladder and wondered where reality had fled to. She was going up a peg-and-rope ladder toward a balloon she couldn't see because it was enchanted. However, the fire consuming the town was more than real, just like the vampires climbing after her.

Reaching over her head for each new handhold and placing her feet carefully, she kept climbing. The overlong hem of the robe was not helpful; the wind kept blowing it under her feet. The burning ache in her shoulder wasn't helpful either.

After a nerve-wracking eternity, the air around her chilled, and something huge seemed to loom over her head. The loud buzzing became a horrendous whirring clearly driven by some kind of engine. Thorn couldn't resist the urge to look up.

A massive wood-planked ship floated directly above her head. The pointed prow on her far left sported a rearing winged unicorn figurehead painted in gleaming gold, the gilded and carved wings stretching out along the ship's body. A spinning propeller whirled at the tip of the unicorn's long spiral horn. Long, broad, batlike wings spread out from the ship's wooden sides, clearly made of fabric stretched across a frame, very like an umbrella. The huge broad-bladed rudder sticking out far behind was made the same way.

Above the ship was the biggest and longest cigar-shaped balloon she'd ever seen. The scarlet and midnight fabric had some kind of interior structure, making the balloon pointed at either end. Thousands of ropes attached it to the wooden ship suspended below it.

She'd never seen anything like it. Sheer curiosity drove Thorn the rest of the way up the ladder.

Close to the curved planks of the hull, the ladder's wooden pins became actual wooden steps that were pegged on the backside to keep the step clear of the ship's hull. Thorn smiled sourly. A good thing, too, or they would have pinched her fingers and toes against the side of the ship something awful.

A bearded man in a dark navy seaman's coat of heavy wool leaned over the brass rail along the edge and looked down at Thorn.

Thorn blinked up at him, startled. "Hello?"

He smiled. "Ah, hello!" He reached down to catch Thorn by the hand. "Welcome, fraulein, aboard the *Valkyrie*." He tugged.

Thorn climbed over the brass rail and stepped down onto the polished deck of the ship floating in midair. Her legs shook under her.

The bearded man leaned over the rail to grab for the next hand.

Thorn tottered away from the rail and stared in wonder. It really was an air*ship*, though it looked more like a carnival ride than anything that might sail on water. From the rearing unicorn prow to the raised stern deck at the ship's rear, the ship was carved, flourished, and painted in scarlet and emerald with gilded scrollwork. Decorative, sculpted brass fittings were everywhere, all gleaming with polish. At the ship's center was a broad brass pipe releasing gouts of steam into the chill air. The pipe was obviously exhaust from the chugging engine hidden below deck. The polished planks under her bare feet trembled with the engine's vibrations.

Around half a dozen men in sea coats and seaman's caps bustled about while shouting back and forth in guttural German. They tugged and adjusted the wrist-thick ropes attached to large iron rings all along the ship's fore and aft, connecting to the monstrous net that held the gigantic balloon.

On the raised poop deck, a massive bearded man gripped the piloting wheel. Standing close by was a small and slender man with closely trimmed dark hair and gold-framed glasses. Like the rest of the crew, he wore a heavy wool coat that fell below his knees, but he sported gold buttons and braiding around his coat cuffs, with more braiding around his small billed cap.

Thorn's brows rose. That was very likely the airship's captain. She turned to see the last of Antonius's black-robed men climbing over the polished rail of the *Valkyrie*. Two bearded men in heavy sea coats hurried to pull up the ladder.

Yaroslav stood with his hands folded behind him at the rail by Antonius. His head was tilted to the side, clearly listening to whatever Antonius was saying, but Yaroslav's mouth was tight, and his gaze was focused on Thorn.

She shivered and folded her arms across her chest. The wind brushing her cheeks and tugging at her long pale brown hair was icy. The cold hadn't bothered her all that much while she was on the ladder, but she wasn't climbing anymore.

A loud bell echoed across the airship's broad, polished deck, accompanied by shouts and whistles. Men scrambled for the ropes, adjusting God knew what. The rhythmic chugging of the ship's engine became louder. The deck gently tipped up, and the tiny ship held in midair by its monstrous balloon rose higher into the sky.

Thorn was finally leaving the town behind on a ship that

flew. She moved toward the brass rail of the ship and looked down. Beneath the rippling pool of magic, monstrous fires raged all across the town with flames that leaped nearly as high as the tall brick chimneys of the factories.

A fist tightened around her heart, and her eyes burned. Only a short while ago she had run down those streets and across those roofs. . . . Her heart nearly stopped in her chest. If Max hadn't driven her out into the snow, she would have been down there still. A sound like falling leaves hissed in her ears, nearly overwhelming the sound of the ship's toiling engine.

Yaroslav pressed his hand on her shoulder. "The Russian army has indeed been enthusiastic."

Thorn started. She hadn't heard him approach. She scrubbed her hands across her damp cheeks and turned to look at him. Her throat was too tight to speak, her heart too shocked. The Russian army had done this? How could they burn a whole town—with people in it?

"It is not quite so bad as it seems." Yaroslav set his arm across her shoulders and turned her away from the rail. "While it is true that much of the town burns, the entire town has not been set alight." His smile was slight, and his gaze weary. "Master Antonius told me that with so many towns infected with the walking dead, the Russian tsar has come to an agreement with the Penumbral court. Together both courts are working to save as many people as they can."

Thorn frowned up at him. "By setting towns on fire?"

Yaroslav sighed. "The fires are to draw out the dead and those they have infected. The untainted will flee."

Thorn tucked her hands under her arms. She couldn't stop trembling. "The dead are *drawn* to fire?"

Yaroslav nodded. "Rather like moths. They need only set the fires, and the unclean fly from their hidden places to destroy themselves." He swept a hand down her hair. "The survivors will return and rebuild anew."

"You sure about that?" She leaned against him. He was warm, and his scent familiar. Her head settled against his shoulder. "You're sure they'll rebuild it?"

Yaroslav sighed. "I have seen many cities fall, and always a new one follows." He tightened his embrace. "Thorn, you are trembling."

"Yeah, I know." She gripped her arms, but she couldn't stop shaking. "So, where are we going?"

"We are going to the winter palace of Prince Rafael."

"Oh, that's nice." She looked up. Yaroslav's face seem to be going away, as if down a long tunnel. The rushing sound in her ears escalated. The voices of the men working around them began to fade under the loud windstorm in her head. She didn't quite notice when her knees buckled. One minute she was swaying on her feet, and the next, the nice comfortable hardwood deck was under her back. She blinked up at the dark sky full of roiling clouds and watched them fade down a long black tunnel.

Someone was speaking. She could barely hear them through the loud rushing wind in her ears. "What?" She was in someone's arms and sprawled across their lap. It smelled like Yaroslav. Her cheek was against his silk shirt. *God, he smells good. . . .*

Fingers pressed into the hollow under her jaw. "Her pulse is weak." It sounded like Yaroslav.

"Too weak and erratic." That sounded like Antonius, from somewhere past Yaroslav's shoulder. "I can barely hear her heart beating."

The arms around her tightened. "I should not have let her climb."

Thorn opened her eyes. She didn't remember closing them. They were still on the deck of the airship. She must have been out for only a few seconds.

Antonius snorted. "How else was she supposed to get on the ship. Fly?"

Yaroslav turned to deliver a tight smile over his shoulder at Antonius.

"You're not serious . . . ?" Antonius leaned over Yaroslav's shoulder, his lips curling slightly. "Count, I am centuries older than you, and I can't fly!"

Yaroslav rolled his eyes. "I am a magus, did you forget?"

Thorn blinked. Yaroslav could *fly?*

Yaroslav frowned down at Thorn and swept his thumb across her bottom lip. "Her lips . . . they are blue." He scowled. "This is silver poisoning. . . ."

"Silver *poisoning?*" Antonius frowned at Thorn. "I thought she had only a graze?"

Thorn sucked in a small breath. How could silver be poisonous? She shuddered hard, and it hurt all the way to her bones. She clutched at Yaroslav's shirt, but there seemed to be no strength in her fingers. She closed her eyes, and a small whimper escaped. *It hurts. . . .*

Yaroslav leaned forward and rose to his feet, cradling Thorn in his arms. He turned to face Antonius. "I need a place of complete privacy to work without hindrance."

Antonius dropped his chin and glanced around. "There's only one place like that on this ship."

Yaroslav's arms tightened around her. "Take me there."

Antonius looked Yaroslav in the eye. "You won't like it."

Yaroslav held the other man's gaze. "Now, Master Antonius."

Antonius hunched his shoulders and turned away. "Follow me." He strode across the deck, with Yaroslav in his wake. Antonius opened the double doors by the ladder to the poop deck and led the way down into the ship's warm bowels.

A dark and very narrow wood-paneled gangway passed by Thorn's eyes in a blur. A doorway on the right opened onto a narrow downward ladder lit with flickering light. Heat poured up from below.

Yaroslav followed Antonius down the steps to a narrow cross-hallway that led left, right, and straight ahead. Every available inch was lined with steaming pipes, fluttering gauges, and huge snakes of wires. Light came from a wire strung overhead that had glowing embers within fist-sized glass bulbs. The overwhelming pulsing chug of massive machinery hammered in Thorn's temples. The sound practically beat against her skin.

Antonius pointed straight ahead. "That passage leads to the ship's engine room." He gestured to the left. "We're going this way." He led them into the narrow walkway. "The spells they're using aren't exactly stable, so don't bump into anything. You could get a nasty burn."

Thorn frowned. *Magic?* It all looked like normal hot-water piping to her.

Antonius stopped at a closed iron door and turned the heavy wheel. The door clunked heavily and swung in, revealing a huge iron-walled chamber. Glowing bulbs occupied all four corners, shedding dim light among deep shadows. A gigantic cage filled the space, leaving maybe an arm's length of clearance all the way around it. He turned to Yaroslav. "This is only place where I know you won't be disturbed."

"A cage?" Yaroslav raised his brow and delivered a tight smile. "Dare I ask?"

Antonius snorted and folded his arms. "This is actually a small cargo hold. The cage is for the plague beast. We're supposed to bring it back alive." He shrugged. "There's a freight door directly overhead. Once we get it in there, we can hoist the cage straight from this hold."

Yaroslav sighed. "Open it."

Antonius rolled his eyes but stepped toward the cage's door. He pushed, and the door swung in. "It's open." He turned to face Yaroslav. "Do you need anything?"

Yaroslav stepped past Antonius and into the cage. His boot heels thunked on the wood-planked floor. "How long until we arrive?"

Antonius looked down at his boot toes. "We'll clear the mountains in less than an hour. We should reach the palace by dawn."

Palace? Thorn blinked. Oh, that was right, Yaroslav had mentioned a prince and a palace.

Yaroslav nodded. "This should not take so long. We will need a place to rest afterward."

Antonius nodded and folded his hands behind him. "I'll put you in my berth."

"Thank you." Yaroslav raised a brow at him. "You may go."

Antonius snorted and smiled. "Possessive bastard."

Yaroslav raised his brow. "And you are not, over your Sophia?"

Antonius chuckled and turned away. "All right, you win." He took the few steps to the door and turned back. "I'll set a guard to make sure you're not disturbed."

Yaroslav nodded gravely. "That would be most appreciated."

Antonius stepped out, pulling the door closed behind him.

Thorn looked up at Yaroslav. "Now what?"

Yaroslav let Thorn slide from his arms, setting her on her bare feet. "Now I take a close look at your aspect to see what damage has been done."

"What?" Thorn's knees wobbled under her. "Again?"

12

"Is . . . this . . . really necessary?" Her arms flung out to her sides, Thorn stared at the plank floor three feet below her and swallowed. She was floating naked, and facedown, in thin air. Yaroslav's fur coat and her backpack had been dropped by the cage's open door. "You didn't do . . . this . . . last time."

Standing at her right side, Yaroslav unbuttoned his snug cuffs and shoved his full sleeves up to his elbows. "Last time, you had not been struck by a silver bullet."

"It's only a graze, a scrape; it should have healed already." She tucked her chin, clenched her hands into fists, and strained against the invisible bonds until her toes curled. Her thoughts scattered under a wave of dizziness, and her sight darkened. She stopped, gasping for breath. That was the sum total of all she could move. *Damnit. . . .*

Yaroslav stepped before her and went down on one knee. "Thorn." He cupped her chin, lifting her gaze to his. "The harm that silver causes is deeper than your flesh." He spoke that incomprehensible word she'd heard before and touched her brow. He rose to his feet and strode along her right side, his fingers trailing down the back of her neck and down her spine. An electrical current shimmered along her skin, following the path of his fingers.

A strong shudder took her. Thorn looked over at her arms and watched the blue streaks of light bloom under her skin. Heat spilled through her, and then sharp needle stabs erupted between her shoulder blades. "Ow, shit . . . !" Fur spilled across bare skin with tiny electrical shocks. She winced and hissed. Her teeth lengthened, making her jaw burn and ache. She moaned, and blood dribbled from her mouth to the planks below her. Her gums were bleeding from her teeth. The base of her spine ached with the extension of her tail. Her claws extended like knife stabs, and her hands and feet burned with the pads that formed on them. The change ended, and she moaned in relief. "Oh, god, that stank. . . ."

Yaroslav rose and stepped to her left side. "It is as I thought."

Thorn sucked in several deep breaths, drained. "What?"

Yaroslav leaned close, peering at her shoulder. "A part of your aspect has been damaged."

She closed her eyes and tried to shift her stinging shoulder. "Is that what hurts?"

"Correct. The magic that allows your transformation has begun to unravel." Yaroslav moved before her and knelt. He cupped her jaw in one palm, again raising her gaze to his. His mouth was tight, and his gaze steady. "I am going to separate your spirit from your flesh. Please do not resist."

"Huh?" Thorn stared at him, not quite sure what he meant by that. "What for?"

With his free hand, he brushed her hair from her brow. "I am going to attempt to rebuild the damaged parts of your aspect. I do not wish you to feel discomfort while I do so."

Thorn swallowed. "It's going to hurt?"

Yaroslav closed his eyes briefly. "A great deal."

A great deal? Thorn winced. *Terrific. . . .* She licked her lips. "It won't heal all by itself?"

He held her gaze. "It is not your body that has been harmed, but your aspect. If left too long, it will fall apart completely."

Thorn frowned. "Will that make me human again?"

Yaroslav shook his head slowly. "Once, that might have been so, but your body has since become reliant on that which binds your two souls, and your two bodies, together."

Thorn shivered. "That's bad?"

Yaroslav sighed and smiled just a little. "It is not bad that you have become accustomed to your dual nature. What is bad is that the original making was improperly crafted and is therefore weaker than it should be."

Thorn bit down on her bottom lip. "A bullet graze really did that much damage?"

Yaroslav sighed and shook his head. "It was not that you were struck by a bullet, but struck by silver. A silver knife would have done the same." He raised a finger. "Silver can be charmed to craft spells or to cut them. The silver in this bullet was charmed to cut, and it has succeeded far better than it would have if your making had been done properly."

"Oh. . . ." Thorn swallowed. "So, you're going to put it back together?"

Yaroslav smiled. "After a fashion. However, it is not a comfortable process, therefore I am going to pull out your spirit, leaving your body to sleep." He lifted his chin. "Are you ready?"

Thorn really did not like the idea of being asleep when someone was messing with her body, but she liked the idea of "a great deal of pain" even less. "All right, fine, do what you need to do." She glared at him. "But make it quick!"

Yaroslav smiled. "I will do my very best." He focused his gaze on hers. "Look for the flames within my eyes."

Thorn looked. Within his black gaze, a spark of red seemed

to move. It was a flame. He really did have flames in the backs of his eyes. "I see it."

"Yes, very good." His voice came from very far away. "Reach for the flames, love."

Some part of her reached for it. And then she slipped and fell—up. She gasped in fright and opened her eyes to find herself staring down at her own body outstretched below her. *Huh? This is some dream. . . .* Or was it? Everything was amazingly crystal clear. She could see the deep blue of Yaroslav's long shirt and the bright blue angular design that glowed from beneath her body's skin. The pattern looked weirdly familiar.

She frowned and eased lower. Her body's design looked a lot like one of those mechanical drawings for wiring she'd seen in her dad's workshop years ago. And there was definitely something wrong with it.

A spot in the lines on her shoulder looked like it had been smeared. The lines connected to it, all across her shoulder blade to her spine, were an angry orange and sparking.

The vampire walked around to her right side and cupped his hands over the center of her back. He spoke. Golden mist erupted from his body, bathing him in a soft golden glow. A ball of scarlet lightning formed between his palms. He spoke again and kept on speaking. A thin line of lightning spilled from the ball in Yaroslav's palms and danced across the smear in the pattern.

Thorn floated closer, trying to catch what he was saying, but none of it made any kind of sense. Apparently it was some kind of mystical chant or incantation. She snorted. *First fairy tales and make-believe, now hocus-pocus. . . .*

Movement above her caught her eye. She turned. A misty white wolf was swimming through the air toward her. Thorn's heart leaped. *Whitethorn?* She hadn't seen the wolf since the day they'd been shoved into the same body.

The wolf collided with Thorn, and the two merged, soul against soul. Warmth and joy burst between them. They parted to dive back into each other. Laughter erupted from her heart and spilled into both of them.

Yaroslav looked up and stared straight at Thorn and then at the wolf. "Exercise calm, if you please."

Thorn stilled. He could see them?

The vampire smiled. "Yes, I see you."

Thorn frowned. "Because of the 'blood' thing?" She frowned. Her voice sounded . . . off.

"Any talented magus can see and hear spirits." He raised a brow at them. "Do not wander off. I need to put you both back when my work is complete."

Oh. . . . Thorn blinked. "All right." She moved through the air to the wolf. They intertwined and floated toward Thorn's body to watch the vampire's work.

The vampire chanted but otherwise didn't move a muscle. The lightning moved across the break in Thorn's pattern, trailing golden light, but its movements were small.

The view got really dull really fast.

Bored, Thorn and floated about the room with Whitethorn sailing in and out of her. There was nothing to see but four plain iron bulkheads and lots of black cast-iron bars. It was less interesting than what the vampire was doing. Passing the room's heavy door, she noticed that it was about two finger widths ajar. Movement beyond caught her attention. She eased closer to take a look.

A black-robed man had his back to the door. Her brows lifted. It was probably one of Antonius's men. She had no clue which one; they all looked alike to her. He was talking to someone standing in the narrow pipe-lined hall, and he was shaking his head. She could barely hear him past the hammering pulse of the ship's engine.

Thorn eased closer, and her head slid right through the door, as though it weren't there. She blinked, startled, and then drifted up to get a look over the robed man's shoulder.

An incredibly beautiful man stood in the hall in a long red velvet robe lined in black fur. His hair tumbled in midnight waves past his shoulders. His mouth was sweetly smiling, and his cheek held a dimple, but his straight black brows were low over his ice-blue gaze. He spoke, his voice low and modulated carefully.

The guard at the door stiffened. His reply held the rumble of a growl.

Thorn frowned. What the heck was going on here?

Whitethorn tumbled into Thorn, knocking her spinning to the side and through the left bulkhead. The two of them spilled into a room commanded by a huge engine surrounded by fast pumping pistons and spooling belts. Pale blue steam spilled from the pipes all around it. Men in coveralls and thick gloves worked around it, shouting to each other in German. They were obviously the ship's black gang, the engineers. Thorn watched, fascinated.

Bells rang, and a gout of blue steam erupted close to Thorn. She felt heat and jerked away from it, frowning. She hadn't felt anything else, but she could feel that. *Weird. . . .*

The white wolf yelped and came sailing for her.

"Thorn!" It was Yaroslav, and he sounded pissed.

Oh, shit. . . . She turned and was immediately back in the cage, floating over her body along with the silver wolf. She blinked. *That was fast.*

Yaroslav glared up at her, his brows low and his lip curled. "I told you not to wander!"

Thorn looked away. "We weren't far. We were just looking at the engine."

Yaroslav pointed up at her. "You are not to go near the engine. It is not safe for you. The magic that powers it is unstable." He pointed downward. "Remain here." He looked down and held his palms her body. "I am very nearly finished."

Thorn followed his gaze. There was an intricate knot-work

design etched in golden light on her shoulder with long trailing gold threads intertwined among her body's original blue design. It was actually quite pretty.

Yaroslav tilted his head and gave her a quick smile. "I'm glad you like it."

Whitethorn playfully wriggled through her, begging for a game of "chase me."

Thorn turned to swipe a hand through the sailing wolf and smiled.

Yaroslav directed the ball of red lightning toward other parts of the blue pattern glowing on Thorn's body. "Your wolf is called Whitethorn. Is that where your name is derived?"

Thorn twisted around in the air to avoid the diving wolf. "I needed a new name for the new me." Her smile faltered. The old one hadn't fit anymore.

"Indeed?" Yaroslav thumbed a long lock of black hair over his ear and glanced up at Thorn. "Are you so very different from before?"

Thorn sighed. How did you explain the melding of wolf perceptions with human thoughts? "She sees the world in a different way, a very practical way." Thorn shrugged. "A lot of human behavior doesn't make sense to her, like modesty or shame or lies. She doesn't understand lies at all because she can always tell when someone is saying something that isn't true." Thorn smiled. "She understands love perfectly, and lust. And family."

Yaroslav moved the ball of lightning to the center of her back, right over her heart. "And that is different from the way you were before?" A golden knot began to appear.

Thorn snorted. "I'm a girl. I'm supposed to be modest and ashamed of my, uh, baser needs." Ever since the wolf had become a part of her soul, none of that had seemed important.

Yaroslav smiled. "I do not see the need to be ashamed of

your . . . baser needs. However, I do believe that modesty serves a purpose."

The wolf twisted in midair and came sailing back.

Thorn dodged Whitethorn's enthusiastic dive and smiled sourly. "Modesty is a real pain in the ass when I have to change shapes in a hurry."

Yaroslav glanced toward Thorn. "Do you not like wearing pretty clothes?"

Thorn rolled her eyes. "Most of that fancy stuff is impossible to move in. Have you ever tried to run anywhere in a steel-boned corset? God help me if I have to change in a hurry. I'd have to rip everything to shreds just to get out of it."

"There. . . ." Yaroslav lifted his palms, and the ball of red lightning extinguished. "My work is complete." He looked up and held out his hand. "Come, it is time."

Whitethorn sailed into Thorn. The two of them melded into one and eased down toward the vampire. Abruptly they fell.

Thorn gasped and shuddered. Her eyes snapped open. She was facing the cage's plank floor again. She was back in her floating body, and it ached. She groaned. "Are we done?"

"We are." Yaroslav collected the fur robe from the floor and came back to drape it around her floating body. "After a good long rest, you will be fully recovered." He tipped her upright and then onto her back to tuck the robe around her like a blanket. "And that is where we go next, to rest." He held out his arms. Something popped.

She dropped into his arms, lip as a rag, and moaned. "I feel like I was hit by a train." She leaned up and wrapped her arms around his neck. It took a surprising amount of effort. "Are you sure you fixed it?"

He cradled her against his shoulder and smiled. "You merely need rest." He pressed a kiss to her brow and walked toward the barred door. "As do I." At the steel door, he called out.

He was answered, and the door swung open, revealing the man she'd seen before, the one in dark robes. The other man, the one in the red robe, was gone.

Thorn sighed and dropped her head on Yaroslav's shoulder. She was just too tired to really care.

13

Thorn shifted under the blankets. A hot weight was flopped heavily on top of her legs, and though the pillow against her right cheek smelled warmly familiar, it was also hard and lumpy. Thorn rolled to her left, away from the stifling heat. Her bare back thunked against a wooden wall. *Huh?* She opened her eyes.

Yaroslav's legs were the heavy warmth practically pinning her. The lumpy pillow was his bare chest and upper arm. He'd taken off his shirt, but she could feel his trousers against her legs. They were on a tiny bed that had been folded down from the wall. The only source of light was a small round window an arm's reach above the bed.

Thorn sat up to get a better look. The curved wall directly across was very close, with barely any space to stand, and the ceiling was low. The door was only a pace or two from the foot of the bed. She frowned. Were they in a closet?

Memory slammed her hard. The walking dead, Max, the vampires in the graveyard, the town in flames, the silver bullet . . . She wasn't against a wall, but a bulkhead on the *Valkyrie*, an airship. The bed under her and the wall against her back vibrated slightly in time to the rhythmic rumbling of the ship's engine. They were flying to some prince's winter palace, located God only knew where.

And she still had a package to deliver.

Thorn scowled and pulled her knees up to her chest, closing her arms around them. How the hell was she supposed to get out of this mess and deliver that package? It was her last one, damnit. Once it was passed to Agent Hackett, she was free. Free after four years of fetching and carrying for the Secret Service, for Colonel Ives—who was dead.

Her breath caught in her throat. The colonel was dead. The man who had brought her back from the wild and then betrayed her was dead, killed by Max.

Thorn shuddered violently, and her heart burned. She closed her eyes to hold in the tears that threatened to fall. She did not want to cry for that man. He didn't deserve her tears. She tightened her arms around her knees, her fingers digging into her upper arms.

A hand closed around her ankle. "Thorn."

She opened her eyes.

The vampire gazed up at her from the pillow, his black eyes half closed. The light cast from the small porthole etched the stark planes of his face and gleamed in the tousled silk of his midnight hair spilling across the blankets.

The fist around her heart eased, and a smile lifted the corner of her mouth. He looked so . . . sweet.

Yaroslav shifted closer. "You are awake. Do you hurt?"

Huh . . . ? Thorn blinked. Oh, yeah, he'd done some kind of hocus-pocus to her, and it had hurt like hell. She shook her head. "That's all gone. I feel fine." She lifted her hands and rubbed her aching eyes. "I've just got a lot on my mind, that's all."

"I should check your wound. . . ." Yaroslav leaned up on his elbow, the light illuminating the strong lines of his collar bones, the contours of his broad chest, and the sleek muscles of his belly.

"It's fine, really." Thorn leaned away but couldn't stop staring. She'd never really gotten a good look at him without his shirt. Each time he'd been without one, she'd been far too distracted to admire the view. She sucked on her bottom lip. The view was well worth admiring.

Yaroslav frowned. "Is it so difficult to allow me to care for you?"

She glanced away. "I'm not used to being . . . cared for."

"So I see." Yaroslav slid his hand up her calf, urging her knees apart. His gaze focused on her exposed feminine flesh, and his full lips curved in a smile. "Perhaps I can offer something else to occupy your mind?"

The small hairs on Thorn's neck rose. He was up to something. "Like . . . what?" She pushed back, but she was already against the bulkhead.

His gaze lifted to hers, and he licked his lips. "I suddenly feel overwhelming curiosity as to your flavor."

"My . . . what?" Interest coiled tight in her belly, and her breath caught. He couldn't be thinking what she thought he was thinking?

"Oh, but I am." Holding her gaze, he ducked his head between her parted knees and pressed a kiss on her inner thigh. His lips parted, and he stroked her thigh with his tongue, leaving a wet trail.

Thorn shivered.

Someone spoke in German, and footsteps thumped past the door.

Every hair on Thorn's body rose. Whoever was outside that door would hear everything that went on behind it. She grabbed for his head, her fingers clenching in his long black hair, and whispered, her voice tight. "We can't do . . . that . . . here."

Yaroslav winced and lifted his chin. "And why not?" He released her ankle to ease her fingers from his hair. "We are alone, yes?"

"The door is closed, but . . ." Thorn was not about to admit that she, a werewolf, was having a fit of feminine shyness. She squirmed to the side and eyed the door. "Aren't we supposed to be arriving somewhere sometime soon?"

"Correct." He surged up onto his knees and grabbed her around the waist. "Which is why we should use what opportunities present themselves." In one smooth, blindingly fast motion, he scooped her up, turned, and dropped her.

She landed flat on her back, her pale brown hair spreading across the pillows. She gasped for breath. *That pushy bastard!* She rose up on her elbows and bared her teeth. "Yaroslav . . . !"

The vampire dropped over her, balancing on his palms, his knees spreading her legs wide. He caught her gaze, and flames flickered in the depths of his midnight eyes. His lips curled back just enough to show his teeth without revealing the points. A growl rumbled in his chest. "Thorn." The rich musk of his arousal scented the air between them.

Thorn froze, staring up at him, her heart slamming in her chest. Thought evaporated. Her nipples rose to hard, aching points, and moisture slicked her thighs. The butter-sweet aroma of her excitement entwined with his musk, filling the room with the intoxicating perfume of raw lust.

His gaze locked on hers; he lowered his head to her breast and licked her erect nipple.

A spark of intense pleasure stabbed downward, encouraging a hot, wet clench in her belly. A small sound very like a whimper escaped her throat. She'd never been this excited in her life. Her knees quivered, and her elbows refused to support her. She slid back down onto the pillows.

"So it is instinct that rules you." He smiled, with just a hint of teeth. "Good." Watching her, he lowered his head to her breast. His flat front teeth closed around her nipple in a tender bite.

The effect was searing, all the way down to her clit. Her back arched, and she gave out a choked cry.

He released her nipple and licked his lips. "Very much better." He eased down onto his belly between her spread thighs and perched on his elbows. His hands swept across the dark gold curls of her mound.

Thorn's flesh shuddered pleasurably under his fingers, and she sucked in a breath. If she was this excited already, what he planned to do was going to make her scream, and loudly. But God in heaven, she wanted it.

His palms spread her open to expose the pink folds. He smiled. "Ah, a succulent feast." His mouth descended. His moist, warm breath brushed her intimate flesh.

Every muscle in her body clenched in voracious eagerness. Thorn bit back a yearning moan.

His black eyes watching her, he opened his mouth on her flesh, and the wet heat of his tongue brushed lightly yet searingly across the tender, oversensitive folds.

She choked and arched up, her body shuddering with violent hunger.

Yaroslav chuckled and wrapped his arms around her thighs to hold her still. "You are very, very ripe, my love." His head dropped, and his tongue delved among her moist folds and then burrowed into her center, seeking her cream.

Thorn nearly screamed. She covered her mouth, barely in time, and struggled to get away from the searing intensity, but his arms held her still for his lashing tongue. Helpless under the onslaught of torturous pleasure, she cried out behind her hands and writhed, her hips rising in time to his working tongue.

He smiled and sucked, groaning his delight. His tongue swirled lightly against her clit.

Thorn arched, and her toes curled. A long moan escaped from behind her hands.

He tapped a finger against her clit.

Erotic lightning struck. She threw back her head and cried out, her hips bucking as climax rose with brutal intensity—and went nowhere. She wailed in frustration and writhed against his mouth. "Please?" The word simply slipped out.

Yaroslav's black eyes creased with amusement. "Please what?" He lowered his mouth and sucked noisily.

Thorn shuddered and trembled as her need coiled tighter but no closer to the edge. Whimpers became cries that escaped her lips, but climax would not come. Something was holding her back, something was missing. "Please!" It exploded from her mouth.

Yaroslav lifted his head, not even bothering to hide his broad grin. "Please what?" He pushed a finger deep into her core and flicked deep within her.

Thorn howled and bucked in time to his finger's possession. "Please! Let me come!"

His smile was full of teeth. "I will have to bite you."

She threw back her head and arched. "So bite me, damnit!"

"As you wish." He pulled fingers from her core and lifted his arm to press her thigh against the bulkhead. He opened his hand on her inner thigh and held it down against the mattress, spreading her wide and holding her perfectly still.

Thorn panted. What was he doing? How the hell was he going to bite her when he was down there?

His mouth and tongue descended to her tortured flesh. His long finger slid back into her slick core. He pressed rhythmically within while his tongue slowly circled her swollen clit.

Searing heat, voracious hunger, hammering need . . . Thorn arched and twisted under him. Gasping cries burst from her lips.

He trapped her leg flat and firmly on the mattress. His

mouth moved from her aching flesh to the crease dividing her mound and the softness of her inner thigh. His tongue darted out, wetting a spot close to her thigh's juncture, and his thumb slowly circled her swollen clit.

Thorn's body stilled. The hair rose on the back of her neck. He was not going to bite her there? She panted in dread and anticipation. She felt the press of pointed teeth against the softest flesh of her inner thigh. Tension coiled, clenched, knotted.

A small but sharp burn scored her inner thigh. A soft whimper escaped. Wet warmth ran downward. . . . Her body released in a brutal explosion of icy-hot fire that blazed up her spine to scour the back of her skull. A waterfall of pleasure crashed down on her.

His mouth closed on the slight burn, and his tongue lapped. His finger plunged, and his thumb flicked across her aggravated clit.

She drowned under wave after wave of glorious delight. Her delighted cries filled the small cabin in time to his sucking mouth.

Yaroslav raised his head from her thigh and licked the crimson smears from his smiling lips. "Good, yes?"

Gasping for breath and trembling with aftershocks, Thorn gazed at the vampire's brutally handsome face and night-black eyes. She nodded. She couldn't form one single coherent thought, never mind actually speak.

He rose from her spread thighs and crawled over her to stare down into her eyes from barely a breath away. "I am glad to have pleased you." His mouth descended to hers.

She opened for his kiss. His teeth gently scored her lips, and she tasted the sweet copper taste of her blood on his tongue. Against her belly, she could feel the rigid length of his erection. She reached down between them to slide her hand into his pants. The silky-smooth shaft was hot against her fingers. Out of sheer reflex, she grasped him and pulled, stroking him from base to the flared head.

He moaned into her mouth and trembled.

Thorn nipped at his bottom lip and wondered what he would look like with her mouth on him. Well, there was only one way to find out. She turned from his kiss and set her free palm against his chest. "Sit up."

He groaned and then leaned up, frowning. "What is this?"

Thorn blinked. He hadn't pulled that thought from her head? He must have been distracted by her hand on his cock. It looked like she wasn't the only one ruled by instinct. She smiled. "It's my turn to taste you."

His brows rose. "Indeed?" He sat back on his knees. The scarce light defined his muscular form into stark planes and hollows. "You wish to do this?"

Thorn licked her lips. "Yep." She looked him in the eye, showing teeth in her smile. "I'm dying to see if I can make you scream the way you made me."

"Is that so?" Yaroslav barked out a laugh. "Very well, you are more than welcome to make the attempt."

He took only a moment to shuck off his pants, tossing them on the floor, and then he knelt near the foot of the bed, facing the pillows and her. He leaned back on one palm and dug his fingers through his long hair, combing it back from his brow. The curving column of his cock arched up from between his knees. The deeply blushing head very nearly brushed his navel. Viscous moisture beaded the tip. "I await your pleasure."

She rolled forward onto her hands and knees, her pale brown hair falling to the blankets. "Ready or not, here I come." Setting her palms between his spread knees, she lowered her head and dropped a light kiss on the top of his right knee. Watching him from beneath the fall of her pale hair, she licked the spot she'd kissed. She licked farther up his thigh and felt his slight shiver under her tongue.

His smile faded.

She lowered her head, dropping down to her elbows to get as low as she could. She worked her mouth until it filled with saliva, and then with a very wet tongue curled it under his lightly furred balls and licked upward over the plump fullness of his sac, and then up the shaft to the moist tip, trailing wetness. He tasted clean. She could smell the soap he'd used under the rich musk of male arousal. She caught his gaze and lashed the tip of her tongue across the very top of the cock head peeking from its sheath.

He sucked in a harsh breath. The head of his cock emerged entirely from its sheath and seeped.

A spark of accomplishment almost made her giggle. *I think he liked that.* She swirled her tongue around the flared edge and then laved across the head. Salty musk tingled on her tongue. The flavor was not quite what she was used to, but it wasn't bad. It didn't have the bitterness of someone who drank beer or ale. It didn't have the numbing burn of someone who drank a lot of those new dark sodas either. It was . . . interesting. There seemed to be some kind of coppery sweetness to it.

Thorn pulled back to focus on his cock and worked her mouth to generate saliva. He was thick and long. She was not going to be able to get all of him into her mouth. That meant keeping her hands on him to make damn sure he didn't shove that thing deeper than she could handle. *All right. . . .*

She licked both of her hands and reached out to smooth her wet palms along the warm length of his shaft from head to root, pushing the sheath back to fully expose the blushing purple head.

His lips parted, and a groan escaped him.

She leaned forward with her very wet tongue extended and twirled it around the very top of his cock head. She widened the circling of her tongue until she stroked the flared edges and then took him deeper, and deeper, to the back of her throat.

Her hands grasped the rest of his length, extending the reach of her mouth. She pulled back slowly while sucking strongly. He slid from her mouth with the sound of wet suction.

Yaroslav gasped, his eyes closing briefly. "I suspect you may achieve your goal."

Her smile broadened. "You made me scream, so it's only fair, don't you think?" She opened her mouth and took him swiftly to the back of her throat. Sucking strongly, she pulled back until he slid past her lips with another wet smack.

He choked and groaned. "By all means, continue with this fairness."

She took him back into her mouth and lashed her tongue under the shaft. *Looks like he hasn't had decent service in a while. Good.*

Yaroslav threw his head back and groaned. "Mother Night, ah!" Braced back on his hands, his hips bucked reflexively, fucking her mouth in short jabs. "You will make me come very swiftly."

Thorn smiled around the cock pumping in and out of her mouth. *That's what you think.* She closed one hand around the base of his shaft, pressing a thumb against the thick vein on the underside, right up against the start of his ball sac. At the same time, she used her other damp palm to stroke what she couldn't get into her mouth. As long as her thumb stayed on that vein, his release could not escape. He would still climax, but he wouldn't fill her mouth with cum. He wouldn't lose his erection either. In fact, it would make it worse.

His hips thrusting, Yaroslav's mouth opened on a choking gasp. He grasped her shoulder with one hand and pushed up with his knees, pumping into her mouth at a frenzied pace. He moaned through clenched teeth.

Thorn felt the pulse against her thumb. He was trying to come. The bastard hadn't even bothered to warn her; he'd intended to come in her mouth. Too bad it wasn't going to happen. *Nice try.*

Yaroslav sat back onto his heels, gasping and groaning. His whole body trembled with denied release.

She nearly grinned. *Surprise!* Well aware that he was more sensitive after his aborted release, she lashed the head of his cock unmercifully with her tongue.

Yaroslav gave a frustrated cry and jerked back, pulling completely from her mouth.

Thorn widened her eyes and looked up at him with her best innocent expression. "What?"

His eyes were narrowed to slits, his cheeks flushed, and he panted for breath, but he smiled. "What is this?"

Thorn tilted her head, keeping her eyes wide, but her mouth tipped into a small smile. "You didn't say 'please.'"

Yaroslav's brows shot up. "Ah?" He folded his arms, and a positively evil smirk graced his lips. "Revenge shall be mine."

She bit her bottom lip. *Uh-oh . . .*

14

Thorn sat up on her knees, facing the frustrated vampire. "Oh, come on!" She folded her arms across her naked breasts. "How hard is it to say please?" She stuck out her bottom lip for good measure.

His smile tightened, and his eyes narrowed. "I was not aware that 'please' was a requirement."

Thorn clenched her teeth. *Stubborn pain in my ass....* "You are not the only one with urges, vampire. Let me have a turn at being on top, damnit!"

Yaroslav's eyes widened, and his brows lifted. "On top?" He released his breath, and his smile softened. "I see. My apologies." He lifted his chin and cleared his throat. "Continue, please."

Thorn blinked. That wasn't quite what she'd had in mind, but it was probably the best she would get, under the circumstances. She took a breath and released it. His potent musky scent beckoned enticingly. She'd take it. *This time.* She leaned forward on her hands.

Yaroslav obligingly leaned back, resting on his palms. His smile tilted up on one side, but his eyes narrowed.

Thorn hesitated. Suspicion curled through her. Watching him, she dropped to her elbows, extended her tongue, and licked up his cock.

His mouth opened, and a soft sigh escaped.

A bit more confident, she licked both her palms, inched closer, and grasped his warm, rigid length. She stroked downward to lower his sheath and then leaned down to twirl her tongue across the tip of his cock head. She took his cock as deep into her mouth as she could and tongue-lashed him.

He groaned, and his head tipped back. "Ah . . . good."

She rested her arms on his spread knees and eased down onto her belly. Sucking strongly, she pulled back, letting him withdraw, only to suck him back into her mouth. She closed her damp palms around him, using her hands to extend her mouth's reach. Her head rose and fell, pumping him in and then sliding him back out. Then again, and again . . .

His body tensed under her. His flavor intensified against her tongue.

She deliberately slowed down and looked up at him.

His eyes were half closed, and his mouth half open. His chest and belly gleamed with sweat, and his nipples stood out in sharp relief. He was getting close.

Good. She tightened her hold on him and slowed further.

He groaned, and his hips twitched, suggesting a rhythm. She matched that rhythm, knowing good and well that his body knew best what would bring him to climax.

He sucked in a sharp breath and sat up to arch over her, breathing hard. He slid his fingers into her long hair at the base of her neck.

Thorn tensed. She didn't want him grabbing her hair and taking over.

He didn't grab; instead, his palms slid down her back, with one hand reaching farther to cup her butt cheek.

It felt kind of good. Thorn relaxed and continued. The flavor of his pre-cum enriched and gained a slightly heady tingle. It wasn't bad, more like the slight burn of fine liquor. He seemed to be producing a lot of it, too. She pulled back to swallow and then took him swiftly to the back of her throat.

He released a soft gasp, and his hand on her butt shifted to the part in her cheeks. His fingers delved downward and brushed her soaked feminine curls. His explorations stilled. "Ah, so this excites you?" His voice was deep and slightly breathless.

Thorn glanced up at him. Actually, no, *he* excited her, but she wasn't about to tell him that. He was too full of himself by far already. She lashed her tongue against the underside of his cock to distract him.

He sucked in a breath and plunged two long fingers into her.

The invasion was sudden, deep, and breathtakingly delicious. Her body clenched around his fingers hungrily. Thorn moaned and sucked his cock a little deeper than she'd planned. Her throat closed tight around it. She pulled back, releasing him, and had to swallow to keep from choking.

She rubbed at the saliva on her chin and glared up at Yaroslav. "What are you doing?"

The vampire smiled and removed his fingers from her body. He raised his hand to his mouth and licked his wet fingers.

Thorn stared, mesmerized by the view of his tongue on his fingers. For all the incredible strength in them, his slender fingers looked so delicate, the long nails lending them grace. His tongue looked positively sinful.

Thorn took a sudden breath and realized she'd been holding it. She glanced away briefly to get her brain functioning again. The sneaky bastard was *trying* to distract her. And it was working. She narrowed her eyes at him. "Do you want me to finish this or not?"

Yaroslav reached down and grasped her by the upper arms, lifting her to her knees.

Thorn stiffened. "Hey!"

He leaned back, pulling her up with him and astride his hips, and then settled back among the blankets. His long midnight hair fell across the bed and slid off the side. "Perhaps we should finish each other?"

She fell forward onto the vampire under her, her hands splaying on his broad chest. "What are you doing?"

The vampire released her arms and wrapped his arms around her, pulling her down and tight against his chest. "Did you not say that you wished to be on top?"

"Uh, yeah. . . ." She swallowed. His nipples were hard points under her palms. "But I meant . . ."

Yaroslav reached up to cup her cheek. "You wish to take command, yes?"

"Well, yeah. . . ." She didn't actually mean to press her cheek against his warm palm, it just kind of happened.

"So, then . . ." He brushed his thumb against her bottom lip. "What is that phrase you Americans use? Ah, yes. . . ." He raised his knees, spreading her wide while pressing his heated length up against her intimate flesh. "Fuck me." He smiled. "Please."

His erection slid against her damp, creaming cleft and the sensitive nub of her clit. Her belly clenched in hungry interest. She sucked in a breath, but that didn't stop the groan from escaping, or her hips from undulating to feel more of him sliding against her. *God, he feels good. . . .*

The vampire groaned, grabbed her butt, and rolled his hips. The hard heat of his shaft sought her, found her, centered, and thrust, sliding deep into her.

Thorn threw back her head and gasped, her knees tightening

against his hips. Without thought, she tilted her hips forward and rocked. His deliciously hard length moved within her, and her excited clit rubbed against his pubic bone. Delight sparked hot and fast. She released a long, low moan.

Yaroslav's eyes closed, and his lips parted with a satisfied sigh. "Yes. . . ."

She leaned forward, pressing her palms on his chest. His cock slid partway out. She fell back down on him, taking him brutally hard. His cock slid into her slick sheath and hit just the right spot within her. She gasped in raw pleasure.

The vampire groaned and bucked under her, meeting her with a thrust. "So . . . strong." He rolled his hips under her, grinding upward. "Is . . . good."

Thorn grinned in sheer feminine conquest. "Glad you like it." She rose again to fall fast and hard, grunting with the impact.

He groaned and bucked under her. "I will come . . . very quickly!"

She closed her eyes and slammed down onto him. She could literally feel him getting harder and more rigid within her. "Mmm . . . isn't that what you wanted?" She rose and fell faster and harder, riding him with ruthless abandon.

"God . . . yes!" He panted and bucked under her, matching her swift, brutal rhythm, his heels digging into the mattress to thrust upward, meeting her stroke for stroke.

The sweat gleamed and ran on both of them. Their panting breaths were punctuated by the rapid slaps of wet flesh against wet flesh. The rich scent of sex perfumed the small cabin.

"Thorn!"

"Mmm?" She opened her eyes and gazed down at the vampire straining beneath her.

His eyes were wide, his cheeks were flushed, and his mouth gaped open, showing all four of his long teeth. He reached up and caught her around the neck, pulling her breast down to his open mouth. His other hand cupped her ass, his fingers digging into the plump, soft flesh. Pounding up into her with hard, swift thrusts, he suckled hard on her breast, his mouth making enthusiastic wet sounds.

Her mouth opened, and she gasped out her delight, her fingers digging into his shoulders, straining to match his pounding rhythm. Climax coiled and tightened into a white-hot, molten mass. Shivers danced up her spine. She was close, very close. . . .

He growled, a low and liquid feline rumbling deep in his chest. His arm locked around her neck, pulling her breast tight against his wide-open mouth. His teeth pressed into the soft flesh around the pale rose areola of her nipple as he thrust up into her with frantic speed.

She sucked in a startled breath. He was *not* going to bite her . . . there? Fear spiked through her, and climax rose to a vicious crescendo—and held, right on the edge. She writhed and twisted but couldn't make herself go past it; she couldn't make her body come. "Damnit!" Her voice was hoarse with raw need.

His gaze pinned hers, and his tongue swirled across the taut flesh pressed against his long teeth surrounding her nipple. His arm tightened, and his fingers knotted in her long hair, holding her breast locked to his mouth.

The hair rose on her neck, and her body froze with fearful expectancy. *Oh, shit!*

His teeth sank into her breast. Two thin lines of scarlet slid from the corners of his mouth.

Icy shock washed over her and then exquisite pain. Erotic fire sharpened by the jolt of alarm lanced straight down to her core. Climax exploded in a violent skull-burning rush of black rapture. Driven to the edge of sanity by the horrific power of her brutal climax, she bucked in his arms and howled out her ecstasy.

Embracing her tightly, the vampire rolled her over onto her back, pressing her into the blankets. He shuddered and then ground his cock into her, pumping stream after stream of cum into her trembling body.

Overwhelmed by the sheer power of her release, Thorn shuddered through the last of her climax in his arms, barely conscious and straining for breath.

The vampire suckled gently, practically purring against her breast. It was almost . . . comforting.

Someone knocked hard on the cabin's door. "Time to wake up!" The voice clearly belonged to Antonius.

Thorn jolted out of a dead sleep. She gasped and tried to sit up, but she was pinned by Yaroslav's naked and sweaty body. She shoved at his shoulder. "Don't open the door!" Her voice was embarrassingly high. She winced. *I sound like a freshly deflowered virgin.*

"I won't. I know better." Antonius's voice held a definite thread of humor. "We're about to dock. You've got about twenty minutes before we disembark."

The vampire rose up on one elbow and rubbed a fist against his eyes. "Thank you, Master Antonius." He looked at Thorn with sleepy, half-hooded eyes, and a smile tilted the corner of his mouth.

Thorn pointed a finger at him. "I don't want to hear it."

Yaroslav's brows lifted. "Ah?" He grinned and sat upright. "Whatever do you mean by that?" He turned and eased his long legs off the side of the bed. "I was merely going to mention that your belongings are by the door."

Thorn snorted. *Yeah, right, sure, that's all he was going to say.* She was sticky all over from sweat and . . . other things. She was going to have to make a quick change to get clean. She eased off the foot of the bed and saw her white canvas bag on the floor. She knelt to collect it and then set it on the foot of the bed to unfasten the buckles.

Yaroslav stood, set his hands on his hips, and stretched with a groan. "If you will hand me the pitcher and the basin in the washstand, I will warm the water."

Thorn blinked. *Warm* the water?

Yaroslav turned and smiled. "Magic can be of practical use, on occasion."

"Oh, okay." Thorn turned and reached for the ceramic water pitcher sunk into the tiny shelf built into the left corner. The washbowl and clean cloths were tucked on the shelf beneath it. She turned and handed everything to Yaroslav.

He set the bowl and cloths on the bed, smiled briefly, and then shoved his hand into the pitcher. There was a brief flash of golden light. He pulled out his hand, and steam curled out of the pitcher. He poured steaming water into the washbasin.

Thorn blinked. "That's handy. Remind me to come find you to heat the water for my next bath."

Yaroslav's smiled broadened. "You may count on it." He dunked a cloth into the basin and crooked a finger at her. "Now then, come, and let me clean you."

Thorn lifted her chin. "I can do it myself."

"Of course." Yaroslav smiled and sat down on the side of the bed. "But I would very much enjoy doing such for you." He tucked his chin, his brows lifted, and he stared at her from under a fallen lock of black hair. "May I?" His bottom lip protruded just a tiny bit.

Thorn winced. "Oh, yeesh, don't pout!" She rolled her eyes and crossed her arms. "You're supposed to be a big bad vampire for Pete's sake!"

Yaroslav sighed and shook his head. "Oh, very well then. . . ." He held out his hand. "May I bathe you? It would give me great pleasure to do so."

Thorn groaned and walked over to him and took his hand. "What am I going to do with you?"

Yaroslav tugged her close, raised the damp cloth, and smiled. "I have a great many suggestions."

Thorn snorted. "I'm sure you do."

15

Thoroughly clean, warm, and snug in her gray sheepskin coat, Thorn leaned over the starboard railing of the fanciful *Valkyrie*, and stared, not quite sure of what she was looking at. With the sun rising above the mountains behind them, the huge airship had nosed its way between snow-covered peaks to descend into a deep and shadowed valley completely surrounded by steep and jagged cliffs. Halfway up the right-hand cliff, morning light spilled across a row of white pillars set back into the cliff facing.

Thorn blinked. It honestly looked like a building was embedded in the side of the mountain. Sunlight spilled along the cliff walls, and light glinted, drawing her gaze farther along the cliffs. The glinting was from the glassed windows of houses set on gardened terraces carved right into the cliff wall. The buildings were all very different shapes, sizes, and styles from each other, but not much more than that. And they were everywhere.

Her mouth fell open. How did anyone get into or out of all those houses? She craned her neck and squinted, but the ship was too far across from the opposite cliff wall to see any real details.

The airship continued along the left side of the valley, making a wide turn that brought the ship all the way around toward the pillars she'd seen earlier.

Thorn trotted across the deck from the shadowy starboard side to the ship's sunlit port side to get a better look. The row of pillars marched in a shallow inward horseshoe curve within the mountainside. The ornate capitals supported a gleaming white architrave featuring an impressive number of statues. Rearing winged horses pulling ornate chariots posed along with sword-bearing figures under a broad peak. Far below, under the shadows of the pillars, a broad black patio, polished glass smooth, arched outward. It looked like the ship was going to pass right over it.

Thorn pushed her long braid off her shoulder onto her back and frowned. It really was a whole building, and the closer the ship got, the bigger and more lavish it appeared.

Yaroslav, wearing his black, fur-lined, ground-sweeping coat with his hood pulled up, leaned close to her left shoulder. "That is the grand palace, the seat of the Penumbral Realm."

Thorn bit down on her bottom lip. "It's huge."

Yaroslav chuckled. "Quite." Keeping his face carefully turned away from the sunlight, he leaned close to her ear. "That is only the facade—the front door, so to speak. The actual palace is deep within the mountain."

Thorn realized that the glints she was seeing, shining from behind the pillars, were windows, hundreds of them. "How deep does it go?"

Yaroslav lifted his chin. "Miles. Many, many miles." He set his gloved hand on her forearm. "You are to go nowhere with anyone but myself."

Thorn snorted. "I can find my way across whole countries. I am not going to get lost."

Yaroslav caught her chin and turned her to face him. "This has nothing to do with getting lost. There are those to whom you would be prey."

Thorn raised a brow and smiled. "I'm not helpless. . . ."

"Thorn." Yaroslav's eyes narrowed, and his fingers tightened on her chin. "There are those within to whom *I* am prey."

The hair on thorn's arms lifted. "What . . . ?"

Yaroslav released her chin and sighed. He looked over at the cliff palace. "Your kind and mine are not the only creatures of fairy tales and make-believe that truly do exist." He smiled tightly. "And we are far from the most dangerous."

Thorn wanted to laugh, but couldn't quite. "What, there are dragons and unicorns, too?"

Yaroslav looked away. "As far as I know, there is only one dragon, but there are indeed unicorns."

"A dragon?" Thorn blinked. "You're kidding?"

"Unfortunately, I am not." He shook his head. "If we are fortunate, you will meet only the Prince."

Antonius walked over to stand at the railing on Yaroslav's left. His hood was also raised to keep his face in shadow. "If she really was made by a heretic, she might have to stand before the Penumbral Senate." He looked out at the palace.

Yaroslav straightened, and his mouth became a tight, thin line. "The senate has convened?"

Antonius looked down at the rail and curled his lip. "There are reports of the plague all the way up into Russia. That's how we gained their army's support."

Yaroslav sighed and gripped the rail. "So swiftly it has spread?"

Antonius's mouth tilted up in the corner, but his gaze was hard. "This century has railway."

Yaroslav scowled and made a harsh sound of pure disgust.

Thorn tilted her head. "Is your senate anything like the senate in Washington?" She'd carried and delivered messages for more than a few senators during the war.

"More like the Roman senate." Antonius waved his hand toward the palace. "This place was built when Rome still ruled the known world."

Thorn blinked. Did he mean *ancient* Rome? She knew a little about Rome from the Latin and Greek the colonel had insisted she learn to read, but she simply couldn't imagine anything being so old.

"I had not expected this." Yaroslav scraped a hand though his dark hair and glanced at Thorn. "The Penumbral Senate does not convene often."

"It does for things like this, and when they do, the world changes." Antonius smiled sourly. "And not always for the better."

Thorn frowned. "The world changes?"

Antonius waved a gloved hand toward the palace. "The last time they convened, they passed the Covenant of Shadows, the ruling to isolate the human race from magical influence." He straightened, tapped his chest, and cleared his throat. "The sleepers shall remain undisturbed." He shrugged. "No more magic for humankind."

Thorn frowned. "Why not?"

"Magic can too easily go awry and destroy all in its wake." Yaroslav sighed and looked over at Thorn. "Nearly a third of the known world's population was lost due to a pair of half-grown human princes armed with less than skilled magi."

Thorn stared. "That's impossible! I would have heard about a war like that." The colonel would have found a way to drum it into her skull. He was very fond of history, especially those that dealt with wars.

Antonius snorted. "Ever hear of the Black Plague?"

Thorn frowned. Actually, she had. "You mean the plague caused by the rats in the Dark Ages?"

"That's the one." Antonius smiled sourly. "A single white rat cursed by a Moorish wizard was sent as a gift from the Turkish crown prince to the Frankish crown prince." He rolled his eyes. "Unfortunately this one rat escaped while being transported by ship, and the curse contaminated every rat it came in contact with."

Thorn shook her head. "But that wasn't a war."

Yaroslav snorted. "No, it was not. It was a childish squabble that nearly destroyed all of the known world."

Antonius stepped back into the shadows to scrape his gloved fingers through his short dark curls. "After cleaning up the mess, the senate ruled that humans were no longer allowed magical knowledge of any kind, saying that they cannot be trusted to keep from killing themselves with it."

Yaroslav snorted and folded his arms. "Humanity has always had the revolting tendency to use anything within reach to commit large-scale genocide."

Thorn winced. They were right. The battlefields she'd skirted during the War Between the States had been perfect examples of humankind's delight in wiping themselves out in large numbers.

Antonius pulled his hood back up to shade his face and rejoined them at the sunlit rail. "Anyway, the senate's ruling forced all of maguskind into exile from all of humanity."

Yaroslav tugged his hood lower, hiding his expression. "With so much of the human population already decimated, it was not difficult to conceal ourselves."

Antonius folded his arms over the brass rail and snorted. "Humans are notoriously short-lived. After four generations, less than two hundred years, no one believed we existed."

Thorn stilled. "Fairy tales and make-believe."

Yaroslav patted her arm. "Exactly."

Antonius stepped back from the rail, moving into the shadow cast by the ship's broad smokestack. "There are a lot

156 / *Morgan Hawke*

more humans in this century." He shook his head. "The Gods only know how the senate will rule this time."

Yaroslav followed Antonius into the shade, dropped his chin, and curled his lip. "Why do you think I wished to find and deal with this heretic as swiftly as possible?"

Thorn turned to look at the immense palace looming closer by the second. She looked straight down the ship's side and discovered that the ship was already overshadowing the patio's broad expanse, and lowering. She looked back up, craning her neck. As large as the towering pillars were, the balloon still topped the palace's decorative peak, but not by much.

Thorn turned around to look at the vampires standing in the shadows. "I thought you said vampires didn't have a problem with sunlight?"

"It won't kill us." Antonius smiled tightly. "But it does slow us down."

Yaroslav looked away. "Sunlight interferes with some of my . . . abilities."

So, vampires weren't all-powerful? Thorn leaned back against the sunlit rail and smiled. "That's nice to know."

Yaroslav lifted his chin, and his brows dripped low over his eyes.

Thorn didn't bother to hide her grin.

Bells rang across the ship's deck.

"Ah . . ." Antonius lifted his chin, clearly looking for something. "We're getting ready to dock." He nodded to both Thorn and Yaroslav. "Count, Miss Ferrell, I'll see you after I make my reports." He trotted across the deck for the doors leading below.

Several shipmen came to the rail by Thorn and began tugging on ropes.

Thorn picked up the canvas pack at her feet and walked over to Yaroslav to get out of their way. She slid her arms into the straps and tugged on Yaroslav's sleeve. "So, how old is he?"

Yaroslav glanced down at her and then turned and looked over at the palace. "Master Antonius? I am not quite sure, but I do know that he witnessed the glory that was Rome first-hand."

Thorn frowned after Antonius. "He's really that old?"

"Yes, however . . ." Yaroslav smiled briefly, "Antonius is not nearly so old as some few members of the senate."

"There are people older than ancient Rome?" Thorn leaned her arm against his and gave him a wry smile. "That's just plain scary."

Yaroslav turned and smiled at her. "Wait till you meet them." He patted her cheek.

Thorn snorted. "Is that a threat or a promise?"

Yaroslav sighed. "Hopefully it is merely a threat."

Thorn blinked. "Huh?"

The ship's steam whistle released a powerful double-tone blast only inches behind her.

Pain stabbed into Thorn's temples. "Ow!" She clapped her hands over her ears and winced.

Yaroslav winced as well. "That was not pleasant."

Insanity broke loose with sea-coated, bearded men running and shouting everywhere. Ropes were loosened and tossed over the ship's sides. Chains rattled loudly. The steam whistle cut loose again.

Thorn moved back over to the sunlit rail and looked down. On the broad black patio under the shadow of the massive pillars, men scurried to catch ropes, securing them to large iron rings bolted into the polished stone expanse. Heavy chains dropped from the airship were pulled through yet more rings. Iron bars were rammed through the broad links to keep them from sliding back out.

A shipman in his dark seaman's coat wearing heavy canvas gloves approached and motioned Yaroslav and Thorn toward the prow and an open portside door.

A rope-and-peg ladder was rolled through the doorway. It unfurled to the polished black floor below.

Thorn winced. Another ladder climb. *Great. . . .* Movement and scarlet caught the corner of her eye. She turned.

Dark navy sea-coated men scattered before a scarlet-hooded and robed man flowing with uncanny grace across the deck toward them. He didn't even move like he had feet; in fact he seemed to sway from side to side. His hands were folded together, concealed by voluminous sleeves, and coal-black curls spilled from under his black fur-lined hood.

It was the man she'd seen earlier, while Yaroslav had been fixing her . . . magic.

He turned his head, facing them, and his movements stilled, utterly. From within the shadow of the hood, his blue eyes seemed to glow, and his deep scarlet, Cupid's-bow lips curved up into a sweet smile that did not reach his icy gaze.

Thorn's wolf soul recognized his swaying movements and his utter stillness very well indeed. *Serpent. . . .* Every hair stood on her body. "That isn't a human."

Yaroslav's hand closed tight on her upper arm, and a low growl rumbled. "Correct, Senator Belus merely has the appearance of one."

Thorn stilled. That was a *senator?* She glanced up at the vampire. "He was in the hallway when you . . . fixing me."

"That comes as no surprise." Yaroslav's brows dropped low over his eyes, and his gaze remained fixed on the senator. "You might even say it was expected."

"Oh. . . ." She looked back toward the senator. "There was another man in the hall, too. I think he was one of Antonius's."

Yaroslav took a deep breath and smiled. It wasn't pretty. "He was there to keep this one at bay."

Abruptly Senator Belus moved, heading toward the sunlit portside door with decisive speed. In the gangway he stopped, turned backward, and then stepped out onto the ladder. He looked over at them again. His deceptively sweet smile broadened, and he began his descent.

The man stationed by the ladder stood very stiffly, eyes wide, and did not offer his hand.

Thorn shivered. She really, really didn't want to get on that ladder with that . . . senator.

Yaroslav led her across the deck to the opposite, starboard side. Standing in the shadow of the poop deck, he looked over the edge. "I, too, have no desire to share the ladder with Senator Belus." He unfastened his long coat and shrugged out of it, revealing a high-collared, black velvet tunic with full sleeves gathered into gold embroidered cuffs. The tunic's full, heavily embroidered hem fell past the tops of his boots. He held his coat out to her. "Put this on."

Thorn took his furred coat. "Over my coat and pack?"

Yaroslav nodded. "The wind will be very cold."

"Okay. . . ." Thorn tilted her head and shoved her arms into the sleeves, pulling on his coat over everything. "What about you?"

Yaroslav leaned close to Thorn. "Are you willing to give me your trust?"

Would she trust him? Thorn arched a brow at him. "With what?"

Yaroslav held out is hand and gave her a tight smile. "Your life?"

Thorn took his hand. "Yes." She believed absolutely that he would do his best to keep her alive.

Yaroslav closed his fingers tight around hers and gave her a blinding smile. "Good." Tugging her close, he sat on the brass rail and set one leg over the side. He scooped her up to cradle her in his arms. "Hold on very tight." He smiled. "And do your best not to scream."

Thorn wrapped her arms around his neck and scowled. "I don't scream."

"Is that so?" Yaroslav's grin was positively evil. "Are you quite sure?"

Thorn looked down over the rail and sincerely wished she hadn't. It was a very, very long way down. The bottom was so far away there were clouds below them, and dawn had yet to reach it. The trees looked smaller than blades of grass. She swallowed. "What are you planning to do, jump over the side?"

His brow lifted. "And if I say yes?"

She froze and then tightened her arms around his neck. She'd agreed to trust him; she certainly couldn't back out now. "Okay."

Grinning, Yaroslav tipped forward and fell into the sky, carrying her with him.

16

They fell from dawn's light into the deep shadows of untouched night.

Clutching the vampire's neck for dear life, Thorn held her breath and managed not to scream, but only just barely. The icy wind burned against her cheeks and made her eyes water.

Golden mist erupted all the way around the falling vampire. Red lightning arced and crackled.

Thorn felt a shimmering electrical current wherever her body met his. It wasn't uncomfortable, but it wasn't exactly pleasant either.

The mist expanded, darkened, and thickened around him, coating him in a second shape that expanded upward and outward. Something rather like a second pair of arms unfolded from his back and expanded. Gleaming midnight rainbow feathers formed and lengthened until he had a pair of enormous wings. A feathered tail spread behind him. His boots took on the appearance of clawed feet.

Thorn shivered. This wasn't like the way she changed at all.

She changed from the inside out. He was changing the outside, and hiding himself within. It was frightening; it was amazing.

And they fell.

Yaroslav's winged form darkened and solidified. He lifted his chin, and his long black hair became a crest of black feathers. Midnight feathers spread all down his body until only the very center of his face remained exposed. His eyes enlarged and turned gold and round, like coins. The hands holding her became clawed, with the skin scaling to the elbow. The long feathers of the vampire's raven wings rustled like leaves.

Yaroslav's wings spread wide, catching the wind and slowing their decent into a long glide. His wings beat forward and fell back, churning the sky, literally swimming on the wind's current. He turned with a head-reeling swoop, and they passed through the ship's shadow.

Flight. . . . It was terrifying; it was exhilarating. Her breath exploded out of her in a peal of laughter.

Yaroslav grinned at her.

Thorn looked up at the bottom of the airship. It looked so small compared to the long balloon that held it. They sailed past the palace's sunlit entry and then past tiered cliffs with ornate houses nestled on them. Where was he taking her? She tried to ask, but the wind ripped her voice completely away.

His shadowy thoughts moved against the back of her mind. *The palace is not where I wish to be.* The tip of his right wing lifted into a bar of sunlight. For a brief moment the feathers blazed with rainbow shimmers; then the feathers broke loose, as though cut, and disintegrated into black smoke.

Thorn gasped. What the hell . . . ?

The vampire abruptly dropped into a sharp spiral. He swore viciously and turned to look at his wing and the missing tips to his feathers. His brow lowered, and his mouth set. Red lightning crackled, and the feathers re-formed.

She stared. Sunlight "interfered"? That looked an awful lot like *destroyed* to her.

Still swearing in at least three languages Thorn couldn't begin to recognize, Yaroslav sailed lower, going deep under the shadow line. He glanced at her, and his thoughts moved against the back of her mind. *Sunlight will not harm me physically, it merely drains my powers.*

Thorn bit down on her bottom lip. *Oh, is that all?* She eyed the sunlight slipping past the surrounding peaks and creeping down the passing cliff walls at a dauntingly fast speed. Wherever they were going, they had better get there soon. They were running out of darkness.

Well do I know it. Yaroslav scowled at the passing cliffs. *It has been too long since I have been here. I cannot find . . . Ah!* His wings pumped, and he rose. *There.*

Thorn turned to look at where he was heading. Dead ahead was an ornate, green, copper-roofed, four-story mansion set into an arching cave hollowed into the mountain's face. The house's lowest level was of rusticated white stone with red brick above it, and the upper levels were timber and white plaster. Blown snow covered the fanciful roof and sharply pointed dormers. *There?*

As she watched, sunlight bathed the copper arabesques decorating the spine of the snow-covered and steeply peaked roof. The slender copper-domed minaret turrets commanding the house's four corners brightened. The circular stained-glass windows of the broad square facing tower twinkled. The snow caught on the gargoyles below the clock's face sparkled.

Hold tight! The vampire pumped his wings hard and then stretched straight out into a soaring glide barely under the burning surface of dawn. Black feathers began to scatter behind them, tumbling away and disintegrating on the wind.

Thorn tightened her hands around Yaroslav. He was flying far too close to the light.

They sailed over the white wall bordering the cliff's edge, and tumbled onto the snow-covered lawn. Thorn rolled right out of the vampire's arms, landing on her belly. She groaned and sat up, shoving snow from her cheeks. "Yaroslav?"

Two body lengths away, Yaroslav was a smoking feathered mess lying on his belly with his wings flopped awkwardly. Abruptly his feathers blew away, scattering in a rustling rush, leaving his human form gasping in the snow. Gold mist curled around him.

Dawn's light spilled over the cliff's edge wall and inched toward the vampire lying in the snow.

"Shit!" Thorn rose and tottered over to him on shaky knees. Sunlight might not actually burn his skin, but it did bad things to his magic. Tripping on the overlong hem of his fur-lined coat, she jerked at the buttons and shrugged out of the coat as fast as she could.

Sunlight brushed against his feet. The gold mist curling around his feet turned to black smoke and then to ash. He groaned and folded into a fetal position.

Thorn tossed the coat over the curled vampire, covering him from head to foot, and then collapsed in the snow at his side. She released a long sigh that became a tired chuckle. "Well, we made it."

"I am pleased for you."

Thorn jerked and turned to look over her shoulder toward the house.

A slender young man glided toward them across the top of the snow in a ground-sweeping scarlet robe. Within the shadow of his hood, lined with black fur, red highlights gleamed in dark curls worn loose and tumbling at his brow and across his shoulders. His rounded cheekbones and pointed chin set off perfectly the full Cupid's bow of his mouth, defining the delicately youthful face of a Renaissance angel. His hands were folded together within the voluminous sleeves. Behind him

strode two large men in hooded black robes bearing un-
sheathed swords.

Thorn rose slowly to one knee. The men with the swords
didn't bother her in the least, but the one in the red robe made
her heart pound in her throat. She didn't know how she knew,
but every drop of blood in her veins was convinced that this
slender young man was the most deadly being she'd ever met.
She couldn't make herself look him in the eyes. Focused on his
left shoulder, she suddenly realized that his robe looked an
awful lot like the snake-man's. Was this another . . . ? She risked
a glance upward. "Senator?"

"I am indeed." Eyes as blue as a summer sky framed by
sooty lashes peered at her from under the fine arch of black
brows. "And who might you be?"

Thorn tried not to flinch. It took everything in her to resist
the urge to change into fur and bolt. "I'm Thorn Ferrell. This is
Yaroslav."

"Yaroslav?" The youthful senator frowned. "Count Feodor
Yaroslav Iziaslavich?"

Thorn frowned. That sounded really familiar. "I think
so."

"Let me see. . . ." The senator dropped to one knee in the
snow and reached for Yaroslav's fur-lined coat.

Terror slammed through Thorn in an uncontrollable white-
hot rush. "No . . . !" She threw her body over Yaroslav's curled
form to straddle him on her hands and knees. The change into
half wolf ripped through her so fast it made her skin burn and
her head throb. Shaking in fear and pain, she laid her tall ears
flat and bared her long teeth at the terrifying young man.
"Don't touch him!" She knew damned well she didn't stand a
chance in hell of taking him, but that wouldn't stop her from
trying.

The youthful senator sat back on his heels, his eyes wide. "A
werewolf . . . ?"

The two men with swords snarled, baring long teeth, and leaped forward, landing only inches behind the senator.

The senator threw up his hand faster than the eye could follow. "No."

The armed men stopped cold.

Thorn froze with them, her heart nearly stopping in her chest. Her snarl died.

Yaroslav moved under her. "Thorn. . . ." He pushed feebly at the coat's hood covering his face. "This is . . ." he groaned, "my prince."

Thorn's ears lifted. This was the famous vampire prince they'd been coming to see? She sat up on Yaroslav's back.

The vampire prince tilted his head to peer under the edge of the coat's hood and smiled. "Welcome, Count. I have been longing to speak with you."

"And I you, my prince." From under the coat, Yaroslav pushed at Thorn. "Off. You are . . . heavy."

Thorn slid off Yaroslav's back and crouched at his side. Embarrassment flooded her cheeks with heat. She'd almost attacked Yaroslav's prince. And yet she could not stop her heart from pounding or her hands from shaking. She still couldn't look at him directly. "I'm sorry for my, uh . . . temper, sir."

"Perfectly understandable, Thorn." The vampire prince rose slowly to his feet and eased two steps back. "However, your master needs care. Will you allow us to carry him into the house?"

Thorn lowered her head, and her ears tipped back. "What about the sunlight?"

The vampire prince waved a hand. "Sunlight merely weakens us. It does not actually harm us."

Yaroslav groaned and pushed to his knees. "It affects my magic, not my body."

Both armed men sheathed their swords and took two steps forward.

Thorn backed away from Yaroslav and them.

The prince rose to his feet. "We will take good care of your master." He tilted his head and smiled, showing a dimple in his cheek. "By the way, I am Rafael."

She shot a narrowed glance toward the terrifying prince. "He's not my master. No one is."

The two robed men looped their arms under Yaroslav's and lifted him onto his feet while keeping his long coat pulled up over his head.

The prince's brows lifted. "Indeed?" He set his hands behind him and looked over at Yaroslav. "Is this so?"

"Not so." Yaroslav groaned and set his arms about the shoulders of the two men helping him. "She is . . . blood-thrall." He sucked in a deep breath. "Thrice over."

Rafael's brows lifted. "Oh?" His chin dropped, and his bottom lip protruded just a little. "Pity." He turned and led the way toward the house.

The two men helped Yaroslav stagger after him.

Thorn trotted after them. "I'm a . . . what?"

Yaroslav waved his hand. "I will explain all later, Thorn."

Thorn stopped in her tracks and scowled. She wasn't sure she wanted to know what the hell a blood-thrall was anyway. She looked over her shoulder at the sunbathed cliffs. It might be better if she left before she got any deeper involved in all this. Unfortunately she wasn't sure she could scale such steep cliffs.

She looked back toward the house. Yaroslav and the prince were gone, but the trail through the snow led directly to the steps of a huge arching portico shading a pair of ornately glassed doors.

Thorn sighed. She should at least find out if there was a trail out of the valley and get something to eat before she took off. She wiped her rough palms down the front of her coat and focused on the wolf so close to the surface. Her power rose in a tide and whispered under her skin. She willed her beast to go back under.

Her heart thumped, and the rising power bled away. The wolf didn't want to.

Thorn blinked. What the hell . . . ? She set her jaw and concentrated. She needed her fur and fangs to go back under. She needed her human form. She refused to be seen as more of a beast than the vampires.

The blood rushed in her ears, and a chill sweat broke out all over her. The wolf didn't want to go. She refused to look like prey in front of all those predators.

Thorn gasped and staggered a step. She couldn't change. Her wolf soul was actually fighting her.

She tried again.

Her belly churned and cramped in refusal.

Thorn dropped to one knee in the snow and gasped for breath to keep from vomiting. She couldn't make herself change. She groaned and rose to her feet. She was going to have to deal with the vampires in fur and fangs. "Stupid wolf instincts."

She took two long strides toward the house and listed to the left. Her balance was off. She stopped and rolled her eyes. It was her tail. Her tail had emerged while she was still fully dressed and it was jammed down her left pant leg. She dug under her coat to unbutton the seat of her pants. She had no clue why her tail mattered to her balance. She walked fine without one as a human, but when she had one she couldn't walk properly if it wasn't free. A judicious tug let it out. She shoved her clawed hands into her coat pockets and continued on toward the house.

This was not going to be one of her better days.

17

Thorn stepped up under the arch of the mansion's portico and pulled the tie from her braid. The flight, the crash, and then her sudden and violent change into her half-wolf form had made a complete mess of her hip-length hair. She fingered her braid apart until her wolf-silver mane spilled loose down her back. She slid the pack from her back and crouched to dig out her brush. There wasn't a whole lot she could do about her appearance, but she had to at least try.

One of the windowed double doors clicked and opened.

Crouched down with one buckle to her pack unfastened, Thorn glanced up, startled.

A tall, slender young man with curly brown hair, in a neat black formal suit, blinked down at her. "Miss Thorn?"

He didn't have that shimmer of "otherness" the vampires gave off, or the heavy disquiet Max had. Good lord, was this a *normal* person? Thorn dropped her ears as low as she could get them and gave him a smile with closed lips to hide her overlong teeth. She eased up on her feet. "Yes?"

"Ah, very good." He smiled brightly. "I'm Thomas." He

stepped back from the door and bowed slightly. "This way, please." His English pronunciation was straight out of London.

Thorn nodded and eased past him into a highly polished golden oak vestibule lit with a graceful brass gaslight chandelier with frosted glass tulip bulbs. The beautifully inlaid pendulum clock on the left wall abruptly chimed the three-quarter hour.

She frowned. The clock face read only a handful of minutes after the hour, but it had chimed as though it was a quarter of the next hour. She shook her head. Someone needed to check that clock.

The young man closed the door behind her and continued to smile, his eyes wide and a trifle unfocused. "This way, please, miss." He stepped past her.

Clutching her canvas bag by one strap, Thorn followed the young man into a broad and brightly lit marble-floored entrance hall and couldn't help but stare. Polished tables set against the walls held exquisite Greek and Roman bronzes and whimsical china knick-knacks. Corners were occupied by tall brightly painted Chinese vases filled with hothouse flowers. The walls sported framed woodblock prints and elegant portraits.

The young man led her to the right toward a sunken indoor garden under a glass-paned cupola skylight, featuring potted tropical trees and flowers around a cherub fountain. An older white-haired gentleman in an extremely formal black-tailed suit came out of the sunken garden to share quiet words with the young man.

Thorn sucked on her bottom lip and glanced about. On the left, a monstrous spiral staircase with an ornately carved, black oak balustrade led upward. Just beyond the staircase stretching to the left was a broad tapestry-hung, window-lined hallway. Directly ahead at some distance away, morning light spilled through monstrous windows across a tapestry-covered grand piano.

As a high-level courier, she'd seen more than her share of elegant manors. This house looked like any other an American senator might live in. However, this was the first time she'd been in one jammed into the side of a cliff.

The young man turned to the left and headed for the stairs. "This way, Miss Thorn."

Thorn followed him to the broad spiraling staircase and looked straight up. The stair wound upward for four floors. Morning light spilled past heavy gold velvet curtains partially covering the narrow glass-paned camber windows marching up the curving outer wall. A huge multileveled, cast-iron chandelier filled the central hollow. However, instead of gaslights or candles, the chandelier was set with fist-sized glass bulbs that held still gold embers.

Thorn shook her head and climbed after the young man. If the house was lit with magic, perhaps it wasn't so normal after all.

They passed two thoroughly human housemaids on their way down. With frilled aprons tied over their black dresses and their hair bound under tiny lace bonnets, they looked like any other housemaids Thorn had seen. Smiling vaguely, the maids nodded at the young man but barely spared Thorn a glance.

Thorn's pointed ears lifted a little. The people here didn't seem to care that she didn't look completely human. She sighed. Considering that they were working for vampires, maybe that was to be expected?

The young man stopped at the turn to the next floor and stepped into a deep arching alcove. He knocked on the heavy black oak door.

Thorn eyed the door, and her heart pounded fiercely. The vampire prince was beyond that door. She could feel him with every beat of her heart.

The door opened inward, and a robed man looked out. His hand was on the hilt of a sheathed sword.

The shimmer of "other" made the hair on Thorn's body rise. This was definitely a vampire.

He focused briefly on Thorn and then smiled at the young man. "Thank you, Thomas." His hand moved away from his sword.

The young man nodded, and his smile brightened. "Of course, sir." He bowed to Thorn and stepped away, heading back toward the stairs.

The robed man stepped back, opening the door wider. "Come in." Another sword-bearing, robed man stood just inside the door.

Ears low and clutching her bag to her chest, Thorn stepped between both men into a spacious room that stretched to her left under an ornate vaulted and coffered ceiling.

Tall windows, heavily curtained in dark gold velvet, marched across the long facing wall. The rest of the walls were painted terra cotta and held tall wilderness landscape paintings in gilt frames. An Arabian carpet in red, gold, and black covered nearly the entire sleek parquet floor. The center of the carpet was commanded by a huge expanse of wrist-thick clear glass resting knee-height on the outstretched wings of a pair of crouching white marble angels. On all four sides of the glass table were pairs of tall gold velvet wingback chairs. Matching couches lined the walls.

At the far end of the room was another closed door flanked by another pair of armed men in black robes.

Yaroslav sat in the farthest wingback chair, facing her, slouching comfortably with his feet up on an ottoman and a scarlet throw across his lap. "Pure happenstance." He lifted a blue and white china cup and smiled at the vampire prince sitting in the wingback on his immediate right. "She bit me."

Rafael was equally slouched with one booted foot up on a matching ottoman. He'd removed his scarlet senatorial robe and tossed it over the back of his chair. His high-necked black velvet tunic was very similar to Yaroslav's, with gold thread embroidery at the wrist cuffs and around the collar. His belt, however, was made of intricately wrought gold links set with deep scarlet cabochon stones.

A Turkish coffee service of etched silver sat between them. A lone blue and white cup sitting upside down on its saucer occupied the opposite corner.

Thorn snorted. They looked positively cozy. Unfortunately her pounding heart and the raised hair all down her spine weren't buying any of it.

The prince lifted his china cup, and his lips curved with evident humor, showing his dimple. "*Bit* you? Surely you jest?"

Yaroslav lifted his chin and smiled at Thorn. "I assure you; practically the first moment we met, she bit me."

Thorn hefted her bag over one shoulder and stepped into the room proper. "Of course I bit you."

A clock chimed out the three-quarter hour on her immediate right.

Thorn stopped and turned to look at the narrow table against the wall. The time on the gilded cherry wood bracket clock wasn't anywhere near the three-quarter hour. She rolled her eyes. Another messed-up clock. She strode toward Yaroslav, taking care to stay on the left side of the low table, across from the vampire prince. "I bit you because you were a total stranger that came into my cave while I was in wolf form." She smiled tightly. "That's what wolves do when they're cornered."

Rafael turned to look at her, and his brows rose over his sky-blue eyes. "So you can assume the form of a true wolf?"

Thorn's throat tightened. He was looking directly at her. The words dried in her mouth. She dodged his gaze, swallowed, and nodded. She looked down at the glass tabletop instead. In the middle of the table was a rather large and detailed brass-framed compass. It was as broad as a dinner plate but only two finger widths in height. She frowned at it. There was something odd about where the needle was pointing.

Yaroslav set his cup on the glass table. "She makes a very lovely wolf, silver as the moon, and quite large."

"Oh?" Rafael glanced at Yaroslav and then directed his gaze back toward Thorn. "May I see?"

What? Thorn jerked her gaze from the puzzling compass. He wanted to *see*? Her body wasn't against it. In fact she had the distinct impression that she'd feel a whole lot more comfortable on four legs rather than two. But that meant exposing herself during her most vulnerable of moments—between shapes. "I, uh . . ." She really, really didn't want to change in front of him, but she didn't want to anger him either. She looked at Yaroslav, not sure what to say.

Yaroslav pushed the lap throw to one side and rose to his feet. He stepped close and eased the backpack from her shoulder. "Allow me to help you disrobe." He set her bag on the seat of the chair beside her.

Thorn froze, staring up at him in shock. He *wanted* her to change in front of this terrifying . . . prince?

Yaroslav tugged at the few buttons to her coat, unfastening them. "She is a trifle shy, my prince, if you would be so kind as to ask the guards to turn their backs?" He worked the coat from her shoulders.

Rafael nodded and lifted a hand. "Of course."

Thorn glanced toward either door. All four guards turned to face the door they watched over.

Yaroslav tossed her coat on the chair, over her bag, and pulled at the shoulder latches to her battered coveralls.

Thorn snapped out of her daze and pushed his hands away from her clothes. "I'll do it."

Rafael leaned to one side and rested his chin on his upraised palm. "You may turn your back to me, if you like."

That sounded like a wonderful idea—she wouldn't have to

look at him—and yet it was an extremely stupid idea, too. One didn't leave one's back exposed to a predator. She shook her head. "I'm okay."

She sat down on the chair to tug off her work boots. They had gotten decidedly uncomfortable, with her toes being clawed. She got them off and winced. She'd torn the hell out of her socks. She sighed, tugged them off, and shoved them into her boots. She got back up on her feet to work on unfastening the hip buttons to her pants.

Yaroslav reached out to fuss with the buttons of her cream flannel shirt.

Thorn pushed at his hands. "Quit that." She turned to the side to take her buttons out of his reach.

Yaroslav followed her around and reached for her buttons again. "I am merely attempting to be helpful."

Thorn turned to the side again to take her buttons back out of his reach. "You don't need to be so helpful."

Yaroslav rolled his eyes. "Very well, then. . . ."

Thorn unfastened her last shirt button. The shirt slid off her shoulders in Yaroslav's grasp and was tossed onto the chair beside her. She froze, her heart beating in her mouth. Her naked back was to the prince.

Yaroslav set his hand on her bare shoulder. "Remain calm." He tugged at the coverall buttons at her hip. "Rafael also wishes to see your aspect." Her pants slid down to her ankles, exposing her entire backside and her tail. Yaroslav shoved her long hair over her shoulder and off her back, exposing the full length of her spine.

Chills raced up her back. She crossed her arms over her breasts and shivered. Light began to glow under the skin of her bare arms, forming the overly familiar blue tracery that marked what bound her two souls in one body. She glanced over her shoulder in alarm.

"I have never seen an aspect such as this." Rafael leaned forward in his chair, and his gaze narrowed. "Indeed, this is the work of a heretic." He raised a finger. "The pattern shows signs of deterioration." He raised his gaze to Yaroslav. "Is this your overlay?"

Yaroslav looked down and nodded shortly. "The original aspect is silver damaged."

Rafael's brows lifted. "To be this fragile, it is a beginner's work, clearly." He smiled slightly. "Excellent workmanship on your part; the transmutation appears to be proceeding smoothly." He eased back in his chair. "I am glad. I would not have wished to lose such an enchanting creature."

Yaroslav nodded and released a breath. "Thank you, my prince." He released her shoulder and took a step away to present a small bow.

Rafael laughed. "So, worried, were we?"

Thorn looked away and nervously rubbed her bare arms. What the hell did he mean by transmutation?

Something tapped her shoulder.

Thorn yelped in shock, and her wolf surged to the surface in a brutally fast change. She dropped to four paws, whirled, and snapped at something blurry hanging right over her head. She missed, and her vision abruptly cleared.

Yaroslav held his retracted hand close and stepped back. His brows dropped low over his dark eyes, and his bottom lip protruded just a bit. "Thorn. . . ."

You idiot! She laid her ears flat back and trembled, a little dizzy on her feet. She had changed much too fast. *You scared the hell out of me!*

Yaroslav folded his arms across his chest. "If you wanted a taste of my blood, you need only ask."

You shouldn't have startled me. She shook herself, settling her fur out of sheer habit.

Rafael chuckled softly. "A very lovely wolf indeed, and so large." He tapped a finger on his bottom lip. "Siberian?"

Thorn lifted her head to focus on the prince of vampires. Her tall ears lifted. Oddly, she felt a whole lot better about him. The prince didn't seem nearly as frightening. It wasn't that he was any less a dangerous predator, it was more that it was easier to see that he was not actually inclined to attack. At least, not at the moment. *Alaskan tundra wolf, actually*.

Yaroslav looked toward his prince. "She says she is a tundra wolf from Alaska in northern America."

Rafael smiled, and his gaze narrowed sharply. "She was made by an American sorcerer?" He rubbed at his chin. "I had not thought to search there. . . ."

Thorn shook her head in the human fashion. *Not American*. The Doctor's accent had been very British.

Yaroslav looked down at Thorn, and his brow lifted. "You did not mention that before."

Thorn looked up at him and tilted back an ear. She was pretty sure she had mentioned it.

Yaroslav folded his arms and lifted his chin. "I do not remember such."

Rafael's smile tightened. "Mentioned what, may I ask?"

"According to Thorn . . ." Yaroslav looked over at his prince, "the sorcerer that made her, the Doctor, had a British accent."

Rafael's brows rose; then he rolled his eyes and sat back in his chair. "Of course. How obvious." He swept a hand down his cheek and smiled wryly. "This plague was released by the Turks. A British sorcerer makes perfect sense."

"The Turks . . . ?" Yaroslav scowled. "Again with a plague?"

Rafael tilted his head to the side. "They released it, but the Assyrian magi could not discover how their human government had gained it. Senator Ashur is quite firm that it is not of their making." He raised a finger. "However, in this century the British and the Turks are coconspirators against Russia, which Bulgaria claims to be a part of."

178 / *Morgan Hawke*

"Bulgaria . . ." Yaroslav lifted his chin, "where the plague first appeared, yes?"

"Exactly." Rafael waved a hand at Thorn. "Now that we have the heretic's signature and his country . . ." he smiled, baring fangs a lion would have been proud of, "an end shall come to this debacle very swiftly."

Thorn suddenly felt a pang of pity for the Doctor.

Yaroslav frowned. "If there is not more than one heretic."

Rafael's smile slipped. "More than one . . . ?"

Yaroslav tilted his head toward Thorn. "There is more than one werewolf."

Thorn looked up at Yaroslav. *Max.*

Yaroslav nodded at her. "Max."

18

"Two?" Rafael sat up in his wingback chair, his sky-blue eyes wide. "There are two werewolves?"

"Indeed." Yaroslav stepped back around the edge of the glass table to the wingback chair by his prince. He tugged at his long tunic and sat. "A very poorly made man beast." He set one booted foot up on the ottoman. "The creature is clearly embattled within as well as without."

"That is to be expected from a heretic's work." Rafael's gaze focused on the center of the glass table. "On the other hand, in spite of the obvious flaws in Thorn's aspect, her dual nature appears . . . united."

Yaroslav reached for his abandoned cup and the coffeepot. "Thorn is at peace with her feral nature, and so gained . . . stability within and without." He poured steaming coffee into his cup. "She is a very remarkable creature." He winked at her and then set the coffeepot back on the tray.

Remarkable? Thorn would have blushed if her wolf form had allowed for it. Instead she shook her shoulder fur just a little, unexpectedly pleased by his praise.

"I agree. Quite remarkable." Rafael tilted his head and aimed his smile at Thorn. "You seem to be a bit more . . . comfortable with my presence, Thorn."

Thorn raised her head, lifted her ears, and gave him a broad wolf grin with her tongue lolling in a friendly fashion. She was a lot more comfortable. The wolf was a far better judge of aggression, or lack of it, than her human side.

Rafael's smile broadened. "Might I touch your fur? It looks so soft."

Thorn dropped her head and tilted one ear back. He wanted to *touch* her?

Yaroslav dropped one hand over the arm of his chair and rubbed his fingertips together. "Do not be afraid. Rafael means you no harm."

Thorn eyed Yaroslav's fingers and wanted the comfort he was offering. She moved to his side and set her head under his hand before she'd considered what her actions might mean. His fingers combed down her heavy neck fur and through her shoulder fur, delivering small, delicious shivers. An overwhelming surge of affection spilled into her mind directly from Yaroslav. She sighed and leaned into his hand. His touch felt really good. To hell with worrying about what letting him pet her might mean.

"May I?" Rafael eased to the side toward Yaroslav and dropped his hand over the arm of his chair, palm down. He smiled as sweet as a cherub. "It would please me greatly."

Rolling under a shivering wave of physical delight, and pressed by the warm affection from Yaroslav, she slid between Yaroslav's chair and the ottoman under his raised knee to Rafael's side. She sniffed at the long-nailed hand the prince offered. His scent . . . Yaroslav's scent held shadows, but the prince's was tinted strongly with what could only be described as ancient night. It was alarming, but his body was clearly not displaying aggression. She held still.

Rafael raised his hand slowly and slid his fingers through her shoulder fur. "Soft as a cloud. How delightful." His voice was barely above a whisper.

Thorn held very still under his hand. His touch felt physically pleasurable, but the pressure of his presence made her heart race.

Rafael set his other elbow on the arm of the chair and rested his chin on his upraised palm. "I do, however, have one pressing question." He stroked down her back and turned his head slowly. His gaze focused on the center of the low glass table. "What do you carry in your bag?"

Huh? Thorn lifted her head in confusion. *My bag?*

Yaroslav stilled, and his gaze shifted to the table, too.

Thorn turned to look at the low table, automatically seeking what they were looking at. The compass—they were both staring at the compass. She puzzled over it. There was something wrong with the needle's direction. Compasses were supposed to point due north; this one wasn't. It was pointing straight at her pack on the chair across the table.

All three of them looked at the canvas bag resting on the chair across the table.

Rafael's hand stopped on the back of Thorn's neck. "Count, would you be so kind as to investigate the contents for me?"

Yaroslav frowned briefly at Thorn. "Of course." He rose from his chair.

Wait a minute! Thorn jerked away from the prince. *That's mine!*

Rafael's fingers closed brutally tight in her neck fur. "Please, remain where you are, Thorn." His voice held the threat of a low growl.

Thorn growled in reply, too frightened by the threat in his voice to react any other way.

Rafael leaned over the arm of his chair and set his other wrist before her. "You may bite me if you wish." His gaze narrowed, but his smile remained. "I assure you, I won't mind in the least."

Yaroslav froze, his hand outstretched to Thorn's backpack. He turned sharply to look at Thorn with wide eyes, and fear pulsed across their mental connection. *Do not bite him! I do not wish to lose you to him.*

Thorn trembled in the prince's hand. Personally, she wasn't ready to die. Her growl turned to a low whine. *But my bag?*

"Count, the contents of that bag, if you please?" Rafael kept his fingers tight and his gaze focused on Thorn. "You heard the clock. You know what I am looking for."

"Of course." Yaroslav lifted the half-open bag from the chair by one of the shoulder straps. The bag tipped, and several things tumbled free. Thorn's brush, a red shirt, a rolled pair of socks, and one paper-wrapped parcel hit the seat of the chair.

Rafael looked sharply over at the chair. "That package . . . ?"

Thorn started. Her package from the colonel. *That's my delivery!*

"Thorn is a courier for the American government." Yaroslav lifted the parcel and frowned deeply. He turned to look at Thorn, his jaw clenched. "Your colonel gave *this* to you to deliver?"

Yes! It was to go to Agent Hackett and then to his superiors in Washington. Thorn jerked back sharply.

Rafael's fingers tightened in her fur. "Open it."

No, don't! Thorn whined and hated the sound coming from her throat. *That's private!*

Yaroslav tugged at the twine, and it broke free. The letter fell to the table. He tore the paper and tugged open the cardboard box. He stared at the contents, and his eyes widened. "This is . . ."

Two clocks, one at either end of the room, chimed out the three-quarter hour.

Rafael turned to face Yaroslav, straightening in his chair

without releasing Thorn from his grasp. He smiled slightly. "So now we know what has set off the house's alarms."

Yaroslav scowled and then walked around the other end of the glass table, away from Thorn. He held out the opened box to Rafael. Inside, on a nest of wool batting, was a finger-length glass vial full of something that glowed a near-blinding violet blue. "This . . . was supposed to go to America." He did not look at Thorn.

Thorn gaped. *He opened my delivery!* She winced. Hackett was going to kill her.

Rafael stared at the glowing vial. "Is that . . . ?"

Yaroslav's jaw tightened. "There is no mistake. The contents are highly concentrated." He set the box down on the glass table. The needle within the compass turned to point at the box.

Rafael tilted his head toward Thorn. "Does she know what this is?"

Yaroslav shook his head. "No."

Rafael frowned. "But the signature . . . ?"

Yaroslav looked away. "So I see."

Thorn trembled in the vampire's grip. Signature? What the hell were they talking about?

Rafael's body relaxed, and his tight grip on her fur eased. "What an interesting puzzle." He leaned back in his chair and set his foot up on the ottoman. "This is growing more curious by the moment."

All the tension bled from Thorn's body. The prince wasn't angry anymore. Exhausted and more than a bit overwarm in her winter-thick fur, she sat down on her haunches and panted.

"Thorn . . ." Rafael's voice was gentle, almost soothing, "where did your colonel get . . . this?"

I have no idea. I'm only a courier, they never tell me anything. The colonel had said that it was connected to the plague, but that was all. And he was dead, killed by Max. She froze. She *did* know where the package had come from. Max had told her. It had come from him.

Yaroslav stiffened, and his eyes widened. His fingers clenched on the box. "This . . . came from *Max*?"

Rafael looked up at Yaroslav. "This is from the other were-wolf?"

Yaroslav looked away and scowled. "Antonius made mention that Max was known to be the plague beast."

Rafael's brows lifted, and a sigh escaped him. "Ah, so . . . ?"

Thorn stilled utterly. Max was the plague beast, and her package had come from him. *I was delivering the plague to America?*

Rafael released Thorn's fur to stroke down her back, calmly. "Thorn, it is obvious that you did not know what you carried."

Thorn glanced up at him. Had he actually read her thoughts? Or had it been a good guess?

Rafael lifted a brow at Yaroslav. "Could Thorn perhaps have been an early experiment?"

"It is possible." Yaroslav tilted his head. "Her making was obviously done nearly a decade ago."

Rafael shook his head. "There is no other option. Remove all trace of the Doctor's aspect from Thorn. I give you sanction for claim." He smiled up at Yaroslav. "I was hoping not to have to do that."

Yaroslav snorted and folded his arms. "You were hoping to steal her."

Rafael smiled. "But of course!"

Now, wait just a damned minute! Thorn slid out from under Rafael's stroking hand and backed away. She focused on Yaroslav and laid her ears back. *You said you can't remove the . . . whatever it is the Doctor has on me.* A low growl rumbled in her chest. Had he lied?

Rafael's brows lifted. "Whatever is wrong with Thorn?"

Yaroslav glanced at his prince. "A misunderstanding." He

moved behind Rafael's chair toward Thorn. "I did not lie. You cannot live without your wolf's soul." He looked at Rafael and then back at Thorn. "However, your Doctor is the maker of the plague."

What? Thorn lifted an ear, and her tail switched in confusion. *Okay, so . . .* She looked from one vampire to the other. *What has that got to do with me?*

Yaroslav glanced away. "The . . . vial will be presented to the senate, which will not only identify the plague's maker, but also allow them to manufacture a cure."

Rafael turned in his chair to face Thorn. "This Doctor is a heretic, and, as such, all his creations would be under mandatory judgment."

Thorn tilted her head. *And mandatory judgment means . . . what?*

Yaroslav stared at her and held her gaze. "A mandatory judgment means that you, as one of his creations, would have to be destroyed."

Thorn jumped back out of sheer reflex. *Destroyed? You're kidding, right?*

"No need to fear." Rafael smiled. "I have given sanction, or permission, to Count Yaroslav for your creation, or re-creation, so to speak. He is going to remake you."

Yaroslav folded his hands behind him and lifted his chin. "I am going to replace the Doctor's spell with mine."

Replace the spell? Thorn sat down on her haunches. *Can I think about this first?*

Yaroslav's brows lifted. "You wish to think about this?"

"What an excellent idea!" Rafael stood up. "I am of the opinion that thinking is best done on a full stomach." He rubbed his palms together and turned to smile at Thorn. "How does breakfast sound? We have some excellent venison steaks."

Every thought in Thorn's head came to a complete stop. *Food. . . .* Her stomach knotted into a hungry and loud snarl.

Her mouth watered, and she was forced to lick her lips. She rose up on her feet and looked up at the smiling prince. That sounded wonderful.

Rafael leaned to the side to catch Yaroslav's attention. "There, it is decided. Breakfast first, and other worries after, yes?"

Yaroslav rolled his eyes. "As you wish, my prince."

"All will be much better after breakfast." Rafael stood next to Yaroslav and patted his arm. "Trust me."

Thorn faced the long room's terra-cotta painted wall. The wolf moved against her soul within her and slid under. She rose from four legs to two. Her white fur became a long silvery mane that spilled past her tall pointed ears and swept down her curved spine to her tail. She groaned. Her body still wouldn't let her take full human form. "Damnit. . . ."

Yaroslav raised the white silk dressing gown one of the staff had brought. "Thorn?"

Thorn lifted her arm and closed her hands to put the robe on without tearing the sleeves with her finger claws. "I can't take full human form." She folded the robe across her and knotted the sash at her waist. "It's like my heart won't let me."

Yaroslav wrapped his arms around her and leaned against her back. "It takes time to accustom one's self to the company of the prince."

"Okay." Thorn turned to smile wryly at Yaroslav. "I got accustomed to you." She pressed a kiss to his cheek. "I can get accustomed to anybody."

Yaroslav snorted and tightened his arms around her. "Do not get too accustomed."

Thorn leaned back against his broad chest and smiled. "Jealous?"

Yaroslav lifted his chin. "But of course."

Rafael chuckled softly at the table behind them. "Continue with this display of affection, and *I* will grow jealous."

Breakfast was served downstairs in an oval room lit with candlelight rather than sunlight. The green and gold, silk-cut, velvet draperies were drawn across all the windows. The curving walls were covered in fine tooled leather. The cream-damask-swathed round table was set with gold-trimmed eggshell porcelain and positioned before a trim white-painted fireplace with Wedgwood inlaid panels in moss green and white.

Thorn eyed the elegant room with more than a little dismay. "I would have been fine in the kitchen."

Both vampires turned to frown at her.

Thorn hunched her shoulders. "What?"

Rafael lifted his chin and sniffed. "My guests do not eat in the kitchen." He took the chair closest to the windows.

Yaroslav pulled out the velvet chair facing the fireplace and nodded at Thorn. "Sit."

"Okay, fine, whatever. . . ." Thorn eased her tail to the side, tucked the voluminous skirts of her snowy robe closed and sat. She tucked her hands in her lap. "But just so you know, I have terrible table manners."

Yaroslav took the chair opposite Rafael and snapped open his napkin. "There is no time like the present to learn them." He lifted a stern brow at Thorn.

Thorn snatched for her napkin and tucked it onto her lap. *Bully.*

Just about every kind of breakfast food imaginable was served by the vaguely smiling staff, along with coffee, tea, and hothouse orange juice.

Yaroslav lifted a pair of steaming steaks onto Thorn's plate.

The savory aroma made Thorn's stomach ache with longing. She groaned. "That smells so good." She lifted her fork and knife and then stopped to eye Yaroslav.

He nodded.

Thorn started cutting and eating with a will, swallowing the bite-size chunks whole. Fangs simply did not allow for chewing. As it was, the tender rare meat practically dissolved on her tongue. She moaned with delight.

Rafael lifted a clear glass pitcher of what looked like water from a tray held by a smiling maid. He filled a single large tumbler and set it by Thorn's plate. "It would be best if you drank this." He set the pitcher back on the tray, and it was carried away.

"Thanks." Thorn took a large swallow from the glass. It tasted incredibly pure, as though it was water and then some. She took a second swallow and then continued to cut and eat.

Beside her, both vampires began to fill their own plates.

Thorn eyed the vampires with interest. Apparently they did not live on blood alone. There went another vampire myth down the drain. She smiled, completely at ease. In fact, she was more at ease than she could remember being in quite a while. She took another swallow of the water. "This water tastes really pure."

Rafael smiled. "That is because it is not exactly water. It is Aquinas."

Thorn held up the less than half-full glass. "Okay. . . ." She smiled. "Never heard of it."

Rafael tapped his lips with a damask napkin. "I would have been greatly surprised if you had." He leaned back in his chair. "It is served only to human staff working among magi." He lifted a coffee cup. "Aquinas eases the human heart of fear and delivers pleasant feelings without clouding the mind."

Thorn raised her napkin to cover a sudden yawn. "Oh, so that's why no one seems to mind my, um . . ." she lifted a hand to indicate her ears, "my appearance."

Rafael nodded. "Exactly." He tilted his head to the side.

"However, it has a different effect on those whose bodies are enchanted."

Thorn smiled at Rafael. "Oh? Like what?" She was forced to raise her napkin to cover another yawn.

Yaroslav eased from his chair to kneel at her side. "It puts them into a very deep sleep."

Thorn turned to look at him. "It does?" Her eyes were so heavy. In fact, so was the rest of her. She tipped toward him and slumped against his chest.

Yaroslav's arms closed around her. "Yes, my love, it does."

Thorn snuggled against his chest. He smelled so good. "Sorry, I'm . . . sleepy."

"I am sure you are." Yaroslav kissed her brow. "Pleasant dreams."

19

She was asleep. At least, she was pretty sure she was asleep; it was so hard to tell. Somebody was carrying her against a warm chest. It smelled like Yaroslav. She sighed. His chest vibrated under her cheek. He was walking somewhere while talking to somebody, but she couldn't quite make out what was being said. Her ears didn't seem to want to work right. She frowned in concentration.

"To borrow from the Americans Master Antonius is so fond of, having her drink Aquinas was sneaky, my prince."

Rafael chuckled from somewhere in front. "Perhaps, but it saves on lengthy explanations that will only end in eventual agreement. Time is not a luxury we currently possess."

Yaroslav's arms tightened around her. "You are sure this must be done immediately?"

"You cannot bring her before the senate wearing that heretic's mark."

"Can I not leave her here?"

"That would be unwise. You said yourself, she was seen by Senator Belus. He is bound to ask damaging questions if she is not with you during tonight's session."

"That Venetian snake. . . ." Yaroslav stepped down, and then again, and then again . . . His boot heels clicked with each downward step. "He has always been overly fond of that which does not concern him."

Thorn frowned. It felt like he was going down a staircase.

"Senator Belus was raised among the Borgias. It is only natural that he acquired their taste for intrigue and blackmail." Rafael sighed heavily. "However, it is his taste for live victims acquired during his time among the *domini canis* that truly concerns me."

Yaroslav growled. "Such poor taste. . . ."

"You were tsar in Kiev; surely you understand his appetite for power?"

Yaroslav groaned. "Only too well. However, after withstanding nearly one full year of being tsar, I regained my sanity. I let my foolish cousin Roman take the throne, and all the petty squabbling that went with it."

Tsar? Thorn's thoughts tripped and stuttered. A tsar was a . . . But that meant that . . . Yaroslav was a Russian *prince?*

"Regained your sanity, eh?" Rafael laughed softly. "Was Byzantium better than Kiev?"

"Byzantium was quieter than Kiev. I was able to continue my more personal interests, with far fewer people attempting to assassinate me."

Rafael snorted. "I see your point." There was a loud metallic shriek and then the creak of a large door. "Speaking of your personal interests, and considering your arrival, do you have the . . . resources to complete this working by sunset?" Rafael's voice, and their footsteps, echoed as though they had entered a large room.

Yaroslav lifted Thorn and then sat her down on a very flat and very hard surface. "I will complete it." Gently he straightened her legs and then cupped the back of her head to lay her back.

"Knowing you, of that I have no doubt. However, to replace

someone else's work, line by line, requires a great deal of power. I would rather you did not collapse before the senate."

"As you have pointed out, it must be done." Yaroslav tugged at the sash at Thorn's waist, freeing the knot to her white dressing gown. "Have no doubt, I will recover."

"Recover, he says. . . ." Fabric rustled and boot heels clicked, as though Rafael paced. "I am not a worker of magic, but I do have great age and the power that accompanies it." His steps stopped. "I offer you a taste of that power."

Yaroslav's hands stilled. "Is it your wish that I . . . remain by your side?"

Rafael chuckled, but the sound held a dark, smoky quality. "If that should be your desire, I would not refuse. The choice is yours. What say you to my offer?"

"I see." Yaroslav released a breath. "I would be honored to accept, under one condition."

Rafael groaned. "Always there is a condition."

Yaroslav snorted and moved Thorn's hands to her sides. "Your essence is potent, my prince. Even a mere sip would be . . . compelling . . . to one such as I."

Rafael sighed. "Very well. What is your condition?"

Yaroslav set his warm palm over Thorn's heart. "Should something happen to me, I would have you take guardianship of Thorn and her descendants."

Rafael drew in an audible breath. "Her descendants? You have gained such knowledge?"

Yaroslav brushed her long hair to one side. "It is a . . . pursuit of mine."

"I see." Rafael's light footsteps came to Thorn's side. "I accept your condition. I should very much like to see this . . . pursuit . . . succeed."

Yaroslav snorted. "I will do my very best to endeavor, my prince."

Fabric rustled, and soft clinking announced the loosening of belts. Someone moved right next to her. She could actually feel body heat. It smelled like Yaroslav.

What was happening? Thorn's body was far too relaxed to lift even a finger, but, damnit, she wanted to see. She focused all her will, all her concentration on opening her eyes. She succeeded in lifting her lids a tiny bit.

Something large loomed over her. It was Yaroslav's bare back. He was sitting right next to her on whatever she was lying on. His head was bowed forward, and a bare arm was around his waist.

The arm belonged to an equally shirtless Rafael, standing between Yaroslav's knees, embracing him tightly, chest to chest. Rafael's eyes were half lidded, and a sweet smile curved his lips. He rested his chin on Yaroslav's shoulder and whispered, "Yes, partake of all you need."

Yaroslav gripped Rafael's bare shoulder. His fingers tightened, his knuckles turning white. He gasped and lifted his head. His eyes were closed tight, and his lips parted. Scarlet trickled from the corner of his mouth. He licked his lips and shuddered. "I did not know you had lived quite so long."

Rafael lifted his other arm while keeping hold of Yaroslav. A jagged wound marked his wrist. "My true age is not something I share with many." He turned his head and licked the wound. The mark disappeared almost instantly. "Nor my blood." He smiled.

Yaroslav turned his head to the side, wincing. "So much power...." He sighed and opened his eyes to look up at the vampire prince before him. "A single drop would have been sufficient."

"And you had a full swallow." Rafael tilted his head slightly, and his smile faded only a hair. "Can you forgive me, Prince of Kiev?"

Yaroslav raised his brow, and a sour smile curved his mouth. "It was not completely unexpected, Prince of Troy."

Rafael winced. "Was I so obvious?"

Thorn started. *Troy?* Wasn't that a place from an old fairy tale?

"You sent Master Antonius to my mountain to collect me." Yaroslav chuckled softly. "If you were trying for subtlety, a battalion was not the way to do it." He groaned and leaned forward, sliding off the . . . whatever it was Thorn rested on.

Rafael stepped back. "I was . . . concerned for you."

Yaroslav stood before the vampire prince and folded his arms across his chest. "I am not quite so helpless as to need a battalion to come to my rescue."

"So?" Rafael's chin rose, and his smile disappeared utterly. "You were a shopkeeper, a clock maker in a small town on an isolated mountain, not the master of a defensible castle. You did not possess an army. You did not even possess stone walls about your home."

Thorn could not believe what she was hearing. Yaroslav was a *clock maker?* Being a shopkeeper didn't go with how she saw him at all. She simply couldn't imagine him living anywhere but in a castle with servants.

Yaroslav bared his teeth. "I am an aged vampire and a sorcerer! Not a mere defenseless human! How could you have so little faith?"

"How could I not be concerned?" Rafael's eyes narrowed, and a liquid growl rumbled. "Your mountain was the only one within a hundred-mile radius to be attacked by a plague that is magical in nature. Clearly someone wanted your life to end!"

What? Thorn would have gasped if she could have. Someone was trying to kill Yaroslav?

Rafael bared his teeth. "I would know who!"

Yaroslav jerked his head to the side, looking away.

Rafael snarled. "Do not look away from me!"

Yaroslav jerked as if struck. He turned his gaze back toward his prince, but his chin was down, and a growl rumbled. "Is this why you bound me by blood?"

Thorn had no clue what the hell "bound by blood" meant, but it didn't sound good.

Rafael sighed, and all the anger drained from him. "You know something this heretic fears, or he would not attempt your assassination. I bound you to protect you."

Yaroslav shook his head. "I know no more about this heretic than you, my prince."

"Ah!" Rafael smiled and held up one long-nailed finger. "But you have more knowledge and experience with spell craft than anyone living." He folded his arms across his bare chest. "If anyone can stop this plague, it is you."

Yaroslav rubbed his jaw with a palm. "Then it is not this heretic we should fear." He set his hands on his hips and stared straight at his prince. "But the one who told the heretic to fear me."

"Agreed." Rafael lifted his chin. "And who knows of your existence?"

Yaroslav frowned and then scowled. "You suspect someone on the senate?"

Rafael shrugged. "Does anyone else know you exist?"

Yaroslav shook his head. "None still among the living."

"So. . . ." Rafael turned and paced back and forth before Yaroslav. He frowned deeply. "It would be so convenient if it was Senator Belus, but he would never cooperate with a user of magic, certainly not a heretic. His hatred for magi would not allow for it."

"Still?" Yaroslav smiled. "One would think he would have accepted his curse by now."

"Certainly." Rafael snorted and continued his pacing. "If he had not earned his curse so richly."

Yaroslav shook his head. "He should not have meddled in the affairs of wizards."

Rafael snorted. "That did not stop him from using the Do-minicans' Inquisition to hunt as many of them as he could."

"Such a childish temper." Yaroslav leaned back against Thorn's resting place. "So now I am bound and bait in your trap?"

Rafael stopped still. "You are bound to preserve your life. It is I who am bait. To get to you, they must first go through me."

"Conspiracy and intrigue..." Yaroslav straightened and combed his fingers through his long black hair. "And you won-der why I choose to make clocks?"

Rafael smiled tiredly. "I am beginning to suspect that the making of clocks might be a wiser occupation for myself as well."

Yaroslav wiped his hands down his trousers. "So...."

Rafael nodded. "So."

Yaroslav shook his head. "I had best work, my prince."

Rafael nodded toward Thorn. "Perhaps you should begin by deepening the slumber of your little she-wolf?"

"Ah?" Yaroslav turned sharply to look at Thorn. The hearts of his eyes blazed gold as a flame. "So stubborn." He raised his palm and held it over her eyes. "Sleep, Thorn."

Weighted darkness pressed down on Thorn. *No!* She wanted to know what had just happened and what was really going on. She wanted to know who Rafael really was...!

"All in due time, Thorn; sleep deeply until my call."

She fought against it. *No, damnit!*

"Yes."

Black waves edged with scarlet lightning crashed down on Thorn's mind and washed her away.

"Thorn."

Thorn jolted hard, and her eyes snapped open. She gasped a deep breath, with her heart slamming in her chest. She was awake. Completely awake and lying on a carpeted floor. She stared at the arching white ceiling, painted to look like a sky with clouds. *What the . . . ?*

Somewhere close by, a clock ticked. Fabric whispered. Someone was there.

Startled, Thorn rolled forward in a swift, smooth movement that carried her from lying on her back to a sitting position and then all the way up to stand on her . . . four paws in the center of a rich Indian carpet. Thorn's fanged wolf jaw opened in complete surprise. She'd transformed into her wolf state so smoothly she'd barely felt it. She held perfectly still, almost afraid to move. She should not have been able to change that quickly.

Shimmering color caught her attention, and she looked about sharply. She was in an oval bedroom fit for a prince. The curving walls were covered in shimmering gold cream silk. At the far end of the room was a huge bed canopied in cut velvet of gold and midnight blue. On the left, matching drapes masked a row of floor-to-ceiling windows. To the right was a pair of doors, and between them a small French Baroque table holding a small pendulum clock.

Her gaze was caught by the brilliant hues of the blue and gold floral carpet under her paws. She reached out and watched her paw extend into a human hand. A slight shiver raced through her, and her entire body returned to human form with uncanny swiftness.

She sat back on her heels and stared at her hands and then stroked her bare thighs. She was completely human. She'd never changed so fast or so easily in her life. She was also completely naked.

"Thorn?"

Startled, she twisted about so fast she fell back on her butt. She winced. *That was graceful. . . .*

Yaroslav was dressed casually in a long black velvet dressing robe with his long black hair pulled back into a snug tail. He sat before a plain, unfinished table pushed up against the wall and scattered with hand tools and small mechanical bits. The scent of fine-grade machine oil was in the air. His brows lifted. "How do you feel?"

"I, ah . . ." She frowned. How did she feel? "I feel fine." Her frown deepened. She felt unusually fine, considering she'd just changed twice in a matter of minutes. Normally, changing that fast, and that close together, would have had her flat on her back with her head spinning from exhaustion. She hadn't even broken a sweat.

Yaroslav nodded and smiled. "That is good."

"But . . ." Thorn bit down on her bottom lip, puzzled, "I shouldn't feel like this. Not after changing like that."

Yaroslav turned back to his table. "You will become accustomed in time."

"Accustomed to what?" Thorn rose to her bare feet and padded toward him. "Did you do something?"

"I did." A miniature gold pocket watch lay in pieces on the table before Yaroslav. He lifted a delicate gear and peered at it. "I remade you."

"Remade . . . ?" The things Thorn had heard, and overheard, ticked into place. She scowled. "That sneaky bastard fed me that water so I couldn't resist, and then you knocked me out and went and did . . . whatever it was you said you were going to do to me."

"Yes." Yaroslav lifted a delicate instrument and set the gear within the open pocket watch. "I redesigned your aspect, erasing all trace of your Doctor."

Thorn blinked. He hadn't even tried to dodge the issue. "What happened to discussing it after breakfast?" She leaned close to watch him work.

Yaroslav lifted yet another tiny gear. "Prince Rafael felt confident that you would eventually agree. However, time was of the essence." He set the gear within and lifted a tiny screwdriver. "He was correct. If we had spent even one hour in discussion, I would not have finished in time." He applied the tiny tool with incredible delicacy.

Thorn watched with interest. He really was a clock maker. "In time for what?"

Yaroslav set the screwdriver to one side and lifted a delicately painted watch face. "The dressers will be here with our attire in one hour." He set the face over the open gears.

"Attire?" She frowned. "But I already have clothes."

"You cannot appear before the senate in . . ." he curled his lip, "dungarees."

Thorn stilled. "The senate?"

Yaroslav turned on his stool and waved his hand at the door farthest away. "The bath is in there." He turned back to the table. "Use care, as the furnace keeps the water quite hot."

"Indoor plumbing?" Thorn clutched Yaroslav's sleeve. "For real?"

Yaroslav smiled. "Prince Rafael is very fond of his . . . comforts."

"Hot damn!" Thorn strode for the other door with determination. "I'm taking a bath!"

Behind her, Yaroslav chuckled.

20

Thorn settled into the huge paw-footed oval tub and leaned back against the smooth white porcelain. The steaming water with its generous froth of bubbles covered her to the chin. Sunbeams poured through the frosted glass windows high on the wall to her immediate right, giving the bubbles rainbow hues.

Thorn frowned at the late afternoon light. They had arrived first thing in the morning. Apparently whatever it was that Yaroslav had done had taken nearly all day to do. Not that she'd had much choice in the matter. She sighed and sank deeper into the hot water. Okay, so she would have agreed, but still, it would have been nice to actually give her consent, rather than have it assumed by the prince. *The sneaky bastard. . . .*

But he sure did live well.

It had been ages since she'd had a hot bath, and never so quickly. Her last decent bath had been in a copper hip tub in her cramped cabin on the ship. This claw-footed tub had two spigots, one for hot water and one for cold, and had filled at an unheard-of speed with water so hot it actually steamed. The pedestal sink occupying the far wall directly in front of the tub also had spigots for both hot and cold. A pull-chain flushing toilet stood beside it. Pure luxury.

Thorn moved to the center of the tub and then leaned back to submerge her head. She came up wiping suds from her cheeks with water spilling down her long hair.

She looked to her right at the low, narrow shelf attached the wall and then leaned to reach beyond the fluffy towels. She grabbed the square, dark amber glass bottle and pulled out the fat cork. Earlier investigation while the tub filled had proved that the bottle held a thick, creamy liquid soap surprisingly light in scent. It made wonderful bubbles, too.

She poured a generous amount into her hand and set the bottle back on the shelf. She closed her eyes and proceeded to work the soap into her long hair. She couldn't imagine being able to bathe like this anytime she wanted to. It was . . . paradise.

The door opened and then closed.

Unwilling to open her eyes with soap dripping down her cheeks, Thorn sniffed to see if she could smell who was there. She couldn't smell a thing beyond the soap.

"Ah, a lovely water nymph." Yaroslav's distinctive voice held humor.

Thorn released a breath she hadn't realized she was holding and went back to scrubbing soap into her hair. "I'm not done yet."

"Oh, I know." The sound of Yaroslav's bare feet padded close. "I have come to assist you." Fabric rustled.

Thorn frowned. "I know how to bathe myself."

"Of course you do." A double splash and the sudden rise of the water in the tub announced that Yaroslav had stepped in right behind her.

Thorn started. "What are you doing?"

"I should think that would be obvious." There was a larger splash, and then his long legs slid along the outside of hers.

"Mmm . . . you run a good bath." He settled behind her. "Very nice." His fingers slid into her soapy hair to massage her scalp. "Allow me." Delicious shivers followed the path of his fingers.

Thorn rocked under the pressure of his working fingers. The sides of the tub were too far away to grab for stability, so she was forced to hold on to his knees underwater. "I can wash my own hair, damnit." She wanted to lean away, but his fingers felt so good. Her groan of pleasure escaped quite by accident.

"Of course you can." Yaroslav chuckled. "However, I will need assistance with mine."

"Oh?" Well, if he needed help, that was different. Thorn relaxed into his fingers. It was only fair that he did hers, too. "Okay."

Yaroslav removed his fingers and leaned to the right, clearly reaching for something on the shelf. "Tilt your head back so I may rinse out the soap."

She did so, and a cascade of bathwater spilled down her head.

"Hold still." Another deluge, and then a nubby cloth was pressed over her eyes. "Very good."

Thorn reached up to take the cloth and patted the water from her eyes. "Okay. . . ." She leaned forward to get up.

He cupped her breasts under the foamy water. "And where are you going?" His finger closed on her nipples in a light pinch.

Thorn's belly clenched with awakening interest. She sucked in a small breath. "I thought I was going to wash your hair?"

Yaroslav pressed a kiss to the side of her neck. "Not quite yet." His hot, wet tongue stroked the side of her throat.

Shivers spilled through Thorn. She didn't even try to hold back her breathy moan.

He released her breasts and set his palms under her thighs. His breath brushed against her throat. "Lift for me."

Thorn lifted her knees, allowing Yaroslav to slide his legs under hers. "Yaroslav?"

Yaroslav caught her under the thighs and lifted her up to straddle his lap. "Yes?" He pulled her back into the cradle of his hips. The hard length of his very erect cock pressed against her spine. He leaned to the side and selected a small green glass bottle from the shelf. He pulled the cork, set it on the shelf, then turned back with the bottle in his hand.

Thorn swallowed. "You want to have sex in the tub?"

Yaroslav shoved her hair over her shoulder with his free hand. "No, I want to . . . make love, I believe is the saying, in the tub." He tipped the bottle, and a thick liquid with the distinctive scent of olive oil spilled onto his palm.

Sex; make love . . . Thorn rolled her eyes. "Same thing. . . ."

"No." He set the bottle on the shelf and then kissed the back of her neck, sending shivers up the back of her skull. "It is not." He rubbed his palms together. "Sex is of the body; love is of the heart." He dunked his hands underwater. He pulled one hand back and slid it between them to caress his shaft. His other hand cupped and then delved into her feminine flesh.

Thorn jolted with the unexpected contact. His fingers moved on her, caressing and exploring her lightly. Too lightly. She groaned and leaned forward, pressing against his palm. The sudsy water sloshed slightly. She could barely think past the pleasure coiling hungrily in her belly. "Anything you say."

"Excellent." He thrust a long, oiled finger into her core and caressed her deep within. "Then you will accept my love?"

Thorn shifted her hips, grinding on his hand while rubbing against his rigid cock at the same time. God, he was good. She groaned. "Anytime you feel like giving it."

He sighed, and his thumb pressed between her plump lips to brush lightly against the nub of her clit. "So?"

A bolt of raw lust speared through Thorn to throb low and hard in her belly. She moaned and tilted forward, balancing

with her hands on his knees while arching back in an un-
ashamed invitation for him to take her.

His breath quickened against her neck, and his hand slid up
to her belly, his fingers spreading wide to hold her. He pressed
forward, deliberately sliding his cock between the cheeks of her
butt. His lips brushed her ear. "Then, will you give me your
love?"

Thorn trembled, and a chill slid through her. Her heart
thumped. "My love?"

"You have mine; I would have yours." His long teeth grazed
the side of her throat. "It is only fair, is it not?"

Thorn shivered, and her heart sped up, thumping hard and
fast in her chest. He wanted her to love him?

"Yes. . . ." He nipped at her throat. "That is exactly what I
want."

Thorn shook her head and pulled away. She wasn't ready to
think about love.

His arms closed tight around her, holding her in his lap.
"Thorn."

She pushed at his hands and tried to rise. "Let me go!"

He held her firmly seated on his lap. "You will stay."

"No!" She struggled. "I won't!" Water and suds sloshed
over the sides of the tub, splashing on the floor. "I don't want
to talk about this!"

Yaroslav held her in place. "We will speak of this, and we
will speak of this now!"

"I don't want to!" Thorn tried to get her feet under her, but
the bottom of the tub was just too slick. More water spilled out.

"So I see." He grabbed one of her wrists, and then the other,
trapping them under his arms and locking her back against his
chest. "But it must be spoken of."

Thorn struggled in his hold, her heart beating in her mouth.

He braced his legs and held on to her. "Thorn, what is this
fear?"

Fear? She stilled in his embrace. Did she fear him? *Yes.* She trembled with a fear she couldn't quite identify. A fear she didn't want to identify. "I just don't want to talk about . . . this."

His lips brushed her temple in a deliberately soothing gesture. "You have desire for me, yes?"

Desire . . . ? Thorn turned to look at the door. Yes, yes, she did. She ached with the urge to have him. "Yes, I enjoy bed sports with you, but that's not—"

"And you would not see me harmed?"

"Of course not!" Red fury gripped her heart. "I would kill any that tried." Her voice came out in a low, liquid growl.

"Then what is this fear?" He stilled utterly. "Do you doubt that I love you?"

Pain throbbed deep in Thorn's chest. *He loves me.* Her throat tightened. "I . . ." Her voice didn't want to work right. "I know you do." It was in his voice when he spoke to her. It was in his hands when he touched her. It pressed against her heart, a warmth like no other. "I just don't know if I can love you back." She closed her eyes to hold in the hurt.

He stilled and then trembled. A chuckle escaped his lips. "How foolish."

Thorn's hurt vanished under a wash of hot temper. "It's not foolish!"

"Oh, but it is." He pressed a kiss to her cheek. "You have loved me all this time."

"What?" Thorn twisted on his lap just enough to deliver her glare. "How can you say that?"

He gave her a breathtaking smile. "Because it is true." He released her wrists to cup her face. "Believe me." He pressed a hot, voracious kiss to her parted lips.

The taste of him brought every thought in Thorn's head to a screeching halt. His teeth raked her tender lips. His agile tongue seduced her into seeking him out and returning his hungry passion.

Without breaking his kiss, he cupped her hips and urged her to turn on his lap. He caught her knee and lifted it, bringing her leg over his legs so that she straddled him on her knees, facing him.

Thorn caught hold of his shoulders for balance and practically attacked his mouth with her tongue and teeth.

He closed one arm tight around her hips and turned away, breaking the kiss. His lips were red and moist from her kisses but set firmly. He turned back to face her, and his gaze was determined under lowered brows. "You love me. There is no doubt."

Thorn groaned and set her brow on his shoulder. He just wouldn't let it go! "How can you be so sure?"

"It is unmistakable." Yaroslav slid a hand down her spine and cupped her butt. "There is no one who sees us who does not see your love. It is as visible as your golden eyes." He tilted his head to catch her gaze. "The only one that does not recognize this—is you."

Thorn bit down on her bottom lip. She did lust after him, and she did care for him. Was this love? A fist seemed to close around her heart. She didn't want it to be love. She couldn't afford to love him. But if it was . . . ? "Yaroslav, what happens when I go home and there's an ocean between us?"

He groaned and slid his hands under her thighs, lifting her from his lap slightly. "More foolishness." He pulled one hand from her and slid it between them. "You belong . . ." the head of his cock nudged the delicate flesh, "with me." He pulled her down, surging into her, filling her.

She threw back her head and gasped, grabbing for his broad shoulders.

He cupped her butt in his palms. "You are . . ." he urged her up, sliding nearly completely out of her body, "mine!" He slammed her back down onto him.

Brutal delight detonated within her. Thorn unleashed a

small shout and arched up. She shoved back down onto him with greedy haste, determined to wash away the ache in her heart with the physical rapture he offered. With his hands on her hips to guide her, she rode him with incredible ease, buoyant in the water. Her moans and gasps filled the sunlit bathroom. Water sloshed.

His mouth sought hers, and they kissed. Their bodies swayed apart and back together, rocking against each other, mercilessly urging the rising tide of ecstasy to a murderous pitch. Groans and panting became frantic gasps and hungry growls.

He arched her back until her head nearly touched the water and sought her breasts with his mouth. His lips fastened on a nipple; then his teeth. He bit down with his flat front teeth and then sucked hard, lashing her swollen nipple with his tongue.

Bolts of delight struck with each pass of his tongue on her nipple. Thorn dug her nails into his shoulders and cried out, drowning in the molten pleasure coiling tight in her belly, stirred by his strong thrusts and his sinful mouth.

Grasping Thorn around her hips, Yaroslav twisted sharply, turning them sideways. He moved forward, until Thorn's back pressed against the tub's curved side, and held her there. "You love me, but I have yet to hear it from your lips." He thrust hard.

Thorn groaned. Love . . . ? *Again?* She shook her head.

He caught her by the hair at the base of her neck and took her mouth in a swift, hard kiss. He ground his cock deep into her.

Thorn moaned into his mouth and threw her arms around his neck. She locked her legs around his hips and writhed against him, impatient for release.

Yaroslav pulled back, breaking the kiss. "Thorn, I would have you say it. Tell me you love me."

Thorn clenched her jaw. She shook her head. Why wouldn't he just let it go? "No."

"Thorn . . ." His brows dropped low over his eyes, and his mouth curved downward, "tell me you love me."

A stab of pain shot through her heart. She turned away. She didn't want to love someone she was going to leave.

"What is this?" He caught her jaw in his palm, forcibly turning her to face him. "You will remove these thoughts of leaving!" His jaw tightened, and a growl erupted from his chest. "I will not allow it."

He would not *allow* it? Thorn bared her teeth and snarled all her anger and frustration in his face. "You can't make me stay with you!" She shoved against him. "I'm not a pet!"

"Oh, but I can." He lunged forward to grab the rounded edges of the tub on either side of her. Pressing against her, chest to breast, he pinned her against the wall of the tub. He smiled, baring all his long teeth. "You belong with me!"

Thorn's temper snapped. She'd had enough. No one told her what to do. "Fuck you!" She shoved at his chest and called on the wolf that shared her soul. The wolf rose in a white-hot rush of joy. Thorn's skin tingled with the onrush of fur. Her ears and the teeth in her mouth lengthened with incredible speed. She snarled, baring her lengthening teeth, and shoved against him with hands tipped in claws. "Let go!"

"You will *not* change!" Yaroslav grabbed for the hair at the back of her neck, forcing her head back, and set his other palm against her forehead. "I forbid it!" Dark, smoky power slammed against the white fire of the rising wolf and shoved her back.

Thorn's skin burned with the retreat of her fur and ears. Her teeth returned to human flatness, leaving an ache in her jaw. She grabbed for his wrist, but her human strength was no match for his. How the hell was he doing this?

He growled and released her forehead. "You forget; I redesigned your aspect." Gripping her hair, he took her mouth in a punishing kiss that sucked the breath from her lungs. He released her, and his lip curled. "Your body is mine."

Thorn gasped for breath, stunned by his possessive anger.

Yaroslav caught her under the calves, forcing her knees up high and wide. He thrust hard into her body, slamming her against the side of the tub. Then again, and again . . .

Thorn arched back with the violence of his taking, shuddering under the hot bolts of delight he delivered with each stroke. She was mad as hell at him, and yet the coals of her banked passion ignited into a firestorm of raw, wanton lust. She could not stop herself from responding to him. Tears spilled from her eyes even as soft, helpless cries spilled from her throat, announcing her desperation for ecstasy's release.

Yaroslav leaned into her, twisting his hips with his hard thrusts. His heated breath scorched the skin of her throat. "Tell me you love me, and I shall let you come." His long teeth grazed her throat, leaving shivers in their wake.

"Please . . ." Clinging to him and trembling uncontrollably, she gasped for breath, barely able to breathe past the ravenous need in her core and the raw pain in her chest. "Please, no. . . ."

His arms tightened around her. "Tell me you love me." His hoarse voice broke. "Please!" His anguish pressed into her mind and against her heart.

Her gasps became sobs. "I don't want to love you, only to lose you."

"You will not." His thrusts eased, becoming long, torturous retreats and slow, decadent advances. "You will not lose me." His lips caressed her brow, pressing gentle kisses. "You cannot lose me, for I will not let you go. I will never let you go." His voice was gentle, coaxing, tender, and yet desperation echoed clearly behind it. "You are mine to the end of your days. I love you."

Tears blinded her and burned down her cheeks. His words sliced through her, shearing her heart in two. It was too late. Her heart was well and truly lost. She sucked in a breath. "I do,

I do love you." Her voice barely made it past the tightness in her throat. "It hurts how much I love you."

His mouth sought hers to deliver a kiss that bruised her lips. He broke the kiss to stare into her eyes. "I will take very good care of you. I so swear." His arms closed around her tight, and he kissed the side of her throat.

She moaned softly, desperate for release, and yet worn to the bone by the battle over her heart.

His teeth pricked her tender skin and then sank in slowly, taking her throat with exquisite care. He removed his teeth and sucked gently, drawing her blood, drinking her soul.

Climax rose in a slow, ponderous, yet unstoppable tidal wave of sheer intensity. It flowed over her, bowing her backward with its unforgiving force. Her breath stopped. Rapture rushed through her in an overwhelming flow of intense pleasure that would not stop. It washed through her so completely, all thought snuffed out to blackness. Somewhere in the distance, she could hear screams.

21

Utterly exhausted, Thorn staggered out of the bathtub, supported by Yaroslav's arms. She curled her lip. "That was a filthy, rotten, dirty trick, you pushy bastard."

Yaroslav pressed a swift kiss to her brow. "I know." He wrapped a fluffy white towel around her and rubbed her skin.

She glared up at him. "Proud of yourself?"

"Truthfully?" Yaroslav grinned down at her. "Yes. You are a very difficult woman to win."

Thorn groaned and rolled her eyes. "I'm not a prize, damnit."

"Oh, but you very much are." Yaroslav rubbed her long silvery hair with the towel. "A great many would have you." He pulled the towel away. "Can you stand?"

"Sure." Thorn stepped back on rubbery knees and grabbed the edge of the tub. "What happened to me washing your hair?"

Yaroslav walked around the tub to grab another towel off the shelf. "Securing your heart was of far greater importance to me." He scrubbed at his damp skin.

"Securing my heart?" Thorn snorted. "What are you planning to do with it? Lock it in a box?"

The vampire stilled and then straightened to wrap the towel around his hips. "And if I say yes?"

Thorn blinked. "That's . . . not possible." But, then, a lot of things she'd thought impossible had proved far too real.

"It is possible, in a sense." Yaroslav collected another towel from the shelf and approached her while unfolding the white, nubby length. "Love cannot be taken; it must be given." He leaned close to wrap the towel around her. "Words of true love spoken from the heart resonate with a great deal of power, which can indeed be bound." He tucked the corner of the towel into a fold across her breasts. "Once gifted, love can be held in such a way as to feel the heart's pulse beating in one's hand." He dropped a quick kiss on her brow.

Thorn tilted her head and stared. Was that supposed to make sense? She sighed and shook her head. "If you say so."

Yaroslav set his arm about her shoulder. "You will see." He urged her toward the bathroom door. "In fact, momentarily." He escorted her out of the bathroom and into the bedroom.

Four people standing in the center of the bedroom turned to stare—two women in maid's uniforms and two men in semi-formal black and white livery, all holding clothes over their arms.

Yaroslav blinked. "Or perhaps not."

Thorn's heart stuttered in her chest. How long had they been there? How much had they heard?

Yaroslav patted her arm. "They are here to dress us."

The maids approached Thorn, and each bobbed a curtsy.

The men approached Yaroslav and bowed.

Dressing proceeded with extreme and near violent haste.

The bedroom door closed behind the exiting staff.

Thorn gripped the long, heavy skirts of her scarlet velvet coat and walked in a circle before the tall looking glass set between the windows. Sunset spilled past the edges of the bedroom's closed curtains, drawing shimmering midnight rainbow hues from the black silk of her high-waisted gown.

She fingered the gold and silver thread of the embroidery weighting the wide collar that banded her shoulders and draped down over her chest. Matching embroidery covered the belling sleeves and edged the velvet coat all the way down to the floor-sweeping hem.

The full-sleeved and full-skirted gown under the coat was simple in design, but the heavy black silk was embroidered within an inch of its life with broad, exaggerated flowers in deep emerald, ruby red, and indigo. The shift beneath was a very soft cream silk. And then there were the loose, voluminous trousers gathered at the ankles into gold-embroidered cuffs.

For all its decoration, the whole thing was surprisingly easy to move in. Thorn turned about in a barefoot pirouette. She stopped, her cheeks heating with embarrassment. *I'm acting like a little girl in her first party dress.* She bit down on her bottom lip and tugged at her full shirts. Well, technically it *was* her first party dress.

Never mind. She thumbed a lock of her long hair behind her ear. The dressers had merely brushed the whole mass straight back and set a small gold-embroidered, pointed cap over it. The cap's slender embroidered band across her brow was all that held everything in place.

She lifted a long lock of her silver hair. It hadn't gone back to its normal pale brown. It was still as silver as her wolf fur, only it had developed black streaks at her temples too, just like the dark streaks that marked her fur. Her brows had also darkened to almost black. She'd tried to change it back, concentrating until her head pounded, but nothing she did would return her to her human coloring. *Damnit. . . .*

She sighed and walked across the room to where Yaroslav preened before another standing looking glass. "Are you sure about me wearing this?" She positioned herself to the side of his standing glass to get a good look at him. "I feel like I'm dressed for a Christmas costume party."

"So?" Yaroslav tugged at the embroidered long collar of his sleeveless, scarlet, velvet, floor-sweeping robe. "It is traditional for my home." He swept a hand down the sleeve of the black brocade coat he wore beneath it, tied with a broad, deep scarlet sash. The only sign of the long deep indigo shirt beneath the coat was the fabric that came through the long slashes in his coat sleeves. His full black trousers were tucked into knee-high black boots with aggressively upturned pointed toes.

"Traditional, eh?" Thorn's brows rose, impressed in spite of herself. He looked positively . . . royal. "So, where is your home?"

Yaroslav raised his chin and swept a hand over the top of his head to the long, sleek braid his midnight hair had been confined to. "I was born in Kiev in Russia."

Thorn nibbled on her bottom lip. "Prince Rafael said you were prince of Kiev?"

Yaroslav winced slightly and nodded. "I was tsar a very long time ago." He smiled. "It was not to my liking, so I gave the title to my younger cousin Roman, who liked it very much indeed."

A knock sounded on the door.

Yaroslav turned sharply to look. "One moment, please!" He glanced down at Thorn's bare feet and frowned. "Where are your slippers?"

"I, um . . ." Thorn's cheeks heated. The slippers in question were made of glove-fine leather, lined in scarlet velvet, and had curled-up, pointed toes. They were also covered in delicate gold thread embroidery that matched her cap. "They're over on the bed." She pointed. She hadn't put them on because they hadn't seemed like real shoes.

Yaroslav rolled his eyes. "Well, fetch them."

Thorn tugged at the edges of her coat. "Don't they have any boots I can wear?"

"Boots?" Yaroslav's brows rose. "Whatever for?"

Thorn clenched her jaw. "Those slippers are too fragile. I'll ruin them!"

Yaroslav smiled. "They are only shoes." He pointed at the bed. "Fetch them, and put them on your feet."

Thorn groaned and went to fetch the delicate slippers off the foot of the velvet-swathed bed. She leaned against the bed and lifted first one foot and then the other to set the slippers on her bare feet. They felt wonderful, but she just knew the pretty things were going to be in pieces by the time the night ended.

Nearly moaning at the thought of the demise of her slippers, she headed back toward Yaroslav.

Yaroslav collected something from the plain wooden table and met Thorn in the room's center. "This is for you." He lifted his hands and displayed a pinkie-thick, coiling silver chain with a ladies' locket watch dangling from it. The silver casing was heavily inscribed with a design that looked vaguely familiar.

Thorn's mouth fell open. "For me?"

"Indeed. I made it quite specifically for you." He popped open the casing so she could see the pale cream watch face with its decorative Roman numerals and delicately filigreed hands.

"It's looks awfully . . . valuable." She took a hasty step back and clasped her hands behind her. "Are you sure you want to give that to me?"

"I do." He opened the chain. "And, yes, it is very valuable. It holds my love for you." He smiled. "Turn around."

Thorn turned her back and felt a tremor rack through her. *A present. . . .* She hadn't had a present since . . . She winced. Since the Christmas before she'd become a werewolf. She didn't even want to think about how long ago that had been.

Yaroslav lifted the watch over her head and set it over her heart. "As long as this watch ticks, you will know my heart beats, even across an ocean." He closed the chain around her neck.

The weight of the watch settled against Thorn's heart. She lifted the watch and stared at it in her palm. It was so pretty and so feminine. She bit down on her bottom lip. You definitely didn't wear something like this with dungarees.

Yaroslav leaned over her shoulder and whispered. "Hold it tight in your palm."

Thorn closed her hand around it. It warmed and expanded and then contracted ever so slightly in a double thump, like a heart beating. "Oh. . . ." She opened her palm, but the watch lay perfectly still. It wasn't moving at all. And yet she could still feel it, beating in her palm. The delicate hairs lifted all over her body. "Is there magic in this?"

"Of course." Yaroslav took her shoulders and turned her to face him. "All my heart is beating in your hands." He lifted her chin and gazed into her eyes. "I would have your solemn promise that you will never give my heart away or leave it behind, even if something should happen to me."

If something should happen. . . A strange sort of pain engulfed her heart and burned in her eyes. "I promise." She opened her eyes. "No matter where I go, or how far, I'll keep this with me."

He smiled. "Thank you." He leaned down, cupped her jaw, and pressed his lips softly to hers.

Thorn parted her lips to receive his kiss. His tongue swept in to deliver exquisitely slow caresses that made her heart twist in her chest and her head reel. Her eyes closed, and she grabbed on to the lapel of his coat while clutching the watch to her heart in her other palm. A single tear slid down her cheek.

He pulled back, releasing her lips. "What is this?"

Thorn opened her eyes and looked away to wipe her palm across her damp cheek. "It's nothing. . . ."

"Ah, my love. . . ." Yaroslav smiled and nudged her hands away, using his thumb to brush away her tear.

A loud, insistent knock echoed from the door.

Yaroslav winced, straightened, and spat out something harsh and bitter.

Thorn smiled and sniffed, wiping at her cheeks. "There goes that tender moment."

Yaroslav curled his lip, baring a long, pointed tooth. "Quite." He turned to scowl at the door. "Yes! Come!"

Thorn almost laughed.

The door swung wide open. "Are you two ready yet?" Antonius bustled in, scowling. He carried an ornate golden helmet with a tall red horsehair crest under one arm. "We're going to be late!" He threw back his swirling blood-red cape to reveal gold-plated, nearly anatomically correct Roman armor. His chest plate actually had nipples. Beneath it he wore a very short white tunic banded in purple.

Thorn's eyes widened. She'd seen Scottish kilts, but those went down to the knees. Antonius's . . . hemline was positively indecent. She could not tear her gaze from his exposed muscular thighs. Her cheeks heated, and she suddenly felt more than a little overwarm. She squeezed her eyes shut and swallowed hard. *Note to self: don't look below Antonius's chest.*

Yaroslav frowned down at her. "Thorn?"

Thorn turned to smile brightly up at him. "Yes?" Her voice came out just a little tight. She glanced sideways at Antonius.

Antonius focused on Thorn. His smile was slow in coming and smug when it got there. "I think I'm going to enjoy playing honor guard tonight."

Yaroslav looked over at Antonius, and his brows dropped low over his black eyes. "Is that so?" He lifted his chin. "Then you may walk behind us, Antonius." He looked down at Thorn and held out his arm in a clear invitation for her to set her hand on it. "Shall *we* go?"

Thorn nearly chuckled. Someone was feeling possessive. She set her hand on his arm and nodded. "Lead the way."

Yaroslav swept out the door, with Thorn clutching his sleeve. Antonius followed close on their heels. Two more men in Roman armor joined them in the hall, and then two more. With breathless haste, they proceeded through a broad room painted in shades of deep red and then to the sweeping spiral stairwell and downward.

They didn't stop at the bottom but turned right into the broad entry hall and then continued straight out the broad front door.

Thorn eyed the snow-covered lawn and jerked to a halt at the top of the portico steps. Her pretty little slippers. . . .

Yaroslav stopped one step down and raised a brow at her. "Thorn?"

Thorn waved a hand out at the lawn. "I can't walk out in that—my slippers will get ruined!" She froze with her lips still parted and then slapped a palm over her mouth and cringed. Oh, god, she sounded like a prissy little girl afraid to get dirty.

Yaroslav shook his head and smiled. "Allow me. . . ." He leaned close and swept her up into his arms to carry her down the steps.

Thorn grabbed him around the shoulders, her cheeks scalding hot. "This is so, so . . ."

Yaroslav strode across the snowy lawn. "It is romantic, yes?"

"It's embarrassing." Thorn clenched her jaw. "I'm a werewolf, damnit."

Behind them, Antonius and at least two of his men did a poor job of stifling their chuckles. Yaroslav laughed outright.

Very close to the cliff's-edge garden wall, a flagstone patio set before a decorative wrought-iron gate had been swept clean of snow. Yaroslav carried Thorn onto the patio and then leaned down and set her on her feet.

Her cheeks still burning, Thorn busied herself tugging at her coat and silk skirts.

Yaroslav stared, delivering the distinct impression that he was waiting for something.

She looked up at him. *What?*

He folded his arms and raised his brow.

Antonius watched the two of them with undisguised humor.

She frowned. He was definitely waiting for something. *Oh, yeah. . . .* She sighed. "Thank you."

Yaroslav smiled and delivered a small bow. "It was my pleasure."

Antonius snorted and closed his eyes while covering his mouth.

Thorn rolled her eyes. First the princess clothes, and now manners. . . . This night was going to be a royal pain in her ass, she could tell. She sighed and turned to stare out the gate. The cliff heights beyond were in full orange-and-violet-sunset display. A deep shadow encroached and spread to cover the lawn before the vampire prince's house. Just past the garden wall, the fanciful *Valkyrie* approached.

Thorn winced. Another balloon ride. *Great. . . .* "I don't know if I can climb a ladder in these clothes."

"A ladder climb will not be necessary." Rafael's voice coming from behind them held clear humor.

Yaroslav turned around. "My prince."

Thorn turned to look, too.

The vampire prince was back in his flowing senatorial red robes, with the addition of a slender black circlet around his brow that shimmered with dark rainbows. Striding across the snowy lawn around him was a veritable army of sword-bearing, black-robed vampires. Rafael stopped before Yaroslav and smiled at Antonius and Yaroslav's men. "I see we have all gathered." He raised a brow at Yaroslav and Thorn. "Finally."

Yaroslav bowed briefly and then raised his chin and cleared his throat. "I had . . . a bath."

Rafael's smile broadened. "So I . . . heard."

Thorn's cheeks heated, and there wasn't a damned thing she could do about it.

Rafael shot a narrowed glance at Yaroslav and softened his voice. "I shall expect both of you to remain close at hand."

Yaroslav didn't quite flinch. "Of course, my prince."

"Thorn." Rafael raised his brow at her. "Please try to avoid biting the senators." He smiled wryly. "No matter how richly they deserve it."

Thorn snorted. "Are you expecting them to deserve it?"

"Absolutely." Rafael's smile tilted upward into a rakish grin. "Incidentally, you look positively enchanting."

Thorn had no idea where the urge came from—she just followed it. She inclined her head, stepped back, and delivered a deep curtsy. She even did it right. "I thank you for your fine compliment." Her granny would have been very proud.

Rafael, Antonius, and Yaroslav stared, eyes wide.

Thorn frowned at each in turn. "What? I do have some manners, you know." She folded her arms and added under her breath, "Just not many."

Rafael grinned and shook his head. "This may be more interesting than I expected."

Yaroslav rolled his eyes. "That is very much what I am afraid of."

Behind them, Antonius snorted. "I just love when Rafael thinks an event is going to be interesting." His voice positively dripped with sarcasm. "He said the same thing about Agamemnon's army."

Agamemnon? Thorn frowned. Where had she heard that name before?

Yaroslav glanced back at Antonius. "I believe I remember him mentioning something similar about Genghis Khan."

Thorn frowned up at Yaroslav. "Is he like Kublai Khan?" She'd actually enjoyed the unfinished poem "Xanadu" by Coleridge.

Yaroslav shook his head and sighed. "Genghis Khan was Kublai Khan's grandfather."

"Ah?" Thorn's mouth fell open. "Then Xanadu is a real place?"

Yaroslav patted her shoulder. "It is indeed a place in China, though it has a different name."

Antonius sneered.

Thorn chose to ignore him.

A bearded man wearing a navy blue seaman's coat and cap appeared at the gate in the garden wall. Antonius strode across the patio to meet with him. Soft words and nods were exchanged.

Thorn frowned. Clearly the man was from the *Valkyrie*, but the airship had just gotten there. She couldn't see how he'd gotten from the ship to the gate so fast. Had he jumped off?

The man saluted Antonius and stepped away.

Antonius returned and delivered a sharp salute to Rafael. "The *Valkyrie* is ready for your departure, my prince."

Rafael nodded. "My thanks, Master Antonius." He nodded toward Yaroslav and Thorn and lifted his chin. "Shall we . . . ?" He turned and strode for the far end of the patio and the gate. Two guards trotted ahead and opened the wrought-iron gate.

Yaroslav and Thorn were swept along to the gate among the prince's black-robed entourage, flanked by Antonius's Roman-armored men. They passed through the gate and turned to the left into a tunnel carved into the cliff with a broad downward staircase. The staircase spiraled down and opened onto a broad stonework dock jutting out into open space. The *Valkyrie* waited at the very end, like any proper sailing ship. An ordinary railed gangway led from the dock to the ship.

Thorn's brows rose. *Must be nice to be the prince.*

22

Among shouts, clanging bells, and the deep, reverberating call of the airship's steam whistle, the *Valkyrie* eased away from the cliff-side dock and headed for the far side of the gorge to the massive palace carved into the mountainside.

The sunset view should have been spectacular. Unfortunately Thorn wasn't able to see any of the panoramic scenery passing by. Pressed against the aft-deck bulkhead, Thorn scowled up at the armored vampires surrounding her. They stood a full stride away, but they were all taller and broader than she was. She couldn't see a thing past them.

Thorn moved to step past them.

Antonius stepped in front of her and smiled. "And where do you think you're going?"

Thorn stepped to the side to go around him. "Over to the side. I can't see anything from here."

Antonius stepped with her, blocking her in. "And anything can't see you either." He stepped toward her. "Be good, and stay where we can protect you."

Thorn backed away. She really didn't like anyone being this close. "I didn't need protection before!"

"You weren't part of the prince's entourage before." He kept coming, forcing her to step back until she was nearly up against the aft bulkhead. "Now you are, and that makes you a target."

She growled; she couldn't help it. "Don't crowd me!"

"Then be good, and stay put!" Antonius set his hands on his hips. "If something happens to you, it's my neck that pays for it."

Thorn snorted. "You're not serious . . . ?"

"I am deadly serious." Antonius glared at her. "Thorn, I take my orders directly from the prince. I am not assigned to guard someone unless there is reason for it."

Thorn folded her arms over her chest. "I'm not helpless."

Antonius sighed, and his smile reappeared. "No, you are not helpless, but nor are you among humans."

Thorn turned away. "Fine, I'll stay here."

Antonius nodded. "Good. I'll do my best to see that you're not crowded, but you will remain under protection. Understood?"

Thorn clenched her jaw. "Yeah, I get it."

Antonius moved away.

Thorn scowled after him. This was going to be a major pain in the butt. She leaned a little to the left and spotted Rafael and Yaroslav sharing a quiet conversation only two long strides away from her.

Yaroslav frowned deeply at the deck, with his arms folded across his chest. Though he nodded occasionally, he didn't seem at all pleased with what the prince was saying.

Thorn strained to listen, but with all the shipboard noise, hearing anything was impossible. She tried listening to his thoughts the way Yaroslav was always listening to hers, but she couldn't feel a thing from him.

Yaroslav glanced up at Thorn and then back down at the deck.

A twinge of disappointment twisted in Thorn's heart. He was keeping her out. She looked away. *More secrets. . . .*

Far sooner than Thorn expected, the airship bumped to a stop. The tone of shouts and whistles from the working shipmen changed.

Yaroslav came to Thorn's side and leaned close to her ear. "Stay close to me at all times." He tucked her hand under his arm, pulling her close.

Thorn didn't get a chance to reply. The vampires moved en masse to the port side of the ship. Held tight against Yaroslav's side, Thorn was hustled down the gangplank onto another jutting stonework dock. She caught only a glimpse of soaring pillars before she was hurried into another tunnel with yet another staircase.

The staircase opened into a broad, arching, and vaulted hallway dimly lit with tiny glowing lights embedded high on the whitewashed walls. Thorn looked about curiously, but with all the vampire guards, it was impossible to catch more than a glimpse of the smooth, shadowed walls. They proceeded down the hallway at a fast march. The thick carpeting underfoot muffled their footsteps.

They passed through a set of ornate and towering double doors of solid brass and stepped onto polished marble. Thorn could see little more than that the room they had entered was huge and circular, with a distant domed ceiling that seemed to be made of glass. Sunset-stained clouds and early evening stars were clearly visible.

The guards parted, and Rafael stepped past them, with Yaroslav and Thorn only a step behind. Finally she could see her surroundings.

The chamber's distant and curving walls were solid gold-flecked marble, and the white floor contained an inlaid, highly detailed map of the entire world. Tables were set three-quarters of the way around the room on upward tiers, with well over a hundred people seated behind them, wearing an incredible array of brilliant costumes under their hooded red robes. One story above, a pillared balcony held even more people in red robes, though theirs were banded in black.

Rafael turned sharply to the right and strode for a broad alcove commanded by a massive black oak table with clawed feet and a matching thronelike chair cushioned with black velvet. The guards followed, and Thorn was swept along at Yaroslav's side. Rafael stopped at the right side of the broad table and turned about to face the gathering in the tiers.

Echoing voices hushed to whispers and then silence.

Yaroslav drew Thorn off to the left side of the table, and they turned to face the staring, silent crowd.

Thorn suddenly realized there was something odd about the people seated in the tiers and gathered on the balcony. A great number of the faces staring at her from under red hoods were not human in coloring or even shape. Many had tall ears, more than a few sported horns and tails, and a few had wings. In fact, the only ones that looked human were the vampires gathered around her.

Antonius stepped forward. "All hail Rafael, High Prince of the Penumbral Realm!"

As one, the people behind the desks stood.

Thorn froze in place. *What?* Her hand tightened on Yaroslav's sleeve. She had thought Rafael was the prince of vampires.

Yaroslav glanced at her very briefly, and the shadow of his thoughts pressed against her mind. *Rafael is indeed the prince of vampires.* He gave her a fleeting smile. *And, also, chosen ruler of all who mankind no longer believes exists.*

Rafael raised his chin. "Welcome, senators. I thank you for your attendance." He swept his robes to the side and took a seat behind the broad table.

Antonius raised his fist. "This court is now in session!"

The brass doors clanged shut.

The people in the tiers sat in their chairs and began to whisper.

Rafael raised his chin. "Ladies and gentlemen of the senate . . ." he held his hand out to the side, "tonight I have acquired that which will end this plague that has been of much concern to us."

A guard set a small box with a paper seal in Rafael's palm, bowed, and stepped back.

Rafael tore off the paper seal and opened the box.

A deep, sonorous *bong* echoed throughout the chamber.

The chamber echoed with waves of startled voices.

"This was intercepted en route from the plague beast." Rafael held up a finger-length glass vial containing a brilliant violet-blue liquid. He smiled. "After close examination, it has been concluded that this is the source of the infection of our cities and our towns."

Thorn's heart slammed in her chest. She knew that vial. It was *her* delivery that had been intercepted.

"Count Feodor Yaroslav Iziaslavich . . ." Rafael tilted his head toward Yaroslav, "our most experienced magus, has already begun decoding the contents to create an end for this plague of the poisonous dead."

Yaroslav bowed to the gathering.

A senator stood. "Then you have succeeded in capturing the plague beast?" The voice was deep and melodious. The senator pushed back his hood, revealing Belus's striking face, but all trace of humanity had been stripped away. His blue eyes were round and slitted, and his hair was no longer black curls but a straight fall of long, slender feathers. The tip of a long scaled snake's tail of gleaming black writhed at the hem of his robes. His gaze focused on Thorn.

Thorn's breath stopped. Was the senator trying to say *she* was the plague beast?

Rafael shook his head. "We have not, Senator Belus. We have merely acquired his delivery before it reached its intended destination."

Thorn released her breath. *Thank you, Prince Rafael.*

Senator Belus's gaze shifted focus to the prince. "But the plague beast is known to be a werewolf, is it not, such as the one beside you?"

Loud whispers broke out.

Rafael nodded. "Yes, the plague beast is known to be a werewolf. I believe Master Antonius can give you more information, as he and his men met the creature during his most recent campaign."

Antonius stepped forward. "My men and I encountered the beast when we collected Count Iziaslavich. Unlike the count's small companion . . ." he nodded toward Thorn, "the plague beast is a large and poorly made, red-furred man creature of deformed proportions."

Thorn scowled. Why did everyone think she was small?

Antonius lifted his chin and glanced around the room. "We strongly suspect the beast was manufactured by the same heretic who created the plague."

Senator Belus nodded. "I see. However, is not the creation of any werewolf, even one such as the count's companion, forbidden?"

Yaroslav stiffened against Thorn's side, and the black oil of his angry thoughts spilled into her. *Foul serpent. . . .*

Rafael raised his hand. "Correct." He smiled, with just a hint of his fangs showing. "Unlike the count, who has gained sanction for his personal companion, the maker of the plague beast has indeed committed a crime."

"Of course." Senator Belus bowed and sat back down.

Thorn wasn't sure if she should be happy the prince had defended her or pissed he'd just announced to the world in general that she was the count's mistress.

Another senator rose. His eyes blazed like two gold stars in a face that gleamed like gold metal. Long, straight black hair spilled to his waist from under his scarlet hood. "With the source for this plague in hand, have you uncovered the identity of the heretic sorcerer who created it?"

Whispers fell to total silence.

Rafael shook his head. "We have his signature, Senator Ashur. However, it is one unrecognized."

Whispers spilled and became shouts.

"How could you not recognize the signature?"

"A signature cannot be disguised!"

"Impossible!"

"A magus cannot change the nature of his power!"

Rafael raised his chin. "We have come to the conclusion that this heretic is not among our peers but is a complete unknown."

Another senator rose. "Are you saying a magus came into power outside our knowledge?"

Several other senators rose and voiced similar concerns.

Rafael raised his hand and waited for the voices to die down. "Senators, I am saying this heretic is not recognized as one of us. We will not know how this heretic came into power unrecognized, or gained the knowledge of this plague's creation, until he is found and questioned."

Yaroslav tugged at Thorn's sleeve. "Come."

Thorn turned and was led to a cushioned bench set against the alcove wall. Seated next to Yaroslav, she could still see the proceedings, but she was no longer under the direct eye of the senators.

More questions were fired, concerning magi capable of magic outside anybody's knowledge and what to do about them.

Rafael's replies remained calm and factual.

The senators calmed, and their questions turned to political control issues of countries and cities Thorn couldn't make heads or tails of.

After a while, Thorn sagged against Yaroslav's side. "I'm a little surprised everybody is speaking English."

Yaroslav chuckled. "They are not. The room is enchanted so that all might speak in their native tongue yet be understood by all others."

Thorn's mouth fell open. "It's magic?"

Yaroslav smiled. "Magic is capable of many things. Some of it is even practical."

Thorn blinked up at him. "Oh. . . ." A yawn came out of nowhere. She raised her hand to cover her mouth. "Oh, sorry. I guess I'm still tired."

"After all that has happened, this is quite understandable." Yaroslav set his arm about her shoulders and pulled her close. "You may rest, if you like. The senate will consist of little more than semantic bickering for quite some time." He smiled. "I will wake you, should there be a need."

Thorn nodded. She wasn't in the mood to argue. She was so tired, her eyes were already closing. She slid down onto Yaroslav's lap and rested her cheek on his thigh, curling up across the bench. He was warm and smelled comfortingly familiar.

The vampire pulled his black robe up over her like a blanket and swept a hand through her hair. "Be at ease. I will watch over you. Your duties are done."

Her duties were done? Thorn felt a chuckle bubble up but was too tired to release it. Oh, she was done, all right. Her last delivery had been intercepted. Hackett wouldn't like it, but that was one of the hazards of courier work. He'd just have to live with it. All that was left was the long journey home and then . . . freedom, at last.

Her heart twisted in her chest. She didn't want to get back on that ship. She didn't want to go back to being treated like an unwanted but occasionally useful tool. No matter how many secrets the vampires had, and how strange the world had become, the vampires had treated her more like a human being than the humans ever had.

And to be completely truthful, she didn't want to leave Yaroslav behind. He loved her. Her fingers tightened on his thigh. And she loved him, too.

Screw Hackett. She'd stay here and be happy, for once in her life. It wasn't as though the army could find her in these mountains. In fact, she'd like to see how the army dealt with living fairy tales and walking nightmares. She smiled. Hackett would probably wet his boxers.

She dreamed . . . of rushing down a dark town street at an insane speed. With her claws, she clung, lying flat, atop the curved roof of a shaking and chugging steam car. The wind rushed down the collar of her flannel shirt and tugged at her dungarees. They were going too fast.

The vehicle took a sudden turn and violently rocked up on two wheels and then slammed back down on all four.

Slammed hard to the side, Thorn hung on but just barely. Furious, she shouted at the driver. "Slow down, you idiot!"

Unfortunately the driver's bench was empty. No one was driving the car.

She crawled forward toward the driver's seat. Someone had to stop the car, or it would crash.

A hand closed on her ankle.

Thorn looked over her shoulder.

Max, completely human in his bowler hat and tinted glasses, stood clinging to the side of the moving car, gripping her by the ankle. The door of the car flapped open against the side. "Your interference is not appreciated."

Thorn jerked at her ankle. "If we don't stop the car, it's going to crash!"

Max smiled, and his teeth became jagged with far too many

fangs. "So?" The car slammed over a bump, and Max's glasses flipped off and away. His yellow beast's eye blazed bright gold, in stark contrast with his human eye of ordinary brown. "Do you honestly think a crash matters to me?" The bones of his hand stretched, deforming into clawed fingers that were neither wolf nor human.

Thorn jerked harder at her ankle. "Let go!"

"I'm sorry." Max's body began to jerk and twitch. "But I just can't do that." He stretched and swelled, tearing his clothes. His bowler hat flew off, revealing the points of ears that were wrongly shaped for either a wolf or a human. "We can't have you running around anymore, can we?"

Thorn dug the claws of her other foot into the rooftop. "Max, if you won't let me stop the car, I'm getting off!" She kicked out, jerking her trapped ankle. "Let go, you beast!"

"That's Mr. Beast—I mean, Mr. Rykov, to you!" Max dug his other clawed hand into the roof of the wildly rocking car and started to pull himself up onto the roof. "You're not stopping this car! You'll make a fine linguist!"

Thorn snarled, baring lengthening teeth. "Max! You're not making any sense!"

"Of course not!" He released a peal of high-pitched laughter that dissolved into barks. "I'm not sane, remember?" He lifted his deformed snout, pointing ahead. "Take a look!"

Thorn turned to stare at the broad expanse of the brick factory wall the car was speeding toward. Her heart slammed in her throat. She gasped in a deep breath and called on her wolf. White fire erupted within her in a wild rush. She rose up on four legs. Her suddenly slender ankle slid out of Max's grasp.

Max screamed. "You're not leaving!"

She launched straight forward from the top of the car and stretched out into a long flying leap. She landed with ease on the factory roof. She leaped again, soaring toward another rooftop. She didn't want to be there when the car crashed.

She turned to look and discovered she had somehow managed to reach the top of a snow-covered mountain cliff. Far below at the base of the cliff, the car exploded. A ragged figure lunged out of the flaming wreckage and began to climb the cliff face. An eerie howl echoed all around.

Thorn stared down at the climbing monster, her heart slamming hard in her chest. He was coming for her. . . .

23

Thorn gasped and opened her eyes to shadows. "Max Rykov, a linguist. . . ." She'd forgotten that she knew Max's last name, what he did, and that he was British—like the Doctor. She sat upright, pushing back the long black coat that covered her. She had to tell Yaroslav and the prince what she'd remembered. She stared at the gold-and-green-velvet-swathed chaise longue she'd been sleeping on and then looked around and blinked. *As soon as I figure out where the heck I am.*

The room was not particularly large, and was square and white-walled with a high, vaulted ceiling. Her gold cap had been removed and set on a long glass table supported by wrought-iron vines to her right. Her long red coat had been tossed over the back of the chair. Behind the chair, floor-to-ceiling curtains had been pulled nearly closed over a broad window, casting the room in deep shadow, though she had no difficulty seeing anything. Before her was the door.

A deep breath told her that the coat she'd been sleeping under was perfumed with Yaroslav's scent. He must have carried her there. She frowned briefly. She didn't remember her

234 / Morgan Hawke

sense of smell being this good when she was in human form. She shrugged and shoved the robe all the way off. She'd think about it later. First she needed to find Yaroslav and the prince. Considering the way they had been hovering over her, they couldn't be far.

She set her slippered feet on the ornate green and gold India carpet that almost entirely covered the polished oak floor. A handful of steps took her to the door. She reached for the crystal doorknob and heard Yaroslav's voice coming from the other side of the door. He wasn't speaking English, so she had no idea what he was saying. Then the prince made a quiet comment in the same language.

Thorn smiled and turned the knob. They were right outside. *Good.* She shoved the door open and was nearly blinded by the bright light. She flinched and threw up a hand to cover her eyes. "I just remembered Max's last name and . . ." Her vision cleared.

In a large room nearly wall to wall with crammed bookshelves, the prince sat to her right in a leather chair behind a broad desk. A silver coffee service was perched on the far corner. He looked up, setting down the papers he held in his hands.

Yaroslav sat with one knee over the other in a black velvet wingback chair just on the far side. His eyes went wide, and his jaw tightened.

Before the desk, in a matching wingback chair with a plain white coffee cup in his clawed fingers, sat Senator Belus. The scarlet hood of his robe had fallen back, and the light from the overhead chandelier turned his long mane of slender feathers to midnight blue. Though he sat like a man, a long snake's tail curled under his chair where his feet would have been. His Cupid's-bow lips curved upward, and his serpent-slitted blue eyes creased in obvious pleasure. "By all means, continue with what you were saying."

Thorn's breath stopped, and her heart gave a painful thump. *Oh, shit. . . .*

The prince sighed and then chuckled tiredly. "This is Miss Thorn Ferrell, from America. Thorn, this is Senator Belus of Venice."

Belus rose from the chair with exquisite and completely inhuman grace. He placed his coffee cup on the edge of Rafael's desk and turned to face her. "Miss Thorn, a pleasure. . . ."

Thorn grabbed her skirts and dropped into a hasty curtsy. She really, really didn't want him to offer his hand. "Please pardon my intrusion, senator."

Belus's smile broadened. "Oh, you are no intrusion at all. I am quite pleased you could join us."

Thorn rose from her curtsy with a smile pasted on her lips. *Yeah, I just bet. . . .*

Belus eased back down into his chair and set his chin on a clawed hand. "Now that the pleasantries have passed . . ." his slender black brow lifted, and his smile sharpened, "why not continue with your little announcement? I'm sure it will prove quite fascinating."

"Um . . ." Thorn swallowed and looked over at Yaroslav. She had no idea what to say.

The vampire sat utterly still in his chair, holding his coffee cup.

Rafael leaned back in his chair. "You may as well continue, Thorn. Senator Belus has been rather . . . persistent on the subject of the plague beast." He smiled tightly. "The senator may as well assist in this inquiry, as he is unparalleled in his techniques to uncover . . . secrets."

Belus blinked and then sighed. "So nice to be appreciated for one's . . . talents."

Yaroslav raised his coffee cup to his lips and didn't volunteer a single word.

Thorn was absolutely positive the prince was trying to tell her something, but she really had no clue what it was. However, if he wanted the senator to know, then . . . okay. She shrugged. "Max's last name is Rykov. He said he was a linguist and part of the British attaché."

"Indeed?" Belus casually retrieved his coffee cup from the edge of Rafael's desk. "And how did you come to know this . . . Max Rykov?"

Thorn tucked her hands behind her and lifted her chin. She knew an interrogation question when she heard one. She took a breath to review and organize her facts and then told him in a clipped and precise military manner about her meeting at the train station and what he'd said during the ride to the colonel's house in his steam car.

Belus's gaze narrowed. "And how is it that you were both going to the same destination?"

"I'm a courier." Thorn smiled tightly. "I was making a delivery."

"Oh?" Belus's eyes widened, but his claws scraped against the porcelain cup. It was a sound too light for normal human hearing, but Thorn heard it quite clearly. "Is that so?"

Yaroslav cleared his throat. "Thorn is a courier for her United States."

Thorn's jaw tightened. "I was. My term of service is over." Only the tiniest trace of a growl showed in her voice.

Belus smiled, but his gaze had chilled. "And is this how you and the plague came to be here together?"

Thorn lifted her brow. Apparently the senator was determined to make her the plague beast. She bit back a sour smile. Too bad she wasn't. She turned to the prince. "May I answer him?" Because there wasn't a darned thing to actually tie her to the Doctor, telling him the whole story with only minor adjustments should satisfy his curiosity.

Thorn. . . . Yaroslav's thoughts pressed against her mind.

Across the room, his gaze focused on hers. *You do not need to explain yourself to this . . . snake.*

Thorn brushed at her skirts and avoided Yaroslav's gaze. *If I don't tell him something, he'll only get more suspicious.*

"Very well. . . ." Rafael tilted his head, and a slight smile played on his lips. "But be brief."

Thorn returned Rafael's slight smile. "Of course." Rafael was probably curious himself. She doubted he knew any more than what Yaroslav had told him, which couldn't have been much. She cleared her throat and faced Senator Belus. "After I made my delivery to the colonel, I was asked to deliver another package. . . ." She leaped clean over her personal issues with the colonel and launched straight into her second meeting with Max on the stairs when he'd been partially transformed. She relayed exactly what he'd said and done.

"On my way out of town, I met with Yaroslav and Master Antonius at the church, and that's when Max tried to reclaim my package. Master Antonius gave chase, but the town was already on fire, so they were unable to pursue him." She nodded toward Yaroslav. "Yaroslav figured out what I was carrying, and the package was turned over to the prince." She smiled. "The end." There, that should shut him up.

Belus's finger tapped against the side of his cup, and he looked away, frowning. "I . . . see." His frown deepened. "You had no idea what you were carrying?"

Thorn shook her head. "I'm not privy to the details of my deliveries. I just carry them."

Belus's gaze turned to Yaroslav. "But the count recognized what you had?"

Yaroslav smiled, showing teeth. "I do have some experience in recognizing . . . curses."

Belus's smile remained, but his eyes narrowed. "Of course." He slouched in his chair and tapped his cup with a clawed finger. "So little do we know about this heretic and his beast."

Yaroslav leaned back in his chair. "The beast is heavily flawed, so it can be surmised that the heretic's knowledge is incomplete. His skills are very likely limited."

Thorn shrugged. "We know he's British."

Belus turned sharply to stare hard at Thorn. "Do we?"

Thorn stiffened. *Me and my big mouth....* "Well, yeah. Max is British, so the sorcerer should be, too, right?"

Belus eased back in his chair. "Not necessarily. . . ." His gaze focused on the floor, and his finger continued to tap on his cup.

Rafael tilted his head to the side and gave a sweet smile. "Are you finally convinced that Thorn is not the plague beast, Senator Belus?"

The senator lifted his chin and then rose from his chair in a smooth glide. "I am." He looked over at Thorn with a smile. "In fact, I am quite pleased that she is not."

Thorn didn't take one drop of comfort from his words.

Yaroslav frowned deeply.

Belus set his cup on Rafael's desk and then straightened, pressing his fingertips together. "May I have leave to hunt this heretic, my prince?"

Rafael took in a deep breath and exhaled. "You have my leave to hunt." He raised a finger and narrowed his gaze at Belus. "With the intent to capture the heretic for questioning."

Yaroslav's expression remained neutral; however, his cheeks seemed to pale.

The senator smiled, and he bowed very deeply. "Thank you, my prince." He straightened and clutched the lapels of his robe. "I shall not disappoint."

Rafael returned his smile a little sourly. "Try to contain your . . . enthusiasm, if you please? The idea is to end the casualties."

Belus glanced away, plucking at a piece of lint on one sleeve. "I shall endeavor to be . . . sparing." He gave Rafael a sideways glance. "And the beast?"

Rafael's brows lowered, and his mouth became a taut, thin line. "The beast is under sanction; it is to be destroyed."

The senator's smile broadened, showing the points of two slender fangs. "Excellent." He bowed to Rafael, nodded to Yaroslav, and left the room, swaying gently from side to side, with a cool smile on his lips.

Thorn's skin crawled, and the hair rose on every inch of her body. There was no doubt in Thorn's mind that Max was a dead man.

Rafael leaned back in his chair and wiped a hand down his jaw. "That was relatively painless." He leaned forward, setting his elbows on his desktop, and picked up a paper. "Now, if only the rest of the senate were so easy to placate."

Thorn did not want to sit in Belus's vacated chair, so she strode around it to Yaroslav's and perched on the arm.

Yaroslav raised his brow at Thorn. "You had not told me of your first meeting with Max."

Thorn crossed her arms and shrugged. "I thought I had."

Yaroslav scowled. "I do not remember such."

Rafael rolled his eyes. "Now, now children. . . ." He shook his head. "We have other things to worry over." He set the paper on his desk. "Such as, what the senate plans to do to the human race in general for being so bold as to have developed a magus all on their own."

Thorn leaned forward. "Do *to* the human race?" She couldn't have heard that right.

Rafael shuffled through the papers on his desk. "There are a great many reasons why humankind was forbidden magic." He tugged a paper from the pile. "Most of those reasons begin, and end, with mankind's creativity when it comes to wanton destruction." He tapped the paper before him with a long finger. "Because of this, there is a strong movement among the senate to remove all governmental control from the human race altogether."

Thorn shook her head. "You mean so the senate can rule the world?" Like the villains in the penny novels?

Rafael smiled. "It is childish in the extreme, but, then, those proposing this plan have no idea what it's like dealing with a human population." He set the paper aside.

Yaroslav shook his head. "Humans are much too independent to allow any but their own chosen rulers and far too prone to rebel at the slightest excuse."

Rafael sighed. "It is simple ignorance. Unlike vampires, who begin their lives as ordinary humans and are made into vampires, the majority of the senators were born the beings they are." He smiled sourly. "They were never a part of human society, so they don't see human society as having value."

Thorn frowned. "You're saying they don't see people as people?"

"Correct." Rafael tapped on another sheet of paper. "Which is why they also propose that the plague should be allowed to run unchecked. . . ."

Yaroslav stiffened. "What . . . ?"

Rafael turned a tight smile on him. "They seem to feel that the plague would be a simple way to thin the population to a more controllable size."

Yaroslav scowled. "Thin it? It is more likely to destroy the human population utterly!"

Rafael sighed. "See what I mean by childish?" He lifted another paper and scanned the text. "This faction here wishes to put a halt to scientific development."

Thorn's mouth fell open. "Why would anyone want to stop science?"

Rafael waved a hand toward Yaroslav. "That is your area of expertise."

Yaroslav folded his arms across his chest and looked away. "It is possible that magic could result from purely scientific inquiries, if pursued within . . . certain areas of knowledge."

"But stopping science . . . ?" Thorn frowned. "Isn't that a little . . . extreme?"

"As you can see, humans are not the only ones prone to panic." Rafael tugged out yet another paper. "It is this, however, that troubles me the most." He frowned at the writing. "It is a plan to control the number of humans that develop into magi."

Yaroslav curled his lip. "Magi are born such. This cannot be controlled."

Rafael nodded. "Yes, of course. This is why families of magus descent, no matter how distant in the bloodline, are already under watch." He set the paper flat on his desk. "However, it is a known fact that magi occasionally develop spontaneously, born to those of no magus blood whatsoever. This faction is proposing that a court representative with attaché be assigned to each human country with the purpose of monitoring for magus ability."

Thorn frowned. "You mean like a police force?"

"More like an assassins' guild." Rafael tapped the paper. "This faction wishes to see all such humans destroyed."

Yaroslav growled. "That would mean the slaying of children."

Rafael smiled tightly. "Something I will not condone." His smile faded. "Unfortunately the majority of the senate feels that the appearance of magi among the greater human population is going to continue." He leaned to the side to grasp the handle of the coffeepot. "And I am forced to agree." He filled his coffee cup.

Thorn slid off the arm of Yaroslav's chair to stand. "You're saying magi are going to start popping up all over the place?"

Rafael sipped at his coffee. "Probability versus such a large and diverse population as the world currently insists that the appearance of maguskind is unavoidable." He leaned back in his chair. "Therefore it is only a matter of time before yet another disaster, such as this plague, is unleashed by yet another unknown and unchecked power."

Yaroslav leaned forward in his chair. "That cannot be allowed to happen."

"Agreed; something must be done." Rafael wiped a hand down his jaw. "But what?"

24

Standing before the desk in Rafael's library office, Thorn glared up at Yaroslav. "What do you mean, I have to stay here?"

"Exactly as I said." Yaroslav leaned over to cup her shoulders. "The prince and I must attend a very private meeting." He pushed, gently forcing her to step backward. "It is best if you remain safe in here."

"Forget that!" Thorn shoved back, but it was like shoving against a tree trunk. Her slippered feet slid on the carpet. "Damnit, vampire, I'm not made of glass! I don't need to be kept safe!"

Yaroslav continued pushing, urging her backward step by step. "No, glass you are not, but you are very precious to me." He pressed her through the doorway and into the sitting room she'd awakened in. "Antonius will watch over you."

She shoved harder and continued to slide backward on her flat-soled slippers. "No, damnit!" He was immovable. Had he always been this strong?

They reached the small room's center, and he stopped. "I

244 / *Morgan Hawke*

will return soon." He dropped a kiss on her brow. "Do not leave this room."

Thorn felt something dark and smoky coil tight within her mind. Her breath caught. "Vampire, what did you just do?"

"You should rest." Yaroslav turned and strode for the door.

She bolted after him. "Yaroslav, this is bullshit...." She stopped cold before she could enter the office beyond. She sucked in a sharp breath. "What...?" She pushed to go through, but her hand wouldn't cross the threshold. Nor would her foot or her knee or her shoulder... no part of her would pass through the doorway. Her body just wouldn't do it.

She was trapped.

Yaroslav strode through the office, headed for the far door.

"Vampire!" Thorn leaned against the door frame to stare after him. "Don't you dare leave me like this, you bastard!"

He grasped the doorknob and did not face her. "Thorn, you have escaped one too many times to be trusted to your own devices." He opened the door. "Sleep well, my love." He closed the door behind him.

He'd left her behind.

Thorn's heart pounded, and a cold sweat broke over her body. The howl tore from her throat. *Don't leave me!*

Yaroslav's thoughts brushed gently against hers. *I will return soon.*

Thorn continued to howl. She couldn't stop herself. The wrenching pain in her heart wouldn't let her.

Thorn dropped the shredded remains of what had once been a green brocade pillow. The ragged scraps of fabric landed on the carpet atop a clump of duck feathers. The entire room was a mess of shredded fabric and scattered feathers. She sighed and wiped with clawed hands at the feathers sticking to her skirts. So much for keeping her temper.

Dragging her wolf-padded-and-clawed feet, she walked

across the room. She sighed heavily and flopped facedown on the graceful chaise longue, leaving her bare feet hanging over the side. Now that she could think past her temper, she was very glad she hadn't torn it apart—just the four matching pillows.

She took a deep breath and willed herself back into human form. The shift was blindingly fast and took hardly any effort at all. Whatever Yaroslav had done had made it much easier to move between forms. She wasn't exactly sure this was a good thing. She really didn't like the idea of suddenly sprouting ears and a tail every time her temper got the best of her.

She groaned and pressed her face into the cushions. It had been years since she'd had such a blinding fit of rage, and it had happened so fast. One second she was completely human, and the next she was a fanged and howling half beast. Somehow her dress had survived, but her toe claws had torn right through her pretty slippers. Damnit.

When she was about halfway through shredding the second pillow, Antonius had come in to check on her.

She'd given him a faceful of screaming fangs and then thrown the remains of her slippers at him. She'd snorted. She might not be able to pass the threshold, but her slippers had gone through to smack against his fancy chest armor just fine.

Antonius had stared in complete shock and then said something. She had no idea what; she hadn't been able to think past the need to rip something apart to relieve her anger. Unable to get to him, she'd raked the hell out of the door frame with her claws, leaving shredded wood all over the floor.

Antonius had jerked back and left after that.

She rolled over onto her back, shoved her hair out of her face, and threw her arm over her eyes. "Stupid vampire. . . ." How could he leave her trapped like this?

Scent tickled her nose. She frowned. Why did she smell . . . snake?

"Is something wrong?" The voice was melodious and very familiar.

Thorn jerked upright on the chair and stared.

Senator Belus stood at the door in a black robe of fine velvet. He glanced around at the falling feathers, and his brows rose. "My, my . . . I see we do have a bit of a temper."

Thorn scowled. "What do you want?" And where was Antonius? Wasn't he supposed to be watching over her?

Belus smiled. "I came to bring you a bit of news." He went to set his hand on the door frame, only to pull it back, staring at the deep gouges left by her claws. "I am guessing that you are . . . confined within this room?"

Thorn snorted. "Good guess."

Belus sighed, a trifle dramatically. "A great pity. I wanted to invite you to see the stars from the observatory."

Thorn almost laughed. There was no way in hell Yaroslav would agree with her going anywhere with Senator Belus. "I'm sorry, but as you can see, I am . . ." what was that word? Oh, yeah . . . "indisposed at the moment." She smiled sweetly, which took some effort. For some reason, her body practically hummed with the urge to change, but she wasn't afraid. Something else was urging her to change. But what?

She lifted her nose. Belus smelled like a common black rat snake. Their bites would make you a little dizzy, but they were far from poisonous. And the wolf rather enjoyed eating them. She stilled. It was her wolf side. Her wolf wasn't afraid of the senator at all—that wasn't why she wanted to change. She was . . . hungry. The wolf wanted to eat Senator Belus. It was kind of funny in a twisted way.

Belus tilted his head, his lips curved upward in a smile. "Well, then, since you cannot come out, might I come in?"

Thorn let a small sneer escape. "I really wouldn't do that, if I were you, senator." She gripped the cushions under her. "I'm having a small amount of trouble controlling my . . . wilder nature."

"Is that so?" His gaze focused on her, and his smile sharpened. "I'd like to see this . . . wilder nature. Would you show me?"

Thorn licked her lips. Her mouth was watering. "I really don't think that would be a good idea right now." The wolf was very hungry.

Belus eased past the door's threshold. "I'm afraid I must insist, as I am rather pressed for time."

Thorn's gaze focused on the man-shaped snake that had moved into her territory. Her eyesight abruptly sharpened, the shadowed room brightening to near daylight. Her control was slipping. She dropped her chin to hide her lengthening teeth. "Senator, I really think you should leave."

Belus sidled a bit farther into the room. "There is no need to be afraid. I have no desire to harm you."

"Oh, I'm not afraid at all." Tall ears rose from her hair and turned toward the senator with complete attention. She rose from the chair to stand on clawed feet. Her tail uncoiled from the base of her spine and slid down one leg of the full trousers under her skirt. She opened clawed hands. "That's why I really think you should leave right now."

Belus tilted his head to the side, his long mane of fine feathers whispering with his movements. "Ears, claws, downy fur . . . how fascinating. Does your change go any further?"

"All the way to wolf, senator." She stepped toward him and listed to the left. Her balance was off. She stopped, and her ears flattened briefly in annoyance. It was her tail; it was caught in her pants. She turned away to grab at her skirts. She needed to free her tail. . . .

He lunged at her, his hands outstretched.

She saw the movement and leaped to the side.

He slid right past her, another whole body length of snake trailing behind him. His hands slammed into the carpet where she had been.

Off balance, she fell, sprawling on the carpet.

He turned swiftly, drawing his snake's body under him. He rose from the floor with grace. The hem of his robes lifted from the floor to expose a tight, writhing coil of a gigantic black serpent.

Thorn came up into a crouch and stared with interest. It appeared he didn't have legs at all. "With all due respect, senator . . ." she looked up at his face, "what the hell do you think you're doing?"

Belus smiled, baring two long, thin fangs. "My apologies, but as I said earlier, I am pressed for time." He dove at her.

Thorn lunged straight for the base of his coil, passing under his outstretched hands. His claws caught in her skirt in passing, ripping the fragile silk. Thorn grabbed the thick, black snake coil, sinking her finger claws into him. The bastard had torn her dress! She bared her fangs, but he was too broad across to get her teeth into him.

Belus shouted in pain and twisted sharply, his coils bucking from her grasp.

Thorn was thrown off the sleek, scaled body, her claws tearing free to leave shallow furrows in his flesh. She rolled across the carpet and landed on her butt and her trapped tail. She yelped.

Hissing, Belus recoiled himself with incredible speed. His lip curled, and his eyes narrowed to bright blue slits. "That hurt."

Snarling, Thorn grabbed the back of her dress and ripped the silk skirting away, leaving only the sleeved top half, and her trousers. "That's what happens . . ." she tore the seat of her pants open, "when you attack a hungry wolf." She tugged her tail free.

He smiled tightly. "Oh, so you do have a tail. . . ." His smile faded. "Wait, a hungry wolf? I'd heard you do not eat others?"

Thorn smiled broadly, baring both her upper and lower fangs. "I don't eat humans, because they taste bad." She lapped at his blood running down her wrist. "You taste just like a rat snake."

His smile disappeared utterly, and his coils withdrew beneath his robes. "Just what are you saying?"

"You mean you didn't know . . ." Thorn licked her lips and rose into a crouch, her finger and toe claws digging into the carpet, "that wolves eat snakes?" She inched toward him on her fingers and toes. "And I really like the taste of black rat snake."

Belus eased back from her, his frown deepening. "You don't say?"

Thorn eased to the side. The best way to kill a snake was by taking out the head from the back. She needed to get behind him. She dashed past him, aiming low to stay under his reach.

Belus twisted sharply and snatched for her.

Thorn skidded to a stop just out of reach, tearing the carpet with her claws, and dashed past him on the other side, forcing him to keep twisting in the same direction to follow her, and then again.

Belus jerked to a halt, finally reaching his body's limit.

Got you! Thorn launched off the carpet, hands out and mouth open, aiming for the back of his neck. Midway in her leap, her body shifted into her wolf shape, the form her body used to hunt and kill. It happened so fast, she didn't have time to stop it.

Belus turned his head, and his eyes widened. He dropped flat to the floor.

Thorn sailed right over him, crashed hard against the wall, and tumbled to the floor. She yelped and thrashed, entangled in her human clothes.

With blinding speed, Belus lashed out with his snake's tail, his heavy coils smashing down on top of her.

Thorn gasped and struggled for breath, her body shifting back into half wolf in sheer shock. She choked and shoved. "Get off me!"

From above her, Belus grabbed both her wrists. "Enough!" His head dropped onto her shoulder, and his slender fangs stabbed into her.

Thorn shouted. She knew good and well that his bite wasn't deadly, but it still hurt like hell.

Belus pulled back, releasing her from his fangs. "That should calm you." He released her wrists, letting her fall back on the floor. His coils retreated.

Thorn leaned up on her elbows. "Bastard...." A wave of dizziness struck. A buzzing started in her ears, and her eyes went out of focus, all the colors running together in a big smear. "What...?" She flopped back on the floor, too light-headed to move.

Belus leaned over her, a great, dark, blurry shadow. "Much better."

25

Barely able to think past the buzzing in her head, Thorn felt hands on her shoulders pushing her over from her back to her belly. Her cheek pressed against the carpet. The sound of ripping silk was loud. Cool air washed against her back.

The shadowy blur that was Belus leaned over her. "Damn...." He sighed. "No matter." He pushed her over onto her side. Using what felt like strips from her torn clothes, he shoved her knees up to her chest and then swiftly tied her wrists to her ankles.

She was lifted into the air, and the world spun. She groaned. What the hell was he doing?

Belus carried her right through the door into Rafael's office and then to the wall behind his desk. Set between two crammed bookshelves was the sliding panel to the dumbwaiter. Belus slid the panel open and hefted her into the box suspended by cables. Folded up with her knees against her chest, she just fit without actually touching the sides. He scooped up all her hair and shoved it in.

As she was lying on her side in the cramped box, Thorn's

sight became crystal clear just long enough to see Antonius slumped against the wall by the office door. His shoulder was bleeding. Belus must have bitten him.

Belus smiled. "Fragile load to train-station office, if you please."

The shelf Thorn rested on trembled and then began to lower.

Belus closed the sliding door to the dumbwaiter, enclosing her in darkness.

Thorn descended.

Somewhere close by, people were shouting. A train whistle shrieked. The stench of green wood, iron, and engine oil burned in her nose. Beneath it, she could smell water, wool, and hay.

Thorn winced, her half-beast wolf ears tipping back to lie against her hair. It was loud, smelly, and annoying, and she was trying to sleep. On top of that, whatever she was curled up on was scratchy. She shifted, and hay crunched under her. Her bare feet slammed against bars. She couldn't stretch out. *What the hell . . . ?*

She opened her eyes to iron bars enclosed by wood planking. The space was not much larger than her curled-up body. *What the hell is this?*

A quick glance around her revealed that she was in a cage clearly designed for shipping a wild animal on a gray rough wool blanket that had been tossed over a pile of hay. Another blanket had been thrown over her. What light leaked in between the planking was yellow, obviously from lanterns.

She leaned up on her elbows, her silver locket watch swinging between her bare breasts. All trace of her clothing was gone. The blanket slid down her bare shoulders to her waist. Bitterly cold air brushed through her light fur. She grabbed for the blanket to pull it up over her.

A lightning bolt of memory slammed through her fogged brain. Being trapped in the room by Yaroslav, Belus, the fight, the bite, the dumbwaiter . . . She jolted hard. *I've been kidnapped?*

A train whistle sounded, and the cage shuddered around her. The yellow light flickered.

Thorn's heart slammed in her chest. She was on a train going God only knew where. She needed to get out of this.

She pushed up onto her clawed hands to sit up, and her head spun. She groaned and slid back down to her elbows. *Belus's venom. . . .* She wasn't going to be able to escape until she was free of the effects. She pressed her brow to her forearm. *I've been kidnapped. . . .* It was so stupid. What the hell could that snake possibly want from her?

The silver watch thumped against her breast just like a heartbeat. *Yaroslav's watch . . . !*

She turned onto her side and gripped the watch with both hands. A heart beat between her palms. She closed her eyes and concentrated. *Yaroslav, where the hell are you?*

Black pain stabbed the back of her skull so hard she yelped and grabbed her head. "Ow! Shit. . . ." What had Belus's venom done to her?

A chuckle sounded, very close to the box. "Oh, dear, you didn't try to use any sort of magic, did you?" It was Belus, and he sounded amused. "I'm afraid the box is sealed against any and all external magic. Nothing gets in, and nothing gets out." His voice changed locations, as though he circled her box. "In case you were wondering, I do indeed know what that watch is for. You may use it later to call your vampire lover when I'm done with you."

Thorn twisted around, following his voice, but she couldn't see a damned thing through the planks. "Where are you taking me?"

"Oh, that's right, I never did tell you my news."

Thorn released a deep, low growl. "Snake. . . ."

"There has been a sighting of the plague beast in the port city of Constantza in Romania."

Thorn dug her claws into the blanket under her. It looked like Agent Hackett was going to have to deal with a werewolf other than her, a crazy one, and possibly the walking dead. It was almost sad she was going to miss it. "Yeah, so?"

"Well, according to my sources, there is an American ship in the port called the *Fairwind*, with a rather interesting passenger list. It includes one Thorn Ferrell."

Thorn winced. She was supposed to go home on that ship. "So?"

Something very like claws scraped across the top of the box containing her cage. "My dear Thorn . . ." Belus's voice purred very close to the box, "if I can find this information, so can the plague beast, which obviously has some interest in you."

Thorn rolled her eyes. "The only interest he had in me was that I wasn't carrying the plague to where he wanted it to go."

Belus chuckled. "I strongly suspect otherwise."

Thorn shook her head. "There's no other reason. . . ."

"Oh, but there is! Do you have any idea how rare werewolves are? They are quite difficult to make. The slightest inaccuracy in any part of their aspect tends to cause insanity, not to mention very short life spans."

Thorn froze. *Short* life spans?

"Consider yourself very lucky. According to what I saw, your aspect is very well constructed indeed, unlike poor . . . Max, I believe his name was? I doubt he has too much longer to live." Belus tsked sadly. "I doubt he even knows he's doomed." He scraped across the top of her box. "But I am quite sure that his maker is well aware of how flawed his creature truly is."

"What has any of that got to do with me?" Thorn tried to sit up again, but her head pounded, and her arms shook. She groaned and dropped down onto the blanket.

"Instinct, my dear she-wolf; the instinct that drives the doomed to propagate has everything to do with you."

Thorn scowled. "You are not making any sense."

Belus snorted. "Allow me to use simpler terms. Max may not know he's dying, but his body surely does. It is the instinct of all living creatures to breed when death is close."

Thorn blinked. "Breed?"

"Oh, yes. Werewolves can indeed beget other werewolves, but only by mating with another werewolf, and it is highly likely that you, my dear, are the only female he knows." He tapped the top of the box. "In fact, you are probably the only female werewolf there is at this point in time."

Thorn frowned. "Then you're planning to use me as *bait*?"

Belus laughed. "Now you're catching on! Yes, bait for both the werewolf and his maker. The heretic very likely knows that his beast is too flawed to survive much longer. I am quite sure he would be highly interested in viewing a creature as finely constructed as you, if only to see how you are made."

Thorn shook her head. "I seriously doubt that the—" She sucked in a sharp breath and coughed. She'd very nearly said, "the Doctor." "—your heretic would be anywhere near Max."

"Oh, but I strongly suspect he is. You see, if Max is as poorly made as I suspect, the silver your Yaroslav shot him with has very likely torn a rather large hole in his aspect. No doubt his maker is scrambling to keep his very useful creature pieced together before it falls completely apart."

Thorn frowned. "How did you know Max was shot?"

Belus snorted. "You forget, I was already onboard the *Valkyrie* when you arrived." His voice was very dry. "I heard it from a number of eyewitnesses."

Thorn winced. "Oh. . . ."

"So all I need do is stroll through the port city of Constantza with you by my side, and either the plague beast, or his
maker, should come to me. Once they do, you are free to go
wherever you will."

"Oh, gee, thanks." Thorn curled her lip. "You honestly
think it'll be that easy?"

"I honestly believe they are that desperate. The werewolf is
about to die, and his maker is about to be in critical need of a
new . . . assistant."

Thorn scraped a hand through her tangled hair. There was
no way in hell she was going to play Belus's little game. She
wanted nothing to do with Max or the Doctor, or Belus, for
that matter. First chance she got, she was getting out of this box
and off this train. Her stomach rumbled. She really needed to
hunt down something to eat.

Belus chuckled. "Ah, so you *are* hungry?"

"Hungry enough to eat a whole cow." Thorn smiled grimly.
"Or a man-sized snake."

"My apologies, but I am not on the menu." Belus's voice
held no humor whatsoever. "I'll see what I can find for you."

Thorn sneered. "Good idea; you might live longer."

Belus actually hissed and moved away from her box. "You
know, I really should have beaten you."

"That would have been a very bad idea." Thorn let her
growl echo in her voice. "Beatings only make me hungrier."

Long minutes passed, and the cold intensified.

Thorn scowled. She must have been put in an unheated boxcar. Unable to take the chill in her half-beast form, she reached
inside and called her wolf's body with all its thick, warm fur.
The change was smooth and practically effortless. The silver
watch chain around her neck was just big enough to accommo-
date her change. She barely felt it within her neck fur.

She blinked. Apparently whatever Belus had put on the box to stop magic, didn't seem to bother her shift between forms. She rose to her paws, and her head swam. She groaned and settled back down on the blanket. Her ability to change might be okay, but her body was still suffering from Belus's venom. She'd have to wait for the venom to wear off. *Damnit. . . .*

She set her head down on her foreleg and stretched out on her belly. The cage was too small for her human length but just fine for her wolf's body. She closed her eyes.

Metal thunked against the wood around her cage.

Thorn lifted her head from her foreleg. *What now?*

There was a metallic screech, and then the rattle of a chain being withdrawn.

Thorn blinked. Was someone opening her box?

A narrow wooden panel slid to the side, revealing a gap near the bottom of the bars. The edge of a pie tin slid through the gap and into her cage, pressing up against the hay filling the bottom of her cage. The scent of raw steak perfumed the air.

Food! Thorn rose to her paws with only the slightest touch of dizziness and hastily dug the hay aside, gouging the cage's plank floor in the process. She grabbed the pie tin with her teeth and pulled it in. It held three large, raw T-bone steaks. *Yes!*

She bit into the first and tore it in half, leaving the bone in the other half. She chewed it to a manageable size and swallowed. It wasn't the best-tasting meat in the world, but it wasn't bad. She preferred venison, while it was still warm and juicy. She bit into the other half, chewed the meat off the bone, then crunched the bone with relish.

A panel on the top of the box opened, and Belus peered through the bars. "Are you actually eating the bone, too?"

Thorn looked up at him, curled her lips back from her long teeth, and growled.

Belus blinked. "My god, you're a wolf." His brows lifted. "I saw you do this before, but I hadn't realized how thoroughly wolf you actually became."

Thorn snorted and tore into the second steak. Well, of course . . . she was a were*wolf*. She changed from human to wolf. Why was everyone always so surprised?

Belus closed the panel. "I will leave you to dine in peace." A door opened and closed.

She crunched the bone from the second steak and realized that the dizziness had completely passed. Belus's venom had finally worn off. It was time to think about escape. As soon as she was done eating.

She swallowed down the bone to the third steak and noticed that some of the thin, watery blood had dripped on the wood floor of her cage. Still hungry, she lapped at it and then dug at it. The wood tore under her claws. Thorn stared at the deep gouges she'd made without even trying. She opened her jaws in a broad wolf grin. They had put her in an iron-barred cage that had a wooden floor. *Idiots!* She went to the opposite corner of her cage and began digging in earnest, the splinters flying behind her.

The wood planks that made the bottom of the cage were fairly thick but no match for her claws. It didn't take long for her to dig all the way through to the floor of the train. Interestingly enough, the train's floor was made of wood, too.

She lifted her head and listened. No one had bothered to check on her to see what she was doing. *Definitely idiots.* She turned back and continued to dig.

Thorn dug until she opened a hole through the boxcar's floor large enough to finally stick her head through. The rattling noise coming through the hole was painfully deafening.

That's when she noticed the flaw in her plan. If she tried to escape through the bottom, she'd be run over by the low-slung, fast-moving train. She'd made a perfectly good escape route she couldn't use.

Out of sheer frustration, she dragged one of the blankets over the hole, covering it so she wouldn't have to look at it. However, it didn't do much to muffle the rattling of iron wheels rolling on iron rails. Thorn flopped down on the hay and groaned. *All that work—for nothing!*

26

Resting her head on her paws, Thorn noticed that the rattling tempo of the iron wheels passing over the rails was becoming wider spaced. It was taking longer to go from rail to rail. The train was slowing down. She lifted her head and looked over at her hole. If the train stopped, she could easily get out through the bottom of the train.

She rose to her feet, dragged the blanket off her hole, and started digging again. Her claws tore into the wood loudly, but she didn't care. She needed to widen the hole enough to let her shoulders pass, and she needed to do it fast.

A door opened and slammed closed. Bolts scraped and thunked into place. "What are you doing in there?" Belus's voice came from entirely too close.

Thorn dug faster. If she had to get out of the hole while the train was still moving, she'd do it. She wanted out of that box.

The panel on the top of the box slammed open. "Thorn? Ah!"

Thorn didn't bother looking; she kept digging. She was too close to escape.

"We don't have time for this!" A hard shove moved the entire box to the side.

Thorn was knocked off her feet. She yelped and fell into the straw. She leaped back onto her paws, but her hole through the floor of the train was gone. She snarled in fury. *Son of a bitch . . . !*

The click of a lock and the rattle of chains announced that the box was being opened. "The train is under attack. We must leave now."

Thorn froze. The *train* was under attack? What was this, the American Wild West?

On one side of her box, the panel and bars slid partway to the side, leaving a small space.

Thorn rushed for it, shoving her long, narrow head through and then her shoulders. She made it all the way out and was brought to a sudden choking stop that swung her all the way around to sit back on her haunches.

Two things became immediately apparent. The first was that she had indeed been kept in a boxcar. It was crammed with shipping boxes and crates. And the other was that she had been brought to a halt by a dog's choke chain around her throat that was attached to a bright silver chain leash.

The leash's end was in Belus's gloved hand, with a goodly length of it wound around his wrist. He smiled from under a smoke-gray top hat set on his long dark curls. His eyes were those of a normal human, if a rather brilliant blue. A gray scarf was carefully tucked within the curly furred lapels of his floor-length, ink-black fur coat, and he carried a thick blackthorn walking cane crowned with a winding silver serpent. He snorted. "Well, now, that was completely predictable."

Thorn laid her ears back and bared her teeth. Every hair on her body bristled. How dare he put her at the end of a chain like a dog? She lunged.

Belus raised his heavy cane. "No!"

Thorn's body locked up, forcing her to an abrupt skittering stop. *Huh?* She backed away and then trotted to one side and then the other at the end of the chain, snarling with the urge to attack, but she just couldn't make herself do it.

Belus's brows rose. "Sit."

Thorn sat. She didn't want to; her body just did it all on its own. Squatting on her haunches, she glared at him and trembled in fury. She didn't know what the hell had just happened, but she knew very well who to blame.

Belus smiled. "Well, well, this obedience chain actually works on werewolves! How pleasant." He lifted his chin. "Listen, and obey! You are not to bite me or make any other attempts to harm me in any way. Nor are you to make any attempt to remove the chain. Is this understood?"

Obey . . . my ass! Thorn growled but nodded her head once. She understood all right. She understood perfectly that she would find a way off this chain, and once she did, he was lunch.

Belus nodded. "Good."

Something heavy hit the door to the next train car.

Belus turned and frowned at the door. "And that would be our cue to exit. I've bolted the door, but I doubt that will last long." He tucked his cane under his arm and swayed toward her. "It seems that plague has been unleashed on this train."

Thorn skittered out of his way. The plague, as in, the walking dead? He had to be kidding!

Belus moved right past her. "And so we must leave before we arrive at our destination." He leaned down and started unbolting the heavy cargo door on the side of the boxcar.

Something slammed into the door, powerful enough to rattle it. It was followed by scratching, more heavy banging, and hideous moaning.

Every hair on Thorn's body stood. He *wasn't* kidding.

Heavy thumps like footsteps sounded on the rooftop right above them.

Thorn's ears rose, and she looked straight up. She hadn't thought the dead could *climb!*

Belus shoved, and the cargo door rolled, clanking and grinding sideways, opening a few feet. A bitter wind full of flying snow whirled into the car. "A human might not survive a jump from a moving train." He turned to look at her. "But, then, neither you nor I are human." His human semblance faded. While the shape of his face remained unchanged, his eyes became large, perfectly round, and slitted, and his dark curls became a mass of long, slender feathers. The slightest pattern of scales marked his hairline.

He rose, the hem of his coat lifting from the floor, revealing the heavy black snake coils that made up the lower half of his body. He gripped the door with his gloved hands and shoved hard.

The door slid open all the way with a hard clanking slam, revealing a swiftly passing forest marching up a steep hillside, covered in deep snow.

An eerie howl echoed from the night.

Thorn knew that howl. *Max. . . .* It sounded like Belus's plan to draw the insane werewolf was already working. But how the hell had he found her?

Belus turned to her and held out his hand, his long nails extending through the fingertips of his gloves. "Thorn. . . ."

A gunshot exploded directly overhead. Something thumped hard on the roof.

Belus looked up, smiling sourly, and tucked his cane into the belt of his coat. "Apparently some of the passengers are still alive." He turned to her. "Though not for long." He ducked low and grabbed Thorn around the chest and haunches.

Thorn yelped in surprise. *What the . . . ?* She twisted in his hold, snarling, but she just couldn't make herself bite him.

Belus locked his arms around her, digging his fingers into her fur. "Stop!" He bared his long, slender fangs, showing his annoyance. "Do not fight me. I do not wish to accidentally strangle you on the chain when we fall."

Thorn stopped struggling, her snarls dying to low rumbling growls. It was not her intent; she wanted to bite him so badly her mouth was practically foaming, but her body refused to cooperate. *Stupid leash . . . !*

"Good." Belus easily lifted her in his arms, as if she were a pup. His body tensed, his coils winding into a tight spiral under him. He looked out the door into the night, watching the forest ahead of them. "Ah, there. . . ." He launched them off the train and into the snowy night.

Thorn was thrown hard against Belus's shoulder. Behind them, crouched on the curved roof of the rapidly passing train, was a huge shadowy figure, a long cape streaming behind him. . . .

Locked together, Thorn and Belus slammed into a snowbank at the base of a fairly steep embankment.

Thorn rolled free of Belus's arms but was brought up short by the chain about her neck that was attached to his wrist. She rose to her four paws and shook the snow from her fur.

Belus rose upright, wiping snow from his coat. "Well, that was less than pleasant." He retrieved his top hat from where it hung at the center of his back by a string buttoned into his coat collar, and set it on his head. He reached into his pocket and pulled out a gold pocket watch. The lid flipped open, and he peered at the watch face, frowning. "We need to attain some distance rather rapidly." He looked over at the still-passing train and then turned to face the trees and raised his cane, pointing. "The most direct route into town is that way." He swayed across the snow up the embankment, leaving a shallow curving trail in his wake.

Drawn by the chain around her neck, Thorn had no choice but to follow.

Belus moved surprisingly fast uphill across the top of the

snow and among the trees—far faster than a man could run, even on a flat, smooth surface.

Thorn loped at his side.

A massive explosion brightened the night and shook the ground under Thorn's feet. She yelped and spun to look back. Beyond the trees, a towering fire lit the night.

Belus checked his pocket watch. "Ah, right on time." He smiled, closed the watch and then led her deeper into the trees at a far slower pace. "In case you are interested, that was the train's engine that just exploded."

Thorn danced to the side in shock. *The train?*

Belus tucked his cane under his arm and shoved his gloved hands deep into his pockets. "I noticed that there were a high number of infected passengers with more than a few already dead in their seats. I decided it might be best if that train did not reach its destination." He tilted his head in a slight shrug. "And so an explosion. Any of the dead or infected that endured the crash will immolate themselves in the resulting fire."

Moving at his side in a long-legged trot, Thorn glanced over at him, ears up. He'd decided this? *He* blew up the train? Who the hell was he to do something like that? What about anyone that might not have been infected? She laid her ears back flat and growled.

Belus smiled down at her. "You do not approve?"

Thorn snapped toward him. Hell, no, she didn't approve of mass murder!

Belus looked ahead and lifted his chin. "Even though I saved the town ahead from an invasion of the walking dead?"

He had a point. Thorn dropped her head low. Damnit, now she didn't know what to think. She just didn't like the idea of innocent people being hurt.

An eerie howl echoed in the distance.

Thorn stopped and looked back through the trees.

Belus snorted. "Oh, was that a friend of yours?" His voice dripped with sarcasm.

Thorn curled her lips, showing her teeth. *That wasn't funny, you bastard.* Maybe she should show him how bad his joke really was. She raised her right front paw and dragged it through the snow, making a line, and then another. And then another . . .

Belus moved behind her to look at what she was doing, and his brows rose. "You're writing?"

Thorn snorted. She couldn't talk to him in this shape, and it was too cold to assume her human form, so this was the best option. It was awkward as hell, but she succeeded in making the letters *MAX* in the snow without stepping on it too badly.

Belus frowned. "Max . . . ?" He looked over Thorn. "That . . . was the plague beast?"

Thorn nodded her entire head carefully in the human manner.

Belus grinned, showing his long, slender fangs. "Excellent!" He turned and slammed the end of his snake's tail across the word, cutting the name in half.

Thorn jumped back to the very end of the chain.

Grinning, Belus lashed his tail across the snow, wiping the word from the snow. "Once I have the name of the heretic from the plague beast, the end of this hunt will be very swift."

She stared at him. Belus actually thought he was going to *talk* to Max? She could have sworn she'd told him that Max was insane, not to mention a man-eater.

"Well, then, Thorn." Belus coiled his tail back under his long coat and tugged on the chain, drawing her close. "Shall we find a cozy spot for a nice long chat?" He looked toward the trees and smiled. "Let's see, on this side of town . . . ? Ah, yes, I believe I know just the place!" He led her among the trees, humming a jaunty tune.

A chat? Trotting at his side, Thorn flicked up one ear at him. Obviously Belus was just as crazy as Max.

* * *

At the top of a steep hill was a massive crumbling building. Shattered spires rose above the winter-bare trees and scraped the roiling, cloudy sky.

"There it is." Belus nodded. "This will do very well indeed." He towed her up the hill toward it.

Thorn's first impression was that it was an abandoned monastery. The rambling building was that spread out. However, once they cleared the last of the trees, she could see that it was a burned-out, brick-walled factory at least eight stories high that went on for several acres. What she had taken for spires were in fact artistically twisted and blackened brick chimneys. Traces of the decorative tin roof clung to what was left of the upper stories. The wind moaned through shattered windows.

It had to be the creepiest building she'd ever seen.

Belus led Thorn along the devastated building's side, passing abandoned pipes and crumbled brick walls. He shoved open a scorched and battered door and proceeded into the half-lit darkness with obvious purpose.

The interior was a maze of narrow, scorched hallways and large rooms filled with the rusted hulks of shattered machinery. The warped tile floors were littered with broken glass, burned bricks, plaster peelings, and tumbled furniture.

Thorn followed Belus up a tilted marble stairwell to the very center of the broad and nearly empty floor above. The floor planks creaked alarmingly.

Belus nodded and then reached down to pat Thorn on the head. "Now, to prepare the stage. . . ."

Thorn snapped at his hand.

Belus leaned down to catch her by the head. "Thorn. . . ." His nails dug into the fur of her ruff, forcing her to meet his snake-slitted eyes. "Be very glad your vampire has officially claimed you. I would take a great deal of pleasure in training you to proper obedience."

Thorn bared her teeth. She would take a great deal of pleasure in eating him at the earliest opportunity.

He released her and moved away, drawing her after him. "Let's see, where shall we begin? Ah, I know . . . with warmth." He shivered. "This body is not suited for winter."

27

In the very center of the abandoned factory's second floor, Belus drew a circle on the floor with the heel of his cane, leaving a trail of pale blue light.

Thorn followed him, nose down, trying to see how he was making light spill out of his cane, but she couldn't figure it out.

Belus completed his circle and then reached into the pocket of his floor-length black fur coat and pulled out a small yellow ball. He held out the ball before him and glanced at Thorn. "Stay back. I wouldn't want all that lovely silver fur to get singed."

Thorn's tall ears rose. *Singed?* She stepped away, moving behind him as far as the chain would allow.

Belus tossed the ball into the blue circle. The ball stopped in midair about an arm's length from the floorboards. He called out a short guttural word. Fire erupted around the ball, creating a miniature sun the size of a human head that floated in midair.

Thorn jumped back, her tail low. *Holy shit!*

Belus held out his gloved hands and sighed. "Much better. . . ."

He reached back into his coat pocket and pulled out what looked like a coil of extremely fine wire. "Now, then, to create my trap." He looked down at Thorn and frowned. "Hmmm . . . I can't afford any accidents, so . . . Thorn, sleep!"

Between one breath and the next, blackness crushed Thorn under. She never even felt the floor hit her cheek.

"Thorn, awaken."

Thorn groaned and opened her eyes to firelight and the distant ceiling of a shattered factory. The floor was hard under her bare back. Somehow she'd reassumed her half-wolf form while she'd been asleep. She wasn't cold, though. She had been laid out close to the floating fire, and a thick fur coat had been tossed over her naked form.

"How very interesting." Belus smiled from where he was seated on a slightly charred chair only a stride away. He was dressed like any other gentleman in a crisp black shirt and a neatly tied and starched black neck cloth tucked under a steel-gray waistcoat, with a black frock coat to cover it all. Well, the top half of him was. The bottom half coming out from under his coat was all shiny black snake. His heavy cane lay across his lap. "Apparently this is your natural form."

Thorn eyed Belus's clothes and realized it was his coat that covered her, but the damned chain was still around her neck and attached to Belus's wrist. She sat up and grabbed her head with her hands. "Ow . . . shit."

Belus tsked. "I suppose I did put you to sleep rather fast, but I could not afford to have you wandering about my heels while I set the wire." He lifted his gloved hand and gestured outward.

Clutching the coat to her bare breasts, Thorn turned to look.

Marching up the long floor were four rows of flat-sided brick pillars that supported what was left of the ceiling. Thorn had to squint, but she could just make out light glinting on what looked like spider webbing strung between the four pillars that surrounded them. "What is that?"

"I believe the modern phrase is monofilament wire."

Thorn frowned and tilted her head to see more glints of light. There was a lot of it strung back and forth between the encircling pillars. "It doesn't look very . . . threatening."

"Which is why it makes such a wonderful trap." Belus chuckled. It was not a pleasant sound. "I advise you, quite strongly, to avoid straying too close. It is derived from silver and designed to cut anything that comes in contact with it, especially creatures of enchantment."

Thorn turned to look at him. "But it's so thin. . . ."

Belus smiled broadly. "I assure you, one thread could cut a man in half. I've seen it do so." He waved at her. "If you would be so kind, I need you to call the plague beast."

Thorn rose up on her knees. "Call him?"

Belus lifted his chin. "Howl, my dear Thorn, as loudly and for as long as you can. Now."

A shimmer of white fire sizzled in Thorn's bones, and she slid into her wolf form and rose to her four paws. She raised her muzzle and howled toward the rafters of the old factory. The long and bittersweet sound sailed high and traveled across the sky like the call of a hawk.

She called again, and then again . . .

A piercing howl that was closer to a shriek finally answered her.

Thorn slid back into her half-human body. "He's coming." She grabbed for the coat and set it about her shoulders. It stank of snake, but she really didn't want to be naked in front of Belus. "He's pretty close, actually." She snorted. "His voice doesn't carry far."

"Excellent!" Belus reached into his coat pocket. "Your throat must be parched." He pulled out a silver embossed hip flask and held it up. "Do not drop it. The interior is glass." He tossed the flask toward her.

Thorn caught it by reflex. "What's in it?"

"Water." Belus's smile turned sour. "I cannot drink spirits."

Thorn stared at the flask in her palm. Howling had dried out her throat. She unscrewed the top and sniffed. It smelled like water. She took a careful sip. It tasted like pure water. She up-ended it and drank down three swallows, emptying it. All of a sudden she realized she'd tasted water that pure before. She stared at the emptied flask in her hand. *That bastard...!* She looked up at him and curled her lip, showing one long fang. "This wasn't water."

"Aquinas is indeed water." Belus smiled. "Merely a very special kind." He tilted his head to the side. "However, the few pitiful swallows in that flask will do no more than calm you." He shook his head and sighed. "It was all I could carry on short notice."

Tension bled from Thorn's body. Her shoulders slumped, and her eyes became heavy. She wasn't exactly tired, just... very relaxed. "You're a total conniving bastard, you know that?"

"Why, so I am." He rose from his chair and scooped her up, coat and all. "But even conniving bastards have their uses."

Thorn wanted to struggle, but she just... couldn't.

Belus sat back down in the chair with her sprawled across his lap, wrapped in his coat. Her head fell back over his arm, her silver hair spilling onto the floor. He cupped her jaw, turning her to face him. "Werewolves can be very useful indeed. Pity you already have a master."

Thorn barely had the energy to turn her head away. "He's not my master."

Belus snorted. "I beg to differ." He parted the coat, and his nails traced down her belly. "What is written on your body clearly states otherwise."

Thorn shuddered. "Don't . . . touch me."

Belus chuckled and closed the coat over her. "Remain calm. I have no designs on your . . . chastity."

"That is very good. You will breathe longer." The breathless growling voice came from the shattered floor directly above.

Belus looked up. "Does our prince know you are here, count?"

Count? Thorn squinted into the shadows above but couldn't make out any trace of movement. That voice was Yaroslav? It didn't sound anything like him.

"Our prince knows you have taken Thorn."

Belus snorted. "But of course. I did not exactly conceal my actions. However, shouldn't you be engaged in decoding a certain plague serum?"

"The serum was very pure and not very stable. It was child's play to decode. Release her."

"I'm afraid I still have need of your rather ferocious little companion." Belus's gaze narrowed, and his mouth curved up into smile. "You are welcome to come down and join us."

Thorn stiffened. "No! Don't! There are wires!"

Whispers of movement came from the deep shadows, and the planks above creaked. "Yes, I see Ariadne's web."

Belus shrugged. "It's only strung around us, not overhead. If you come straight down you will not encounter them."

"Why should I? Do you have a use for me also?"

Belus chuckled, low and vicious. "You know better than most what use I have for maguskind." He tilted his head. "However, I strongly suspect you would give me a terrible case of indigestion."

A board creaked above. "If not poisoning."

"Quite." Belus's lip curled. "Out of sheer curiosity, how did you get here so quickly?"

"Oh, I have my ways." Something twirled lazily downward from the shadows above. It was a black feather. A huge black feather. It fell into the light, gleamed briefly, then disintegrated into smoke.

Thorn stared. *Ah, so that's why his voice is off.* He was in his winged shape. She frowned. Could that have been Yaroslav she had seen on the top of the train?

The chugging snarl of an approaching steam-powered vehicle caught Thorn's attention. She turned to look beyond Belus's shoulder toward the stairwell.

Belus turned to her and frowned. "What is it?"

She frowned. "I think it's a steam car."

Belus lifted his brows. "A steam car?"

Thorn nodded slowly. "Coming this way."

Belus looked up at the ceiling. "Count, it seems we are about to have company." His serpent appearance faded into that of a normal human, his booted feet crossed at the ankles. "Would you care to assist me while I question our guest, whom I surmise is the plague beast?"

"The plague beast?" A shadow shifted at the left side of the shattered floor above.

"What better way to find the master than by asking its servant?"

"Is that why you've spun Ariadne's web?"

Belus shrugged. "I thought it an efficient method, as the beast is under sanction."

Thorn stilled. "Under sanction" meant sentenced to die. They were talking about the deadly wire and Max.

"I see." A board creaked, and plaster peelings fell from the ceiling. "Would you care to put out that bane fire?"

Belus smiled, showing his slender fangs. "And take the chance that I might be attacked by hostile magic?" He snorted. "I think not."

On the floor below, something rumbled and then crashed. The floor planks trembled. A screaming howl burst from close by.

Thorn's heart slammed hard, and the fur rose all down her spine. That sound might have been Max, but it was the sound of pain and terror, not anger. The wolf sharing her soul suddenly awoke, bringing forth the sharp sizzle of white fire that seared deliciously through her blood. Her mind cleared completely. "Something's wrong. . . ."

"Something certainly is." Belus grabbed the hair at the back of her neck, jerking her back against him. He caught her jaw, forcing her head back to lock gazes with her. "You should not be this alert."

Thorn grabbed for his wrist, wincing. "Let go!" Pain stabbed into the back of her skull and blazed down her spine. Her back arched, and she gasped. Writhing sharply, she fell off Belus's lap and landed on her side, groaning. Broken lines of blue flickered under her skin, hinting at a pattern. Delicate swirls of bright yellow erupted and intertwined, snuffing out the blue lines one by one, creating a different pattern entirely.

"What is this?" Belus knelt over her, grabbed Thorn's coat, and yanked it off her. He stared at the conflicting pattern appearing all over her body. A smile bloomed. "So, that is your little secret." He stood and laughed. The sound was deep and full of triumph.

Thorn shuddered under the onslaught. Abruptly the pain stopped. She sucked in a deep breath and sat up carefully. She watched the gold lines fade under her skin. Whatever it was that had just happened was over.

A dark shadow dropped from the floor above, landing heavily on the floorboards three strides away. Yaroslav rose from his crouch in his customary black fur coat, his long hair still bound in its neat braid. Black feathers floated down from above and disintegrated into smoke and ash. "Belus. . . ."

Belus turned and crossed his arms, his smile broad, but his eyes narrowed. "You have no reason to fear, count. The prince said quite plainly you had his permission for her . . . claim."

"But I did not give my permission for her theft." The voice was crisp, sharp, and pure Oxford English.

Thorn knew that voice. She had not heard it in many years, but she would know it anywhere. She twisted sharply, coming up into a crouch, every hair on her body bristling.

A bearded man in a bowler hat and a long winter coat stepped from the far staircase and strode toward them. He stopped at the edge of the light, just beyond the glinting threads. The light reflected on his round spectacles and gleamed down the silver walking stick he carried. "I will ask you, politely, to return my property."

Belus lifted his chin. "And who might you be?"

"I am Dr. Richard Marcus Townsend, a professor of alchemy at Oxford. That child is my creation."

"Oh?" Belus pursed his lips, and his brows rose. "But what of your other creation, the one called Max?"

"I'm afraid Mr. Rykov is . . . not quite himself at the moment." Dr. Townsend tilted his head slightly to the side. "Might I know who I am speaking to?"

Belus smiled. "But of course! I am Vicompte Belsarius Antimony Svorsa of Venice." He held out his hand toward Yaroslav. "This is Count Feodor Yaroslav Iziaslavich of Kiev."

Dr. Townsend raised his chin. "Ah, count, would you happen to be any relation to Master Feodor Yaroslav Iziaslavich, the watchmaker? I have a matter of some urgency to address with him."

Thorn stilled. *What . . . ?* He knew Yaroslav?

"I am." Yaroslav took a single step toward Belus and Thorn. "However, I am sad to say my grandfather passed away last month."

Dr. Townsend shook his head. "My condolences on your loss."

Yaroslav's brows rose. "If I recall, my grandfather exchanged letters with a Professor Phillip Townsend, a doctor of philosophy in Oxford?"

The doctor smiled. "Oh, yes, that was my paternal grandfather." He reached into his coat pocket and pulled out a gold pocket watch at the end of a chain. "In fact, I inherited this rather peculiar watch from him, but it stopped running. I was hoping Master Yaroslav could repair it."

Yaroslav smiled tightly. "I'm afraid that is no longer possible."

"A pity. . . ." Dr. Townsend shook his head sadly. "You see, my interests in the arcane began with this watch."

Belus lifted his brow at Yaroslav. "You don't say?"

"Oh, yes, a watch that ran without ever needing to be wound?" The doctor tucked the watch back into his pocket. "It piqued my interest quite a lot. Unfortunately it stopped the day my grandfather died. I took it apart and could get it to tick for short periods of time, but I couldn't quite master the technique of keeping it running."

Belus continued to smile at Yaroslav. "That does sound rather . . . interesting."

Yaroslav snorted and spoke under his breath. "All the interest in the world does not make a talent appear without previous potential."

"So, count . . ." the doctor leaned forward on his walking stick, "would you happen to share in your grandfather's . . . interests?"

Yaroslav's gaze narrowed. "It could be said that I do."

Dr. Townsend clasped his hands together. "Splendid, simply splendid! I have so many questions to ask you!"

Yaroslav smiled tightly. "And I have quite a few for you as well. Shall we begin with why you created a plague of the walking dead?"

Dr. Townsend stilled. "Ah . . ."

"And why did you make me a werewolf?" Thorn rose to her

feet and stepped forward, wanting him to see her nude body and what it had become.

The doctor waved a hand distractedly. "My child, all scientists experiment. . . ."

What? Thorn's hands fisted at her sides. "I was an *experiment?*"

Dr. Townsend smiled. "One of my first successes, I might add."

Thorn's mouth fell open. Warping a human being into something else was a *success?*

Yaroslav crossed his arms. "And the plague of dead? Was that, too, an experiment?"

"Oh, no, that was by request." The doctor sighed. "The Turks are having troubles with the Russians, so I was asked to create something for the Turkish war efforts. It was just something I threw together." He shook his head. "Why they released it among the farmers in the Balkans is beyond me. It was supposed to be released in Russia."

Thorn scowled. *Oh, and Russia would have been so much better?* Was this doctor out of his mind?

Yaroslav's jaw clenched. "Those creatures appeared in my grandfather's town in Walachia."

The doctor smiled. "But of course! I wanted to impress him with my work!"

Yaroslav's hands fisted. "They destroyed the town utterly."

Dr. Townsend shrugged. "These things do happen."

Belus lifted one finger. "If I might ask, you were asked to . . . make the dead walk, by whom?"

Dr. Townsend looked away. "By . . . someone of influence in the diplomatic community."

Yaroslav frowned. "Your government knows about your . . . work?"

"They know." The doctor lifted his shoulder in a small shrug. "They just don't quite believe it. However . . ." he smiled, "I have acquired some rather influential financial support for any research I care to explore. In return, I do my patriotic duty, when asked."

"Your patriotic duty?" Thorn gasped. "Do you know how many innocent people your plague has killed?"

Dr. Townsend shook his head and sighed. "My dear child, that's what wars do. They kill people."

Yaroslav shook his head and turned away. "Towns end, an appropriate name."

Belus smiled at the doctor. "Why don't you come into the light so we can have a proper discussion, Dr. Townsend?"

28

Dr. Townsend, creator of the plague of walking dead, and maker of both Max and Thorn, lifted a hand to adjust his round spectacles and frowned. "I would love to stay and chat. However . . ." he lifted his silver walking stick, "it seems there is a rather interesting collection of thread strung between the pillars." He brought his walking stick down amidst the wires.

A shower of sparks danced along the cane.

The doctor hastily pulled back his cane. "Ah, my mistake, it is very fine wire, and it seems to be somewhat electrified." He ran his gloved hand along the length of his cane, and his brows rose. "Not to mention deucedly sharp. You've quite scarred the silver." He cleared his throat. "And so I believe I shall decline your invitation." He lifted his chin. "So if you don't mind, I'd like to have my creation returned. I have a rather urgent matter that needs my attention."

Thorn crossed her arms over her breasts and curled her lip, showing one long fang. "I am not going anywhere with a homicidal lunatic like you!"

"Now, now . . ." Belus glanced at Thorn. "Let's not lose our temper to name calling."

"Fine." Thorn grabbed the chain he held. "Can we lose this instead?"

Yaroslav stepped closer. "I would see that chain off *my* companion." His hands closed on the sheathed knives at his hips.

Belus lifted his brow. "I see your point." He turned to Thorn. "Do you promise not to try to eat . . . the snake?"

Thorn shot Belus a level glare. "Does the snake promise to leave me the hell alone?"

Yaroslav stepped close to the pair of them and frowned from one to the other. "Thorn does not eat people."

Thorn smiled at Belus, showing her teeth. "Snakes taste different from people. I find them quite delicious."

Yaroslav's brows rose, and he looked over at Belus. "You don't say?" His mouth twitched into something vaguely resembling a smile. "How very . . . appropriate."

Belus shot Yaroslav a glare. "I want your oath that you will you keep control of her appetites."

Yaroslav sighed and turned to Thorn. "I'm afraid the prince would not be amused if you ate one of his appointed senators."

"Was that supposed to be reassuring?" Belus's voice dripped with sarcasm.

Beyond the gleaming threads, the doctor frowned. "A senator? To what prince? What country do you people represent, anyway?"

He was ignored.

Thorn rolled her eyes and sighed as dramatically as she could. "Oh, all right. I won't eat the snake." She narrowed her eyes at Belus and growled. "As long as he promises to never try something like this again."

Belus rolled his eyes in an equally dramatic gesture. "Oh, very well. . . ." He smiled. "I promise I will never use you without your permission again."

Thorn tilted her head. That didn't sound quite right, but it was probably the best she could get at the moment, and she really wanted the chain off. "Fine. Agreed." She tugged on the chain. "Get this off me."

Belus reached out to grasp the choker chain around her neck and lifted it up over her head and off. "There."

"Thank you." Thorn lashed out with a hard, fast, jabbing punch, using every ounce of power she could muster. It landed perfectly in Belus's belly.

Belus folded over and staggered back two steps, gasping for breath.

"Enough." Yaroslav grabbed Thorn's upper arm, pulling her back, but his mouth twitched upward, and his eyes were creased with barely disguised humor.

Belus slowly straightened, glaring at Thorn. "That was . . . sneaky."

"Yeah, I know." Thorn curled her lip in a vicious smile. "But, hey, I kept my promise not to eat you."

Yaroslav slid out of his coat, revealing a pair of long knives buckled at his hips and strapped to his thighs. "Thorn, don't pick on the sn—the senator." He draped his coat over Thorn's bare shoulders. "We shall leave you to your . . . entertainments." His voice dropped to a soft whisper. "Don't forget—the prince wants him alive."

"Excuse me. Hello?" The doctor raised his silver walking stick. "My creation, if you please?"

Yaroslav scowled at the doctor. "She is not your creation anymore. She is mine."

Thorn stiffened and glared up at Yaroslav. "What . . . ?"

Yaroslav clapped his hand over her mouth. "Doctor, your original aspect was misaligned and profoundly flawed. In fact, it was so very poorly constructed I was forced to replace her making entirely, removing all trace of your mark on her. And, as such, she is no longer yours. "

Thorn grabbed Yaroslav's wrist. Damned possessive vampire! She yanked his hand off her mouth. "Yaroslav!"

"That is entirely beside the point!" The doctor straightened sharply. "I made her. I want her back!"

Thorn aimed a snarl at the doctor. "Go to hell!"

Yaroslav set his arm over Thorn's shoulders. "Fear not; he will see hell." He glanced at Belus and smiled pleasantly. "Sometime quite soon, in fact."

Belus smiled right back and licked his lips.

Yaroslav turned away, encouraging Thorn to turn with him. "Good-bye, Dr. Townsend."

"Stop!" Dr. Townsend raised his silver cane, waving it. "You don't understand! I need her!"

Belus straightened the lapels of his coat. "*You* don't understand, doctor. She has already gone beyond your reach."

The doctor gripped his silver cane and raised it. "*Nothing* is beyond my reach!" He slammed the heel of his cane on the floorboards. "Come!"

Something huge crashed, making the floor shake and dust fall from the broken rafters. It sounded to Thorn like it was large enough to be one of the big machines on the floor below.

Something heavy and metallic scraped at the bottom of the stairwell.

Thorn froze and then turned back to face the stairs.

Yaroslav turned with her.

A horrific and agonizing bellow came up from below.

Belus lost his smile. "What in hell's name was that?"

Something huge, with one glowing golden eye, dragged itself up the stairs. Its breaths wheezed painfully from its chest, and it stank foully of dog, hot engine oil, and rot. It stopped at the top of the steps and growled.

"Oh, my god. . . ." Thorn's heart slammed in her chest, and her stomach churned with revulsion. Her entire being, wolf and human, rejected it utterly. It was an unwholesome, unnatural, twisted thing. It was a thing that should not live. It was a thing that needed to be wiped from existence. And yet there was a trace of something familiar in its scent. "It's Max."

Yaroslav stiffened. "That . . . thing?"

"Gaaa!" Belus tugged out a handkerchief from his sleeve and covered his nose. "Is it supposed to smell this . . . dead?"

The doctor lifted his hand, palm open, to the thing on the stairs. "Alas, Max is no longer the man he once was."

Max crawled from the stairwell, pulling himself along the floor. His head and jaws were misshapen, caught between human and beast. His one wolf yellow eye gleamed, reflecting the light, and the eye still human reflected nothing. His back was hunched, and his legs had lost all trace of human shape to become the haunches of a beast. The knobs of his warped spine showed plainly through the patches of red and gray fur that covered him sporadically. And, still, he had no tail.

Light gleamed on metal.

Metal? Thorn frowned, using her wolf's eyes to pierce the shadows. That couldn't be right. . . .

Max's right arm had been replaced entirely by a geared machine that ended in blades instead of fingers.

She sucked in a sharp breath. "What did you *do* to him?"

The doctor sighed and shook his head. "It seems Max took a silver bullet in the hand. I'm afraid my attempts at . . . repairs were not quite as successful as I could wish. I was forced to replace his entire arm." He set a gloved hand on Max's filthy, disfigured head.

Max looked up at the doctor and whimpered. "Home? Ma . . . ster?"

The doctor shook his head slowly. "Not yet, Max. I need you to get something for me." He pointed his silver cane past the gleaming threads.

Max turned to look toward Belus, Yaroslav, and Thorn. He

still had one plain brown human eye, and it was swimming with tears.

Thorn cringed. He was in pain. A lot of it.

The doctor stroked Max's warped head. "Bring the little wolf to me." He smiled. "You may eat the others."

Belus rolled his eyes. "How very melodramatic!" He took two steps back to his abandoned chair to collect his silver serpent walking stick. "What is this, a penny dreadful?"

Yaroslav frowned and drew the pair of long knives buckled at his hips. "I am indeed seeing a resemblance."

Max moved out from under the doctor's hand and approached the gleaming threads. He sniffed. "Bad. . . ."

The doctor lifted his chin. "Max, use your new hand."

Max raised his metal arm and raked it down the threads. The wires sparked, stretched, snapped, and wrapped around the metal arm. Electrical current danced along the wires. Several whipped out to slash his shoulders, leaving long, vicious cuts.

Max jerked his head back, releasing a scream of pain and fury.

Yaroslav eyed Belus. "Ariadne's thread was a good idea."

Belus scowled. "*Was* being the operative word."

Max bit at the sparking wires wrapping him. He yelped, and his mouth came away bloodied.

Thorn took a deep breath. "I'll take care of Max. You two can have the lunatic doctor."

Yaroslav and Belus looked at her sharply.

Yaroslav shook his head. "Absolutely not!"

Belus laughed. "Are you insane?"

"No, I'm not." Thorn jerked her thumb toward Max. "He is. You don't stand a chance of fighting something like that."

Yaroslav scowled. "And you do?"

Thorn snorted. "I am a wolf. I'm faster than he is and experienced at taking down large prey. He's just a dog, a scavenger used to taking down weaker prey."

Belus waved his hand toward the lumbering Max. "Excuse me, but in case you hadn't noticed, you are not even half his size!"

"So?" Thorn scowled. "Size has nothing to do with it." She dropped the coat from her shoulders. "I've killed grizzly bears before." She smiled, showing all her long teeth. "And eaten them."

Belus's brows lifted at Thorn. He turned to Yaroslav. "She's terribly bloodthirsty. Are you quite sure you can handle her all by yourself?"

Yaroslav bared his teeth. "Thorn . . . !"

She ignored him and let the white fire take her, only this time she asked for all of it. The feral half of her soul roared outward in a blaze of pure glory, but this time it did not stop at a wolf's body. She expanded further, taking on mass, breadth, and height. Her forepaws remained closer to clawed hands, with forelegs muscled like human arms, and yet her haunches and tail were that of a wolf.

Thorn shook her body and lifted her entirely wolf head, and her ears flicked forward. The room looked so . . . small. Both Yaroslav and Belus seemed tiny.

Belus's brows rose, and he stepped back, away from her. "All right, now I am impressed."

Yaroslav stepped back also. "Thorn, I did not know you could do this."

Thorn turned her long muzzle toward him. She couldn't speak this way, so she reached for her connection to the vampire. *Neither did I.* She shrugged.

"Ah, you are loud." Yaroslav winced.

Belus pointed at Thorn. "She did not do that before?"

Yaroslav moved around Thorn's haunches, keeping a careful distance from her huge tail, and stood by Belus. "I suspect I may have rebuilt her aspect a bit too well."

Bleeding and wounded, Max growled and hunched down.

Thorn focused on Max. He was going to jump. She laid back her tall ears and bared teeth the length of knives. Her growl echoed low and deep. He was still larger than she, but not by much.

Max jumped, his clawed hands out. Saliva and blood dripped from his wide-open mouth and crooked teeth.

Thorn launched herself at the monstrosity that was once a man. Arms out, she caught him around the chest, biting down on his left shoulder, sinking her long fangs into flesh and bone. Her momentum slammed him back against the far wall.

Dr. Townsend shouted and ran for the staircase.

Thorn twisted her head, tugging at the foul-tasting fur and flesh in her mouth while digging in her claws.

Max screamed and dug his claws into her sides. His natural claws barely reached through her dense fur, but his metal claws scored long, vicious cuts down her ribs.

The brick wall crumbled under the combined weight of the two struggling werewolves. They fell out and one story down onto the debris-littered ground below.

Thorn landed on top of Max and jumped away. She shook herself and felt the burn of cuts. She turned to face him again.

Max rolled over and pushed upright on his warped legs. He looked from side to side, taking in deep sniffs, and then focused on her and screamed, spread his misshapen arms wide, and ran at her.

Thorn bared her teeth in a wolf grin. *Nearsighted idiot.* Four legs were far superior for speed and balance. She darted in and ducked low under his charge to grab his ankle in her jaws. She bit down, snapping the fragile bones, and kept going, dragging him facedown through the snow.

Max screamed in fury, but there was a high-pitched note of terror in his voice as well.

She dropped him and turned.

Max flipped onto his back, kicking out with his one working foot.

Thorn trotted out of range and circled, grinning for all she was worth. If she could get behind him, she could break his neck. And then she would eat. She was far too hungry to care how foul the meat tasted.

Max scrabbled onto his hands and limped toward her, slashing with his claws. His mechanical arm wheezed and steamed with his motions. The armpit stink of fear rolled off his skin.

She dove in, her jaws open to grab his other ankle. She closed on the bones and crunched.

Max threw himself backward, his mechanical hand slashing at her, scoring long cuts on her shoulder.

Thorn reared back, his ankle in her jaws, throwing him onto his back. She released his ankle and lunged back in to bite down on his upper leg, hunting for the big artery that ran up the inner thigh.

Max howled out his terror and grabbed at the thick fur around her neck.

Thorn twisted her head sharply, pulling her head free of his claws and ripping his leg open in the process. Blood spattered the snow and steamed.

Max somehow pushed upright and crawled back, away from her. His screams became sounds of utter terror.

Thorn dropped low and stalked after him. Max was about to die, and he knew it. She licked her black lips. Dinner was about to be served.

Max's body shimmered and shrunk to something that very nearly resembled a human. His mechanical arm became a weight too heavy for him to move. Max grabbed for it and fought with the weight that held him pinned but couldn't budge it from the snowy ground. He stared at her, his eyes wide, and shrieked. "Doctor! Doctor! Save me!" Tears streaked down his misshapen yet very nearly human face. "Please . . . please . . . somebody help me."

Thorn stopped and crouched low in the snow. His fear should have been music to her ears, but it wasn't. It was pitiful. Her growls died to silence. Max had been an educated man before someone else had made him into a monster. Someone else had made him something that could never return to being human.

Thorn took a deep breath and released it. There was no hope for Max. None at all, but he didn't need to suffer. Clearly he had suffered enough. She rose to her paws and moved toward him.

Max froze, his screams silenced by pure terror.

She moved to his side and licked his cheek. He tasted awful.

Max shivered and then blinked up at her. "You're going to kill me." It wasn't a question.

Thorn nodded slowly in the human manner.

Max blinked rapidly. "I . . . I haven't been quite myself lately." He grinned, but there was too much fear in it to be a true smile. "Actually, I haven't been myself in quite a . . . while."

Thorn shook her head. No . . . no, he hadn't.

Max swallowed and shivered hard. "I can't go back, can I?"

Thorn's ears lowered. No, he was long past that possibility. She slowly shook her head again.

Max closed his eyes. "I . . . see." Tears spilled. "If I think about it, I . . . I really don't want to live this way . . . anymore." He opened his eyes and looked over at her. "Can you make it, um . . ." he took a shaky breath, "quick?"

Thorn nodded.

Max swallowed again and then nodded. "All right." He leaned back, lying out in the snow. He stared at her. "You're very beautiful, you know. Even like this." He raised his nearly human hand and wiped at his cheeks. "I was never . . ." he sucked in a breath and winced, "I was never anything more than a monster." He closed his eyes. "Okay, enough drivel. I'm ready." He lifted his chin. "Do it."

Thorn rose, silent in the snow. She dropped her head in a fast lunge and crushed his entire neck in one bite, snapping the bones and killing him instantly.

Thorn released Max, and he fell back in the snow.

She lifted her muzzle and howled, long and sweet.

29

Yaroslav came running out of the shattered factory, his coat on and flapping open around him. "Thorn!"

Thorn turned to look and moved toward him. Her great beast form dissolved until she had only her human body. The tears welled up and exploded out of her. She dropped to her knees in the snow. "I killed him."

The vampire threw off his coat and wrapped it around her. "I know, I saw." He pulled her into his arms and held her curled up against his pounding heart. "It was a mercy. He was in great pain."

Thorn nodded but couldn't stop crying.

A hideous scream echoed from within the factory.

Thorn stiffened. "What was that?" She wiped at her cheeks and looked up at the factory.

Lightning danced behind the shattered windows.

Yaroslav looked up at the factory with her. "That would be the doctor receiving just punishment for creating one such as Max. Not to mention a plague of the dead."

Thorn frowned. "Belus?"

"Oh, indeed." He turned and carried her away from the factory toward the road. "Dr. Townsend will not die. However, by the time Belus is through with him, he will wish he had."

Another scream rent the night, and then another.

Thorn shuddered. "What is he doing to the doctor?" She shook her head. "Never mind, I probably don't want to know."

Yaroslav snorted. "For his incurable habit of meddling in the affairs of others, Belsarius Svorsa was cursed into becoming a lamia, a creature that feeds on the blood of humans, but he also feeds on magic. By the time he is done, the doctor will never be able to work another spell again, so long as he lives." Yaroslav stopped. "Well, now, this is of interest."

"What . . . ?" Thorn turned to look.

On the road before the factory was a steam car.

Yaroslav grinned. "This is most excellent. Now we do not have to walk into town!"

Thorn blinked. "You can drive one of these?"

Yaroslav lifted his chin. "I have some idea of how one works."

Thorn rolled her eyes. "Never mind. I'll drive."

Yaroslav frowned. "You . . . ?"

Thorn grinned. "Well, yeah. I'm from Long Island City. Everyone had a steam car of one type or another in their back shed. Poppy let me drive his on the back roads." She slid from his arms. "All we have to do is get the boiler water hot and keep the pressure stable."

Yaroslav shoved his sleeve up past his elbow. "Show me where this water is kept. . . ."

Thorn blinked at him. "You're going to hocus-pocus the water?"

Yaroslav frowned at her. "Hocus-pocus . . . ?"

Thorn rolled her eyes. "Use magic on it?"

"Ah. . . ." Yaroslav raised his hand and wiggled his fingers.

"I am indeed going to hocus-pocus." He lifted his chin. "Where is this boiler?"

The trip down the road, while full of fits and starts and quite a bit of grinding gears, was moderately uneventful. At least until Antonius came galloping up the road with six of his men.

Laughing wildly, Antonius leaped from his horse onto the coach box of the moving steam car and clambered into the seat to throw his arms around Yaroslav.

It seemed that Yaroslav's antiserum had been released into the drinking water and dropped from the sky from balloons like rain. Apparently it worked very well indeed. Those infected but still living who drank the water recovered, and the rainfalls melted the dead on contact.

Antonius poked Yaroslav in the chest with a finger. "But you are in big trouble for leaving without telling the prince where you were going, or even *that* you were going."

Yaroslav curled his lip. "It was urgent!"

Antonius sat back on the coachmen's bench and propped his booted foot on the dashboard. "I'm sure it was, but I'm telling you right now, the prince was not amused."

Yaroslav shook his head. "Yes, yes, I will deal with the prince's judgment on my return. . . ."

Antonius leaned close. "You're taking the train, right? The royal box is waiting at the station for you, scheduled for an express transfer."

Yaroslav scowled. "Is it so urgent I return immediately?"

Antonius nodded, and his smile disappeared. "The senate has passed another ruling."

Yaroslav cringed. "Do I want to know . . . ?"

Antonius smiled tightly. "Let's just say that you and the rest of us vampires are going to be very busy for quite some time."

"That does not sound promising."

Antonius shrugged. "It could have been a lot worse. For

some reason, Senator Belus was missing, so a couple of the more radical possibilities didn't even come up." He grinned. "Thank God for minor miracles, eh?"

Yaroslav scowled. "Thank God, indeed."

Thorn was barely awake when Yaroslav drove onto the rail station in the dead of night. The vampire carried her out of the steam car. She was wrapped in nothing but his long fur coat. He strode across the mist-shrouded platform, where a train sat already waiting.

A door was opened by a conductor, and Yaroslav stepped up into a blue velvet and gilt private car.

Thorn moaned in his arms. "This train is not going to have walking dead on it and then explode, is it?"

Yaroslav chuckled. "No, this one will not."

Thorn got no more than a glimpse of a small dining area before her gaze was caught by the full-size, curtain-draped sleeper bed. "Wow...."

Yaroslav tugged back the blankets on the bed and set her down among the sheets. "Sleep."

Thorn struggled upright. "I can't." She pressed her hands against her burning belly. "I'm too hungry. Is there any food in here?"

Yaroslav stared down at her, and his brows lowered. "There is my blood."

Thorn grimaced. *Blood, great....* She sighed. "Okay, fine."

Yaroslav blinked. "You are not going to argue?"

Thorn shook her head. "Too hungry."

Yaroslav unbuckled the belts to his sheathed knives around his long shirt. "I thank God for minor miracles." He rolled his belts around the knives and set them on the floor by the head of the bed. He unbuttoned his long, dark shirt at a rapid pace, revealing his spectacularly muscled chest and belly.

Thorn stared in fascination. "You're getting undressed?" Not that she minded in the least. He was damned nice to look at.

Yaroslav grinned and sat down on the edge of the bed. "I am hungry, too." He tugged off his boots.

Thorn blinked. "Oh. . . ." The warmth of excitement stirred in her belly. She licked her lips. "Okay."

Dressed in only his pants, he sat on the edge of the bed, turned, and held out his hand. "Come to me."

She crawled across the bed to him and took his hand.

He encouraged her to sit across his lap.

She frowned up at him. "I'm not a child."

Yaroslav sighed. "Only too well do I know this." He snorted. "Indulge me in my small pleasures, will you not?"

"Oh, all right." Thorn huffed, as if she were put upon, but the smile sneaking onto her lips ruined the whole effect. "If it makes you happy."

"It does." Yaroslav nodded firmly, his bottom lip protruding slightly. He curled his arm around her and held his forearm under her nose. "Drink."

The scent of his skin, and the blood pulsing under it, brought Thorn's hunger roaring forth. It was more than she could bear. She opened her mouth on his forearm and bit down.

He released a small gasp and groaned.

She pulled her teeth back out and covered the puncture from her teeth with her mouth. She sucked in a mouthful of copper fire and swallowed. His flavor wasn't quite something she would ever find truly delicious, but she had definitely acquired a taste for it. Heat burned down her throat and expanded in her stomach, replacing her hunger with warm and intoxicating contentment.

"Yes. . . ." He sighed. "Good, very good." His arm curled around her, keeping his forearm tight against her mouth. He stroked her brow with his free hand.

She curled up against his shoulder and drank. She had a nice view of the car's decorative arched ceiling and Yaroslav's face. He was here, with her. He was safe. The enemy had been found and destroyed. The man who had occupied her nightmares for so many years was finally wrapped in the coils of a nightmare of his own.

It was . . . comforting.

She sighed and relaxed. The heat in her stomach curled up into her mind, and while it didn't erase her thoughts, it did make it far easier not to think of anything at all.

Yaroslav smiled, carefully hiding his long teeth, and pressed his hand to her cheek. "We are feeling better, yes?"

She blinked at him and then nodded and smiled.

"Very good." He pushed her upright on his lap, off his arm. "And now it is time to serve your punishment."

Raw, sweat-inducing alarm snapped Thorn right out of her comfortable stupor. She twisted to look at him. "Punishment?"

Yaroslav cupped her jaw in his hand, his long nails digging in slightly. His gaze bore into hers. "Yes, punishment." He smiled, but his eyes were narrowed and flickered with flames, betraying his banked fury. "This is the second time you have put your life in extreme danger. I will not tolerate such behavior."

Thorn grabbed for his wrist. "You can't mean that?"

"I should have dealt firmly with you the last time. I will not be so remiss again. This time, you will be spanked."

"I will be . . . what?" Thorn stared. She couldn't have heard that right.

"Spanked." He tugged sharply.

Thorn tumbled across his splayed knees, her feet kicking up in midair. Her hands scrabbled for something to hold, but there was nothing but the floor and the edge of the bed. "I thought you were . . . hungry?"

"Oh, but I am." He pulled her into position across his knees. "I will indeed feed, directly after you are thoroughly punished."

She struggled. "You can't do this!"

His arm pinned the back of her legs, steadying her across his lap. "I not only can, I most assuredly will." He wound her hair around his fist. "The best way to deal with punishment is to simply endure. If you do not resist, it will be over with swiftly." He leaned over and smiled, showing the tips of his fangs. "However, I hope you do resist. I find that far more entertaining."

Thorn scrabbled to grab the side of the bed. "Are you insane?"

"No, I am very, very angry." His palm circled on one vulnerable butt cheek and then the other.

He *was* angry; she could feel it pulsing at the back of her mind. *Oh, my god! He's really going to do this!* She expected the ripple of fright that brought the hair up on her arms, but the warm throb of hungry arousal took her completely by surprise.

From the corner of her eye, she saw him raise his hand. "Don't!" Then she heard a loud crack. Half a second later, her right butt cheek was on fire. A hiss escaped her lips.

"There's no need to be brave. I have you well in hand. Feel free to wriggle all you like. In fact, you may also scream." He raised his hand again.

She flinched at the sharp slap; then her other butt cheek was on fire, too. She bit back a moan and could not stop herself from writhing on his lap to relieve the sting. She knew damned well she could change forms to get away from him, but the coil of erotic tension tightening in her belly was too delicious to give up on. "Look, I'm sorry, okay?"

"It is far too late for apologies."

She didn't see him raise his hand again, but she certainly heard the quick succession of slaps and felt the fiery results.

He stopped.

She groaned in agonized relief.

"Hmmm . . . your arse is becoming quite warm to the touch." His voice was soft, almost a purr. He explored her burning butt with long nails that felt more like talons on the marks he'd made. "Ah, your arse is blushing very nearly the exact shade as the heart of a rose."

She hissed under his fingers. "God!" She couldn't stop her writhing. "Nearly?"

"Fear not." He leaned over and smiled at her. "It will soon be the exact shade." His finger slid down the seam of her butt to explore her soft core. "How nice, your cream has begun to drip. I believe you are enjoying this." He slid a finger into her.

She gasped with the delicious sensation.

"In fact, I believe you are enjoying the warming of your arse very much indeed." He flicked something tender and exciting deep inside.

She jolted with carnal hunger and moaned.

He chuckled. "What a lovely sound." He pulled his finger free. "Now, then, no more mercy. I expect to hear you scream."

She clenched her jaw and bared her teeth. "I won't scream, damn you."

"Oh, but you will." He chuckled. "I know just the instrument to encourage you." He looked away. "Now, then, did I not see a hairbrush somewhere?"

30

Thorn froze. *A hairbrush?* He was going to use a hairbrush on her?

Yaroslav leaned to one side of the bed. "Ah, yes. Here it is. The prince believes in leaving his private car fully equipped with interesting conveniences, such as this nice flat-backed, round brush, like my mother used to use on me." He showed the broad ivory instrument to Thorn, who was sprawled face-down across his knees. "I'm afraid this will sting a great deal." His hand rose and fell with inhuman speed.

She heard the slap of ivory on flesh and then felt the stabbing burn. She yelped in surprise. He was right. The brush stung like hell.

He leaned close. "Was that a scream, my love?"

"No!" She could not hold still across his lap. "No, it wasn't a scream."

He pursed his lips. "Are you very sure?"

She tried to turn to look at him, but his hold on her hair was too snug. "Yes! Damn you, it wasn't a scream!"

"Good." He sat up. "I'll stop when you scream." He gave her three quick smacks, one right on top of the other.

She gasped with the pain and moaned.

He chuckled. "I will stop when you scream." He gave her three more smacks on the other cheek.

She writhed and gasped. "Son of a fucking bitch!"

"Ah, please continue to writhe in that fashion. You are making me quite deliciously hard."

Thorn's temper snapped. "Sadistic bastard!"

He leaned over her. "Oh, so you noticed?" The brush landed sharply, twice, once on each cheek.

She almost screamed that time. She barely stopped herself.

He chuckled. "Still resistant?" The brush landed, and landed, and landed . . .

She let out a screech that nearly deafened her.

He flinched back. "I think I can safely say you have indeed screamed."

She was lifted up from her humiliating position and set across his knees. She hissed as soon as her butt made contact with his hard leg. And yet she shivered with a brutal need she didn't quite understand and really didn't want to think about.

He wrapped his arms around her. "We are finished." He pressed a kiss on her brow. "Bravely done."

Thorn's heart contracted and ached. He thought her brave. She closed her eyes. Fresh, hot tears slid down her cheeks in a sudden rush. She blinked in surprise. Tears? *What the . . . ?*

He smiled as his thumbs brushed her damp cheeks. "Ah, good, very good." His voice was very soft.

"Good?" She leaned close and pressed her brow against his. "But, I don't know why . . ." She sniffed. "Why I'm . . ."

"Why you are crying?"

"Yeah . . . that."

"It is release. The Greeks call it catharsis. All you had locked within you is escaping. Pain releases all the emotions at once." He took a deep breath and released it on a sigh. "When the pain of the heart runs very deep, physical pain is sometimes the only release."

"That is so strange." She dabbed at her eyes.

He looked away. "Not as uncommon as you would think."

She leaned back to look up at him. "You . . . ?"

"Of course." He offered her a linen handkerchief. "I have lost many loves in my long life."

She took the handkerchief. He was a vampire. He had lived, and would continue to live, far longer than any human could. She couldn't imagine the amount of hurt he had endured. "I'm . . . sorry."

"It is a condition I have become accustomed to." He kissed her brow. "Enough about sadness. Do you feel better?"

She nodded.

"Good." He picked her up and set her on the bed. "On your hands and knees, if you please." He pulled his buttons free and dropped his pants.

Her eyes were drawn to his violently hard and rigidly upright cock. She licked her lips. The scent of his arousal rolled from his skin, electrifying her. Her body thrummed urgently, and a spat of moisture dampened her thighs.

He grasped the length of his cock and stroked back the tender foreskin, exposing his violently blushing, and slightly dripping, cock head. His eyes were dark, wide pits. He licked his lips. "Turn about, and rest on your forearms."

She turned with speed and positioned herself in front of him. Relief at last . . . *thank God!*

His cool hands closed on her warm butt, spreading her cheeks.

A shiver shook her.

"Oh, your arse is nice and warm." The head of his cock rubbed against her aching and moist opening; then he pressed for entry. He surged hard and slid within, groaning in obvious pleasure.

She moaned. Tight fullness, exquisite ache, dark pleasure . . . He filled her, and her heart leaped to have him there.

His hands cupped her hips. "Oh, yes. . . ." He sighed, pulled back a little, then thrust hard. He gasped and trembled within her. "My apologies . . ." he sounded breathless, "but I have this overwhelming need to fuck you."

His need was overwhelming? Thorn just about snarled. "Don't talk about it—hurry up and do it!"

He pulled back and proceeded to hammer into her.

The sounds of wet flesh striking wet flesh, and groans of hunger, filled the small room.

Delicious and ruthless pleasure coiled tightly within her core. She shoved back against his merciless plunges, greedily encouraging her body's climb to orgasm. The leading edge of climax rose violently fast and beckoned. A fine trembling shook her thighs. She clutched the blankets with whitening knuckles.

He groaned and slowed the pace. "Patience, my love."

"Screw patience!" She shoved back onto him.

He gasped and caught her around the waist, pulling her upper body off the bed. He growled, raising the hairs on her neck. "You will learn to obey!"

"Obey, my ass!" She was sitting right on the vicious edge of an explosion that was going nowhere fast. If he didn't let her come soon, she was going to kill him slowly and painfully. She clenched her teeth. "I want to come, damnit!"

Holding her trapped firmly against his body, he shoved one knee up on the mattress. He reached up and cupped her breasts in his warm palms, pinching and rolling the swollen tips between thumb and forefinger.

Thorn whimpered with the exquisite fire stirred by his fingers.

He thrust in earnest, pistoning and grinding up into her body. "You may come when I so will it—not before."

She tried to grind back down on him, but this position kept her practically immobile. She wailed in boiling frustration.

The vampire gasped. His hot mouth and velvety tongue caressed the long muscle along her shoulder.

Climax rose within her, hot and fast, cresting and holding on the edge of madness. She felt the scrape of his long teeth and trembled. "Please . . . please . . ." She knew damned well she was begging, but she really couldn't care less.

He pulled free of her body.

She cried out in denial, only to be turned to face him and shoved down onto the sheets. She sprawled on her back.

He came over her and surged within her in one brutally hard thrust.

She arched up from the mattress, howling in carnal welcome.

He bared his long teeth and thrust hard into her, then again, and again . . . "Now—now you may come." His head dropped, and his teeth sank into her shoulder.

Release exploded through her in a hot, wet rush of brutal glory that burned up her arching spine and ripped a scream from her throat. She bucked frantically under him, her nails scoring his butt and thighs.

He ground into her, riding her climax, moaning against her neck.

She came down from her release panting under him and soaked in sweat, the air perfumed with the rich musk of lust.

His tongue stroked the bite on her shoulder. "Thorn. . . ." His mouth found hers in a leisurely but thorough kiss.

Thorn kissed him back, glad to her soul to have him exactly where he was, safe in her arms.

His arms closed tight around her, and he rolled to his side, their bodies locked in carnal intimacy and their legs entwined. His tongue swept deliciously against hers. A purr boiled from his chest. He pulled back and stared at her with eyes dark yet hooded with sleepy heat. "My love. . . ." He brushed the hair from her damp brow and then pressed a kiss there. He pulled her against his heart. "And now, to sleep."

A knock at the door awakened Yaroslav and Thorn.

Yaroslav opened the interior door to admit a conductor pushing a breakfast cart and an attendant carrying a pair of suit presses with a change of clothes for each of them.

Breakfast was eaten while the suit presses were opened.

Half a piece of toast hanging from her mouth, Thorn pulled out the frilly white blouse embroidered in red, the green velvet skirt, the pair of white lacy petticoats, and then the black velvet bodice embroidered in red silk. She was not amused. The striped stockings and the frilly bloomers were even less cause for amusement. However, this time, sensible boots had been provided.

She finished her toast and turned to glare at Yaroslav. "Was this your idea?"

Yaroslav turned, holding a white men's shirt that was nearly as heavily embroidered in red thread as her blouse. "No, it was not." He frowned and lifted black velvet trousers also trimmed in red embroidery. "I suspect we are seeing my prince's sense of humor. This is Russian festival attire."

Thorn lifted the green velvet skirt. "Do I have to actually wear this?"

Yaroslav sighed. "I do not think we have much choice in the matter. We are expected before the prince upon arrival."

Thorn groaned. "I don't even know how to put all this stuff on!"

Yaroslav stepped up behind her and wrapped his arms around her, embracing her. "I will help you." His lips caressed her throat, leaving delicate shivers in his wake.

Thorn lifted her chin and groaned. "Oh? You're actually going to help me get into clothes, as opposed to out of them?"

Yaroslav sighed. "Unfortunately we have time for little else. The train will reach the station soon."

Thorn stuck out her bottom lip. "Damn, that's a pity."

Yaroslav pressed a kiss to her brow. "Yes, I know."

They stepped off the train in an obscure little town in the heart of the mountains.

Thorn eyed Yaroslav and pulled her green wool cloak close about her shoulders. He had chosen to wear his black fur rather than the bright red wool coat with all the gold thread and tassels. She was almost disappointed.

A waiting pony cart took them to the very far side of town and a very old hotel set tight against a cliff face.

Yaroslav nodded to the desk clerk and walked straight down the hall to a pair of very old doors set into marble arches. They opened onto a hallway that ended in a very modern, wrought-iron-gated, elevating lift set into a shaft that rose straight up into the mountain.

Yaroslav opened the gate, ushered Thorn within, and cleared his throat. "This is Yaroslav. The main office of the Penumbral Senate, if you please. I am expected."

Thorn had overheard Antonius saying that Prince Rafael had not been amused. Standing across the hall from the closed door to the prince's palace office, staring at the ridiculously high, arched, and vaulted ceiling, Thorn had no problems believing it whatsoever.

Rafael was shouting at Yaroslav loud enough to wake the dead in what she suspected was pure Russian. She was almost glad she had no clue what the prince was saying.

She looked across the hall at Antonius, posted directly in front of the door in his plain black robes and armor. He was wincing. That couldn't be good.

Thorn cringed. Well, at least heavy objects weren't being

tossed around in there, so there was some hope. She looked up the deserted hall to the tall, arched window at the far end.

She'd been in that hallway since dawn—only an hour after they had left the train. The lift had brought them straight into the palace—and she had absolutely no idea how.

Silence fell in the prince's office.

Thorn stared. Was that good, or was that bad?

Antonius frowned; then his brows lifted. He stepped hastily to the far side of the doorway and straightened.

The door opened. Prince Rafael stepped into the open doorway and glanced about. His jaw was tight and his body rigid with tension. He spotted Thorn and crooked his finger. "Come in, Thorn." His smile was not pretty in the least.

Thorn stiffened. *Uh-oh. . . .* She ducked her head and walked across the hallway, shivering with uneasiness.

Yaroslav occupied the wingback chair on the left of Rafael's desk. He rubbed his brow and scratched at his jaw. Spotting her, he smiled tiredly and held out his right hand.

Thorn strode for him and took his hand. She leaned close. "Are we going to live?"

Rafael stalked past her and curled his lip. "You will live. Unfortunately, because of your untimely absence, you will not be living here." He stepped behind his desk, tugged at the long skirts of his robes, and sat.

Thorn scowled. "I didn't ask to be kidnapped!"

Rafael waved his hand. "I know, I know. . . . However, this did not stop the Penumbral Senate from choosing you as a Penumbral representative for the United States of America. Which means . . ." he looked over at her with a sad smile, "you are to be sent back to your home country."

Thorn stiffened. "What?" She looked at Yaroslav and then back at the prince. "But I don't want to go back."

The prince sighed and shook his head. "But you were not here to say such, and so you were chosen in your absence."

"Why me?"

"Because . . ." Rafael leaned back in his chair and set his chin on his fist, "you are the only maguskind from America who has ever presented themselves before the senate."

"But . . ."

"But wait . . ." Rafael raised his hand. "This gets better."

Thorn choked. "Better . . . ?"

Rafael cleared his throat. "You know of the Covenant of Shadows, the edict passed to isolate the human race from magical influence and familiarity?"

Thorn frowned. "I think I remember it being mentioned."

Rafael nodded. "Well, while you two were out gallivanting across the countryside last night, the Penumbral Senate passed the Nox Noctis Decretum. It is an edict creating a special judicial branch of the court to monitor and enforce the separation between the Mundane world and the Penumbral Realm."

Thorn frowned. "So, what does that mean exactly?"

Yaroslav sighed deeply. "It means the court has appointed an office of enforcement to watch the human race for unanticipated magus talents."

Rafael folded his arms across his chest. "It's a type of police force, I guess you could say."

Thorn looked at Rafael in alarm. "And what do they do if they find one of these . . . talents? Kill them?"

"No." Rafael scowled. "I will not condone the murder of innocents." He leaned back in his chair. "Wild talents are to be sent here," he stabbed a finger onto his desktop, "where they will be educated and integrated into our society. Or, at least, that's the general idea." He smiled. "I plan to put in motion a mentor-apprenticeship program."

Thorn frowned. "Is that what I'm supposed to do as a . . . representative? Police the people of America?"

Rafael rubbed his jaw and shook his head. "No, you will

have other duties. As there are more vampires than there are of any other maguskind race, and most of them already live among humans in just about every city of the known world, one of them will be chosen to act as enforcement officer."

Thorn frowned at the prince of vampires. "Was that your idea?"

"Actually, no, though I am not complaining." He smiled. "High Prince notwithstanding, I am in far closer contact with my own people. This gives me direct control over how the wild talents are collected and treated once they get here." He leaned forward in his chair. "Which leads us right back to you returning to America."

Thorn squeezed Yaroslav's hand. "But I don't want . . . !"

Rafael nodded. "To leave Yaroslav behind, yes, I know." He stared straight at her. "And so, as the head of the judicial branch representing the Nox Noctis Decretum, I appoint Count Feodor Yaroslav Iziaslavich, prince of Luske, as judicial officer to America, to monitor and enforce the separation between the Mundane world and the Penumbral Realm. You may choose your own staff to assist you in your duties."

Thorn blinked. "Huh?"

Rafael grimaced. "He gets to go with you."

Thorn froze. Yaroslav was coming to America with her?

Yaroslav patted her hand and smiled. "Of course, you will have to marry me and make an honest man of me first."

"Marriage?" Thorn bit down on her bottom lip. "I really don't know if that would be a good idea. . . ."

Yaroslav curled his lip. "You will marry me."

Thorn growled in reply. "Is that so?"

Yaroslav grabbed the back of her neck and pulled her down onto his mouth for a searing kiss. His fingers tightened in her hair. He released her mouth but not her neck and glared at her. "I will convince you."

Thorn glared right back. "You can try."

"I will succeed." He pulled her back down for another hot, wet kiss. Moans erupted between them.

Rafael's brows lifted. He turned away and opened a drawer on the far side of his desk. "I think I shall take this moment to see what properties are available in what American cities." He smiled. "As a wedding present."

Epilogue

January 1877

The Fairwind, *American Line steamship*
En route to New York City, United States of America

Agent Hackett, fine, upstanding representative of the United States Secret Service, sat behind his elegant golden oak desk, wide-eyed with his mouth slightly open. He blinked rapidly. "I'm sorry, but I don't believe I heard you correctly." He shook his head slightly. "Could you say that again?"

Thorn smiled. "Sure." Dressed in a deep green velvet gown trimmed in black braiding, with matching bonnet and shoulder cape, she leaned against Yaroslav's arm. "I would like you to meet my husband, Master Yaroslav Iziaslavich, a watchmaker from Walachia."

Yaroslav tilted his head toward Hackett in a slight bow.

Agent Hackett leaned back in his chair. "So you . . ." He held out his hand and waved it. "How did you . . . ?" Red crept into his cheeks. "How could you . . . ?"

Yaroslav's brows lifted. "I asked; she accepted. Is this not the usual manner?"

Hackett froze with his hand out and his mouth open. He dropped his hand to the desktop and closed his mouth with a snap. "I see." He frowned at Thorn.

Thorn kept her smile perfectly neutral. Yaroslav had asked, all right, but it had taken a very long night of being tied to the bedposts while screaming through orgasm after orgasm. Yaroslav was surprisingly creative when it came to using not only his body but whatever came to hand as an instrument of love play. Eventually she had given in out of sheer exhaustion.

Hackett frowned at Yaroslav. "Are you also a . . . ?" His other hand twirled about in a circle. He cleared his throat. "A . . . ?"

"A werewolf?" Yaroslav smiled carefully, hiding the points of his teeth. "Oh, no, I am something else entirely." Shadows seemed to grow in all the corners of the room.

Hackett stiffened and then swallowed hard. "I, ah . . . see." His voice came out a trifle high-pitched.

Thorn leaned over the desk and set down a sheet of paper. "Here is my formal resignation. Since my term is officially over, I don't see how you should have any problems processing it." She smiled and didn't bother to hide her pointed teeth or the way the desk lamp reflected in her eyes. "Do you?"

Hackett seemed to wilt before her eyes. "Washington is going to kill me. I was supposed to get you to sign on for a new term."

Yaroslav lifted his chin, and the shadows in the tiny cabin deepened. "My wife will not be working in the army."

Hackett nodded hastily. "Yes, yes . . . I understand completely." He grabbed the sheet of paper and shoved it into a drawer. "I will see that your resignation is properly filed."

Thorn nodded. "Thank you, Agent Hackett." She turned away, and Yaroslav turned with her.

"Wait. . . ." Hackett rose from behind his desk. "Where are you going?"

Yaroslav turned back and smiled. "We are going to our honeymoon suite, of course." He turned away and opened the cabin door, letting in the night wind off the Adriatic Sea. "Good night, Agent Hackett." He guided Thorn out of the cabin and pulled the door closed behind him.

Thorn burst into giggles. "When you came out with"—she deepened her voice—"'I am something else entirely,'" she giggled again, "I thought he was going to pee his trousers!"

Yaroslav's smile sharpened just a hair. "He was rather entertaining to torment."

Thorn looked up at him. "Did Prince Rafael really give us a house in upstate New York?"

Yaroslav nodded. "I have heard of this house on the Hudson. I believe he went by the name Van Winkle at the time."

Thorn frowned. "Really? That sounds familiar." How did she know that name?

Yaroslav looped his arm through Thorn's. "So, now that that is done, Mrs. Iziaslavich, I should very much like to explore the silk stockings you are currently wearing."

Thorn lifted a brow at him. "Oh, would you, Mr. Iziaslavich?"

Yaroslav smiled. "I am quite curious as to what you taste like while wearing them."

Heat spilled into Thorn's belly and coiled tight. She licked her lips. "Well, I must confess . . . that I just don't see how I could deny you a chance to indulge in your curiosity."

Yaroslav grinned. "Excellent." He leaned down and pressed a soft kiss to her lips under the stars. "I love you, Thorn Iziaslavich."

Thorn's smile faded. Directly over her heart, the silver watch thumped with the steady rhythm of a heart beating. "I love you, too."

"Good." Yaroslav leaned down and scooped her into his

arms. The froth of her petticoats ruffled over his arm in the night breeze. "I am hungry, wife. It is time for you to feed me!"

Thorn threw her arms around the vampire's neck. "Then, by all means, let's get you fed!"

Yaroslav strode down the deck with determination in his stride.

Thorn's laughter pealed out across the sea and under the stars.